Elijah's Awakening

BOOK 1

CHRONICLES OF THE WATCHERS

—◆—

J. WILLIAM HAUCK

White Ladder Books

Visit **jwilliamhauck.com**

On the cover: An ancient Sumerian depiction of a sky deity known as the Anunnaki.
According to legend, these beings taught and guided humankind.

ALSO BY J. WILLIAM HAUCK

Your past is a part of you, but not as much as the present, for what you do next will determine the future.

CHAPTER 1
EMERGENCE

JEBEL IRHOUD
THE FIRST AGE
100,000 B.C.

The small, wiry man recoiled as the flash of lightning arced across the darkening sky. His sunken eyes scanned the desert plain as his snarled brown hair lifted in the breeze. The crack of thunder caused him to jump and raised the hairs on his arms and neck. Wearing animal skins about his chest and loins, he lifted his spear with one hand while steadying the dead caribou across his shoulders with the other.

Tauta, as he was known in his tribe, spun in the sand as distant streaks of light danced across the sky, roiling the black, billowing clouds into a dozen shades of blue and gray. With nostrils flared and dark eyes wide, Tauta searched for danger. He saw nothing but the windblown plain and smelled only the distant rain and his dead caribou. He turned back the way he had come and looked for movement. He knew it would be hard to tell if danger lurked downwind in the steady breeze.

Tauta scanned the horizon; his long, stringy beard bent in the wind.

Convinced he was alone, the hunter shifted the weight of his kill on his shoulders, turned, and continued across the windblown plain.

While it was sometimes risky, Tauta liked to hunt alone. But his kill was getting heavier with each step, and he now wished another was with him. Maybe his son Rata; he had wanted to come, after all. Rata was old enough to learn the ways, but Tauta feared for him after narrowly escaping a jackal two days before.

Tauta stopped when another streak of blinding white light shot into the ground a few hundred steps ahead. The roar of thunder quickly followed and caused Tauta's hairs to stand even taller. With his heart pounding, the wiry hunter shifted the weight of the dead beast on his shoulder and resumed his desert march. The smell of rain was growing closer, but he still had to go through the valley and over the rocky hills to reach his people. He knew he would be wet and cold by then. Tauta pushed on as the thin blades of grass bent across his bare, calloused feet.

After a hundred steps, Tauta's wide nostrils flared. There was another scent. His wary eyes scanned the plain before him. He saw the rocky hills in the distance and the desert brush bending in the stiffening breeze. The wiry man looked to where the lightning had come down and noticed a strange glow. He stopped, turned back the way he had come, then glanced at the rocky hills. They were closer but still far away. Tauta again caught the unusual scent. With his thick brow bent in concern, he turned and crept toward the strange glow.

As he approached the edge of a broad ravine, Tauta's eyes widened. Down inside the hollow, he spotted a lone tree glowing with what his people called the "sky-light." Tauta had seen it before in the grass on the plains when the angry clouds sent down their light, but it seldom lingered.

Tauta was watching the flames dance across the top of the tree when a man moved out from under it. Tauta raised his spear, his eyes wide, his jaw tight. He disliked the river people and would not give up his kill easily.

The unsettled Tauta eyed the stranger. He wore unusual skins and had an odd scent. The wary hunter stiffened when the man held out his empty hands and waved Tauta toward him. The hunter glanced at the rocky hills. It was raining there now.

Tauta looked for others and wondered if it was a trick of the river people. Seeing no one else, he looked for a way into the ravine. With one eye on the stranger and the other on the rocky slope, he carried his kill down the hill, balancing with his spear. At the bottom, the air was calmer, and the unfamiliar scent stronger. Tauta eyed the dancing flames atop the burning tree in wonder before remembering the peculiar man. He turned to the stranger standing beneath the tree, just twenty steps away. Tauta cocked his head and thought, *The sky-light does not frighten him.*

The stranger waved the hunter closer with a disarming smile.

Unwilling to share his kill, Tauta lowered the lifeless caribou to the rocky ground. He tightened his grip on the crude spear, a shard of flint bound to a pole by dried leather strips. Tauta would need it to remove the animal's skin and slice its flesh, but he could also use it to scare the strange man. He had done so before when one of the river people had come too close.

As Tauta stepped closer to the stranger, he noticed the sky-light was also on the ground, not far from the man. Tauta's eyes narrowed when he spotted a rabbit hanging from a stick above the flames, its skin gone, its pink flesh white. Tauta's eyes widened, and his nostrils flared as he realized that was the source of the smell. His mouth watered at the strange but tantalizing aroma.

"Come," welcomed the stranger, waving the hunter closer.

Tauta turned to the man. Now on level ground, he realized the pale-skinned stranger was much larger than him and stepped back.

"Come," smiled the stranger.

Tauta saw the man had a smooth face like a boy, flowing brown hair, and eyes the color of the day sky.

"Come, eat," beckoned the large stranger.

Tauta's thick brow gathered as he realized he understood the man's words. *Where is he from? He's not of the river people.*

"You are safe here."

Tauta gulped. He wanted to believe the stranger but feared it was a trick. He breathed in the cooking rabbit's aroma and licked his lips. After hunting all day, he was hungry. *Maybe it is not a trick.* Tauta stepped closer.

With a warm nod, the large stranger moved to the roasting rabbit. Kneeling beside it, he turned the wooden skewer on which it hung.

Tauta moved nearer. He was too close to escape the large man if it was a trick, but he could still use his spear. He turned to his kill resting on the rocks behind him, then back to the cooking rabbit. "What do you?" he grunted.

The stranger looked up from the rabbit with a smile. Using a shard of flint, he sliced off a piece of its meat, blew it off to cool it, and then held it out for Tauta.

Tauta's mouth was watering even more now. *If it is a trick, it is too late*, he told himself. He stepped closer, reached out his hand, and took the slice of meat from the stranger's palm. But when he felt its heat, Tauta recoiled and dropped it in the dirt.

The stranger held back a laugh, then cut another slice off the rabbit. After blowing on it, he handed it to Tauta.

Tauta stared longingly at the savory cooked flesh, then cautiously reached for it. Feeling its heat, he tossed it from hand to hand as it cooled.

The stranger nodded approvingly, then cut a piece for himself, blew on it, and put it into his mouth. The closely watching Tauta blew on his slice of the rabbit as well, then took a bite.

The blue-eyed stranger grinned as Tauta's face lit up.

With a nod, the chewing Tauta patted his belly. "Good. Good." With one hand still on his spear, he reached out for more, and the stranger obliged.

By the time the roasted rabbit was reduced to bones, Tauta's spear was on the ground next to him. The wiry hunter turned from the dying fire to the large stranger sitting beside him and nodded thanks. He then patted his chest and grunted, "I am called Tauta." His smile revealed brown and missing teeth.

"I am called Eli," grinned the large stranger.

"Eeel-lie," Tauta repeated. He turned and pointed to the dying flames.

"That is called *fire*," nodded Eli. "I will teach you."

NEW YORK CITY
APRIL 2020

A LARGE HAND reached out from under the comforter to quiet the buzzing alarm. After its third blind tap, the noise stopped. Eli rolled on his back and sighed as the remnants of a dream faded.

Eli's blue eyes opened and closed as he reconciled the past with the present. He ran a hand through his thick, wavy hair, breathed in determination, and pulled himself up from his bed. After looking across the light-streaked bedroom, he rubbed his face, glanced at the clock, and got to his feet.

After a cold shower, Eli dragged a comb through his thick brown hair. He gazed into the mirror and stroked his square chin. He studied the eight-inch comet-shaped scar that ran diagonally from his left shoulder. It was a sad reminder of a life lost.

After disappearing into his closet, Eli emerged in running shoes, joggers, and a sweatshirt. With a sigh, he made his way to his small Westside apartment kitchen. He reached for the TV's remote control, and the flat screen came to life.

"It's day twenty-four of the Coronavirus quarantine. With cases steadily climbing in the Empire State, Governor Cuomo says there is still an urgent need for ventilators, and fears more drastic measures may be needed to win this fight..."

Eli sighed and reached for a box of muesli and a bowl. He placed them on the counter before turning to his refrigerator. Eli hadn't even opened the door when he remembered he was out of milk.

With a tired shake of his head, Eli turned off the TV and moved to a window. He pulled up the blinds and looked through the dirty glass to the street below. The virus had silenced Amsterdam Avenue's usual morning rush, and the street was empty of passersby. Eli moved to the door, unlatched its bolt, and grabbed his worn mask hanging from a coat hook.

Eli had just locked his door when he heard a small dog's bark. He turned to a frail old woman layered in green plaid holding a pointed-eared Yorkie. "Hello, Missus Wissenberger. How are you today?" he asked, his voice deep and subdued.

"I'm still here," she whined with a hint of an accent.

"You really shouldn't go out without a mask, Missus Wissenberger. I told you to let me know if you need—"

"Eli, you worry too much. I've lived through much harder than this. Besides, I've got one here somewhere in my purse," she said with a dismissive wave.

Eli noticed the small, faint numbers tattooed on her forearm. He knew well the horrors she had faced as a child in Poland. "All right. Please let me know if you need anything."

"What I need is what you got! How do you stay so young looking? Twenty years you've lived here and haven't aged a day! Still not a wrinkle on you! And look at me? I'm a wrinkled old witch. I used to be a looker! Just ask my George—rest his ornery soul. Ahh, it doesn't matter," she muttered, fumbling for her key. "If the virus doesn't get me, the boredom will."

Eli forced a smile. "Have a nice day, Missus Wissenberger."

"Yeah, yeah," she replied, disappearing into her apartment.

Eli sighed, then stepped into the elevator.

After exiting the building, Eli breathed in the brisk morning air through his mask; it tasted like yesterday's bad breath. He nodded as he passed a man carrying groceries. The man wore two masks. Eli recognized the fear and uncertainty in the man's eyes before he looked away. It was a look Eli knew well.

A woman approaching from the end of the block saw him and crossed into the street, never making eye contact. Suspicion and aloofness were common in the city, but Eli had noticed it even more with the pandemic's uncertainty. Eli thought the anonymity of the masks made it worse. Anonymity was something else Eli knew well.

When Eli reached the corner market, a line was waiting to go inside. He stopped six feet behind a man wearing a backward Yankees hat and a red bandana pulled up over his nose. Eli waited and watched shoppers emerge from the small market carrying bags of needed food and supplies. Through their masks, he saw some with triumphant looks while others appeared beaten down in defeat. Eli glanced up at a robin happily chirping atop the store's awning, oblivious to the dreadfulness below.

Soon, a masked worker in a store apron holding a clicker waved Eli into the market. He passed the sanitized shopping carts and entered the picked-over produce department as he made his way to the milk aisle at the back of the store. Upon spotting a backup of shoppers waiting for potatoes, Eli turned down a side aisle and nearly ran into a woman holding a handbasket. "Oh, sorry," he said, coming to a stop. His eyes narrowed as he recognized her petite and attractive features, though partially hidden by a wrapped scarf pulled up over her nose. Her harried but deliberate eyes were dark, like chocolate, her skin creamy smooth, her brunette hair slightly tousled under her scarf.

The woman made brief eye contact with Eli before walking around him. Eli turned and watched her disappear around an aisle, then muttered, "Michelle?"

Eli followed the brunette down the aisle, his eyes riveted on her in wonder. He told himself what he saw was not possible—or was it? His life had been filled with the impossible. *Could it be her?* he wondered as she stopped to look over the few remaining cereal boxes.

Eli pulled his gaze away when the dark-haired woman turned to him. He reached for a jar of peanut butter and followed her out of the corner of his eye. Eli noticed her trim shape under her sweater and jeans, and his mind flashed back in time. He saw a woman gleefully dancing in the sunlit sheers of a window. He saw her lovely brown eyes looking into his as they floated in a pond. He smelled the sweetness of her breath as her lips neared his. "Michelle," he breathed.

CHAPTER 2
THE YOUNG NURSE

The gray-haired hospital administrator stroked his mustache as he eyed the trim young lady standing across from his desk. With deep brown eyes, silky skin, and neatly done up chestnut hair, he thought her striking. The doctor's approving gaze instinctively lowered to her amble bust, but his eyes narrowed at her simple dress and moth-eaten sweater. "You wish to have a job here at Saint Louis Hospital?" asked Dr. Joffre.

"Yes, sir," nodded the brunette, her fidgeting hands across her middle, her chocolate eyes fixed on the administrator's desk.

"Madame...?"

"Mademoiselle," gulped the young woman. "Michelle LaRue Duvall."

"Ah, yes. It's here on your application," nodded Dr. Joffre. "I see you are a graduate of La Salpêtrière's nursing school."

"Yes, sir," nodded Michelle, meeting eyes with the doctor, but only for a moment.

"We have had some fine workers come from there. What makes you think you would be a good nurse here at Saint Louis?"

Michelle gulped and looked into the doctor's scrutinizing eyes. "Because...I want to help people."

"You can do that working in a bakery or a laundry. Why my hospital?"

Somewhat taken aback, Michelle stood a little straighter. "Because I want to help people get better. I want to help them heal."

"That is clearly a doctor's concern," shrugged Joffre.

"That should be everyone's concern," replied Michelle.

Dr. Joffre studied Michelle, then said, "I like your pluck. And your appearance."

Michelle's head lowered as she muttered, "Thank you."

"You would obey a doctor's orders?"

"Of course," replied Michelle, looking up at the stern-eyed man.

Dr. Joffre nodded. "Very well. I shall hire you as a nurse's assistant for now."

"But, sir, I've been through the nursing school," insisted Michelle.

"Then that should make you quite proficient at emptying bedpans and changing sheets."

"Yes, sir," muttered Michelle, lowering her head.

"You'll move up from there, depending on your usefulness," said Joffre, his eyes lowering from her breasts to her slender hips.

Though uncomfortable with the implications of his comment, Michelle forced a smile and said, "Thank you, sir. I won't disappoint."

Dr. Joffre smiled and nodded. "I'm sure you won't."

MICHELLE WAS CHEERFULLY HUMMING when she topped the stairs of her apartment floor. She smiled politely at a passing neighbor, found her key in her worn handbag, and opened the paint-peeled door.

After closing and locking the door, Michelle turned with a grin to the frail, gray-haired man sitting near the fireplace reading a book with a magnifying glass. "I got the job, Papa!" she said, hanging up her worn sweater.

François Duvall looked up from his book with rosy, sagging cheeks.

"That's splendid, my dear! Perhaps you have found your calling in life. When do you start?"

"Tomorrow morning. Do you think I will make a good nurse?" asked Michelle, moving into the tiny kitchen and pulling on an apron.

"Of course! You will be wonderful," smiled François. "It is your gift. Like your mother, you have the healer's touch; rest her soul."

"Thank you, Papa," replied Michelle, touched by her father's encouragement.

"How much is the pay?" asked François, returning to his book.

"I'm not sure. I didn't think to ask," blushed Michelle. "I was just excited to get the job!"

"Well, I'm sure it will be better than nothing. Every frank helps."

Michelle sighed as she eyed her father, a vestige of his former self. It saddened her to see his age affecting him so. She knew her father's health was failing and had gone into nursing in part to learn how to care for him. Something she was unable to do for her mother. Michelle smiled when François looked up at her, stroking his cheek with his bony fingers.

Michelle hoped she could make a difference.

CHAPTER 3
BLACK HAND

SARAJEVO, BOSNIA AND HERZEGOVINA
SPRING 1914

The night air was still as the pale yellow moon crested the trees of the cemetery. With the day's warmth fleeting and not a frog or cricket to be heard, an eerie silence filled the shadows. Huddled on the grass amidst the tombstones, a young man pulled his coat tight as he stared at a headstone with dark, foreboding eyes. The inscribed name, Bogdan Žerajić, was just visible in the shadows. The young man gave a heavy sigh and shook his head in despair. To some, Žerajić was simply a failed assassin, a would-be murderer, a bad shot. To others, like young Gavrilo Princip, he was a hero whose final defining act was a bullet to his brain. Gavrilo mourned the man, but even more, he mourned his country.

It had been more than thirty years since the German decree that gave Bosnia and Herzegovina to Austria-Hungary. Wars had come and gone since then, but still, Austria ruled. Žerajić was not the first to hunger for a free Bosnia, and his failed assassination of the Austria-appointed governor had inspired many. There were secret societies filled with such men who ached for a chance to free their land. Nineteen-year-old

Gavrilo had such aspirations and often fantasized his bullet would put an end to Austrian rule and unify all Yugoslavs.

Gavrilo reached for the half-empty bottle of vodka beside him, took a drink, and sighed.

"Why do you sit?" came a penetrating voice from the shadows.

Gavrilo spun in the grass. "Who are you, lurking there?" he gasped, his dark-ringed eyes wide, his black pencil mustache quivering in the moonlight.

"Why do you sit?" repeated the large man as he emerged from the shadows, his combed-back hair and trimmed beard a murky red.

"What business is it of yours?" huffed Gavrilo, pushing back in the grass.

"Do not be afraid, young lion," said the large man, the moonlight glinting off the pocket watch chain under his long black coat.

"Who are you?" Gavrilo gulped. "A constable? I've done nothing wrong!"

"I am no one for you to fear." The stranger's green eyes narrowed. "Why do you sit when there is so much to do?"

"I don't know what you mean."

The stranger's eyes moved to the gravestone. "You mourn your land. You seek change. Revolution. You seek freedom...*power*."

Gavrilo nodded nervously.

"There are others like you, you know. Others who want the same thing."

"A free Bosnia? Out of the clutches of the bloody Austrians?"

"You have said it," the green-eyed stranger grinned.

"Who are you?"

"Someone who can help you."

"Are you part of the Black Hand?" Gavrilo gasped. He had heard of the secret society and longed to be a part of it.

The green-eyed stranger's chest swelled. "I *am* the Black Hand."

"WHAT DO YOU SEE?" asked the tall gentleman as he gazed across the

Miljacka River, his short white hair and beard contrasting sharply against his dark three-piece suit and top hat.

The curly-mustached police captain turned from the man he knew as Cyrus White. "I see a city street, Cumurja Bridge, a muddy river, the usual morning traffic."

"Captain Radulevic, certainly you see more than that," frowned Cyrus.

The police captain, wearing a dark gray uniform and black officer's hat, glanced at Cyrus's fine suit and fancy cane. He wondered if the elegantly engraved ball atop the cane was brass or actual gold. Radulevic despised arrogant men, no matter what their cause. But the enigmatic Cyrus had helped him with a prior case that had earned Radulevic a promotion. "If it's the archduke you're worried about, don't bother. My men have everything in hand for tomorrow."

The fine lines of Cyrus's cheek wrinkled as he gave the captain a condescending smile. "Don't forget what is at stake here, Captain."

Radulevic huffed. "It's hard to get excited protecting someone like Ferdinand. I can't say too many would cry should he or any other Austrian be killed. Not here, at least."

Cyrus's eyes narrowed, and he squared up to the captain. "You have no idea the events such a thing would set into motion."

Radulevic turned away with a bent brow and huffed, "I am a keeper of the law and the peace, of course. The archduke will be fine. I'll have sixty of my best men lining the street. I don't know what you're all worked up about." He pulled a pipe from his pocket and clenched it in his teeth as a horse-drawn wagon clopped past.

Cyrus gave an uneasy sigh, then turned to his associate, standing a few feet back in a suit and hat. He was tall, like Cyrus, but younger, with brown wavy hair and crisp blue eyes. "Let's go, Elijah. There is still much for us to do."

Eli nodded, picked up a black leather bag at his feet, and followed Cyrus across the street.

They were in the middle of At Mejdan Park when Eli, walking beside Cyrus, asked, "Are you sure it will be enough?"

"You doubt me?" Cyrus asked with a sideways glance.

"They've failed us before," warned Eli.

"What do you mean? They fail us every time," quipped Cyrus.

"But this time it's different," Eli insisted.

"You don't have to tell me that. And I shouldn't have to remind you of your place here," glared Cyrus.

"My place here?" fumed Eli. "You treat me like it's my first time!"

"Yes!" Cyrus stopped and turned. "Your place here! There's a reason you are not on your own."

Eli shook his head as Cyrus turned and walked on. "What am I supposed to do?" asked Eli as he followed behind Cyrus. "Just watch as everything we've worked for is destroyed?"

Cyrus glanced back at Eli. "Not here."

"But this is important!"

Cyrus stopped and turned to the frustrated Eli. "Not here."

Eli sighed. He watched Cyrus continue across the park, then shook his head and followed.

———

GAVRILO PRINCIP, Muhamed Mehmedbašić, Trifko Grabež, and another man seated at the back of Café Ramis turned when the door opened. Hunched in their seats, their wary eyes stared across the empty café as Vaso Čubrilović and Nediko Čabrinović entered. After scurrying to the back of the café, the two young men sank into their chairs with harried looks and heaving chests.

"You're late," snapped Trifko.

"We ran," huffed Vaso, pushing up his dirty, round-rimmed spectacles.

"Don't worry, he's not here yet," shrugged Gavrilo, sipping his beer.

"Did you bring them?" asked the thick-mustached Trifko.

"No, Danilo has them," replied Vaso.

Trifko nodded.

"I have mine," grinned Gavrilo, pulling a pistol from his coat.

"Put that away! Are you crazy?" scolded the older Trifko.

"Tomorrow is the day," beamed Gavrilo, hiding his pistol.

"Quiet," warned Trifko.

"There's nobody else in here!" protested Gavrilo.

Trifko anxiously shook his head.

"After tomorrow, it will no longer be a secret," gulped Nediko.

"We'll be the heroes of Bosnia!" said Gavrilo with a proud nod.

"We'll be dead," sighed Vaso.

"It's an honor to die for a free Bosnia," breathed Gavrilo.

"What happens if they catch us?" fretted Trifko.

"You mean, if you don't take your cyanide?" asked Vaso.

"They will torture you first—until they get what they want, then they will kill you," said Nediko, staring into his glass.

"What about the others?" asked Vaso.

"Others? You mean the major?"

"Danilo said the major and even some of the police are on our side. What about them?"

"I don't know," muttered Trifko.

The café door opened, and all eyes turned to see the wiry Danilo Ilić and a much larger man enter.

"Who's that?" gulped Vaso, eyeing the red-bearded stranger.

Gavrilo's eyes widened as he recognized the visitor in the cemetery. His combed-back hair and trimmed beard seemed redder in the light of the café, but his green eyes were just as piercing.

The chairs at the table squawked as the men nervously pushed back across the tile floor to make room. All eyes were on the approaching red-bearded man, who wore a fine suit and stood eight inches taller than Danilo.

"This is Mister Stormbrewer," said Danilo with a nod to the large man.

Trifko tried to hide his concern. Stormbrewer was not a Bosnian name.

"Is he-is he Austrian?" squeaked Vaso.

"No," the large man replied with an amused grin. His green eyes moved to Gavrilo, and he gave a subtle nod.

Gavrilo nodded back.

"Everything is in order. Tomorrow is the day," whispered Danilo. "Ferdinand arrives by train and will be taken first to the barracks to inspect the troops. He is scheduled to leave there at ten o'clock in the morning. Just as we thought, they'll drive him along Appel Quay to the town hall. There will be five or six cars. Muhamed, you'll be in the garden outside Mostar Café. Vaso, you'll be there too, with a pistol."

Vaso nodded.

"Don't I get a pistol?" frowned Muhamed.

"No. We only have four."

"What am I supposed to do? Spit?" scoffed Muhamed.

Lu Stormbrewer's green-eyed glare caused Muhamed to sit back and lower his head.

"Ned, you'll be further down, on the river side of the street, if they don't have a good angle."

Nediko gulped.

"Popović, Trifko, and Gavrilo will be further still, just in case something goes wrong," Danilo added, his eyes filled with concern.

"Nothing will go wrong," Nediko muttered, his gaze distant.

Trifko was trying not to look at the menacing red-bearded man when he said to Danilo, "What did you bring us?"

Danilo turned to Lu Stormbrewer.

The seated men leaned back as Lu lifted a carpetbag onto the table and opened it. He reached inside, removed three new Belgian FN handguns, and set them on the table. Beside them, he lay what looked like a five-inch-long and three-inch-wide block of black clay impregnated with bits of steel. At one end was a wooden cap with a small brass lever.

"What is that?" asked Trifko.

"It's a bomb," Danilo nodded.

"I get to throw a bomb?" gasped an excited Muhamed.

Danilo nodded.

"How does it work?" frowned Vaso.

Danilo glanced at Lu. Then, pointing to the bomb, said, "See the lever on top? You flip it and then throw it."

"It has a ten-second fuse," added Lu in perfect Bosnian.

"Ten seconds? You don't have to light it?" asked Muhamed.

"No. Once you start the fuse, you cannot stop it. Ten seconds, so you must time your throw," explained Danilo.

"How deadly is it?" asked Trifko.

"It will kill anyone within six meters," replied Lu.

"Why does Muhamed get to throw it?" asked Vaso.

"There are three more," grinned Danilo.

Lu opened the bag further, revealing the remaining clay bombs and what appeared to be a thick, ten-inch-long pewter candlestick holder. He pulled two of the bombs from his bag and placed them on the table. The would-be assassins gleefully gazed at the deadly devices like boys receiving shiny new toys.

"Can we practice with them?" Vaso fretted, already knowing the answer. Even their pistol practice had been limited because of the hard-to-find ammunition.

"No. We only have these," replied Danilo.

Looking into Lu's bag, Gavrilo curiously eyed the pewter cylinder's ornate engravings. "What is this?" he asked, reaching in.

Lu's large hand came down hard on his. "That is not yours," he glared, pulling Gavrilo's hand away from the ancient weapon.

"Sorry," Gavrilo gulped.

Lu removed the last bomb, glanced back into his bag at the pewter blazerod, and then closed it.

STANDING ON THE BALCONY, Eli gazed across the river as city lights glistened off its tranquil water, and the warm night breeze stirred his brown, wavy hair. Eli heard accordion music coming from a café down the street and the clop of a horse-drawn wagon crossing the bridge. Distant laughter and conversation drifted through the night, but it wasn't only vocalized expressions he heard; Eli perceived many of the thoughts and feelings behind them. When properly focused, Eli's discernment told him much about the person beside him, often without a word. Sometimes it was more than he wanted to know. Dealing with mortals was a trial of distractions; the larger the group, the more confusing. It had taken him hundreds of years to learn how to filter through their random and discordant conveyances and turn them off when necessary. But occasionally, in the peaceful hours of the day, Eli liked to listen and try to understand better those he served.

Eli watched a couple walk along the riverbank holding hands. They stopped and kissed. Eli wondered what it would be like to hold a woman close, to share an affinity, a loving bond unspoiled by space and time. That a mortal's time was brief didn't bother him. He thought only eighty years of love and devotion to another better than an eternity alone. Eli breathed in the smells of a world not his own and closed his eyes.

"I don't see it," said Cyrus, turning a book's page as he sat in a wing-back chair beside a flickering table lamp.

"See what?" asked Eli, looking back from the balcony.

"Your fascination with it all," replied Cyrus, not looking up from his book. "Some might say it's a distraction from your work."

Eli's eyes narrowed as he looked back across the black, glistening river. "Some might say it *is* my work."

Cyrus's eyebrows raised, but his gaze remained on the text of the old leather-bound book. "It could be perceived as a weakness."

"A weakness?"

"You heard me."

Eli shook his head. He watched the lovers walking hand in hand, then looked away. "My caring for them should never be seen as a weakness."

Cyrus glanced across the room at Eli. "It was once before."

Eli turned back to Cyrus, eyed him for a moment, then left the room.

CHAPTER 4
THE GRAND PRECEPT

JEBEL IRHOUD
THE FIRST AGE

Eli gazed contentedly off the hill across the valley. Beyond the snaking river, the savannah's scattered trees, brush, and grass stretched to the brown, misty hills. He saw a distant herd of grazing caribou. His blue eyes moved to the river when a flock of waterfowl took flight, startled by a hunter carrying his kill along the river bank.

The sound of children playing drew Eli's attention to a cluster of simple huts made from sticks and mud. His eyes narrowed, and a hint of a smile formed as the naked children ran and laughed. He watched them chase around the huts as men and women went about their daily chores. Hunting and gathering were familiar skills to the plains people, but Eli and the others had introduced them to new skills and understanding. Cooking with fire would allow their bodies to absorb energy from their foods better and boost their strength, stamina, and brainpower. Reverence and knowledge of The Holy and Great Ones, the chief designers, had been taught and were readily embraced. The watchers would next introduce agriculture, making the primitives even more self-sustaining.

It was easy for Eli to see the caretakers among the indigenous. While clothed in similar skins, they stood more than a head taller than the primitives. Eli felt satisfaction with what they had accomplished. To guide and teach fulfilled their purpose. But such a task was not a simple one. There were other forces at work. Even now, chaos and conflict lurked in the simple mind of the burgeoning man. Eli knew the road ahead would be long, arduous, and painful.

Eli turned as a shadow came over him. He saw the tall watcher silhouetted in the afternoon sun. "Lu, how's the dam coming along?"

The red-bearded Lu sank on the rock beside him and gave a restless sigh. "Fine, until two of them got into a fight about how to place the rocks. Yesterday, they knew nothing about damming; today, Hoocha is an expert."

Eli grinned and turned back to the huts. He saw Tauta and his son Rata tending to a fire and roasting a boar. The gift of fire had given Tauta eminence, and he was now the leader of the primitive clan. Eli wondered how Tauta would deal with his newfound authority. He had seen such perceived greatness unravel men but had judged Tauta as able. Eli knew time would tell if his judgment was true.

"Do you ever wonder what we're doing here?" Lu asked, leaning on his knee.

"What kind of question is that?" frowned Eli, seeing Lu was serious. "You mean...helping them?"

"But are we helping them?"

"Of course we are. Look what we've taught them already!"

"What if we weren't here? Would it make any difference?"

Eli glanced at the green-eyed Lu. "To them or us?"

"They've been here a million years already. Why not let them figure it out on their own?"

"Because that's not how it's done."

"Says who," mumbled Lu. He looked across the valley beyond the river and the scattered baobab trees, then sighed, "We're wasting our time."

Eli pretended not to hear him.

"Don't you see? We could do so much more! We're gods to them!

They would worship us if we let them! They would do whatever we commanded!"

Eli turned to Lu, baffled by his comment. While the watchers could discern the simple minds of the primitives, they had no such reach into each other's minds. Their mutual understanding was based on honest communication, something Eli now questioned with Lu. "I'll forget you said any of that," breathed Eli.

"Well, it's true," Lu insisted.

"You've been listening to Semjaza."

"What if I have?" shrugged Lu.

"That's not how it is to be. I shouldn't have to tell you!" glared Eli. "It goes against our fundamental purpose."

"According to who? Cyrus?" sneered Lu.

"Cyrus, Raguel, Raphael, all of them. But above all, the Grand Precept."

"Ah, yes, the Grand Precept," Lu muttered mockingly. "The law that usurps all other laws."

Eli looked across the valley, unsure if he should take Lu seriously.

Lu studied Eli for a moment. His gaze returned to the huts when Tauta's woman, Chiacha, emerged from her mud shelter. She had a young child on her hip nursing from her breast. Lu had noticed her before and thought her striking for a primitive. "You know we've been here too long when their women start looking good."

Eli's eyes widened. A smirk formed as he turned back to Lu. "You're having fun with me, aren't you?"

When Lu's expressionless face broke into a disarming grin, Eli snickered and shook his head. "I don't understand your humor," Eli muttered as he got up from the rock and walked away.

"You wouldn't," breathed Lu as his lustful gaze returned to Chiacha.

LU'S NOSE wrinkled as he watched the men and women listening to the famous Eli sitting atop a rock in the middle of the village, like a king. Lu saw the wonder and awe in their eyes, and it annoyed him. Leaning against a tree, he counted more than thirty gathered. Seated to Eli's right was the wise and virtuous Inyanga, the clan's priestess, her dark braided hair draped on her white woven frock. Beside her sat an attentive Tauta, the clan's beloved ruler. Lu had suggested the clever Ulaah lead the clan, but Eli's seniority gave him authority in such decisions. Authority Lu thought was misplaced.

Eli's fame had spread from the plains people to the river people and beyond. The hill people had even joined Tauta's clan and were building huts near the river dam—huts Lu had shown them how to build. In the past months, Lu's irritation with Eli had grown to contempt. While the noble Eli professed no interest in his dominion and power over the primitives, Lu knew it was all a ruse. How could one not crave such power? he wondered.

Lu listened for a time to Eli's direction, but his gaze turned to the comely Chiacha when she approached carrying skins filled with water. Her eyes widened, and she quickly looked down when she saw the mighty Lu, as if unworthy to behold his presence. Lu liked the name the primitives had given them: The Shining Ones. He thought it denoted a certain majesty, and was deserving, coming from a people so simple and base.

When Lu moved in front of Chiacha, she stopped and lowered her head. He reached a large hand to her chin, lifted it to look into her eyes, and smiled. Chiacha's proportions were pleasing to him. She was taller and leaner than most of the other indigenous women, and her breasts hung prominently. The trepidation on Chiacha's face lessened as she looked into Lu's green eyes. She forced a nervous smile.

Seeing the others were still absorbed in Eli's words, Lu took the skins of water from Chiacha's hands and set them on the ground. She watched the water spill and vanish into the earth. Lu's hand ran down Chiacha's bronze-skinned arm. Then, with a lustful grin, he led her into a mud hut.

***

THE SUN HAD SUNKEN behind the brown hills, streaking the dusty sky with a hundred shades of orange and pink. The fire pit in the center of the huts was aglow, and the sounds of villagers eager to be fed filtered up the hill. Lu saw the squinty-eyed Ulaah sitting beneath a sprawling tree, his arms folded, his jaw tight. Lu moved beside him, pulled down one of the tree's sausage-shaped fruit, and bit into it.

"I do not like Tauta," hissed Ulaah. "Why does he lead us?"

Lu's gaze turned to the glowing fire pit. He saw Tauta and his son cutting and serving portions of the caribou they had roasted. Fire had made Tauta a leader, but his service to the growing clan had made him loved. Lu's eyes narrowed. "He leads because Eli chose him."

"Did *you* choose him?" asked Ulaah, looking up at the red-bearded Lu with the eyes of a child.

"No." Lu shook his head distastefully and tossed the rest of the fruit aside. "I would have chosen you."

Ulaah's chest swelled. He looked back down at the village for a time and then muttered, "It is not right."

Lu watched a raven swoop down on a scurrying field mouse. With the writhing rodent clutched in its talons, the black bird's beak quickly tore it apart. "Would you like to be their leader?" Lu asked, eyeing the feasting bird.

"Yes, but the time has passed. The people have chosen Tauta."

"The time is never passed," muttered Lu.

"They *like* Tauta," snarled Ulaah. "Even the new people like him. And he's made peace with the river people. I do not like the river people."

Lu eyed Ulaah, sizing him up a final time. "Do you want this power?"

"Power? I do not know the word," frowned Ulaah.

"The feeling of flying above the clouds—above the others," Lu explained, watching the raven feast. "You could rule them. They would look up to you as they do now Tauta. You would have power over them. They would be *your* people."

Ulaah's face lit up with the possibility. "I would like this thing. How do I get this power over Tauta?"

Lu studied the eager Ulaah, then shook his head. "No...I fear you lack the will."

"No, no, Ulaah lacks nothing!"

"There are things you would have to do. You're not yet ready."

"I am ready!" exclaimed Ulaah, moving in front of the turning-away Lu.

"You would have to swoop down on your prey, like the raven, without thought, without fear," said Lu.

Ulaah gulped and nodded with uncertain determination.

"Would you be willing to do anything for this power?"

"Anything?"

"Yes." Lu pointed to the disemboweled field mouse and the raven about to take flight. "Would you be willing to kill?"

"To take a life?" Ulaah asked, recoiling at the thought.

"Yes," breathed Lu, his eyes narrow.

"Eli and Inyanga have taught us it is forbidden."

Lu shrugged. "I didn't think you were ready."

Ulaah sank onto the rock, his eyes wide in thought. He watched the raven flap its wings into the fiery sky. Then, with a determined nod, he turned to Lu. "Yes, if it would give me this power, Ulaah would do it... but how?"

"How does Tauta kill a caribou or a boar?"

Ulaah's face wrinkled in troubled thought. "He takes its blood with his knife."

Lu nodded. "That is how you kill."

Ulaah's shoulders sank at the idea of spilling another's blood in anger.

"I didn't think you were ready," muttered Lu, getting to his feet.

"Wait!" Ulaah raised a halting hand, his simple mind struggling. "Wouldn't the gods be displeased?"

Lu eyed Ulaah. "I would not be displeased. Am I not a god?"

"Eli says you are not."

"Then maybe you should get your advice from Eli," shrugged Lu.

Ulaah looked at Lu blankly as he tried to reconcile the red-bearded man's words with everything the others had taught him. Then, with a hardened brow, Ulaah nodded. "I would spill blood for this power."

"Would you spill Tauta's blood for this power?"

"Yes," Ulaah eagerly replied.

Lu's eyes narrowed. "Would you spill the priestess' blood for this power?"

"Inyanga?" Ulaah gulped and then gave a determined nod.

Lu grinned as he studied his pupil. He liked what he saw. "I will teach you the dark ways so that you may obtain this power over the people. They deserve a leader such as you."

"Yes, teach me," Ulaah pleaded, almost in a frenzy.

"I will teach you, but you must first take an oath to follow me."

"I will do it! I will swear to follow you as my god!"

Lu's green eyes swelled with delight.

As Eli walked along the river path, he surveyed the new huts the villagers had built. Their workmanship had evolved, and the people now needed less direction. They were learning, and it pleased Eli. He saw the fields near the river where green stalks of corn and knee-high tails of grain waved in the gentle breeze. He noticed the watcher, Duhmee, with her long, golden hair, helping women water the crops. She had taught them well. Near the huts, he saw the loving Jophiel teaching a group of children huddled around her. Not far away, two adolescents chased chickens back into a pen made of bound branches. Eli chuckled when one of the chasing boys slipped and fell into the mud.

Eli breathed in the fresh morning air and nodded contentedly. His fellow caretakers had taught the clan well, and it would soon be time to move on.

When Eli turned back from the fields and noticed Chiacha with her large, protruding belly, his face filled with concern. Chiacha's countenance had dimmed in recent months, and Eli wasn't sure if the strain of pregnancy or something else weighed her down.

A scream from the river spun Eli. It wasn't a child's playful cry, but the harrowed shriek of a woman.

Eli rushed past the huts, along the river to the rocks by the dam, and slowed to a stop. His eyes widened when he saw a bloody Tauta sprawled across the rocks, his throat cut, his carving knife still in his lifeless hand. Beside him lay the priestess, Inyanga, her frock stained red from a bloody knife wound in the middle of her back.

"Look!" gasped a horrified villager. "Tauta took the blood of our priestess!"

"Then he cut his own throat, just like he does the caribou!" cried another. "What does it mean?"

Eli sank to his knees before his lifeless apprentice. He shook his head in dismay as more villagers gathered. "How did this happen?"

Not far away, in the brush by the bank of the river, a wide-eyed Ulaah watched. The power would now be his.

ATOP THE HILL, in a clearing that overlooked the valley, the ivory-cloaked Cyrus sat before the watchers on his council seat, holding a scepter topped by his golden orb. Eli and the others listened as the grand overseer spoke sternly.

Inyanga's murder and Tauta's apparent suicide were no small matter and had brought the overseer to their collective. Eli feared the consequences would be far-reaching, affecting not only the plains people but also the caretakers and their stewardships.

Eli looked down off the hill into the village. In its center, where Tauta usually prepared and roasted his game, his son Rata sat around an empty fire pit with saddened villagers.

Eli's gaze returned to the others gathered there. He saw Duhmee, a teacher of agriculture, her lengthy hair braided, her face heavy with concern. He saw Danjal, a master of the healing arts, who knew this wound would not quickly mend. Beside him, the lovely Jophiel, a purveyor of wisdom and learning, stared at the ground. Even she, who always found the best in the worst, was low.

Eli turned to the gray-bearded Cyrus. As overseer, his guidance was esteemed by most in the council, but not by all.

"Two of them died," shrugged Gadreel, the round-headed teacher of crafts who wore his long black hair pulled back in a bun. "They die all the time."

"This is different. It was murder," glared Jophiel.

"But what would possess Tauta to murder the priestess and then take his own life?" questioned Danjal.

"You're assuming that Tauta stabbed her and then cut his own throat," frowned Eli.

Cyrus's eyes shifted in thought.

"You are suggesting something different?" asked Jophiel. "The evidence speaks for itself."

Eli sighed and shook his head.

Cyrus's gaze turned to Lu, drawing in the dirt with a stick. "You are quiet in this matter, Luqiel?"

Lu wrinkled his nose. He did not like that name. "What more is there to say? Tauta murdered Inyanga and then cut his own throat. Perhaps the burden of leadership was too great. Tauta always seemed... troubled if you ask me."

"Perhaps something else happened."

All eyes turned to Eli.

"What do you suggest?" questioned Cyrus.

"There could have been a third party." Eli looked at Lu.

"A conspiracy!" laughed Gadreel. "They are not sophisticated enough to devise such a plan!"

"Perhaps *they* did not devise the plan," muttered Eli.

"Are you suggesting one of us?" scoffed Gadreel.

"Any such involvement would violate the Grand Precept," proclaimed Jophiel.

"And would be grounds for expulsion," added Cyrus.

"If there are no other revelations or pointless allegations, I suggest we adjourn. There is much damage to repair," insisted Jophiel.

Cyrus looked over the council, then nodded his approval.

Eli and the others were coming off the hill when a frantic woman rushed up the trail toward them. "Come!" she gasped, waving to Danjal, her face full of worry. "Chiacha gives child!"

Lu lowered his head at the announcement. He knew what would follow.

"What's the matter?" asked a concerned Danjal as he approached.

"Chiacha, she bleeds! Come!" cried the frantic woman.

Lu held Gadreel back as the council hurried down the hill toward the village. They then descended a branching trail that led toward the river.

Upon reaching the village, Eli and the others followed the frantic woman through the maze of mud and stick huts.

The sound of a crying newborn resonated within the mud hut as Eli and the others entered.

Danjal was already kneeling beside the bronze-skinned Chiacha, whose naked body was sprawled and bloodied, her eyes lifeless and staring. Danjal's eyes widened when he picked up the bloody infant screaming between Chiacha's legs. He turned back to Eli standing in the hut's entry and gasped, "It's a halfborn!"

Eli's shoulders sank when he saw the large baby boy, its flesh ivory, its head topped with red tufts of hair.

Eli and the others stepped aside as Cyrus pushed into the hut. The sight of the crying, twisting infant filled Cyrus with rage. "BRING ME LU!"

CHAPTER 5
INSURRECTION

Sarajevo
28 June 1914

Sunday mornings were usually quiet in Sarajevo. With the shops closed, the streets would have been empty if not for the visiting Archduke Franz Ferdinand. But with the presumptive heir to the throne of Austria and Hungary scheduled to visit the town hall, many eager Sarajevans lined the streets for a chance to see him and the lovely Duchess Sophie. But not all those waiting were fond of the man.

Young Gavrilo clutched the coat pocket holding his pistol as he stepped through the crowd. His dark-ringed eyes peered out from under his black hat as he watched the streetcar, loaded with eager faces, rumble by, its bell a gentle warning to those scampering across the tracks ahead. Gavrilo's dark eyes widened when he spotted the red-bearded Lu Storm-brewer standing in the shadows across the street behind the growing crowd. Gavrilo gulped and looked up the street as cheerful people continued to arrive. It angered him there were so many misguided Bosnians. *Today that will all change*, he told himself.

Gavrilo glanced back at Popović, who anxiously clutched the burlap bag that held his bomb. Gavrilo thought he could make out its brick-like shape through the tan fabric, but told himself no one would know what it was if they saw it.

Gavrilo's eyes narrowed when he spotted the brass buttons, black tunic, and red cuffs of a policeman, backing people off the cobbled street with a glance and a wave. Gavrilo looked further up the street to the Mostar Café. It took him a moment to find Muhamed in the crowd, but when he did, Gavrilo nodded approvingly. When he turned to the tall Stormbrewer across the street, he was gone.

Sunlight glistened off the golden orb atop Cyrus's staff as he walked along the river's parapet, eyeing the crowd of spectators jostling for a spot to see the archduke.

Further up the street, near Cumurja Bridge, Eli shook his head disapprovingly. He counted only ten policemen in the crowd and wondered where Captain Radulevic was. "Not enough. It won't be enough," he muttered. Eli glanced at Cyrus. He had warned him of the pending tragedy, but now it was too late. Their hands were tied. All would be lost if Radulevic and his police didn't stop the assassination.

Eli scanned the crowd. There were men in suits wearing bowlers or straw hats and women in long dresses wearing feathered hats or holding parasols. He saw wide-eyed boys in sailor shirts and knickers, and dainty girls holding flowers. Some wore traditional clothing: elaborate and colorful dresses on the women and burgundy, brimless hats on the men. Small black and yellow Austrian flags waved everywhere. All seemed eager to see the archduke and duchess. Eli feared what they would really see.

Cheers turned Cyrus's gaze up the crowded street. A procession of six cars approached with puffs of smoke trailing each.

Standing below Café Mostar's awning, Muhamed clutched his bomb under his coat as the cars approached. Through the waving flags and arms, he spotted Ferdinand in the third car back. The future emperor wore a light blue military dress uniform, brightly adorned with medals and brass buttons, with a green peacock-feathered hat atop his head. Beside him sat his wife Sophie, the Duchess of Hohenberg, in a white dress and veiled hat. With the car's fabric top down, Muhamed knew he needed only to arm the bomb and throw it into the car to fulfill his mission, but his body tightened as the vehicles approached. He glanced at Vaso, standing six feet away. His hand was inside his buttoned coat, his eyes wide, his body rocking in interrupted surges, like a windup toy about to be let loose.

Muhamed's mouth was parched, his muscles aching as the archduke's car neared. His eyes met Ferdinand's. The archduke's eyes were gray and calm, and he had a smile under his dark, curled mustache. Beside him sat the lovely Sophie, waving a white-gloved hand.

Losing his nerve, Muhamed released his hold on the bomb and pulled his trembling hand from his coat as the car motored past. He turned to the white-faced Vaso, still clutching his pistol, and waited for him to pull it out and shoot. The cars passed by.

Muhamed released a dejected sigh as his mind raced with what might have been. He looked across the street to a furious Danilo glaring at him, and the towering Stormbrewer following the cars behind the crowd, his brow bent, his green eyes determined.

Cyrus raised his cane when he spotted the red-bearded man moving through the crowd. "He's here! I knew it! Lu is behind this!"

Eli's head spun as Cyrus ran past him. He too had spotted Lu, but there was nothing he or Cyrus could do.

Nediko Čabrinović gulped as the cars approached. His eyes flashed to the café where Muhamed and Vaso had stood, and he wondered what had gone wrong. He felt the bomb in his coat pocket and breathed in courage. He started to pull it out but stopped when a policeman looked his way. Nediko's eyes flashed to the frantic Danilo. He knew he must act now, or it would be too late.

Ferdinand's car was twenty feet in front of him when Nediko pulled the bomb from his coat, twisted its lever, and threw it. It would have been a perfect throw, landing inside the archduke's car, but the driver sped up when he spotted the strange object flying toward them. The waving Ferdinand never saw the bomb as it narrowly missed his head and bounced off the car's pulled-back canvas top, landing on the cobbled street behind them. Before the driver of the following car knew what was happening, he was on top of the bomb. The violent blast ripped through the vehicle, shredding its driver and passengers with shrapnel. The metal fragments shot into the waving crowd and caused panicked shrieks as hot shards cut through men, women, and children.

Soldiers raced up from the rear, past the blown-open car, to check on the archduke, but his driver and the two leading cars had already sped away.

Amid the confusion, a frantic-eyed Nediko took his cyanide capsule from his pocket, bit down on it, and leaped off the parapet into the river.

An exhilarated Lu stood tall in the chaos as terrified spectators fled, trampling one another. Police whistles blew as the smoke cleared, revealing bodies on the cobbled street, some writhing in pain, others motionless, their blood spilling in-between the cobblestones. Lu's charged eyes turned to the archduke's car as it motored away. Determined, he started after it.

While the blast had caused nearby survivors to flee, it had drawn in others curious to see what had happened. Lu was pushing through the shifting crowd when he came face to face with the overseer.

"What have you done?" cried Cyrus, standing firm with one hand on his cane.

"Get out of my way!" raged Lu. But when Cyrus, still ten feet away, moved to block him, Lu angrily pulled a thick pewter rod from his coat and pointed it at the overseer.

Cyrus's eyes widened before a blinding light shot from the rod and blew him back off his feet. Lu's chest swelled at his might. He glared at the motionless Cyrus with a snarled lip as people rushed past. When he spotted Eli racing to Cyrus's aid, Lu raised his blazerod and fired at him. But the bolt missed when Eli dove to the street and shot through a policeman instead, knocking him ten feet back and leaving a smoldering hole in his chest.

Eli looked up from the street in disbelief as Lu dashed through the crowd with coattails flying. Eli leaped to his feet and chased Lu down an alley, but when he rounded the corner, Lu was gone.

Upon remembering Cyrus, Eli raced back and pushed through the crowd. "Cyrus, are you all right?" cried Eli as he kneeled beside his mentor. "What did Lu do?"

"He has a blazerod," gasped Cyrus.

Eli's mouth fell open at seeing the burn wound on the overseer's chest. "Where did he find a blazerod?"

"There's no time," wheezed Cyrus. "You must protect the archduke. There is still a chance, but...you must act quickly."

Eli looked at those around him for help, but he knew they could offer none. His worried gaze returned to the fading Cyrus. "I can't leave you."

"My time is finished," breathed Cyrus. "I've failed them." His eyes softened. "It's up to you now, but..." Cyrus slowly shook his head. "I fear there is too much for you to overcome."

"What must I do?"

"You must stop Lu. You know what he means to do."

"He cannot be trusted ever again," seethed Eli.

Cyrus choked down a swallow. "I fear all is lost."

"I can do it," Eli nodded. "I can handle Lu!"

Cyrus's eyes closed. "You will not succeed. They will be too much for you."

"I can stop Lu! I've done it before!"

"I'm not talking about Lu." Cyrus's eyes pulled open. They were cloudy and dull. He gazed up at the people gathered around them, watching with morbid curiosity. The overseer raised a weak and shaking hand and pointed at the mortals. Then his eyes closed, and his hand fell to the street.

Eli's shoulders sank as Cyrus's body relaxed. He angrily shook his head, looked up into the sky, and cried, "Arghh! It's not supposed to be this way!" Eli's anguished eyes moved to Cyrus's cane and its golden, ball-shaped handle. He watched as the engravings that wrapped around the orb faded and then disappeared. Eli's jaw tightened. He grabbed the cane, pulled the golden ball from its shaft, and pushed it into his coat pocket.

"Stop! You can't take that! It's his!" yelled an onlooker in the crowd. "He just robbed that man!"

Eli glared at the accuser as he jumped to his feet and pushed past him.

THOSE IN THE grand hall stood as the doors opened, and the archduke, his wife, and entourage scurried inside.

Unaware of the assassination attempt, Mayor Curčić stood at the podium as a small band played a welcoming anthem. "We are so fortunate to have with us, Archduke Franz—"

"Mister Mayor! I came here on a visit and am greeted with bombs! It is outrageous!" bellowed Ferdinand as he stormed to the head of the hall, his light blue uniform still wet with specks of blood not his own.

A flurry of gasps and shocked whispers ran through the crowd.

Speechless, the mayor bent his ear as his police chief whispered of the attempted assassination. The mayor straightened up and gasped, "Your Grace, my sincerest apologies! I—"

Ferdinand raised a halting hand, his dark curled mustache twitching.

The mayor gulped as the duchess whispered calming words into her husband's ear. After a moment, the composed archduke sat back up, pulled down on his blue tunic, and nodded. "Now you may speak."

ELI SLOWED to a walk as he neared the Sarajevo town hall. He paid no attention to its grand Moor-styled arches, ornately scalloped roof trim, and tan and brown-striped stone exterior. Eli's eyes were on the five remaining cars of Ferdinand's motorcade, surrounded by wary-eyed police and soldiers. "Is he all right? Is the archduke still alive?" Eli asked as he approached a soldier with a rifle.

"Stop right there," ordered the soldier, raising his rifle not to shoot but to block Eli's advance.

"Where is Captain Radulevic? I must speak to him!"

The soldier turned to an approaching policeman who, with narrow eyes, asked, "Who are you?"

"A friend. I must speak with Captain Radulevic. It's a matter of life or death."

The pencil-necked policeman surveyed the large Eli. "I'll try to find him. Keep him here."

The soldier nodded, took a step back, and then pointed his rifle at Eli's feet.

. . .

INSIDE THE GRAND HALL, the archduke looked over the seated crowd of loyalists from the podium as he continued with his prepared remarks. "...and today, it pleases us to visit your grand and lovely city. While today may not have been the warmest of welcomes," he paused as those gathered nervously laughed, "I see in this people an expression of their joy at the failure of the attempt at assassination—*my* assassination." Ferdinand's eyes swelled, as if only then realizing he had nearly been killed.

"I CAN'T FIND THE CAPTAIN," reported the pencil-necked policeman. "Who did you say you are? And what do you know about the attempt on the archduke?"

"Who I am doesn't matter," Eli glared. "You must act swiftly if you are to save the archduke!"

"What are you talking about? He's safe inside."

"He is not safe!"

"Is that a threat?" asked the policeman, stepping back and reaching for his pistol.

"It is not a threat, sir. Those that would have him dead will not rest," warned Eli.

The policeman gulped, glanced around at the soldiers and police gathered, and said, "I think he should be safe. Who would dare come against him now? Besides, an entire garrison is on its way from the barracks. He will be well protected."

"How long does he mean to stay in there?"

"What business is it of yours?" snapped the policeman.

"I'm trying to help you."

"Perhaps you are a trickster, trying to get information," surmised the policeman, his eyes beady.

Eli shook his head and looked around those gathered for signs of danger.

"YOUR GRACE, I'm so terribly sorry," groveled the mayor as he fidgeted with his Turkish hat in his white-gloved hands.

Ferdinand shook his head as those gathered filed out of the hall. "I must say, it was a bit of a shock having a bomb thrown at me!" He puffed out his chest at his bravery. "And in a way, a strange compliment, I should think—that some crazed soul should want me dead."

"Not much of a compliment for me, Your Grace," muttered Governor-General Oskar Potiorek.

"Your Grace, the hall is surrounded by soldiers," announced Baron Rumerskirch, the archduke's chamberlain.

"Very well," nodded a sober Ferdinand as he glanced at his wife. He clasped his gloved hands together and said, "Should we get on with the program?"

"The program, Your Grace?" asked Rumerskirch.

"Yes. The tour of the city," Ferdinand nodded.

"Your Grace..." Rumerskirch nervously smiled.

"I have come to this fair city to see my people. I should not disappoint them."

"Certainly, Your Grace...but after what has happened—"

"Nonsense. One cannot live one's life ducking from bombs!" Ferdinand huffed.

Baron Rumerskirch's eyes flashed from the archduke to the other ministers of state gathered. "Very well, Your Grace. We shall have the garrison line the streets of your parade route."

Governor-General Potiorek rubbed his chin beard in thought. "I'm afraid we can't have that. They will not have the proper dress for such an occasion."

"Such an occasion?" gasped Rumerskirch. "Saving the future emperor of Austria and Hungary's life?"

The insulted governor-general squared up to the baron and scoffed, "Do you think Sarajevo is full of assassins?"

"What of those injured in the blast?" asked Duchess Sophie, her delicate brow bent with concern.

The ministers stopped and turned, not used to hearing from the duchess in such matters.

"Uh, I believe there were sixteen or twenty casualties, Your Grace," reported the baron.

"How many were ours?" frowned Ferdinand.

"Those in the next car back, Your Grace. Four."

"The rest were Sarajevans? People in the crowd?" Sophie asked.

"Yes, Your Grace."

"How many were killed?" whispered Sophie, looking as if she might cry.

"That, I don't know, Your Grace. They were taken to the hospital," the baron replied.

Ferdinand knew his wife's mind and wasn't surprised by what came next.

"My dear, don't you think it a noble cause for us to visit those harmed in this heinous act? They were here to see us, after all." Sophie said with sad eyes.

Ferdinand turned to his ministers. Then, with a nod to his wife, he said, "Yes, my dear. I think we should do just that. We shall go to the hospital."

"Your Grace," protested Baron Rumerskirch.

Ferdinand raised a halting hand, vetoing his chamberlain.

Moved by the archduke's courage, the diminutive but feisty Count Harrach stepped up and said, "Your Grace, I shall ride on your running board. Any assassin's bullet will have to get through me first!"

THE PUTTER of starting engines turned Eli's head. "What's going on?" he asked, pointing to the men coming down the hall's steps to the waiting cars.

"Never you mind," replied the pencil-necked policeman. "Lieutenant, see that your men keep him here," he said, pointing at Eli.

With his light blue tunic and green feathered hat, Ferdinand stood out like a giant peacock in a herd of sheep as he descended the steps with the white-dressed duchess in hand. "Where's he going?" Eli asked as another soldier approached.

The soldiers looked at Eli blankly.

Eli removed Cyrus's golden orb from his pocket and studied its face for direction, but its surface was plain and smooth.

"What's that?" gasped a soldier, raising his rifle.

"He's got a bomb!" shouted another.

"No, it's not a bomb!" Eli insisted, tightening his grip on the golden ball.

"Put it on the ground!" demanded the thin-necked policeman, his pointed pistol quivering in his hand.

Eli looked at the policeman in frustration and set the orb down.

"Now, step back from it!"

Eli stepped back. The anxious policeman holstered his pistol and reached down for the ball. He studied the simple golden sphere with a furrowed brow. It had an opening for a cane on one end and a grooved circle on its opposite. "What is it?"

"Nothing that concerns you," glared Eli.

"We'll see about that. For all we know, you're the one who threw the bomb!" barked the policeman. He glanced at the soldiers gathered and said, "If he tries to run, shoot him," before leaving with the golden orb.

Eli sighed as two rifle muzzles raised to his head.

YOUNG GAVRILO STARED in the shop window as he considered what might have been. It had only been thirty minutes since the failed attempt on the archduke's life, but he could already feel the hope of a free Bosnia slipping away. He wondered where the others were. If they were caught, Gavrilo knew it would only be a matter of time before the Austrians beat his name out of them. He felt the pistol in his coat pocket and wondered if he should save them all the trouble and kill himself, like his hero, Bogdan Žerajić, had done.

Gavrilo's focus moved to his reflection in the window. He saw his dark-ringed eyes and thin mustache. He wondered what his life might have been like had he been born an Austrian or a Turk. A large shadow moved behind Gavrilo, raising the hair on the back of his neck as if a brisk winter breeze had crossed him. He gasped when he noticed the red-bearded Lu in the window staring at him. Gavrilo spun to the large man. "I-I don't know what happened! I don't know where they are!"

"Quiet!" barked Lu. "You have another chance. He will be delivered to you. Be ready, and do not disappoint me."

Gavrilo gulped as the red-bearded man walked away. He heard a flurry of excitement and turned toward the river and Latin Bridge, where people were hurrying along the street. "What's happening?" he asked, reaching out to a rushing man holding his hat.

"The archduke is returning!" the man exclaimed before scurrying off.

Gavrilo's body tightened, and he felt for his pistol.

THE LAST OF the archduke's procession had motored down the street when Eli turned to the soldiers guarding him. "He's gone. Now can I leave?"

"Not a chance," growled the soldier, his arm quivering from his rifle's weight, its muzzle a foot from Eli's head.

Eli surmised the situation and what was at stake. The rule of doing no harm was paramount, as was his oath to never force a mortal's mind, but stopping Lu was critical, and Eli thought extreme measures were justified. He wondered if the Holy and Great Ones would agree.

Eli's determined gaze moved from the soldiers to their rifles trained on his head. With the others having followed after the motorcade, there was not another soldier in sight.

With no time to waste, Eli looked the nearest soldier in the eyes and said, "There is no need for you to hold me here. I am not a threat." The watcher's persuasive gaze turned to the other. "Lower your rifles, and let me leave."

The soldiers blinked as they processed Eli's suggestion. One and then the other lowered their rifle. "You can leave now," muttered one, glancing at the other.

"Thank you." Eli was about to turn when he spotted the long-necked policeman emerging from the town hall, his hands empty of the orb.

"Captain Radulevic says to let him go," huffed the policeman.

"Where's the orb?" asked Eli with penetrating blue eyes.

"If you're talking about your gold ball, you'll have to take it up with the captain."

Eli sighed in frustration. Knowing there was no time to lose, he turned and ran after the departed motorcade.

. . .

GAVRILO'S EYES widened at the sound of the approaching vehicles. Fearing he might be out of position, he pushed through the crowd to get closer to the bridge, but when the first of the cars turned onto Franz Joseph Street, Gavrilo knew they would be coming right past him. *It's just as Stormbrewer said! The archduke is being delivered to me!*

Gavrilo changed direction and pushed through the crowd to the street. He had to be close enough not to miss. Gavrilo felt the cold steel of the handgun and knew the next seconds would make him a hero and change his country forever. He watched the first car motor past with three men in black suits and one in a blue soldier's uniform. Then came the next. Gavrilo's throat tightened when the third car turned, and the archduke's green peacock hat came into view. Gavrilo tasted the bile of hate churning in his gut. His hand tightened on the pistol's grip. *I cannot miss.*

The squeal of a car's brakes turned Gavrilo's attention. The lead vehicle had stopped, which in turn halted the second and third cars. They had taken the wrong turn.

Gavrilo's steely gaze moved to the archduke's car. It was stopped eight feet before him. He looked into the calm gray eyes of the man who would be the next emperor—the man who would again rob Bosnia of its freedom. Gavrilo stepped out into the street, raised his arm, and fired. The bullet ripped through the archduke's throat and spun his head. Gavrilo turned his pistol on the Governor-General, but when the car lurched, his bullet pierced Sophie's abdomen instead. She cried out as a crimson stain spread across her white dress, then slumped onto her husband's legs.

"NO!" yelled Eli at the sound of the gunshots. He raced around the corner, then stopped and watched in horror as men tackled Gavrilo to the street. With clenched fists, Eli raised his head to the heavens and released an agonized, "NOOO!"

IT WAS NEARLY MIDNIGHT, but the angry clashes between the

archduke's supporters and his enemies were far from over. A gunshot echoed in the distance as Captain Radulevic made his way back home. He wondered when the anti-Serbian demonstrations would end.

The police captain stopped and turned when he heard the rustling and looked back down the darkened lane. The flickering gaslights illuminated glowing pools of cobblestone bordered by shrubs and creeping vines swaying in the warm night breeze. He waited, expecting another to enter one of the pools of light, but there was no one.

Still in his police uniform, with a canvas bag hung from his shoulder, Radulevic's nervous eyes scanned the shadowy lane. The trickle of murky water running down the center gutter reminded him of the puddled blood near the bomb blast. He pushed the disturbing images from his mind and turned to resume his walk home.

Radulevic hadn't taken a step when a cat darted out from under a bench and stopped in the road before him. He reached for his pistol, then gave an uneasy sigh when he realized what it was. The cat's green eyes eerily glowed in the gaslight before it slinked into the blackness. With a tired sigh and shake of his head, Radulevic walked on.

While the archduke's assassination shocked many, murdering a political figure, even a popular monarch, was not uncommon. Assassination was the disenfranchised tool of change, and the House of Habsburg was not immune to it. The archduke's uncle, Emperor Franz Joseph, barely survived an attempt on his life as a young man. While loyalists mourned the death of Ferdinand, others quietly celebrated. But even the most strident separatists took issue with Duchess Sophie's killing.

As he passed through the shadows, Captain Radulevic congratulated himself for capturing the assassin, Gavrilo Princip, and the three co-conspirators. He hoped their trials and hangings would satisfy the Austrian loyalists. Radulevic considered the young revolutionary. Princip was barely nineteen years old. All of them so far were but boys—idealistic, foolish young men. The thought of the detective work necessary to unravel the assassin's plot excited the captain. He wondered what surprises the interrogations would bring and how far-reaching the conspiracy was.

While Radulevic was no champion of the archduke or the Austrian government, he doubted the killings would change anything. He hoped they would at least put the feeble pro-Serbia movement to rest, but he doubted even that. He wondered what the morrow would bring.

Unlocking his cottage door, Radulevic stepped inside, looked back down the dimly lit lane, and then closed and locked his door. After striking a match, he moved to a nearby lamp and lit its wick. He replaced the lamp's glass chimney and adjusted the flame until its warm light filled that corner of the room. The captain moved the lamp to his small dining table, removed his bag from off his shoulder, and set it on the table.

On the wall above the table hung a grainy portrait of his late wife, who had died from diphtheria two years before. Radulevic lovingly nodded to her as he removed his police cap and laid it on the table. He ran a hand through his curly black hair before undoing the top buttons of his red-collared tunic. He then removed his pistol belt and laid it across the back of a dining chair.

The captain opened his bag and took out a thin, half-eaten loaf of bread and a wedge of cheese. He uncorked a nearby bottle of wine, filled a glass, and sat at his table. The captain cut a piece of cheese and put it in his mouth, then reached into his bag and removed the four-inch golden ball. He placed it on the table beside the lamp. Radulevic eyed the shiny sphere as he ate the cheese, his lips smacking. He reached for a fat link of cured sausage, cut a piece, and pushed it into his mouth.

Radulevic's eyes narrowed as he studied the ball that had rested atop Cyrus's cane. It had been an enigma to him as long as he had known the equally mysterious Cyrus White. His eyes narrowed as he remembered the sphere's unusual engravings, but the ball appeared smooth to him now, except for the circular groove at its top. He thought he saw something in the center of it and held the ball closer to the lamp. When he felt the grooved circle, a glowing fleur-de-lis appeared and then faded. Radulevic's eyes widened. He touched the orb again. This time a faint Egyptian ankh appeared. When the image faded, he shook his head in dismay and touched the sphere a third time. Nothing happened. He rubbed it more vigorously, but when it remained unchanged, he set it back on the table before him.

Radulevic took a bite from his baguette and thought back to the bomb-strewn street. He shuddered at the memory of the smoldering car and the blood and bodies scattered around the blackened crater. The blast had thrown one of his men thirty feet and carved a five-inch smoking hole through his chest. Radulevic had never seen anything like it. It was not far from there that the captain had found the lifeless Cyrus. He remembered seeing Cyrus's cane without the golden orb. But when Radulevic returned, not ten minutes later, Cyrus's body was gone. Radulevic had even searched the hospital. It was as though Cyrus had vanished.

The captain studied the strange golden ball as he sipped his wine.

"What you have is not yours," came from the shadows.

Radulevic spun in his chair, nearly falling over. "Who's there!"

Eli stepped into the light with piercing blue eyes and a bent brow.

"You! How did you get in here?"

Eli held out his open palm to receive the orb.

"I could arrest you! How dare you break into my home!"

"You would arrest me for claiming what is rightfully mine?" asked Eli.

Radulevic pushed back from the table, knocking over his chair. His eyes were round as he reached for his pistol belt that had fallen on the floor.

Eli watched the captain fumble with the holster flap before finally brandishing the revolver.

"I could shoot you! It is well within my right!" gasped Radulevic.

"I'm here for the orb."

"What is it? Why is it so important to you?"

"It belongs to me now."

"It's gold, isn't it? That's why you want it!" said a flustered Radulevic, tightening his fingers around the revolver.

"The orb belongs to me. It is not yours," Eli calmly repeated, his hand still extended.

"It's evidence. You can't have it! And what did you do with Cyrus's body?"

Eli's eyes narrowed. "I did nothing with his body."

"Someone took it! When I went back, it was gone!"

Eli stepped closer to the agitated captain.

"Stop! I'll shoot! Perhaps you're a conspirator!"

"You know I am anything but that."

"So you say! I should arrest you!" barked Radulevic, sweat glistening on his forehead.

When Eli reached for the ball, Radulevic pulled the trigger. A flash and a loud *pop* echoed through the darkened room.

Eli's body stiffened, and he winced as if being poked by a stick.

The captain's eyes widened. He was about to fire again when Eli stripped the pistol from his hand. "What are you going to do to me? Kill me? I'm an officer of the law!" gasped Radulevic.

Eli tossed the revolver across the room, then took the golden orb in hand.

Radulevic's jaw slackened when a strange glowing script appeared on the side of the orb between Eli's fingers. When the writing faded, and Eli approached the round-eyed captain, Radulevic gulped and backed up against the wall. "What are you going to do to me?"

Eli raised his empty hand and placed it against the frightened captain's forehead. "Calm yourself. You will forget this," whispered the watcher with blue, penetrating eyes.

The captain's panic faded as Eli pulled his hand away. Radulevic stared blankly across the shadowy room as the watcher walked out the door with the orb.

CHAPTER 6
BLOOD AND SORROW

General Franz Conrad von Hötzendorf wrinkled his nose as he studied the telegram. He stroked his gray mustache and looked across his desk at the red-bearded Lu. "Are you sure?"

"Germany has promised their support, have they not?" asked Lu.

Hötzendorf vaguely nodded.

Lu's green eyes penetrated the general. "You are the chief of staff. You serve Francis Joseph the First, Emperor of Austria, Apostolic King of Hungary, King of Bohemia, Dalmatia, Croatia, Slavonia, Illyria, and Galicia Lodomeria."

Hötzendorf straightened in his chair.

"How many times have you asked the emperor to go to war?"

"Many," nodded General Hötzendorf, staring across the office.

"You want only the best for the Austrian Empire, and so do I."

The general nodded.

"But who bent the emperor's ear each time you asked for war, causing him to disregard your pleas for a stronger, greater Austria?"

Hötzendorf gulped. "The archduke."

Lu's green eyes narrowed. "In a way, the Serbians did you a favor."

"Yes," Hötzendorf breathed, his gaze still distant.

"Then there is the question of Russia."

"Yes, Russia. They are becoming a problem," muttered Hötzendorf.

"Emperor Wilhelm himself has said war must come with them sooner or later if Germany is to survive."

"Yes, he has said that," nodded Hötzendorf.

"Sooner is always better than later, I like to say. You must strike before the Russians become too strong and move to crush Austria," urged Lu.

General Hötzendorf breathed in, swelling his light blue tunic with all its medals, then nodded resolutely. "Herr Stormbrewer, you are a loyal advisor and friend to the Austrian Empire. We should be in your debt."

Lu leaned back and grinned. "Perhaps you will ingratiate me with Kaiser Wilhelm."

SARAJEVO
JULY 1914

IT WAS a hot summer day in Sarajevo. The windows of Eli's quarters stood open, allowing the warm summer breeze to gently stir the window sheers. Wafts of lilac from along the river sweetened the otherwise hot and stale air.

Eli's blue eyes were dim and distant as he sat at the table before the dull golden orb, his shirt open, his dark flowing hair disheveled. A month had passed since his failure, and the sphere was still quiet. For Eli, nothing had changed, but the world beyond his windows was on the verge of upheaval. Austria and Hungary had declared war on Serbia, and Eli knew, like a game of dominos, other countries would follow. Germany would support Austria, which in turn would bring in France and then England. And then there was Russia. Eli closed his eyes. It had all been foreseen. The world would burn.

Eli's heart ached as he considered what would come. He was no stranger to such anguish. He had witnessed countless wars, plagues, and famines. Human pride, hate, and cruelty were all too familiar to him; so were the pain and suffering they brought. It grieved him that such things were unnecessary. Eli knew he and his kind had made a difference. The watchers had brought about good. They had allowed the best of humanity to flourish and shine. But even in the grandest and purest of times, dark forces lurking in the shadows like a panther ready to pounce, stirred up hatred, envy, and greed. The veneer of good rarely withstood such attacks. The cycle had repeated itself more times than Eli could remember. He had lamented his failures and basked in his successes. Maybe too much so, Cyrus would have said.

Eli looked down at his smooth, muscular chest to the scar on his abdomen where the captain's bullet had struck him. While the bullet would have easily slain a man, Eli thought it strange that it had left even a mark on him. In the past, it would not have done so.

Eli sighed. He reached for the smooth orb and ran his fingers along its surface. It faintly glowed at his touch but then faded again. Eli wondered if he was being punished for not doing enough. He wondered if he was no longer worthy of receiving direction. He wondered if his power had left with Cyrus.

Eli considered Cyrus's warning that he was perhaps too invested in the human cause. He remembered Cyrus telling him his fascination with humanity would be his downfall. Eli didn't know how that could be. He didn't know how he could do his work any other way.

Eli's face saddened when he thought of Lu and his treachery. Destroying Cyrus was just the latest of his many betrayals. A part of Eli wanted to go after him, to hunt Lu down and destroy him for what he had done, but such acts of vengeance against his own kind were forbidden. Eli wondered when the Holy and Great Ones would intervene and dispense their retribution. He had wondered that for a very long time. He shook his head as he considered his impatience. It was a human characteristic.

Eli moved to the open window. He looked across the river and watched a streetcar carry its passengers along Appel Quay. When it passed Latin Bridge, his gaze moved to Franz Joseph Street. It struck Eli as odd that the archduke—the man next in line for the Austrian throne

—was murdered on the street named after the man sitting on that throne. Eli wondered if the flowers that marked the spot were still there. His tired eyes moved further up the riverfront to where Cyrus had lain. Eli wondered what had happened to Cyrus's body as he looked down at the golden orb in his hand.

Eli breathed out a restless sigh and shook his head. He could do nothing more staying in Sarajevo. That time had passed. He had hoped by now to know what to do, where to go, and how to stop the growing storm, but all was dark to Eli. Not even the orb gave him direction.

Eli turned back into the room and moved to a small rosewood box resting atop the table. Its wooden finish and inlaid stones were aged and faded. He opened the box to a formed, red velvet interior, laid the golden ball inside, and closed its lid.

PARIS, FRANCE
3 AUGUST 1914

THE YOUNG FRENCH nurse was making a hospital bed when the commotion arose down the hall. After finishing her work, Michelle brushed a strand of her chestnut hair back behind her ear and turned at the clatter of hard-soled shoes rushing down the corridor. She moved to the hospital room door, the six beds behind her empty but for one. Her chocolate brown eyes widened at the muffled shouts, and she started down the hall, passing a boy on crutches, to see what had happened. Atop Michelle's pinned-back hair was a white nurses' hat. Beneath a white apron with a red cross on its chest, she wore a sky-blue nurse's dress. When Michelle reached a cluster of eager-faced nurses exchanging anxious whispers, she stopped and asked, "What's happening?"

A seasoned nurse with streaks of gray turned to Michelle. "You haven't heard? France has declared war on Germany!"

Michelle gave a slight gasp and put a hand to her breast. "What does that mean?"

A younger nurse with red, tear-filled eyes turned to her and said, "It means our men will go off to war."

"Don't be so dramatic," said another. "We have the best army in the world!"

Michelle's worried eyes shifted in thought as the other nurses continued their chatter.

When Doctor Joffre appeared in a long white coat, the nurses quieted and moved against the wall. "What is the meaning of this?" He asked with a bent brow.

"War has just been declared, Doctor," replied an anxious nurse.

"Yes, yes, I know. Get back to work," Joffre huffed as he passed by.

"But what does it mean for us? For the hospital?" asked a nurse.

"It means you are about to graduate from bedpans and bed sheets."

Michelle watched the doctor disappear around a corner, wondering what might change with a war.

"All right, everyone. You heard the doctor. Back to work," ordered the old nurse.

Michelle didn't move as the other nurses returned to their work. When the head nurse turned to leave, Michelle reached for her arm and said, "What does it really mean for us?"

The graying old nurse looked at her sadly. "It means we will watch many of our finest young men die."

Michelle lowered her head as the old nurse turned and walked away.

SARAJEVO
SEPTEMBER 1914

THE TREES on the hills and along the street were changing color. The green, life-giving leaves were now burnt orange and blood red. Some thought the fall colors were a lovely thing to behold, but Eli saw it differently. The brightly colored leaves would soon wither and fall and be blown by the wind and crushed underfoot until there were no more. Only barren gray branches would remain.

Eli considered the cycle of life as he sat at the outdoor café. He watched a young mother pushing a baby in a carriage. She stopped beside him to situate the blanket that insulated her infant son from the cool fall breeze. Eli saw the baby's plump cheeks and curious eyes. He considered the infant's mortality. He would soon be a boy, playful, rambunctious, and full of life. Then an adolescent, craving attention and dealing with the pressures of youth and the uncertainty of pending adulthood. Next, he would be a young man, driven by passion, wanting for love and fortune. Then a father with the worries of providing for his own. He would soon bury his mother—the woman who swaddled, loved, and raised him. He would mourn her loss, but not for long. His survival would become paramount until his children lowered him into the ground. Would he be a great man? Eli wondered. Would he be a general? An artist? A simple laborer? Or would he be a pauper? Would he be well-loved? Or would he be loathsome and despised? It was a complex formula dependent on an infinite number of variables. Over and over, it happened. The cycle fascinated Eli. He was envious of man's journey, as short and potent as it was.

When the baby began to fuss, the mother bent down and offered comforting words. Eli gave a faint nod as the young mother looked up at him and smiled. He watched as she pushed her carriage away.

Eli returned to his newspaper and tea. When a shadow passed by him, he looked up. The young waitress had blonde braided hair pulled back under a small red hat.

"More tea?" she asked, her soft blue eyes wide with infatuation.

"No, thank you, Ana," Eli smiled. She had served him nearly every day for the past few months, and he knew her persona well. Upon first meeting, he had seen in her a kind, nurturing woman, but Eli perceived her future to be filled with pain, suffering, and loss. Eli tried not to think of those things, having developed a fondness for her.

The waitress' chest softly heaved as she took in Eli's handsome features. "What does the paper say today?"

Eli glanced at his newspaper. Knowing she couldn't read, he was tempted to tell her all was right in the world, but he knew better. "The Germans have invaded France," he sighed.

Ana's face filled with concern. "What of the Austrians?" she asked as she balanced a tray with two empty glasses.

"They are now fighting in Russia and Serbia."

"My brother is with them," she breathed, looking down.

Eli felt her worry and fear.

Ana gulped, then inched closer to Eli. "I always see you here alone."

Eli nodded.

Ana gave a reticent nod, started to turn, then stopped. Breathing in courage, the waitress turned back to Eli. She tilted her head as she fumbled for the words. "If-if you would enjoy my company, maybe..."

Eli's smile faded. He could see her interest in him and wondered why she was lonely. Ana was lovely, young, and shapely—qualities that would attract most men. He tried to deny his attraction to her, telling himself it was more of a feeling of interest than primal longing—that would not be appropriate for him.

"I'm sorry. Forget I said that," Ana said, turning.

"Ana, wait." Eli reached for her.

When Ana stopped, her tray tipped, and a glass fell to the patio, shattering. "Oh, stupid me," she muttered.

"No, it was my fault," frowned Eli. He lowered to a knee and began gathering up the shards of broken glass.

"Be careful. I'll get a wastebasket." Embarrassed by her clumsiness, Ana felt the other diners' eyes on her.

When she returned, Eli emptied his hands of the broken glass and offered a harmless smile.

"Your hand. You're cut," Ana breathed, pointing to the small puddle of blood forming in his palm.

Eli's brow furrowed in dismay, and he muttered, "It's not possible."

Ana carefully wiped the blood from his palm with a white table napkin, expecting to see an open wound where the glass had sliced him. But when she removed the napkin, the small red fissure closed before her eyes, leaving only the smooth, meaty flesh of Eli's large hand. Blinking in wonder, she looked into Eli's eyes. "I thought it... You were bleeding." Ana gasped when the crimson stain on the napkin faded to white. "I'm seeing things," she muttered, getting to her feet.

Eli reached out to Ana, but she turned and left. He sat back in his chair and stared at his hand.

CHAPTER 7
THE VISITOR

I t was a lovely sunny day. The green rolling hills were alive with baaing sheep, and the tall trees danced with chirping birds. But a growing cloud, which changed from white to gray, dimmed the fields and quieted the trees. With the shrinking rays of sunlight, dreariness turned to desolation. The sheep turned to dust, and the fluttering birds fell to the once green earth and vanished. The dark and empty fields stretched for miles. Where once pastures and forests lay, there was a barren waste, a sea of tree stumps jutting from the oozing mud. The northern sky was darker still. Roiling clouds filled with man-made lightning and thunder rocked the ground. The wasteland moved past, as though viewed by a soaring eagle, slowly at first, and then faster, until the lines of barbed wire and trenches filled with gray-uniformed men were a blur. Towns and cities followed, all in ruin. The eagle flew across a great river, through the plumes of smoke over a city. It circled a gray, domed palace with jutting flags, black, red, and gold. The eagle lit on a thick, stone window ledge and looked through the wrinkled glass, past the men in uniforms with proud mustaches, to a tall man in a dark cloak with red, combed-back hair. The red-bearded man turned and glared out the window with fiery eyes.

Eli catapulted up in his bed with his chest heaving and gasped, "Lu!"

It was not the first time Eli had dreamed the dream. He drew in a ragged breath and looked across the room. He saw the small streams of water running down the window from the beating rain.

Eli pushed aside the covers, pulled on his robe, and moved to the window. His heart was still pounding as he stared across the storm-swept river. Months had passed, but Eli was still in Sarajevo. He felt shameful and alone.

Eli's gaze moved to a nearby table and the rosewood box that held the orb. He had not opened it in weeks. Beside the box lay a knife. Eli studied the knife, then reached for it. He turned his hand and pricked his palm. Bright red blood puddled up from the prick. Eli counted how long it took for it to fade away to only a faint mark. *Thirty seconds.* There were dozens of such marks on his hand, and each had taken longer to heal. *What is happening to me? Am I being punished?*

Eli looked out the window at a man hurrying along the street, pushing an umbrella into the rain, but the watcher's thoughts were elsewhere.

A knock came at his door.

"Yes, what is it?" Eli asked, looking back.

The tall door opened with a creak, allowing the hallway light to spill into his darkened room. At the door stood a middle-aged woman in a dress and sweater. "Good morning, Mister Eli. What would you like for breakfast?"

"Nothing for me this morning, Missus Jovanović," Eli said, unable to hide his dejection.

"Can I get you anything?"

"No, thank you." Eli sighed, turning back to the rain-streaked window.

Mrs. Jovanović eyed her unusual tenant silhouetted in the window. "I don't suppose you'll be going out today?"

"No," muttered Eli.

"Well then, ring if you need anything." Mrs. Jovanović closed the door, casting the chamber back into shadow.

Eli watched a half-empty streetcar roll through the rain going in one direction, while a small boat motored up the river in the other. He saw a baker standing inside his door waiting for customers, and a mother holding an umbrella urging her three small children around puddles. Eli considered the rigors of human life and how difficult it must be.

When the room lightened behind him, Eli sighed and said, "What is it now, Missus Jovanović?"

"I have never gone by that name," replied a feminine voice, young but rich in tone.

Eli spun from the window to a woman standing across the room. She wore a flowing white gown and glowed like alabaster. "Charmeine! What are you doing here?"

"Hello, Elijah," she said with a gentle smile. "I've come to check on you."

"Check on me?" frowned Eli.

"Yes," she softly replied, her eyes those of a caring sister. "You can hide no longer."

Eli stiffened. "I'm not hiding."

The glowing Charmeine looked upon Eli knowingly.

Eli sighed and shook his head. "I don't know what's happened. Ever since...ever since Lu took Cyrus..."

"Yes?"

"The world has been dark to me. Even the director is quiet."

Charmeine recognized the distress in Eli's eyes. Her gaze turned to the rosewood box. "How can the domain sphere speak to you if you are not listening?"

Eli moved to the table and opened the box. He removed the orb and held it up for the messenger to see.

Charmeine's glowing eyes moved from the dull orb to Eli. "You are needed, Elijah. Lu and his followers are moving unchecked. The world grows darker each day. Death and chaos abound as you sulk in your room."

Eli looked down. "I don't know what it is I am to do."

"You have guided these mortals for a very long time. Must you be told to do everything?"

Eli sighed. He glanced at his hand. "There's something else."

"What is it?"

"I feel I'm...*changing*."

"Changing? How?" Charmeine asked, her golden eyes discerning.

"When I prick my hand, I bleed."

Charmeine laughed.

"I don't see what's so funny about it," frowned Eli.

"Perhaps you are finally getting what you have always wanted."

Eli shook his head, as if not understanding.

"That doesn't work with me, Elijah. You have long thirsted for mortal life. Cyrus himself warned you of this. Perhaps the Great Ones are granting your wish."

"But...it's not my wish."

"Is that so?" questioned Charmeine.

Eli straightened up and dropped his hand. "You've come to tell me I can still matter? That I can still guide mortals?"

Charmeine's face grew serious. "The time for teaching is long past. Your numbers have dwindled to but a few while the forces of evil have grown. The balance is tilted. The evil influence of Lu and his followers must be countered before it grows too late and all is lost."

"I fear a great cataclysm," Eli breathed. "Like before."

"That was the before time. We are nearing the end times. But Lu does not wish that. His only hope of maintaining power is delaying the end. He wishes to overcome good with evil."

"But the Holy and Great Ones could surely stop him, like before."

"They have vowed never again to interfere. The ennoblement of man is up to man—and those who still hold the power of persuasion."

Eli gulped. "You're talking about me."

"That is your calling."

"What must happen? How does humanity fulfill its destiny?"

"The balance must be restored. Evil must be countered. The way must be prepared by a forerunner before the *Ihidaya*, the Enlightened One, can return. But you know these things, Elijah."

"Am *I* that forerunner?" asked Eli searchingly.

Charmeine's golden eyes narrowed. "You are not."

"Then what is it I'm to do? The domain sphere is silent! How am I to do it alone? Cyrus is gone!" fumed Eli.

Charmeine studied Eli, surprised at his human outburst. "Elijah, you are capable of acting without Cyrus. You have done so for thousands of years."

"But not without direction!" Eli insisted, pointing to the orb.

"Lu means to rule unchecked. He will come for the rest of you."

"The rest of us?" Eli's brow furrowed in thought. "He has a blaze-rod. That's the only way he can harm us."

"That is not the *only* way," replied Charmeine.

Eli drew in a beleaguered breath. "What if I'm not enough?"

Charmeine smiled. "You have been enough before."

"But...what of my weakness?" asked Eli.

"Which one?"

Not amused, Eli held up his pricked palm.

"Consider it motivation. Time is flowing."

"But time is only an obstacle to mortals," frowned Eli.

"That is right," Charmeine replied with a departing nod.

Eli watched as the room dimmed, and Charmeine faded away.

Moving to a chair, Eli sat and cradled the orb, expecting it to come to life. He waited for it to give him a directive or to open a travel portal —anything that would allow him to act, but nothing happened. An hour passed, then two. All day he waited and watched the orb, but it remained dim.

The rainy day turned to night.

When the rising sun swept across the morning sky, a dejected Eli returned the orb to the rosewood box and shut its lid. He shook his head in frustration. To Eli, the answer was clear. He was no longer wanted.

With stern, determined eyes, Eli moved to his wardrobe, removed a worn leather suitcase, placed it on the bed, and began to dress.

BERNE, SWITZERLAND
20 DECEMBER 1914

THE THIN, balding man was sitting at the library table reading from *Das Kapital* when the large shadow moved over him. Intent on the text, scribbling notes in the margins with a pencil, he finally shook his head and said, "Move, you're blocking my light."

"You enjoy Karl Marx?" came the penetrating voice.

Vladimir Lenin looked up from his book. He had the air of a professor with narrow, inquisitive eyes and wore a dark mustache and goatee. "Do you know Marx?" Lenin asked, eyeing the large, red-bearded man.

"I knew him," Lu nodded, his look almost boastful.

Lenin shifted in his seat. "Some say he's a revolutionary, but I say he's a brilliant economist and philosopher."

Lu grinned. He could see right through the man.

Lenin studied Lu. "Who are you?"

"My name doesn't matter."

Lenin gulped. "What-what can I do for you?"

"Why are you here in Switzerland when you are anything but neutral?"

"I-I don't know what you mean."

"This place is not your home; it is Mother Russia. She beckons you."

Lenin's eyes narrowed. "How do you know me?"

"Your countrymen are at war."

"Yes, I know. They are oppressed by a tyrannical government. A tsar who is not worth his weight in salt!"

"Millions of your countrymen will die...for him."

Lenin's jaw tightened. "There's nothing I can do."

"There's always something one can do." Lu bent down to Lenin's ear and whispered, "Can't you hear them? The proletariat, the workers, cry out for you."

Lenin's face went blank. He glanced around the library, then said, "You mean...revolution? That was tried once. We failed."

"That is because you went about it the wrong way," shrugged Lu.

Lenin studied the large man. Then, in realization, he said. "The Austrians put you up to this, didn't they? They seek a divided Russia so they may prevail in the war!"

Lu laughed. "They seek what every nation, what every monarch, what every politician seeks: power. Pure, boundless, power. If you do what I say, I will see that you get it."

Lenin's face brightened, and he closed his book.

LARISSA, GREECE
23 DECEMBER 1914

ELI WAS GAZING out the train window when a pot-bellied man wearing a suit and straw hat hefted his bag onto the overhead shelf. Eli nodded politely when the man motioned to the vacant seat across from him, but he would have rather been alone. Eli glanced at his leather shoulder bag beside him. Its flap had fallen open, exposing the rosewood box holding the orb. Eli closed the bag and turned to the window. He wondered why he had bothered to bring the sphere.

Eli heard the train's whistle, followed by the screech of iron wheels spinning on iron tracks. He gazed out the window as they rolled past Larissa Station. The smell of burned coal filtered into the car until the train was up to speed. Eli half-watched as passing buildings changed to crudely plowed fields.

"Is Athens your home?" asked the pot-bellied man, removing his hat to a balding head.

Eli turned to the traveler. He perceived he was a kind man in need of conversation. Eli smiled politely and said in Greek, "No."

"Business then?" the man prodded, still uncertain he was speaking to a fellow Greek.

Eli sighed, then shook his head. His fleeing Europe was the opposite of business. "No, vacation," Eli finally said with an uneasy smile.

"Ah, yes. Athens is very nice this time of year," nodded the man as he pushed a loose strand of thin black hair back atop his head. "Me, I'm on business. Sales."

Eli politely smiled.

The businessman eyed Eli, coveting his thick brown hair, then asked, "Are you German?"

"No," frowned Eli. "Why do you ask?"

"Many Germans vacation in Athens. I just thought—"

"I'm not German."

The businessman shrugged, then unfolded his newspaper.

Not wanting to know of the war, Eli looked out the window. When he felt the gaze of another on him, the watcher turned to a pasty-faced man seated four rows ahead, looking elsewhere. The wiry traveler had long, stringy hair and wore a cheap suit. Eli sensed something unusual about the man, partially hidden by a seat. When Eli looked away, the pasty-faced man's sunken eyes returned to him.

Eli's inadvertent gaze settled on the newspaper headline before him, "GERMANS CAPTURE ANTWERP!" He sighed in frustration and looked out the window.

Eli's tired gaze faded into the past as the fields moved by him. It wasn't his first time in Greece. He thought of those whose paths he had crossed ages before, Archimedes, Hippocrates, Socrates—brilliant, gifted men who would forever change the world and humanity. *The work was different then*, he told himself. *It was simpler and more rewarding.* Eli thought of Cyrus and imagined him saying, *"Needing a reward for one's work is not part of the creed."* Eli sighed. Things were different now. Cyrus was gone, and Lu and his followers were raging. Eli shook the thought from his head. *There's nothing I can do.*

Eli watched the passing fields turn to trees. After a few minutes, his eyes grew heavy, then closed.

The watcher's eyes shot open when he felt someone near him. He saw the balding businessman asleep in the seat across from him, and the wiry man in the cheap suit hurrying away with a leather bag. Eli's gaze returned to his empty seat. His bag—the orb—was gone!

Eli jumped to his feet and hurried after the stringy-haired man, but when the scraggly thief saw Eli following, he darted to the end of the car, out its door, and into the next. Eli chased after him, slowing to squeeze past a woman and her daughter.

By the time Eli entered the next car, the thief was exiting at the far end. When Eli raced past the conductor, the flabby-jowled man spun his head to see what the commotion was.

Eli entered the last car to find the stringy-haired thief standing at the rear door, his chest heaving, his dark, empty eyes glaring at the watcher. *A halfborn.* "What are you doing here?" seethed Eli as he slowly approached.

"I'm taking what is rightfully ours," snarled the ghoulish man.

"That is not yours. Give it to me!" Eli demanded as passengers in the car stirred in their seats.

The sunken-eyed thief shook his head. "I will not!"

Eli stepped closer. "I will take it!"

The pasty-faced thief shook his head.

"You should not be here!" fumed Eli. "Your kind has been long forbidden!"

The ghastly thief loathingly stared down the approaching Eli, then growled, "We are everywhere."

"What's going on here?" cried the conductor, entering the car.

Eli considered how best to handle the matter. From experience, he knew halfborns to be a treacherous lot. "That man stole my bag," Eli replied with a pointing finger.

"Give it back, son. There's nowhere to go," scolded the conductor from behind Eli. Passengers were turned and watching now.

"It is not yours!" snarled the thief as he clutched the bag, his sunken eyes darker still.

Eli moved closer, his brow bent, his jaw tight, his arm reaching for the bag.

The ghoulish thief pulled a revolver from his coat and pointed it at Eli. Gasps from watching passengers filled the car.

Eli stopped. His eyes widened as he remembered Captain Radulevic's bullet. That was months before when his change had first started. He wondered what a bullet would do to him now. Eli shook away the thought and stepped closer, but when he saw the halfborn's finger tighten on the trigger, he dove into an open seat. The revolver's loud *crack* echoed through the car as shrieking passengers ducked in their seats.

When Eli got to his feet, the rear door was open, and the halfborn was gone. He rushed to the door and scanned the empty tracks and olive trees for the thief and his bag, but the halfborn had disappeared. Eli shook his head as he considered the ramifications of not only losing the orb but of having halfborns once again among men.

A woman's scream turned Eli. His mouth fell open at the conductor lying on the aisle floor, staring at the ceiling. The watcher rushed to the lifeless man. He had a bullet hole in his chest and a crimson pool growing beneath him. Eli's knees weakened, and his legs faltered as he lowered to the floor. He touched the pooled blood, then turned his hand and stared at the sticky crimson on his fingers. *What have I done? I could have stopped the bullet and spared his life. He was innocent! He should not have died. It wasn't his time!*

Eli looked from the lifeless man to the open train door. *Lu has opened the abyss. I have to do something, but what? The director is gone.* Eli's jaw tightened, and his eyes swelled with determination. He could hide no longer.

CHARLEVILLE-MÉZIÈRES, FRANCE
GERMAN SUPREME ARMY COMMAND HEADQUARTERS
27 DECEMBER 1914

GENERAL ERICH VON FALKENHAVN was a handsome man with a cleft chin, short gray hair, and a neat mustache. He quietly listened to the two arguing generals seated across from him at the large table, their thick mustaches dancing, their fingers pointing and wagging.

With the war stalled, Kaiser Wilhelm had appointed Falkenhavn Prussian Minister of War two months before. Unlike his predecessor, Falkenhavn had centralized his decision making, leaving the other generals frustrated as they argued their war strategies in vain.

"Generals," Falkenhavn frowned, "I have made up my mind. The plan will proceed as I have directed. You are dismissed." He watched the fuming generals get up from the table and file out of the dark-paneled room.

The tall mahogany door had not been closed long when a side door opened, and a large red-bearded man in a suit entered.

"They disagree with the plan," Falkenhavn frowned. He knew the emperor's patience would not extend indefinitely and feared the army's lack of progress might lead to his demise as well.

"They cannot foresee the end," shrugged Lu as he sat, filling the chair. He studied the general. He knew Falkenhavn's ambitions well and found him a suitable pawn.

"When will we see progress?" Falkenhavn asked, nervously twisting the end of his mustache.

"There are many pieces in motion. Pieces you cannot comprehend. In this, you must trust me, as Kaiser Wilhelm does."

Falkenhavn gulped and nodded. A knock at the door turned his head. "Yes?"

A young lieutenant peered into the room and said, "There is a visitor at the main gate, sir."

"A visitor?" Falkenhavn huffed. "Who is it? I'm expecting no one."

"He says he is here to see Herr Stormbrewer. He says only that his name is Gik."

"Gik?" Falkenhavn glared.

"He is for me," Lu said, turning to the door.

The general gasped when a bony man in a baggy suit entered the office. "My god, does he have cholera?"

Gik looked at the general with dark, sunken eyes and shrugged.

"He does not look well!"

"He is a sad remnant from another age," Lu said, waving Gik closer.

Falkenhavn turned to Lu, not understanding his meaning.

Lu's gaze moved to the leather bag in Gik's bony hand. "You have something for me?"

Gik's hollow eyes flashed to the general.

"It's all right," Lu nodded, waving the halfborn closer.

Gik set the bag on the table beside Stormbrewer, then backed away.

Lu's face filled with satisfaction when he opened the bag and saw the rosewood box. After setting it on the table, he opened it to the gleaming golden orb.

"What is that?" Falkenhavn asked, his eyes wide as he stretched to see it.

Lu held the director in his hand and breathed, "It is everything." He set the orb back into its box and turned to Gik. "What of him?"

"He still walks the earth, as do the others," Gik replied, looking down in shame. "I must have *it* to defeat them."

Lu considered the halfborn's request, then reached into his coat, removed his pewter blazerod, and set it on the table.

"What is that? A weapon?" Falkenhavn asked, even more intrigued.

"I am entrusting you with this," said a stern-eyed Lu. "There is not another. Finish the work that should have been completed long ago."

"Yes, master," The halfborn approached Lu, bowed as if he were royalty, took the pewter cylinder, and stepped backward toward the door.

"Do not disappoint me," glared Lu.

Gik looked up from the weapon, wiped the stringy hair from his eyes, and hissed, "I will not."

CHAPTER 8

THE FRONT

PARIS, FRANCE
5 JANUARY 1915

Gare de l'Est, or Station of the East, was a sea of commotion with trains coming and going and everywhere men in uniform. Eli's nose wrinkled as he stepped off the train. He smelled the trepidation and uncertainty. With the Western Front only sixty miles from Paris, fear of an advancing German Army gripped the city. The Germans might have already sacked Paris had it not been for the hundreds of thousands of British troops who had helped the French hold the line. With both sides dug into trenches that stretched the width of France, and artillery that rained down day and night, advancements on either side were measured by steps.

Despite the stalemate, hundreds of thousands of men had already died. Whether from machine gun bullets ripping across open fields or artillery shells dropping from the sky and exploding, it was the same. On one August day alone, nearly thirty thousand were killed. And that was just on the Western Front. The Eastern Front, where Austrian and German forces battled Russian and Serbian, was even more deadly. Now battles even raged at sea. It was just as Cyrus had foreseen; the world was at war.

As Eli scanned the crowded train platform, it was easy to spot the French soldiers in their sky-blue coats and caps. The British troops' olive-drab uniforms and broad steel pot helmets stood out less. Eli saw the frightened faces of young men waiting to be moved to the front and knew many would never come home.

Walking along the crowded platform with his suitcase in hand, Eli turned as a train with white cars bearing red crosses rolled into the station. Moving through the shifting crowd, he made his way toward that platform. His face saddened at the nurses in white dresses attending to wounded men on stretchers as orderlies in smocks carried them to waiting ambulances. The thought he was just seconds from stopping the archduke's murder and preventing it all scourged Eli's soul.

As the watcher turned from the hospital train and continued through the crowded station, his eyes were drawn to its enormous arched ceiling. He saw pigeons resting high on the trusses, below the skylights and the gray sky. Soon he was outside the station in the large, fenced-off courtyard, where four lines of dour-faced soldiers inched their way toward the trains. Only one row moved out. Beyond the gate, more men in uniform crowded in as cars puttered along the street and horse-drawn wagons delivered supplies. Eli looked up into the gloomy sky. He knew the sun was somewhere above the clouds and missed its warmth.

As Eli neared the exit gate, the line of travelers slowed. A policeman with a pencil mustache in a round, flat hat checked papers. Several more stood nearby with pistol belts and serious faces.

"Papers, please. Have your papers ready," repeated an officer, his thumbs in his pistol belt, as the line inched forward.

"Where are your papers?" asked the pencil-mustached officer when Eli finally reached the front of the line.

"I have no papers," replied Eli in flawless French.

"You must have papers to enter the city," glared the officer. "Where are you from?"

"I used to live on Rue Cler, not far from the tower," Eli truthfully replied, although it had been more than a hundred years. "I've come to help with the war."

"Ahh, a loyal Frenchman," the officer nodded approvingly. "Where are you coming from?"

"I've come from Greece," Eli shrewdly replied. He knew the French officials would have no tolerance for someone coming from Austria-Hungary.

"See that line over there?" the officer pointed to the corner of the court where two dozen men stood. "They're waiting conscripts. Go stand with them. You'll be at the front serving your country in a week."

Eli turned to the group of disheveled farmers. Some looked lean and haggard; others were restless and eager for a fight. Eli picked up his suitcase, gave a determined nod, and moved to join them.

THE WESTERN FRONT
28 JANUARY 1915

THE DISTANT THUNDER of artillery had stopped, and Eli thought he had heard a chirping bird. He turned to the tree on the side of the country road, but its remaining branches were dead and empty. He scanned the western sky but saw only low, gray clouds.

"Move to the right!" yelled a sergeant as a column of infantry trudged toward them on the muddy road with horse-drawn wagons following.

Eli saw the long, weary faces of soldiers returning from the front lines. Some had heads wrapped in bandages or arms hung in slings. Others walked with limps. Those who rode in the wagons were even more battered and stared blankly into the gray sky or across the barren fields. Eli's gaze moved from one man's dull blue, mud-caked uniform to his own. Though small for him, Eli's blue wool greatcoat was bright and fresh, but for the bullet hole in its breast that had claimed its previous occupant. Over Eli's shortened hair, he wore a blue-gray kepi. Gray putties wrapped his thick calves, exposing muddy boots below and dark blue trousers above. A black leather ammunition belt with suspenders rode over his greatcoat. He carried a drab canvas pack on his back, while a canteen hung on one shoulder and his rifle on the other.

Eli noticed the replacements before him staring wide-eyed at the passing survivors. He could taste their apprehension as they wondered what their fate would be. Eli had seen similar looks and sensed such dread far too many times before. While death was a normal part of mortality, he thought the angst brought by war was like no other.

Eli thought of the battles he had prevented. He considered the countless lives he had preserved, allowing them to pass on as old men rather than young. Men were not the only ones to perish in war, he reminded himself. Terrible things happened to women and children as well—some things worse than death.

As they marched along the road, the fields became increasingly scarred by craters and abandoned trenches. They had passed a hospital tent two miles back, but Eli couldn't forget the dozens of cots and blankets lying across the field filled with the wounded and dying. He could still hear their moaning, groaning, and frightened cries. Each suffering sound, each bloody, lifeless body, was a painful reminder of his failure in Sarajevo. He and Cyrus had been tasked with preventing the archduke's assassination and stopping the deluge of death and misery that would follow, but they had failed, and Cyrus was no more.

Eli turned his hand over and eyed his knife-pricked palm. While before impervious to mortal harm, something had changed in him. It seemed with each day he was becoming a little more human. For the first time, Eli understood the fear men felt—the jeopardy of life—and it thrilled him. Whether it was a curse or a blessing, he wasn't sure. A part of Eli wanted to fulfill his measure, to teach and guide those he was with, but another part wished simply to soak in the percolating emotions and sensations and live the short but thrilling life of a man.

Eli felt the rifle on his shoulder. He knew he could not use it to kill or maim and wondered what consequences that would bring.

The horizon disappeared as the new arrivals entered a trench shored up by wooden planks, corrugated tin, and sandbags. Even though Eli stood a head taller than the other French soldiers, the sandbags and earthen walls robbed his view of the beyond. Eli's nose wrinkled at the stench of mud and unbathed men as they walked along the wooden planks, and muddy water sloshed up on his boots. The line of new arrivals stretched far ahead but soon disappeared as the channels turned left and right into the earthen maze.

As they continued north toward the front line, they passed side trenches that ran thirty to forty yards east and west before jogging left or right. First was the reserve trench, where bored Frenchmen sat, smoked, and laughed at jokes dark or bawdy. Then came the support trench with the company's headquarters. Along its walls ran telephone and telegraph wires that disappeared into dimly lit doorways that sank even deeper into the earth. Inside, officers in bright-colored uniforms decided who would live and die.

Fifty yards closer to the front was the covering trench. In it, tired men waited with rifles or behind machine guns while brave men peeked over the edge with spy glasses. It too had bunkers, giving a place for men to sleep and rats to eat.

Twenty yards farther north lay the front line, where frazzled men waited for the order to charge to their deaths across a desolate plain known as No Man's Land. This scarred and cratered killing field, which varied from twenty to two hundred yards or more, held no life at all. Where trees once stood, there were blackened and splintered stumps. Ten-foot-wide craters, filled with bloody rainwater and twisted corpses, dotted the expanse, making it look more like the moon's surface than a French pasture.

It was difficult for Eli not to discern the men he passed. He saw light in all of them, although some shined brighter than others. He felt their promise and potential. If they survived, some would be distinguished men and leave a profound mark on humanity. Some would simply exist, while others would be a bane. That was *if* they survived, Eli reminded himself. It grieved him to feel so powerless.

IT HAD RAINED MOST of the day, and the clouds hung low in the swirling gray sky. Despite the freshness of the rain, the air in the trench was thick and stale.

"Hey, do you want a smoke?" asked Jean-Pierre, offering his pack of cigarettes to Eli, sitting beside him.

Eli turned to the eager-eyed young man, who had a thin mustache and a tuft of hair on his muddy chin. "No, thank you." Jean-Pierre had stayed close to Eli since he and the other replacements had arrived two days before, but Eli was reluctant to respond to the man with more than just pleasantries. He knew most humans enjoyed friendships—relationships that seemed to bond them together, even in the most trying times—but the concept felt uncomfortable to Eli, who was used to more formal relations.

Jean-Pierre lit his cigarette, then pushed his blue cap back with a mud-stained hand. "What did you say your name is?"

"Eli."

"Eli the Giant," smirked Jean-Pierre.

"I'm not a giant," frowned Eli.

"You're huge. You've got to be two meters! What did your mother feed you?"

Eli started to answer, then simply shrugged.

"You don't smoke, you don't drink, you don't curse—but I still like you," grinned Jean-Pierre. "With looks like you, I bet you have been with plenty of women, no?"

Eli turned to Jean-Pierre. He had inspected the Frenchman's persona on their first meeting and perceived an ordinary, unexceptional man. But Jean-Pierre was not entirely void; he had a charismatic quality that drew others to him. It was a quality that intrigued Eli.

"What? You toy with me!" Jean-Pierre scoffed. "You haven't been with a woman? Or maybe you just don't like to tell, eh?" The Frenchman's eyes narrowed as he took a drag from his cigarette. "When we get back, I'll take you to the best brothel in Paris. When they see you, they'll let you in for free!" he laughed. "They'll probably give me a discount for bringing you! Ha! I can't wait to get my hands on one of those beauties!"

Eli's pleasant smile faded, and he turned away as Jean-Pierre continued his lustful chatter. Eli looked down the crowded trench and thought of the women he had felt an attraction to. They were not a few, but their appeal was more akin to a boy's crush on his teacher. And unlike Lu and the others, they were cravings he had never acted on. He thought of Ana, the waitress in Sarajevo. He knew she was drawn to him. Eli wondered what would have happened had he acted on her invitation. He shook the thought from his head and stared down the trench.

While there were many things Eli could discern, such as an individual's unique gifts or the consequences of one's actions in the complex matrix of life, the repercussions of his own works were less clear to him. Eli's gratification came by serving, guiding, and protecting mortals—that was his purpose—but human passion had long intrigued him.

Eli knew mutual attraction was a large part of the formula for propagation, but he didn't understand how such allurement formed. He knew the act of copulation was the practical outcome of that formula, but he wondered why it was used so freely when its consequences were so profound. He knew love between a man and a woman could be lasting and fulfilling or fleeting and painful, but he didn't understand why.

Eli remembered Plato teaching of love in the shade of the Parthenon. Eli understood Philia; affection for mortals was in his nature. It was romantic love or Eros, with all of its facets, that fascinated the watcher.

As Eli's mind drifted, his gaze settled on a soldier huddled and shivering near the bend of the trench. The soldier's rifle leaned against the sandbags, his head down, his glasses speckled with rainwater. While Eli had discerned the personas of most of the soldiers in his platoon, this man had somehow eluded him. He nudged the prattling Jean-Pierre. "Who is that at the end of the trench?"

Jean-Pierre paused and turned. "That guy with the glasses? He's called Sébastien. He won't get you any girls. Maybe a book on female anatomy from the college in Paris," Jean-Pierre laughed. When he realized Eli was sincere in his question, Jean-Pierre's grin faded, and he shrugged. "No one knows him very well. I'm surprised he's still alive. He doesn't seem very savvy, if you know what I mean."

"He has no friends?" asked Eli.

"He was friends with Gaubert until..."

"Until what?"

"Until he got it last week," sighed Jean-Pierre.

"He was killed?" Eli asked, turning back to Sébastien.

"Sniper's bullet. Fast."

Eli nodded. "But he's not your friend?"

Jean-Pierre wrinkled his nose. "No, he and I are too different."

Eli cocked his head. "But you want to be my friend."

Jean-Pierre shrugged, puffed on his cigarette, and said, "You and I are much the same, no? Women think we are beautiful. They want to have us, eh?"

Eli surveyed Jean-Pierre's face. He thought his missing teeth and foul breath might make him less of a prize. "Have you had any friends die?"

Jean-Pierre's gaze moved to his cigarette. He tapped the ashes off and nodded. "Two."

"What are their names?"

"I don't want to talk about them," Jean-Pierre scowled.

Eli nodded, then turned back to Sébastien. Eli saw in him a tremendous intellect. He envisioned an older, bearded Sébastien teaching at a university. He saw him treating sick people in a hospital and working in a laboratory. Eli's blue eyes narrowed. *This man will cure diseases.* Eli sighed. *That is if he survives the war.*

PARIS, FRANCE

FRANÇOIS DUVALL STOKED the fireplace and sat back in his chair. He had just picked up his book when Michelle entered with a sack of groceries. "Ah, welcome home, my dear," he said with a sparkle in his eye, his thinning white hair oiled back on his head.

"Hello, Father," said a tired and bothered Michelle, hanging up her coat near the door.

"How was your day caring for our brave wounded?" asked François.

"Dreadful," sighed Michelle. Still in her nurse's uniform, she moved to the small kitchen and pulled a long, skinny bread loaf and some vegetables from a sack.

"Oh. Do you want to tell me about it?"

"No, not really," said Michelle, now intent on making their dinner. François didn't bother to open his book.

"It's all so awful!" said Michelle, throwing up her arms. "Day after day, I watch these poor soldiers die, and there's nothing I can do!"

"You are comforting them—giving them your compassion. That is something."

Michelle sighed. "It's not enough."

François's brow furrowed. He recognized more than the weight of caring for the wounded was bothering his daughter. "How is your friend, Maurice?"

Michelle stopped her potato cutting and lowered her head. When she wiped away a tear, François got up from his chair. "Did something happen to you two?" he asked, shuffling closer.

Michelle tried to compose herself. She looked at her father with teary eyes, and said, "Maurice has joined the army. He's gone."

"Oh. You should be proud your friend is defending our country."

"No, you don't understand. Maurice and I are no longer together."

"Because he went off to war?" asked François.

Michelle's shoulders slumped. "No. Because he was...because he was sleeping with Juliette!"

"Your nurse friend?" asked François with raised eyebrows.

"Now she will be getting his love letters from the front." Michelle lowered her head and cried.

"I'm sorry, my dear," said François, putting his arm around her. "You deserve better."

Michelle turned and laid her head against her father's sweater. "Why does it have to hurt so much? Why is everything so sad?"

"Because that is the whirlwind of life, my dear," said François, stroking her back as she sobbed. "But don't despair. You will find happiness even amidst the storm."

Michelle shook her head. "I'm done with men, except for you, Papa."

François smiled. "My dear, have faith. You will one day find your soul mate."

Michelle sighed, looked up at her father with tear-streaked eyes, and forced a smile. "You always make me feel better."

François gave a loving nod. "That is what fathers are for."

THE WESTERN FRONT

IT WAS FIRST LIGHT. No Man's Land—the hundred-yard expanse of barbed wire, rain-filled craters, and rotting corpses—was quiet.

"Be ready!" grunted the fierce-eyed sergeant as he stomped through the trench, his breath visible in the frosty morning air, his mud-stained hand clutching his rifle. "We go over on the whistle."

The line of men pressed up against the trench wall shifted nervously, rubbing their hands and moving their feet to keep warm.

"Prepare to fix bayonets," muttered the young lieutenant, his wide, frightened eyes fixed on his pocket watch.

"Prepare to fix bayonets!" echoed the sergeant, eyeing the ladders the men would climb to escape their miserable crack in the earth.

Eli watched Jean-Pierre and the others as they prepared for the charge. He felt their fear as they muttered words of self-assurance, clutched rosaries in cold, stiff hands, and whispered prayers through faltering lips.

"Two minutes," gulped the young lieutenant.

"Two minutes," repeated the sergeant as he walked the line, slapping men on their backs and giving brusque, heartening nods.

Eli noticed Jean-Pierre's trembling hand reach for his sheathed bayonet.

"Men, fix bayonets!" quivered the young lieutenant's voice as he raised his whistle to his lips.

"Fix bayonets!" snarled the sergeant, removing his from its sheath.

A wave of *clicks* ran through the line as the men fastened their long stabbing blades onto their rifles.

"Remember, look for the holes in the wire," Jean-Pierre whispered, glancing back at Eli. "You're so big, it will be hard for them not to hit you, but stay low to the ground. Move as fast as you can, and follow me. Don't shoot until we get to a good hole. You're as good as dead if you shoot standing in the open!"

Eli glanced at Sébastien in another line. He would climb the next ladder over. Eli wondered if anyone had given him such advice.

Eli's eyes widened at the shrill sound of whistles up and down the trench. He felt the fine hairs on the back of his neck stand and a surge of heat rush through him. The sensation was gone in an instant, but Eli marveled at it just the same as frantic-eyed men scrambled up the crude, muddy ladders with rifles on their shoulders.

The *tzing* of enemy bullets ripping through the air above the trench came next. Eli looked away when the first man up the ladder fell back with a hole in his face, his rifle spearing the bottom of the trench with its long bayonet.

"Artillery! Where's the artillery!" cried the lieutenant as he looked at his watch. "Where's the covering fire?"

After climbing the ladder, Jean-Pierre pulled his rifle off his shoulder and charged across the open field as German bullets ripped past him. When he realized there was no covering fire, he dove into a shell crater and slid into a pool of water at the bottom.

Jean-Pierre shook his head in dismay when he looked back to the frail Sébastien standing in the open, frozen in fear. "What are you doing? Stay low! Get down!"

The petrified Sébastien dropped his rifle as bullets *zipped* by him but remained standing.

Not wanting to watch him die, Jean-Pierre was about to look away when he spotted Eli dashing across the open field toward the frozen Sébastien. Eli had no sooner pushed Sébastien to the ground and fallen on top of him, than a torrent of German machine gun bullets cut through the two men coming up behind, blowing them back onto the muddy field.

"Fall back! Fall back!" was the cry as men who had dodged bullets turned and scampered back to the safety of the trenched earth.

Jean-Pierre cringed at the *whizzz* and *thud* of bullets cutting through the backs of retreating men, dropping them on their faces. "Holy God! What are they doing to us?" cried Jean-Pierre as those not shot fell back into the trench. He watched Eli pull Sébastien from the ground and carry him back.

Furious at the botched charge, Jean-Pierre breathed in courage, clawed his way out of the muddy crater, and raced back to his line.

The round-eyed Jean-Pierre fell into the trench, his muddy chest heaving, and he gasped, "What the hell was that? I know the Germans want to kill us, but now we're helping them!"

"Thank you," said Sébastien to Eli, his legs wobbling.

"What were you doing?" scolded Jean-Pierre as he pushed past two other soldiers. "You can't stand up like that! Do you want to die?"

Sébastien breathlessly shook his head, his muddy glasses crooked.

"You! Where's your rifle?" yelled the crusty sergeant as he bore down on the still trembling Sébastien.

"I have it," replied Eli, handing Sébastien his.

The sergeant's eyes narrowed. "Where's yours?"

"I must have left it out there," Eli calmly replied.

"He saved Sébastien's life. I saw it," explained Jean-Pierre.

The sergeant wrinkled his nose. "Your rifle is for killing Germans! You don't leave it to save him or anyone else! That goes for all of you smelly rats! You only have to think about one thing, and that's killing the Hun! Nothing else!" Moving to the rifle stuck bayonet-first in the mud, the sergeant pulled it free and shoved it into Eli's thick chest. "Don't lose this one!" The sergeant pointed to the dead, faceless soldier lying in the mud and barked, "Someone get him out of here!"

Sébastien gulped as two men hauled the body away. He waited for the sergeant to leave before whispering to Eli, "You saved my life."

Eli shrugged off the thanks.

"So, you're a hero," grinned Jean-Pierre.

"I am no hero," muttered Eli.

"You saved *him*." Jean-Pierre pointed to Sébastien.

Eli shrugged.

"Hey, what's this?" asked Jean-Pierre, noticing the bloodstain on Eli's coat arm. "You caught one! Take off your coat!"

Eli looked down at the red stain on his biceps and pulled off his coat.

"Doesn't that hurt?" frowned Jean-Pierre, finding Eli's lack of concern odd.

"Not really," Eli replied. But when he saw the other men's distress, he added, "Maybe a little," trying to fit in.

Jean-Pierre poked his finger an inch into Eli's oozing wound and shook his head. "It went right through. Doesn't it hurt?"

"I would think it would hurt a lot," cringed Sébastien.

Eli grimaced and clutched his arm. "Yes, it hurts now." It was an unconvincing performance.

Jean-Pierre scratched his head.

"You should get that looked after. You could lose your arm if it gets infected," worried Sébastien.

Eli pulled his arm back.

"Here, wrap this around it," Sébastien said, pulling a clean white handkerchief from his coat.

Jean-Pierre's eyes widened. It was the first pure white thing he had seen in weeks. He turned and yelled down the trench, "Hey, where is Doc? We got a man shot in the arm!"

"He's caring for others. You'll have to wait," grumbled the sergeant as he righted a toppled ladder.

Thirty minutes passed. The new friends were sitting on the trench's firing step, listening to Jean-Pierre complain about the failed assault, when a grumbling soldier with a gray mustache and drooping eyes pushed through a cluster of men.

"Who's shot?" grunted the medic, a cigarette dangling from his lips.

Both Jean-Pierre and Sébastien pointed to Eli.

The old medic pulled off the bloodstained handkerchief, dropped it to the muddy ground, and then roughly examined Eli's arm. "Don't waste my time. It's just a scratch."

Eli picked up the muddy handkerchief, shook it off, and handed it back to Sébastien with an appreciative nod.

"Huh? He got shot right through!" exclaimed Jean-Pierre as the old medic huffed off. But when Jean-Pierre looked back at the bullet hole, there was only a shallow scratch. "What the hell?" he frowned, blinking his eyes. "You were shot through! I saw it!"

"So did I," added Sébastien, adjusting his glasses.

Eli looked at his arm, shrugged, and said, "It feels better."

CHAPTER 9
FRIENDS AND FOES

Nestled in the heart of the city, the House of Charity had been in operation for more than a hundred years. Dedicated to caring not only for the sick and afflicted, it housed an orphanage and a women's shelter. While doctors, nurses, women, and children came and went from the shelter, one face endured. Jophiel had been the matron of the House of Charity longer than anyone could remember. Despite her longevity, she maintained a remarkably youthful appearance that some joked was because she was an angel. Others said God kept her young because he could find no one else to do her work with such love and devotion. The tall and lean Jophiel, who usually wore her black hair up on her head, laughed away such remarks.

The sound of playing children echoed off the large hall's stone walls, its high, arched ceiling reminiscent of a cathedral. Jophiel contentedly watched the playing children. Her gaze moved to a small crippled boy abandoned by his parents. He had been there for months, and it heartened her to see him finally experiencing joy.

Jophiel smiled at the young nun supervising the children, then turned and moved down a corridor. She was nearing the childbirth center when she saw an unfamiliar, stringy-haired man in a dark, baggy suit peering into the nursery. Her gait slowed, and her eyes narrowed as she realized who he was. "What are you doing here?"

Gik's nose wrinkled at her presence. He turned from the window, his dark, sunken eyes gleaming. "I have found who I seek."

"Shall I have you removed?" Jophiel asked, unconcerned.

"Where are the other watchers?"

"I will tell you nothing. You're an abomination we should have removed long ago!"

Gik stepped toward her, his nostrils flared, his dark eyes unblinking. Jophiel did not move.

Gik removed the blazerod from his coat.

Jophiel saw the pewter weapon and took a step back. "Where did you get that?" she gasped.

Gik raised the blazerod, and its end began to glow. "Tell me where they are."

Jophiel stiffened and defiantly proclaimed, "We are across the world and will never leave."

"Yes, you will," snarled Gik, before shooting a bolt of light through her.

The Western Front
18 February 1915

THE AIR inside the bunker was stale, and the light dim, but it was warmer than the trench outside. Between the thick poles, which supported planks and beams that spanned the ceiling, stood crude wooden bunks where tired and bored men lay on beds of chicken wire.

Eli sat on the bunker's damp floor beside Sébastien as Jean-Pierre relaxed on the edge of a cot next to another man. At the end of the bunks, tepee-shaped racks propped up their rifles. A flickering lantern cast uneasy shadows on those sleeping or trying to warm as men spoke in hushed voices of home or girls.

As Jean-Pierre finished his tale, Eli watched a fat rat scurry along the row of bunks, dodging one swatting hand only to be struck and flung, squealing through the shadows, by another.

"Anyway, that was last summer," sighed Jean-Pierre, not caring if anyone was listening.

Sébastien watched Jean-Pierre light a cigarette, then pushed up his glasses and asked, "Do you think any of this will matter?"

"You mean the fighting? The dying?" Jean-Pierre asked, shaking out the match.

Sébastien nodded as Eli listened.

Jean-Pierre shrugged. "I can tell you we've been in this same lousy trench for two months. We haven't moved. The Hun haven't moved. How many charges have there been? How many dead men are lying in that field? How many have been eaten by rats and birds? Or torn apart by shells exploding on top of them? Too many." Jean-Pierre shook his head and sighed. "I just hope my children aren't fighting in this same damn trench," he said with a hint of levity. Then his face dimmed. "That is, if I live to have children."

Sébastien looked down glumly as Jean-Pierre smoked and Eli listened to other hushed conversations. After a time, Jean-Pierre shook his head and said, "I don't think it will matter."

Eli saw Sébastien staring at the floor in thought but said nothing.

After another long silence, Sébastien pushed up his glasses and asked, "What do you think will happen?"

"When it's over? I don't know," shrugged Jean-Pierre.

"No, when we die," said a troubled Sébastien.

"Oh," Jean-Pierre nodded. "That's easy; we visit St. Peter, and he gives us a harp and wings, isn't that right, Eli?"

Eli's eyes widened, but he decided it best not to comment.

"No, I'm serious," frowned Sébastien.

"I don't know," muttered Jean-Pierre.

"I didn't use to believe in God," shrugged Sébastien. "I used to think religion was all a joke. Now...I hope it's true."

Eli pulled his knees to his chest and thoughtfully nodded.

"What do you think, Eli?" asked Sébastien.

Eli considered the question, then said, "When it is time, we will return from where we came."

"Aah," grunted Jean-Pierre, "Dust to dust."

Eli shook his head. "No, not that."

"You mean, to live with God?" asked Jean-Pierre. "That's what I said the first time."

Eli faintly nodded.

"Do you think any of this will matter?" questioned Sébastien.

"You mean the war? The fighting and dying?" Jean-Pierre asked.

Sébastien nodded.

"I don't know," whispered Jean-Pierre.

"What do you think, Eli?"

Staring across the crowded bunker, Eli muttered, "It saddens me."

Jean-Pierre snickered. After three weeks, he was used to Eli's enigmatic yet simplistic responses.

"But why are we even here?" persisted Sébastien.

"You mean dug into the dirt, freezing our asses off while the dirty Hun drop shells on our heads?" glared Jean-Pierre. "Because they want what is ours, and we have to stop them!"

Eli raised his head. "So, you kill one another."

"I don't think the Hun have to worry too much about you," chuckled Jean-Pierre. "The dirt and the sky, yes, but the Germans are safe. Three weeks, and I haven't seen you hit one of them!"

Sébastien laughed.

"I must be a bad shot," shrugged Eli.

A smirking Jean-Pierre shook his head. "I'm sure you do many things well, but shooting Germans is not one of them."

Eli thought for a time, then looked up and asked, "Why do men have to fight and kill one another? Why can't they live in peace?"

Sébastien turned to Eli, noticing his use of *they* instead of *we*.

"You must not have been raised with brothers," huffed Jean-Pierre. "We fought about everything: who was smarter, who was stronger, who was better looking, who would get the last roll at dinner."

"But you didn't kill each other," replied Eli, not hiding his concern.

"No... We stopped at that, but I still hated them," whispered Jean-Pierre as he stroked the tuft on his chin.

"Do you hate them still?"

Jean-Pierre considered the question, then shook his head and muttered, "No... I would give anything to be with them." Embarrassed by a tear, he quickly brushed it away.

"We-we can be your brothers," whispered Sébastien.

Jean-Pierre nodded, and more tears followed, faster than he could wipe them.

Sébastien put a comforting hand on Jean-Pierre's arm.

Eli watched his friend sob and felt an aching in his chest. He was somewhat used to such feelings, being compassionate by nature, but what Eli felt now was different. It was more intense than anything he had felt over the thousands of lifetimes he had spanned. He wished he could cry.

After wiping his last tear and gathering himself, Jean-Pierre turned to Sébastien and asked, "Will you go back to the university after?"

Sébastien shrugged. "I don't know. It doesn't seem very useful now."

Eli's face filled with concern. He had seen Sébastien's potential and the impact he would have on the world. "You mean to become a doctor and help people? You no longer think that is useful?"

"How did you know I wanted to study medicine?"

"I thought you wanted to be a bridge-builder," frowned Jean-Pierre.

"That is what my father wanted, but..." Sébastien stared blankly at Eli.

Eli shrugged. "I just thought you would make a good doctor. You could help a lot of people. You could save lives."

Sébastien's gaze faded across the bunker. "No one cares much about saving lives anymore," he sighed.

"They will again," Eli said with an encouraging nod.

"Me, I'm going back to the factory," shrugged Jean-Pierre. "Get fat on pastries and drunk on wine while I sleep with every whore I can find!"

Eli raised a quieting hand.

"What? It's true!" insisted Jean-Pierre.

"No, did you hear that?" Eli asked with a gathered brow.

"Hear what?" asked Sébastien.

A low-pitched *thud* shook the bunker walls and caused dirt to fall from between the overhead ceiling planks. Then there was another.

"Artillery barrage!" cried the sergeant, sticking his head into the bunker. "Be ready for an attack!"

Jean-Pierre rolled out of the cot and grabbed his rifle from the rack as the ground shook.

"What if one lands on top of us?" Sébastien asked, looking up at the underground ceiling.

"Have you seen the craters their shells are leaving lately? A meter of dirt won't do much, but it will save someone from digging our graves."

Eli handed Sébastien his rifle, then reached for his own.

After twenty minutes of shelling, the bunker was thick with dust and nervous anticipation. Every ear was fixed on the rhythm of the explosions. As the deep, resonating impacts grew further apart and then stopped, the men waited for the whistles—the signal for them to leave their hole in the ground and defend their line.

When the whistle came, the men charged from the bunker with rifles ready. Jean-Pierre was the fourth man out, with Eli and Sébastien close behind. Outside, the trench had caved in at the far end from a shell, but was otherwise empty and intact. Eli watched as men climbed onto the shooting steps and leveled their rifles at the charging Germans. Jean-Pierre was already firing when Eli got onto the step.

The watcher looked across the smoky expanse to the freshly mounded earth of new craters and the twisted rolls of knife-edged wire. The shelling had blown open a section of the razor wire fifty yards away, and soldiers with spiked helmets were funneling through the gap toward them. French bullets *popped* and *cracked* through the air, and German soldiers slumped back onto the wire or fell on their faces as others slipped through. Eli's face was filled with worry as he clutched his rifle, but he didn't fire.

"HUN IN THE LINE!" came from their left.

When Eli turned, he saw two German soldiers rounding the bend, twenty yards away, racing down the trench toward them. One was firing his rifle, the other preparing to throw a grenade. Two French soldiers were shot off the firing steps before Eli could react. Seeing the next bullet would be for Jean-Pierre, he raised his rifle and fired.

Jean-Pierre watched with wide eyes as Eli's bullet punched through the first German's spiked helmet, dropping him back on his knees. After cycling the rifle's action, Eli chambered and shot again, striking the next German with the grenade in the center of his chest. Falling to his knees, the grenade dropped to the trench's frozen floor before exploding and spraying hot metal shards. Two more Frenchmen fell, crying out in agony. One of them was Jean-Pierre.

Eli lowered his rifle and stared slack-jawed at the two Germans he had killed. *What have I done?*

"Jean-Pierre!" cried Sébastien, rushing to his writhing friend as more Frenchmen climbed onto the steps to fire.

When Eli saw the wounded Jean-Pierre lying on the bottom of the trench, he dropped his rifle and rushed to him, knocking two other men aside. "Jean-Pierre! Are you okay?"

Resting in Sébastien's lap, Jean-Pierre's eyes were dull and heavy as they shifted to Eli. "See...you are a hero," he breathed as blood trickled from his mouth.

"No, I'm not." Eli grimaced at Jean-Pierre's chest and belly wounds.

When Jean-Pierre saw his escaping blood, he sobbed.

"I'm sorry," groaned Eli. "I was trying to protect you."

Sébastien was sobbing now too.

Jean-Pierre weakly shook his head, then muttered, "I don't think I'll be able to show you that brothel in Paris."

"MEDIC!" yelled Eli, knowing nothing could be done.

Jean-Pierre's eyes closed, and he licked his parched lips. "Tell my mother... Tell her...I'm sorr—" His head sank against Sébastien's chest, and his arm slipped to the muddy earth.

"German bastards!" bellowed Sébastien, shaking his head in grief.

Eli sank to the ground beside his two friends and stared down the trench as the rifle fire continued.

THREE DAYS HAD PASSED. Dozens had died in the German assault, but the front line had not moved.

Sébastien handed Eli a tin of soup from his filthy hand, then sat on the firing step beside him with his own. "You should eat. You'll feel better," urged Sébastien.

Eli set the soup on the sandbag beside him and shook his head.

"We both miss him. He was our friend," sighed Sébastien.

Eli looked up into the gray sky. It wasn't just that he missed Jean-Pierre, the first mortal friend Eli had ever known. It was more than that. Eli had once again failed. Not only was his friend dead, in a strangely impulsive move, he had taken two lives—something the watcher had sworn never to do.

Eli's destitute gaze lowered to the muddy trench boards as he considered how far he had fallen. Taking human life was a serious violation of the Grand Precept. He wondered if he was any better than Lu. Eli didn't know what consequences he would face, but he was sure any punishment would be deserved.

While the pain and remorse Eli felt were unlike anything he had encountered, he attributed those sentiments to his failings, rather than the flow of mortal sensations and emotions steadily growing within him. While Eli once longed to experience such feelings, he wondered now if that was his punishment.

Eli looked at the other men in the trench. Their once blue uniforms were pasted brown by the stinking mire, their lean and haggard faces empty. Most of them had lost friends. All of them had lost hope.

"Only two more days," nodded Sébastien, trying to cheer up his friend.

Eli pulled his sad gaze up from the muddy trench planks. "What?"

"We go back to Paris in two days," Sébastien said, trying to smile. "What will you do?"

Eli considered the question. "I will find Jean-Pierre's mother. I have his last letter."

Sébastien nodded sadly. "Can I go with you?"

"Yes," breathed Eli.

Sébastien looked up into the sky as a hole in the clouds opened, allowing sunshine to spill down onto the cold, dreary waste. "How did you know I wanted to study medicine? I never told anyone here." His gaze turned to Eli to see his response.

Eli shrugged. "I just thought you would be an excellent doctor. You could help many people."

Sébastien nodded, and his gaze moved down the trench. "I would like that." He turned back to his friend. "Eli, I don't remember you ever speaking of your plans after the war. Maybe it was because Jean-Pierre did all the talking."

A thin smile formed on Eli's face.

"What will you do? Find a woman? Have a family?"

"I don't know," muttered Eli.

"You have to think positively. You can't let all of this ruin you," urged Sébastien, motioning to their bleak surroundings.

Eli turned to Sébastien, struck by the irony that a mortal was coaching him. For an instant, Eli wanted more than anything to confide in his friend, to tell Sébastien who he was, what he had seen, and why he was so heartbroken. But Eli only nodded.

"Be ready! Be ready! The Huns are on the line!" warned the sergeant as he ran through the trench.

In their month at the front, the two friends had lived through dozens of charges and shellings. They had frantically dug men out from collapsed bunkers. They had tended to and carried off the remains of men hit by shells or pierced by bullets. They had stared spellbound into the freezing night sky as flairs lit the clouds on fire and floated to the ravaged earth. They had listened to those caught in the crossfire of a failed charge, lying in the middle of No Man's Land, crying, moaning, and whimpering—sometimes for days—until their last breath. While half of their company had been killed or wounded, little else had changed. They were in the same rat-infested trenches, and so were the Germans.

Eli turned and raised his head to the crack in the sandbags that gave him a view across the crater-filled wasteland. He saw the spikes of German helmets sticking out from their trench seventy yards away. They were preparing to charge. Eli took his rifle in hand. He thought of the two Germans he had killed three days before. He thought of his dead friend, Jean-Pierre. Eli feared he might kill again.

Eli's worried gaze moved to the frail Sébastien, peering through the sandbags across the line. Eli wished he could take him away and hide him until the war had passed. Eli no longer knew what he should do. He felt lost in a world he once understood—a world he had helped shape. But everything was changing. He felt all he had worked for was crumbling around him.

Eli breathed in the musty air and listened to the rustling of anxious men moving into position. He watched the young lieutenant inch up to the trench's edge on his right. He knew what would happen next.

It started with the distant *thud-thud-thud-thud* of German machine gun fire and the *zip-zip-zip* of rounds ripping through the air inches above the trench. The whistle of incoming artillery rounds was followed by a storm of tossed earth as German shells careened toward the French trenches.

Eli saw the lieutenant's head snap back as a round punched through a sandbag. Eli stepped down from his firing shelf beside Sébastien and hurried to the young lieutenant twisted backward in the trench, but the hole in his head left no question.

The whistle of an artillery round dropping from the sky spun Eli. "NO!" He saw Sébastien turn to him with wide, knowing eyes and watched helplessly as the shell descended, exploding a foot behind his friend. The blast of light, earth, and wind hurled Eli down the trench and obliterated everything around him.

CHAPTER 10
THE FROZEN DEAD

While the Cathedral of Saint Gervais and Saint Protais was mainly intact, German shelling had reduced its western transept to a heap of rubble. The thick stone pillars inside its nave stood like trees surrounding a hundred men lying on stretchers, draped in gray wool blankets. In between the rows of groaning, moaning soldiers scurried six nurses and two doctors—too few to mend or comfort those suffering and dying. In one corner of the east transept, between broken stained-glass windows, hung a painting of an angel descending to shepherds. Below that, two orderlies struggled with a cot that barely held a large man, whose cut-open, mud-stained, and bloodied uniform revealed multiple shrapnel wounds, including a gaping five-inch-wide chest wound. The large soldier's face was likewise peppered by dirt and shrapnel. The orderlies grunted as they lay the wounded Eli down beside the other new arrivals.

"What are you doing?" snapped Doctor Faucheux from the next row. He stepped over two men to better see the new arrival. His once white smock was smeared red with blood, and his scowling face aged by the terribleness of what he faced daily.

The breathless orderlies slumped their shoulders as they looked at the doctor numbly.

"See his injuries? He has no chance! Why did they even bother to bring him? Take him outside with the others. He'll be dead in minutes."

The orderlies strained and grunted as they hefted Eli's stretcher back out of the cathedral-turned-hospital into the snow.

Dr. Faucheux tiredly shook his head, then returned to his dreadful work.

A DAY PASSED, but Dr. Faucheux had no fewer patients to tend to. In need of a break, he passed the wood-burning stove that barely heated the torn-open cathedral, donned his coat and hat, and pushed open the heavy door. Once outside, Faucheux breathed in the fresh, cold air, lit a cigarette, and shook out the match. His haggard eyes closed as he breathed in the soothing nicotine, and his tense shoulders loosened as he exhaled.

Faucheux eyed the stacked, snow-covered pews removed from the nave to make room for the wounded. He wondered how long before the benches would be turned to firewood to heat his hospital.

To the doctor's left were rows of bodies awaiting burial. A dusting of snow covered the most recent arrivals, and a thicker layer smothered those from the days before. With so few blankets, Faucheux could not afford to use them to cover the dead—they were needed to keep the living warm. For that reason, he was grateful for the snow, which hid the severed limbs and blood-stained uniforms.

Faucheux turned to the north as the distant thunder of artillery registered. It was an all-too-common sound now. The doctor counted the distant *thumps* and wondered how many more torn bodies would be sent to him. He wondered when the next train would come to move the wounded to Paris. He wondered how they would evacuate if the Germans broke through.

After finishing his cigarette, Faucheux was about to return to the cathedral's relative warmth when he noticed the large soldier lying on the frozen earth amidst the other corpses. While snow dusted Eli's body like the others, it was not as thick. Faucheux's brow furrowed when he saw the faint puff of breath coming from Eli's mouth. His eyes narrowed when he remembered the torn and bloodied man from the day before. *Still alive. How can that be?* Faucheux had long marveled at the fighting spirit of those who refused to die. He shook his head when another faint puff of breath rose from Eli's mouth.

Faucheux left the shelter of the arched stone entry and made his way around the snow-covered corpses to the still Eli. He flicked his cigarette into the snow, then stooped and hovered his hand over Eli's open mouth. The exhaled air, though faint, was warm. Faucheux shook his head and wiped the snow off of Eli's chest. His flesh, burned and torn, was cold. Faucheux felt a fist-sized wound where a shell fragment had entered below Eli's right breast, tearing through his ribs and lung. He didn't need to turn the man to know there would be an equally large hole in his back. *Yet he's still breathing. How can this be?*

The groan of the opening cathedral door turned the perplexed doctor.

"Doctor Faucheux, we need you inside," called out an old nurse.

Faucheux nodded, got to his feet, and started back to the cathedral. He stopped at the large door and glanced back at the still-breathing Eli in wonder before returning inside.

NOT AN HOUR HAD PASSED when Faucheux returned to the outdoor morgue. The still-breathing soldier had occupied his thoughts as he tended to a dozen other men. When Faucheux pushed open the door, he expected to see the large soldier dead, with no steam escaping his lips, but to the doctor's dismay, Eli's body was gone. Faucheux scratched his head as he looked at the depressions in the snow where adjacent bodies had lain. They were also gone.

Faucheux's puzzled gaze moved across the snowy street to a wagon stacked full of bodies being taken for burial. The doctor's eyes widened at the possibility the soldier was still alive. *Impossible*, he told himself, before realizing it was a miracle the man had even survived the shell blast at all. "Wait! Wait!" yelled Faucheux as he chased after the horse-drawn wagon.

"What's wrong?" the bearded gravedigger called back, hearing the doctor.

"Wait!" Faucheux huffed, trudging through the snow. "I need to check on one of those men."

The bundled gravedigger glanced back at the frozen bodies stacked in his wagon like planks. "I don't think there is much you can do for them," he morbidly laughed.

Faucheux hurriedly moved around the wagon, searching for Eli between the stacked men's stiff arms and legs.

"What are you looking for?" frowned the gravedigger.

Faucheux stopped and shook his head. "I don't know. Maybe I'm just seeing things. Too many days watching men die."

The gravedigger nodded. "Can I go bury them now?"

"Yes," Faucheux sighed.

The gravedigger urged his horse on, and the large wagon wheels crunched through the snow.

"Wait!" Faucheux cried, seeing a puff of breath coming up from between the bodies.

"What is it?" grumbled the gravedigger. "I'm freezing my ass off!"

"I think one of them is still alive!"

The gravedigger watched with wide eyes as the doctor climbed onto the wagon and tried to push a body aside.

"Are you crazy?" scoffed the gravedigger. "They're all dead! They're frozen solid!"

"All of them?"

The gravedigger shrugged.

"Help me!" strained the doctor as he finally managed to push one of the bodies to the side, only to have it slide off the wagon onto the snowy street like a log.

"You're making a mess now!"

"Then help me!" cried the doctor.

The grumbling gravedigger shook his head, climbed over his seat, and took the shoulders of a frozen dead man while Faucheux lifted his feet. After moving three more dead soldiers, the doctor spotted Eli.

Faucheux climbed on top of him, put his ear to Eli's mouth, and listened for air. He felt and heard him breathing. Faucheux pulled back an arm and slapped Eli's cold face. His eyes widened when he saw movement beneath Eli's closed eyelids. "He's alive. This man's still alive!"

PARIS, FRANCE
24 FEBRUARY 1915

THE MORNING LIGHT streaked through the tall windows of the ballroom. The grand dance floor, which once hosted magnificent waltzes and extravagant gatherings, was now filled with rows of wounded men in hospital beds. Even the orchestra stage held convalescing soldiers. Any hint of perfume that might have lingered in the air had months before been replaced by the pungent fetor of disinfectant and camphor mixed with the occasional stench of rotting flesh. Orchestra music and polite conversation had given way to groaning, quiet sobbing, and comforting whispers.

Moving among the beds, from reaching arm to reaching arm, were nuns in white gowns and winged hats, and nurses in white aprons over light blue dresses.

It was a sad yet hopeful place.

The dark goateed doctor hovered over the unconscious Eli as he surveyed his injuries. "So, this is the miracle man?"

"Yes, Doctor Boucher," nodded Michelle.

The doctor looked at the chart, then back at the patient. A bandage wrapped Eli's head, and stitches ran along his pronounced cheekbone. Boucher's eyebrows raised when he pulled back the hospital bed sheet and saw multiple bruises and wounds across Eli's muscular chest. Some wounds were sewn closed, while others were simply bandaged.

The young nurse fidgeted when Dr. Boucher peeled back the stained bandage below Eli's right breast.

The doctor looked at the chart and frowned. "I used to know Faucheux, but I think being so close to the front has cost him his better judgment."

"How do you mean, Doctor?" asked Michelle.

Dr. Boucher turned and offered a charming, self-important smile. He had been keen on her since first noticing her large brown eyes and pearl-white smile days before. His eyes lowered to the red cross on her white apron, protruding from her notable bust. He thought she had lovely proportions—*a perfect specimen*. Boucher pointed to Eli's chest. "This wound he described is nowhere near as large. Look at it. Besides, it would be impossible to survive such an injury. Impossible."

"And yet he lives," whispered Michelle.

Dr. Boucher's eyes narrowed. "You say he lives, but he clearly does not. He is *comatose*," Boucher said the word with such vigor one would have thought he had invented the term. "Most likely from infection. I'm sure he is rife with it. I expect gangrene to emerge within the day."

"Maybe he is just healing," Michelle meekly replied.

Dr. Boucher shook his head, amazed at the nurse's beautiful ignorance. He surmised he could get her into bed with a glass of wine and a few impressive doctor stories. It usually took little to seduce such women, and from her looks, he guessed she would be well worth the effort. "Normally one's ribs and lungs do not grow back in three days, not when there is, as Faucheux says, 'a hole I can put three fingers through.'"

Michelle looked down in embarrassment.

Dr. Boucher tossed the chart onto Eli's legs, then shook his head. "I'm sorry. I demeaned you." He formed a crafty smile. "Perhaps you would allow me to make amends. Dinner? Maybe dancing?"

Having worked at the hospital for nearly a year, Michelle knew her place and understood the power of such men. She looked at the doctor with astute eyes, unwilling to step into his trap. "There is no need for apologies, Doctor. I should have known better than to make such an assumption."

Dr. Boucher's smile faded. "Well, perhaps another time." He eyed her white nurse's cap over her pulled-back chestnut hair. "Lovely."

Michelle fought off a blush.

Dr. Boucher started to turn, then paused. "And what is your name again?"

"Michelle," she replied with a polite smile.

"Of course. The perfect name for a goddess. Now take care of my patient," Dr. Boucher grinned as he turned and strutted away.

Michelle's smile faded, and she turned back to Eli.

After carefully redressing Eli's rib wound, Michelle placed a gentle hand on his forehead and checked for a fever. She noted his pale, glistening skin and wondered what horribleness he had seen.

While Eli was the lowest of rank, only a private, Michelle found him nobly handsome. She wondered if he was kind or burdened by his good looks, as so many beautiful men were. She wondered if he would someday awake so she might have an answer.

After returning Eli's chart to the foot of his bed, Michelle pulled the bed sheet back over his muscular chest and then moved to the next wounded soldier.

"How are you today, Louis?" Michelle asked as she placed the damp sponge on the wounded man's shoulder and gently cleaned off the dried blood and iodine.

The young soldier, whose arm had been amputated above the elbow, stared up into the ballroom's chandelier.

"Where are you from?" Michelle asked, hoping to brighten the young man's dreary face, but he stared blankly past her.

The mindless chattering of a man, the next row over, caused Michelle to shake her head sadly. With a face full of concern, she returned the sponge to the washbasin and looked to the next bed, where a middle-aged man, recovering from a bullet wound, slept. Michelle was about to fetch fresh water when she noticed Eli, two beds over, stirring. Pausing, she watched Eli to see if she had imagined it but saw no further movement.

After returning with a fresh basin of water, Michelle slid a chair beside Eli's bed and said, "Good morning, Elijah. How are you today?"

She expected no response and got none.

"I would ask you how you slept, but you seem to be an expert at it," Michelle grinned. She began to hum, but stopped when she pulled Eli's bed sheet down to his pelvis and saw some of his bruises were gone. Her eyes narrowed when she saw the stitched wound on his thick biceps. The day before, it was raw and gathered, but it was now smooth and pink, with only the binding thread to deform it. Michelle's soft humming resumed as she gently guided the sponge across his chest and surveyed the other wounds that had likewise improved. She thought him unusually trim and fit, like a field boy she had once cared for.

After sponging Eli's chest, Michelle folded the sheet down to his knees and continued bathing him.

"How is our miracle man today?"

"Good morning, Doctor Boucher," replied Michelle as she respectfully pulled the sheet up to Eli's waist.

"I hope I didn't startle you," grinned the doctor. Then, with a smirking glance at Eli, he added, "If you're lonely for a man, I assure you, I can do better than he."

"I'm quite fine, thank you, Doctor," Michelle said respectfully.

Dr. Boucher's smirk faded. "I thought of you last night when I dined. So tragic to do so alone."

"Yes, that is tragic," Michelle sighed, hiding her scorn as she gazed down the row of maimed and wounded men. She wrung out her sponge and forced a gasp when half of the water missed the basin and landed on the doctor's shiny oxfords. "Oh! I'm so sorry!"

Dr. Boucher took a step back and shook the water from his shoe as he eyed her questioningly.

Michelle hid her devious grin as she moved the basin to a nearby table, then returned to her patient. "Doctor, Elijah seems to be improving daily. Just look at this arm wound; it's completely healed. Shall I remove his stitches?"

"He has a name now," frowned Dr. Boucher.

"I suppose he's always had a name, sir."

Dr. Boucher stiffened. "And how is his miraculous rib wound? Gangrenous, as I predicted?"

"I haven't looked, sir."

"Well, shall we have a look?" Boucher paused then, turning to the watching nurse, said, "Prepare yourself. The stench and sight of gangrene are often overpowering."

"Yes, I know," nodded Michelle.

Dr. Boucher made a face when he peeled back the dressing to the open wound. "What is this?" he asked, seeing an encapsulated shard of rusted iron protruding from the shrunken gash.

"That doesn't look like gangrene," said Michelle.

"Indeed not," frowned Boucher. "Fetch me some large forceps."

"Yes, Doctor," Michelle said, hurrying off.

When she returned, Dr. Boucher pulled the jagged piece of rusted iron from the wound.

"What is it?" asked Michelle.

"Shrapnel," Dr. Boucher breathed, trying to understand what he was seeing. "His body has pushed it out, like a sliver under the flesh. Extraordinary."

Michelle pointed to the open wound and said, "Doctor, I believe it has shrunken from yesterday. Maybe Dr. Faucheux was correct in his assessment."

"Impossible," huffed Boucher, though less convinced.

Michelle eyed the doctor. For the first time not put off by his arrogance, a thin smile formed.

Two rows over, a pasty-faced orderly with long stringy hair paused pushing his linen cart. His head turned, and his nostrils flared as if catching a familiar scent. He stared past the doctor and nurse at the wounded man lying before them. "I have found him," breathed Gik.

CHAPTER II
BEAUTY AND THE BEASTS

Michelle was changing the sheets on a bed near Eli when she heard the muttering. She paused and turned to see Eli stirring in his bed. After quickly stuffing the pillow into its cover, Michelle situated the wool blanket over the empty bed and then moved to Eli's side. He was still unconscious, though his face was glistening with sweat. She placed a hand on his forehead to check for a fever, but he had none.

Michelle's face filled with concern as Eli twisted under his sheets and muttered unrecognizable words, as if in a bad dream. "Elijah, *hush*, be still," she whispered, tenderly stroking his arm. In the six months since the war had begun, Michelle had lost count of how many men with war nightmares she had comforted. "Elijah, you're okay. You're safe here." She listened for meaning to his babbling, but it was all incoherent. Michelle watched with worried eyes as Eli's stirring turned to twisting.

Concerned Eli might be having a seizure, Michelle scanned the hall for Dr. Boucher and found him tending to a patient near the stage. She hurried to him, glancing back twice at Eli.

"Doctor Boucher!" she gasped, nearing the handsome doctor.

"Nurse Michelle," he grinned.

"Doctor, I think a patient is having a seizure!"

Boucher's grin faded. "By patient, I'm guessing you're referring to your Elijah."

Michelle anxiously nodded.

"You've taken quite a liking to him, it seems."

"He is a patient under my charge, sir," Michelle replied, glancing back at Eli.

"Very well, let's see this seizure," said Boucher under his breath as he brushed past Michelle.

Eli was twisting in his bed as they approached. Dr. Boucher roughly felt the watcher's head for a fever, then clutched his wrist for a pulse. With a heavy sigh, Boucher dropped Eli's wrist, turned to Michelle, and huffed, "Your miracle patient is having a war terror. I should think you would have seen enough of those by now to know."

"I was afraid it was a seizure," Michelle helplessly shrugged. "He's come so far; it would be devastating to lose him now."

Boucher huffed, jealous of her concern for a simple soldier.

"I think it's stopping." Michelle moved around the doctor and placed a calming hand on Eli's arm.

Boucher nodded. "Just as I said, a war terror." He pulled back Eli's damp bed sheet. The doctor's eyes narrowed when he noticed the stitches were gone from Eli's arm, face, and chest. Only his large chest wound remained bandaged. He told himself it was hardly remarkable that the more superficial wounds had closed in a week; any healthy man could so heal. It was the degree to which they had healed, with barely a scar visible, that dismayed the doctor. Such healing would typically take months—if they were to heal so well at all. "I see you removed his stitches without my consent."

"I didn't, sir," said Michelle.

"Well, someone clearly did," huffed Boucher.

Michelle gulped and reached a hand into her apron pocket. "They fell out, sir." She opened her hand to the partially dissolved threads.

"What?" Boucher asked in dismay.

"I gathered them this morning when I bathed him."

Boucher shook his head, then turned back to Eli. He tore off the last chest bandage, expecting to find the same wound. But when the gaping hole he had previously measured was only a pink depression, Boucher stepped back, scratched his head in confusion, and muttered, "Unbelievable. This can't be."

Michelle's puzzled gaze moved from their calming miracle patient to the baffled doctor.

"I'm sending him to the hospital," said Boucher.

"The hospital? But...he's in a hospital."

"Not this place! A proper hospital! Saint Louis. I need to run tests. He needs to be x-rayed."

Michelle was unable to hide her amazement as she studied the sleeping Eli. "Doctor, may I accompany Elijah?"

Boucher shook his head. "That wouldn't be possible. You're needed here."

Michelle lowered her head and sadly nodded.

"Unless..." Boucher's brow raised with a crafty grin.

"Yes?" Michelle's uncertain gaze returned to the doctor.

"If you were to agree to dine with me tonight, I think I could arrange such an excursion."

Michelle glanced at Eli. She swallowed her concern and turned to the doctor. "All right. But I have nothing fancy to wear."

Boucher's grin broadened. "You need not worry about that. I'm sure whatever you wear will suffice."

THE RAIN HAD STOPPED, and the clouds had parted, revealing a yellow half-moon that reflected off the slow-moving River Seine. Michelle held her coat tight as she walked along Boulevard du Palais, stepping to avoid the puddles. When the street opened up to the magnificent Notre Dame Cathedral, she barely gave its golden-lit facade a glance. Michelle was more concerned about what lay ahead.

When Michelle spotted the doctor standing below a gaslight on Pont Saint-Michel, her throat tightened, and her gait slowed. "Good evening, Doctor Boucher," she nodded. She thought him handsome standing in the moonlight in his debonair coat and bowler hat, but questioned his motives and her decision to join him for the evening.

"Good evening, Michelle," Boucher grinned, tipping his hat but not taking his gaze off her. "I offered to pick you up at your residence in a carriage."

"Yes, I know, but it's not so cold, and it's stopped raining," Michelle replied with a nervous smile.

"But that's not the real reason," Boucher said as they continued across the bridge.

Michelle hesitated. "I live with my father."

"And he would not approve."

Michelle didn't answer.

They continued up Saint-Michel to the glowing windows of a fine restaurant. Michelle had passed the place many times but had never entered. Her eyes widened as they went inside. She smelled the delicious aroma of fancy food and expensive wines, and saw men in fine suits and women in elegant dresses. While impressed by the extravagance, it felt wrong to be amidst such excess while so many young men were fighting and dying just hours away.

Michelle felt Boucher's eyes on her simple dress as the maître d' took her worn coat and handed it to a hat girl. "I'm sorry," she blushed, "This is my finest dress."

"On the contrary, it looks lovely on you," Boucher gleamed as his eyes lowered to her hint of cleavage. "Your nurses' apron does not do you justice."

Michelle gulped. Fidgeting with her hands, she followed the maître d' to a darkened corner of the restaurant that was partially obscured from the other diners by a green velvet curtain. She felt the doctor's eyes on her as he pulled out her chair at a table set with glistening china, brilliant silver, and sparkling crystal.

After an hour of dinner, wine, and listening to Boucher's self-aggrandizing stories with hardly a word, Michelle cleared her throat and asked, "Doctor, what do you make of Elijah's extraordinary healing?"

"I think it best not to speak of work while at dinner," said Boucher with a condescending smile.

Michelle tried to hide her bewilderment. "But it seems that's all we've spoken of—your surgical successes—the lives you've saved."

Boucher sipped his wine to hide his irritation.

"Have you ever seen a man heal so remarkably?"

Boucher forced a smile, but it quickly faded. "You say heal, but you forget he is still comatose. His brain is not active. He may well be a magnificent vegetable for the rest of his existence—something I would hardly call a life. That, my dear, is not healed."

Michelle reflected on the words, then said, "What do you think the tests will show?"

"I don't know," bristled Boucher. "That is why we are doing the tests tomorrow." He leaned forward with a charming smile then, gazing into Michelle's eyes, said, "I must tell you, you are a lovely woman."

Michelle blushed and looked down at her half-eaten tart.

Boucher reached a hand to hers. Michelle pulled back at first but then let him touch her. Her body tightened as the doctor slid his chair closer. She could see the other diners through the velvet curtain's gap as Boucher's face neared hers. Michelle forced a swallow down her dry throat. She looked unblinkingly into his eyes as his goatee pricked her face. She didn't move when he kissed her. She felt his hand on her knee. Michelle's chest heaved as he pushed his hand along her thigh. She pulled back with a gasp. "Doctor Boucher, do you think this appropriate?"

"Very appropriate," he breathed, sliding closer.

Michelle pulled back, her face flushed. "Doctor, thank you for this dinner, but I must get back to care for my father."

Boucher eyed Michelle in dismay. "The night is young. Can't your mother care for him?"

"My mother is dead," said Michelle, fighting back emotion. "Besides, I have work in the morning."

Not understanding how she could refuse him, Boucher gaped at Michelle as she pushed back her chair and left the table.

MICHELLE PRETENDED NOT to notice Dr. Boucher watching from three rows over as two orderlies moved Eli onto the stretcher. Unconscious for the ten days she had cared for him, Michelle wondered if the doctor was right and that Eli might never awake. She watched as the two orderlies, one short and stalky with beefy arms, and the other bony with long stringy hair and a gaunt, pasty face, hefted Eli from the bed.

Wearing a short brown cape over her nurses' uniform, and carrying her handbag, Michelle followed the stretcher-bearers between the hospital beds to the main ballroom door. After exiting into the crisp morning air, she went down the steps to the waiting ambulance truck with red crosses painted on its open rear doors. She waited for the workers to load Eli into the back, paying little attention to the sunken-eyed Gik and his frequent glances at her.

Once Eli's stretcher was situated, Michelle climbed into the back of the ambulance, sat on the bench nearest his head, and placed her bag under her legs. She adjusted the wool blanket under Eli's arms as the pasty-faced orderly sat beside her, and the driver closed the door. When she felt Gik's eerie gaze, she turned and gave him an uneasy smile.

While the ambulance's small windows let in light, the morning's dreariness made the truck's confines even darker and more suffocating. Michelle quietly hummed as rain dotted the windows, and the truck lumbered down the street.

Still sensing Gik's discomforting gaze, Michelle squeezed Eli's hand. Her eyes widened when Eli stirred under the wool blanket. "Elijah? It's okay. I'm here with you," she whispered, watching the ghoulish orderly out of the corner of her eye.

When Eli groaned and shifted in his cot, as if awakening, Gik's nostrils flared. He reached into his smock's pocket and removed the blazerod.

"What's that?" Michelle asked with concern, thinking it was a heavy candle holder—a formidable club.

Gik ignored her and pointed the blazerod at Eli's chest.

When Michelle saw the rod's glowing end and the venomous look on the orderly's face, she instinctively grabbed his arm.

"Let go of me!" shrieked Gik. "I must destroy him!"

"No! Stop! What are you doing? Help!" cried Michelle as she fought against the bony Gik. She screamed when a bolt of light shot from the rod's end, grazing Eli's thigh and causing him to shudder.

Gik shoved Michelle aside and aimed the blazerod at Eli.

The rod's end was glowing brightly when Michelle lunged at the wild-eyed Gik. She pushed the blazerod away just as a flash of light shot from it and blew a six-inch hole through the ambulance's side.

"Help! Stop him!" shouted Michelle as the pale attacker fought against her. When the ambulance lurched to a stop, she cried, "HELP ME!"

Michelle was still wrestling with the gangly attacker when the ambulance's rear doors opened. She was about to warn the driver of the weapon when Gik turned the blazerod and shot a bolt of light through his chest. Michelle recoiled in horror as the driver flew ten feet back and slid along the rain-soaked street.

When the wild-eyed Gik turned the strange weapon on Michelle, she helplessly screamed and pushed back on the bench seat away from him. "Please, don't!" she pleaded as the rod's end glowed orange and then white.

"You should not be here," snarled Gik.

Michelle gasped when Eli's hand shot up from the cot and grabbed hold of Gik's wrist. She screamed and ducked as the blazerod pointed at her, and another bolt of light punched a hole through the ambulance's roof.

Pushed back in the corner, Michelle watched slack-jawed as the previously comatose Eli bent Gik's arm back. Her eyes darted to the orderly, his ghoulish face screaming without sound as he fought against Eli's lone arm. With the snap of a breaking bone and a haunting shriek, the pale Gik released his hold on the blazerod. It fell to the ambulance floor with a metallic *clang*. Eli's arm dropped off the cot when the howling Gik pulled his bent and broken arm free.

Michelle watched in disbelief as the ghoulish attacker leaped from the ambulance and stumbled down the street, clutching his dangling arm. She turned back to her patient with wide eyes. "Elijah! You're awake! Are you okay?"

Eli's face glistened with sweat, and his heavy eyes drooped as if fighting off sleep.

"Elijah. Elijah! Wake up! Stay with me!" Michelle cried, shaking his arm, but he didn't respond. She felt his glistening forehead for a fever, then his chest through his sweaty hospital gown. His heart was racing. "Elijah. Elijah, it's okay. I'm here with you." Michelle gasped when she realized people were watching her from outside the ambulance's open rear door.

"Are you okay, mademoiselle?" asked a stout man with an umbrella.

"What's happening here?" barked a flat-nosed policeman, pushing through the small crowd. "What happened to that man?" he asked, pointing to the ambulance driver with a smoldering chest wound.

Michelle gulped and tried to calm herself. "A wild man nearly killed my patient! We need to get him to the hospital!"

"Is he a war hero?" asked a wide-eyed boy, looking around the others.

"Maybe it was the dirty Bosch!" screeched a flabby-jawed woman.

The policeman's wary gaze moved from the ambulance's blown-open walls to the dead driver sprawled on the street fifteen feet away. "Move back! Move back!" he barked at the gathering crowd.

"Look, he's on fire!" cried the boy. With gasps, the others gathered around the ambulance driver to see the flames coming from his chest.

Michelle's heart was still pounding when she turned back to the unconscious Eli. She felt a warm flutter surge through her but quickly dismissed it as a girlish infatuation for the man who had just saved her life.

Michelle was about to place Eli's arm back on the cot when she spotted the rod-shaped weapon on the floor by her feet. She looked to see if anyone was watching, but the crowd was more interested in the burning driver. Michelle reached for the blazerod but stopped short of touching it. After breathing in courage, she picked up the strange weapon. Though it looked like pewter, it was warm to the touch. She studied its ornate engravings, then felt the lip at its base, where a candle might go if it was a candlestick, but the hole was shallow and black as obsidian.

Upon seeing the spectators still standing around the dead driver, and the policeman damping out the flames with his coat, Michelle pushed the strange rod into her bag and snapped it closed.

. . .

MICHELLE'S FEET were dragging when she topped her apartment building stairs. It had been a long and traumatic day. After answering the policeman's questions as best she could, and finally getting her unconscious patient to the hospital, Michelle sat with Eli, hoping he would again awake. But despite her best efforts, Eli's slumber persisted.

Fearing another attack on her patient, Michelle spent the next eight hours beside his bed. Finally convinced Eli was safe in the hospital, she left him for home.

Michelle moved to a dim wall sconce outside her apartment door, opened her handbag, and reached for her key. She hesitated when she spotted the blazerod inside. Michelle had nearly told the police about the strange weapon but doubted they would believe her. She wondered why someone would want Eli dead, then reminded herself a war was raging. Michelle wondered who Eli was and if his unusual healing abilities had anything to do with it. She shook the muddled thoughts from her head and told herself she was too exhausted to figure anything out.

Michelle retrieved her key and moved to her gray, paint-peeling door. She heard a sound behind her and glanced over her shoulder at the darkened staircase. Michelle gulped as she remembered the frightful attacker and feared he might be lurking in the shadows. With her heart pounding, she fumbled with the key, inserted it into the lock, and quickly opened the door. After stepping inside, Michelle closed the door and hastily turned its locking bolt. Her chest was heaving as she stood with her back to the door. She swallowed her fear, took a deep breath, and calmed herself.

Across the darkened room was the flickering glow of the fireplace. Michelle pushed a button that brought to life the incandescent bulb over the small kitchen table, then moved into the compact kitchen and set her bag on the table. She pulled off her nurses' hat and cape and hung them on a nearby rack. With her pulse slowing, Michelle sighed at seeing her father slumped in the soft chair near the glowing fireplace.

"Papa," she whispered as she moved to him and pulled the shawl from his lap. "Papa, come, let's get you to bed."

The old man's droopy eyes pulled open as he lifted his head. "Hello, my sweet," he grinned, his voice tired and raspy.

"Papa, let's get you to bed," she repeated, reaching for his hand.

"I can manage," he wheezed. As he pushed up from his chair, the thin gray strands of hair atop his head fell forward.

After helping her father to his bed and closing the door, Michelle returned to the kitchen table and opened her bag. She stared at the engraved pewter rod resting inside. Michelle would never have believed the power of the strange weapon had she not seen it. She hoped the French or British were behind its invention but feared it was German ingenuity, as they seemed especially adept at creating instruments of death.

Michelle gulped, then reached into her bag and carefully removed the blazerod. She held it up to the light to better examine its engravings. While futuristic in its deadly function, it seemed to her worn and archaic. With the luster of pewter, Michelle thought it odd to feel warm to the touch. She remembered its glowing end and carefully peered down the rod's darkened barrel. Within a depression lay a black onyx lens. Michelle turned the blazerod, searching for rivets or screws but found none.

With a tired sigh, Michelle looked around the kitchen for a place to hide the strange weapon. She opened a cabinet and stood on her toes to reach the top shelf, then turned to a bookcase across from the fireplace. Michelle moved to it, removed several books, then laid the rod at the back of the shelf. After replacing the books, she gave a satisfied nod and turned out the light.

CHAPTER 12
THE AWAKENING

Michelle was sitting on the edge of Eli's bed, studying his striking features while wiping his brow with a damp sponge, when his eyes pulled open. With a gasp, she removed her hand and leaned back, uncertain how he might react.

Eli slowly blinked his eyes, trying to make sense of his surroundings. Michelle moved a little closer when he muttered unrecognizable words. She could tell it wasn't gibberish, like the days before; they were formed words—a sentence but in another language. "Oh... You're awakening. Can you hear me?" she whispered with an uncertain smile.

Eli blinked as he tried to clear his vision. "Who-who are you?" he asked, his voice weak and raspy. Eli's eyes widened when the nurse came into focus.

"My name is Michelle." She felt a warm surge flow through her as she gazed into Eli's blue eyes for the first time. "I have been caring for you for the past three weeks."

Eli tried to sit up, but the effort was too great.

"Your body is tired. Ease yourself. It will take time for your strength to return."

Eli turned his head but saw only white partitions on either side. "Where am I?"

"You're in Paris. In a hospital," Michelle replied with brown, searching eyes.

Eli's brow furrowed. "Paris." He said the word as if not knowing its meaning.

"How are you feeling, Elijah?"

The watcher's muddled eyes moved to her. "Elijah...is that my name?"

Michelle's face filled with concern. "It was the name on your papers. Do you not remember?"

Eli looked at her blankly.

"You had a letter in your pocket, written by someone named Jean-Pierre. Is that your friend?"

Eli's eyes shifted, as if unraveling an impossible riddle.

Michelle put a comforting hand on Eli's arm. She had seen amnesia before in wounded soldiers, particularly after surviving a blast. "Do you not remember your name?"

Eli shook his head.

"Do you remember where you were when you got hurt?"

Eli's eyes drifted down his blanketed body. "No."

"Do you remember anything before that?"

Eli gulped and shook his head.

"Do you recall your childhood? Where you grew up? Your parents? Anything?"

Eli looked at her with a hollow bleakness, then muttered, "What happened to me?"

"They brought you from the front. You were badly wounded," Michelle explained, unable to hide the concern in her eyes.

Eli's gaze drifted as he searched for something familiar, but there was only the calming woman and the white fabric panels beside his bed. He closed his eyes, and a tear ran down his cheek.

"I'm sorry," Michelle whispered, tenderly stroking his arm. "But with this terrible war, maybe it's better you don't remember what you've seen."

Michelle's heart ached when she saw Eli's fear and confusion. She had seen so many men destroyed by the war it was easy to forget each one's agony.

When Eli reopened his eyes, he saw the red cross on Michelle's white apron and asked, "You're a nurse?"

"Yes."

"You have been caring for me?"

"Yes," breathed Michelle.

"For how long?"

"Almost a month."

"What happened to me?"

Michelle shook her head. "I don't know. You were wounded at the front."

"There is a war?"

"Yes," nodded Michelle.

"What is the year?"

"1915."

"The month?"

"March."

"Who is fighting the war?"

"We're fighting the Germans. The British are helping us."

"Who's winning the war?"

"Nobody, it seems." Michelle sighed. "The fighting is spreading all over, and the Germans keep thinking of more terrible ways to kill our boys. They are despicable monsters!" She thought of the latest weapons: poison gas and guns that spit fire across fields, cooking men in their trenches. Michelle shuddered at the memory of the blazerod, an even more terrifying weapon. She wondered why the Germans had targeted Eli in the ambulance. Her brow furrowed when she remembered him fending off the ghoulish attacker with one arm. *It was almost like a reflex. Who is this man?* she wondered.

Eli winced as a fragment of a memory of men fighting with spears on chariots flashed through his mind.

"Are you okay?" asked Michelle.

"I-I must get up. I shouldn't be here." When Eli tried to sit up, a jolt of pain ran up his hip. "Ow!"

"Be still, Elijah. You must rest," urged Michelle, laying him back down. "I have water here for you. I'll call for some soup. You'll have to take it slowly. Your body has weakened."

Eli lay back on the bed as images of men fighting and killing flashed through his mind. "My body hurts."

Michelle looked over him with concern. "Where do you hurt?"

"All over. Here," Eli said, hovering a hand above his chest, "and my leg," he added, wincing at its mention.

Michelle tried to hide her uncertainty. Unlike Eli's other wounds, the blazerod's thigh burn was still red and oozing. "I'm sorry, but with how badly you were injured...it's a miracle you're alive."

"A miracle?"

Michelle considered saying no more, but his recovery was too extraordinary. "You had a hole in your chest from a German shell—the size of a man's fist. You had a dozen smaller wounds as well. I watched them heal in a week. The way you have healed—I've never seen anything like it! Neither has Doctor Boucher."

"Who's Doctor Boucher?"

"He was your doctor."

Michelle reached for a glass of water on the side table. She held it to Eli's lips with one hand while she supported the back of his head with her other. The watcher's blue eyes met hers as he drank down the water, and she smiled.

WHILE ELI'S strength had not fully returned, and his recent leg wound made walking and standing painful, it was the strange darkness that he felt that was most disturbing. The mystery of his past was only part of his bleakness. He felt an uneasiness, a peculiar foreboding, as if he had committed a great omission.

Eli was staring at the hospital ceiling when he noticed someone at the foot of his bed. He weakly smiled when he saw it was the kind nurse, Michelle.

"How are you today, Elijah?" asked Michelle warmly.

Eli saw the compassion on her face but nothing more. He felt blind but didn't know why. His gloom returned.

"Are you not feeling well?" Michelle asked with concern.

Looking as though he might cry, Eli forced down a swallow, then gave a faint shrug. "I don't know. I feel empty inside. I feel darkness around me. Sometimes it's suffocating."

Michelle moved to Eli's side and felt his cheek for a fever.

The warmth of her touch radiated across Eli's face and caused his pupils to widen momentarily. They locked eyes, and he breathed in Michelle's fragrance.

"What's the matter, Elijah?" she whispered.

Eli blinked out of his stare. For a moment, he had forgotten his pain. "I feel all alone... I-I don't know who I am."

Michelle sat on the side of Eli's bed and gently stroked his cheek. "You're not alone. I'm here with you. When people lose their memory, it often comes back."

"Often?" whispered Eli.

Michelle nodded.

"I feel I should be doing something. That I should be somewhere else."

"That is very common for soldiers coming from the front. They feel they have abandoned their friends. Do you remember any of your friends?"

An image of Jean-Pierre flashed through Eli's mind, but he didn't know who it was.

Michelle's face swelled with compassion when she saw Eli's pain. "It is perfectly okay to be sad. You're still healing on the inside too. It will get better." She moved her hand from his cheek and looked over Eli's handsome features. "Elijah, do you remember anything at all?"

Eli's gaze moved to the white partition. "I sometimes see faces and places but don't know where they're from."

"I'm sorry. I wish there was more I could do," whispered Michelle.

When Eli saw her eyes welling with tears, he said, "I've made you sad."

Michelle wiped away a tear and forced a smile. "I'm sometimes lonely too."

Eli cocked his head. "But...you know who you are."

"I sometimes wonder," muttered Michelle, her gaze drifting.

"You have no family?"

"I have my father," Michelle tearfully shrugged.

"But not your mother?"

"No," Michelle said with a sad shake of her head. "She died."

"I'm sorry," breathed Eli. He watched Michelle wipe away her tears, then asked, "Why does it hurt so much inside?"

"I don't know, but it does, doesn't it?" Michelle sighed. "I was much younger when my mother died. I remember the priest telling me that God allows us to feel pain so we can also feel joy." Her gaze grew distant. "I just wish there was more joy to feel now."

Eli found Michelle's hand and wrapped his fingers around it. "When I see your face, when I feel your touch, it makes me feel happy."

Michelle's smile forced more tears down her cheek. "You make me feel happy as well, Elijah."

"Does that mean we're friends?"

"Yes, I think it does," beamed Michelle.

Eli's face grew serious. "I don't remember if I have other friends, but I think you're my favorite."

Michelle laughed. "You're one of my favorites too, Elijah." She stood, and her face grew serious. "But I am still your nurse, and it's time for your walk."

Eli's face dimmed. "Walking does not make my leg happy."

Michelle laughed and reached for Eli's hand.

ELI QUIETLY WATCHED as Doctor Boucher examined his healed wounds, roughly poking and prodding him, and every so often muttering, "Extraordinary. Amazing." or "I've never seen anything like this."

"Good morning, Elijah," beamed Michelle as she rounded the partition to Eli's bed. "Are you—Oh, Doctor Boucher," she gasped, not expecting to see the doctor standing over Eli.

Boucher glanced at Michelle. "Elijah, you are very fortunate to have your private nurse."

"She's taken wonderful care of me," Eli replied. He sensed Michelle's uneasiness with the doctor but little else.

"I granted your request to accompany my patient to the hospital for testing. That was three days ago. I haven't seen or heard from you since," frowned Boucher.

Michelle gulped. "I've been here caring for Elijah."

"I see that. What of your duties at the auxiliary hospital?"

"I've transferred here," Michelle replied, clutching her hands.

"That's very nice, but Doctor Joffre, the hospital administrator, is a personal friend, and he's unaware of any transfer request."

Michelle looked down. "I may have forgotten to submit the paperwork."

Boucher shook his head. "Today I learned the ambulance driver was killed. He had a hole blown through his chest and ignited on fire!"

Eli's brow furrowed as a fragment of the attack flashed through his mind.

"They said the ambulance was all but destroyed! What happened?"

"I-I don't know really. It all happened so fast." Michelle shrugged. "An awful man attacked us. He was dressed as an orderly. I think he was a German agent."

"A German Agent?" scoffed Boucher. "None of that matters. I'm here to make sure my patient is tested and to bring you back to the auxiliary hospital."

"But who will care for Elijah?" gasped Michelle.

"I assure you, there are other nurses. Besides, his wounds have healed, and he'll soon return to the front."

"No, you don't understand; he's forgotten everything! He doesn't know who he is!"

Boucher turned to Eli. "Is that true? Do you have amnesia? Or are you another malingering coward?"

Eli's eyes narrowed. He did not like Dr. Boucher.

"It doesn't matter," huffed Boucher. "They don't need you for that kind of care. There's an entire hospital wing for the shell-shocked and weak-minded."

"It's not just that; Elijah was wounded in the ambulance attack," explained Michelle.

"Yes, I saw his blistered thigh. How did he get burned? What weapon did that?"

"The same one that killed the driver," Michelle replied, feeling Eli's curious eyes on her.

Boucher sighed.

"Please, doctor. Elijah is our miracle patient! I've seen so much progress with him; I want to see it through!"

Boucher's crafty gaze moved from Eli to the alluring nurse. "I suppose I could make arrangements with Doctor Joffre...if..."

Michelle's eyes lowered. "Are you asking me to dinner again?"

"I believe I am," Boucher said with a charming grin.

Michelle glanced at the watching Eli, then nodded to Boucher, "All right."

Eli's jaw tightened as he eyed the conniving doctor.

"Unfortunately, I have another commitment tonight. Tomorrow night, perhaps?"

Michelle nodded.

A triumphant Boucher stepped closer to Michelle, lifted her chin with his hand, and waited for her to smile. When she did, he nodded approvingly and said, "Now take my patient to x-ray. They're waiting for him."

"Yes, doctor," Michelle dutifully replied.

Eli watched the doctor leave and the smile fade from Michelle's face. He waited for her to finish writing in his chart, then asked, "Why do you let him treat you like that?"

"It doesn't matter."

"I think it does."

Michelle sighed. "He's a doctor, and I'm a nurse. Why does it matter? I'm doing it for you."

Eli frowned in confusion. "You're doing it for me?"

Michelle gulped. "Yes."

"Because we're friends?"

Michelle made eye contact with Eli, then said, "Yes...I guess."

"Thank you."

Michelle looked down at Eli's chart and nodded.

"You are very kind to me."

Michelle smiled, "You are easy to be kind to."

"You enjoy caring for people, don't you?"

Michelle nodded. "I wish I could do more."

Eli studied Michelle. "You have a nurturing soul...I can tell."

They locked eyes, and she said tenderly, "Thank you, Elijah."

"Your days must be very long if you treat all of your patients as you do me."

"I don't," breathed Michelle, lost in Eli's blue eyes. She felt her heart flutter. It was stronger and more real than what she had felt before with him. It reminded her of the days after she had met her former lover, Maurice, and it scared her. She tried to deny what it meant. Michelle pulled back. She wondered if she was spending too much time with Elijah. She told herself she should move to another patient but didn't want to.

For the weeks she had tended to him while he lay unconscious, Michelle had wondered who Elijah was and what he would be like. Now he was awake, but because of his amnesia, she was no closer to understanding the mysterious Eli. Even so, she found his presence intoxicating and now questioned almost everything she did.

Gathering herself, Michelle got up from the bed, forced a dispassionate nurse's smile, then said, "I'll check on you later."

Eli's gaze followed Michelle as she left the room. He then sank back into his pillow and stared at the ceiling.

CHAPTER 13
THE FREAK COLLECTORS

The violin music in the restaurant was soothing and the *Coq au vin*, a chicken dish braised with wine, mushrooms, and bacon, was sublime. Michelle had purposely diverted her thoughts from the enigmatic Eli, and to her surprise, she was enjoying herself with the handsome doctor. The wine mixed with Boucher's seducing flirtations were swaying Michelle. Even his flouting of money seemed less off-putting to her.

Seeing he was making progress, Boucher poured more wine into her glass and nodded to the man playing the violin, who then moved beside their table. The music and the wine eased Michelle further, but her thoughts occasionally returned to Eli.

When the piano near the dance floor began plinking out a melody, Boucher leaned closer with a clever grin. "Would you care to dance?"

Michelle blushed. "I'm afraid I'm not very good."

"Nonsense." Boucher stood and reached for her hand.

Boucher's eyes followed Michelle's slender hips as she got to her feet and moved past him to the dance floor.

After three songs, Boucher saw Michelle was enjoying herself. It surprised him when her smile faded. "What's the matter, my dear?"

"I'm sorry. I've been rude."

"How so?"

"I fear I've been entirely preoccupied with our patient."

Boucher grinned. "On the contrary. I find your devotion to your patients impressive and very appealing."

Michelle's face brightened, but then her brow again furrowed. "Doctor, what did you learn from Elijah's tests yesterday?"

"Please, I told you to call me Leon," grinned Boucher. His smile faded when he realized Michelle was still waiting for a reply. He waved a dismissive hand and said, "Nothing notable."

"Please, we both know he's remarkable. Did his tests show anything...anything unusual?"

"No," Boucher lied.

"And his x-rays? Did they show any more shrapnel inside him? Or give any clue to the cause of his amnesia?"

Boucher studied the striking nurse. Fearing he might not get her into his bed without answering, he frowned and said, "The x-ray showed nothing," which was true. Not even Eli's bones were visible. The image was just a white haze.

"That's good," smiled Michelle.

"Yes," Boucher nodded, and they continued to dance.

Michelle tried not to blush as the doctor eyed her.

Boucher's yearning gaze moved from her gentle lips to her sultry eyes. Then, with a crafty grin, he asked, "Would you care to walk along the Seine?"

"A walk along the river? That would be splendid," Michelle replied with a smile not forced.

While the night air was brisk, the song of an accordion and the chatter from an outdoor café were warming. Michelle took Dr. Boucher's arm as a clopping horse pulled a carriage past them. Boucher grinned contentedly.

The moon had just broken through the clouds, the Eiffel Tower was aglow, and the gaslights reflected off the lazy river as they walked along the path. Michelle thought the evening was perfect. Her tranquil gaze moved to a couple passionately kissing in the shadows. Michelle noticed the man's uniform and wondered if they had been lovers before the war or if it was a rushed leave romance. She wondered if the soldier would return from the front. She wondered if she might find him someday in the hospital.

As they continued along the riverfront, they passed other couples, arm in arm, moving in and out of the shadows. Michelle felt the heat of their desires, intensified by the uncertainty of the times. She wondered about her situation. She looked up at the handsome Dr. Boucher. He was wealthy and highly esteemed. *I could do worse than him.* The thought, while comforting, was also conflicting.

When they passed into the shadows between the lamp lights, Boucher stopped and pulled Michelle close to him.

Michelle gulped as she gazed into the doctor's yearning eyes. She felt her face moving toward his. Her heart was pounding when their lips touched. Her body tightened, then relaxed as Boucher pulled her against him. She felt comfort in his passion and power.

After several minutes of kissing, the doctor pulled back, gazed into Michelle's tranquil brown eyes, and breathed, "Spend the night with me."

Michelle's eyes widened as she considered his invitation. While drawn to him, her better sense prevailed. She sighed. Then, fearing she might be making a mistake at his refusal, she whispered, "Do you think it is a good idea for us? With you being a doctor and I..."

"*Shhh.*" Boucher placed a finger to her lips. "You needn't worry about that. I know best."

"You know best for you, perhaps," bristled Michelle.

Boucher's eyes narrowed. "What do you mean?"

Michelle pulled away, as if blinking out of a trance. She had heard the stories and knew she wasn't the first woman—or nurse—to be lured into Boucher's bed. Shocked at how close she had come to falling for his cajoling, Michelle bit her tongue and said, "Thank you for a lovely evening, Doctor, but I think it best for me to leave now."

Boucher's chest heaved with desire. He had heard such refusals before and considered them veiled invitations. He stepped closer and pulled the apprehensive Michelle into him. "You don't mean that," he breathed, his lips hungry for hers. "I will give you a night like no other."

Michelle pushed back. She feared he would take what she no longer wanted to offer. "No, I must leave now!" she blurted.

"Are you refusing me?"

Michelle forced a smile. "Doctor, you are very persuasive, but I don't think tonight."

Boucher's jaw tightened. "It's that damn Elijah, isn't it?"

"I don't know what you mean."

"You know exactly what I mean! You've lost your objectivity over him."

Michelle's face went blank.

"It has been known to happen, of course. Nurses become infatuated with their patients, just as patients do their doctors. It is, of course, unhealthy in the extreme. The next man deserves your unbiased care as much as this so-called miracle man does."

Hearing the truth in his words, Michelle gulped and looked down at her shoes. "Forgive me, Doctor, but he is extraordinary. Even you must admit so."

"Extraordinary or not, I'm removing you from that hospital!"

"Doctor, please!" Michelle gasped.

"Then come to bed with me," said Boucher with a look of desperation.

Taken aback, Michelle gulped and defiantly shook her head. "I will not be coerced by you."

"Coerced?" Boucher glared.

Michelle stepped back. "I've-I've heard the stories about you."

"Stories?"

Michelle gulped. "I wouldn't be the first nurse to be drawn into your lair." She fought to hold her tongue, knowing her work as a nurse hung in the balance, but she couldn't. "I'm frankly shocked at myself for even considering such a vulgar and repugnant request!"

"*Vulgar*? And *repugnant*?" seethed Boucher. "I've dined you. I've wined you." He grabbed Michelle's arm. "I will have you!"

Michelle slapped Boucher's face.

The doctor staggered back and looked at her with stunned eyes.

"Maybe you should have saved your money and your time and just found a street whore!"

"How dare you speak to me that way! Do you have any idea what I can do to you? To your freak, Elijah!"

Michelle pulled back. "What are you talking about? This has nothing to do with Elijah."

Boucher shook his head. "I should have known better than to have fallen for a tramp! We'll see how you like patching up men at a field hospital!"

"What?" gasped Michelle.

"I'm moving you to the front! Perhaps they will benefit from your ungratefulness!"

"No! What about Elijah? He's my patient!"

"He is not your patient! And he is not your worry! After tomorrow, it won't matter anyway!" seethed Boucher, turning away.

"What does that mean?" pleaded Michelle, moving in front of the fuming doctor.

"It means the Army is collecting him tomorrow."

"But he's not ready to return to the front!"

"I don't think they care about that. They're more interested in how he so remarkably heals. They'll most likely dissect him like a frog, then watch him grow back! I would have never supposed such a thing, but how valuable would a soldier be that cannot be killed? Shoot him, allow him to heal, then stick him back on the line! Incalculable! There, does that satisfy your obsessive curiosity with the freak?"

Michelle looked at Boucher in dismay. "You are cruel and heartless!"

"Enjoy your time at the front. Now get out of my way!" snarled Boucher as he stormed past.

THE HOSPITAL ENTRY WAS BUSTLING. Bloodied and bandaged soldiers on stretchers were being carried in through the large, arched doorway and tended to by nurses and doctors. Some of the greeting staff were fresh and eager-eyed, while others dragged and wore drawn faces.

The gray-haired and mustached hospital administrator, Dr. Joffre, hardly noticed the chaos. It was just another day with a fresh shipment of wounded men from the front. Skirting along the wall of the entry, he reached out a welcoming hand to the large red-bearded man in a fine suit and greatcoat. "Doctor Stormbrewer, I presume."

"Doctor Joffre," Lu nodded, his crisp green eyes gathering in all before him. "This is my assistant, Monsieur Gik."

Joffre's gaze moved from the intimidating Stormbrewer to the gaunt and sickly man in a baggy suit at his side. "Is he quite all right?"

Lu glanced at Gik. "Yes, he's Romanian and cursed with a rather unsightly appearance."

"Romanian," Joffre frowned. His eyes lowered to Gik's deformed hand protruding from his coat sleeve. He thought it strange to see the hand turned, as if it were backward, then rotate under his sleeve to its proper position. Joffre blinked his eyes, uncertain of what he had just seen, then motioned them toward his office. "This-this way, please."

Lu glared at the stringy-haired Gik, then followed the doctor. Not only had the halfborn failed to dispatch Eli, but he had also lost the blazerod, forcing Lu to take matters into his own hands—something he loathed to do. Lu preferred having mortals or, in Gik's case, half-mortals to do his work.

"When I received your telegram, I was quite confused," said Joffre, glancing back as he walked. "How exactly did you hear about our wonder patient?"

"Such news travels quickly," replied Lu, his voice deep and menacing.

"The Army has sent you, but you don't look like the military type," observed Dr. Joffre, pushing open his office door.

"I am an Army advisor," replied Lu, lowering his head to enter the administrator's office.

"Have you found others like him with such remarkable healing abilities?" asked Dr. Joffre.

"I'm afraid I cannot discuss such matters," said Lu tersely.

"Ah, yes. Army secrets. I understand," nodded Joffre, trying not to look at Gik. "Do you think the enemy would be after such a man?"

Lu's green eyes narrowed. "Perhaps, if they understood his value. Why do you ask?"

"There may have already been an attempt on him," replied Joffre.

"Oh?"

"Yes, there was an incident with the ambulance."

"Incident?" questioned Lu.

Joffre scratched his head and gazed out the window. "Yes, an ambulance driver was killed when he was being brought here. A strange weapon blew a hole through him, and the ambulance was all but destroyed! Some say it was a German agent."

"No doubt." Lu gave his ghoulish assistant a glaring, sideways glance, and Gik hung his head and stepped back behind him.

"What will the Army do with him?" asked Joffre, turning back to his guests. "Experimentation? As a scientist, I understand the value of research, but as a physician, I find it abhorrent when conducted on humans."

"Fortunately, you need not worry about that," glared Lu.

Joffre gave an uncertain nod.

"We are in violent times. I'm sure even a man of your noble morals understands the importance of defeating one's enemy."

"Yes, of course." Joffre gulped. "Would you care for tea or coffee?" he nervously asked, offering them seats across from his desk.

"No," Lu replied with piercing green eyes. "Perhaps you could take us to him?"

About to sit, Joffre sprung back to his feet. "Yes, of course. He's not far from here, in the south wing."

Lu and Gik followed Joffre out of the office and down the crowded corridor as the doctor nervously rambled. After turning down another hallway, Joffre paused outside a large room with six partitioned beds partly visible through a hall window. "He's right in here."

When the eager Lu started to enter, Joffre raised a halting hand and said, "Doctor Stormbrewer, when do you plan on taking our patient? Today?"

Lu considered killing the annoying doctor then and there, but the corridor was too public of a place. "Perhaps. I would like to see him first."

Satisfied with Lu's response, Dr. Joffre turned and entered the room.

Following behind Joffre, Lu reached into his coat pocket and felt the golden orb. While he would have rather had the blazerod the inept Gik had lost, Lu knew the domain sphere's power could be just as effective at removing his rival and less messy. Lu eyed the wounded soldiers as they passed each open partition. He thought them weak and frail and not deserving of life.

When Dr. Joffre reached the second to last bed and saw a thin man with a bandaged face and arms, he stopped and scratched his head. "That's not him."

The stern-eyed Lu pushed past the doctor and barked, "Where is he?"

"I don't know. This was his bed! Nurse, where have you moved Private Mansel? Nurse!"

"Yes, Doctor?" A short, heavy-set nurse waddled to his side.

"Where have you moved Private Mansel?" demanded Joffre.

"I don't know, sir. The bed was empty when I got here this morning. I thought he had been discharged."

"Discharged! No! Find him!" yelled Joffre.

"Yes, Doctor!" The nurse waddled out of the room.

"Where is the nurse who brought him here?" barked Joffre.

"Michelle? She was moved to a field hospital," replied another nurse.

Lu's eyebrow raised as he searched the room for clues.

"Nobody knows where he is, Doctor Joffre!" gasped the waddling nurse as she hurried back into the room.

Joffre shook his head in dismay before turning to the seething Lu. "I'm sorry. I don't know where he is."

"It seems your patient has fled," glared Lu. "Tell me about this nurse, Michelle."

CHAPTER 14

RENEGADE

Eli slid his queen across the worn chessboard, then looked up at the white-haired François Duvall.

"You've beaten me again, haven't you?" grinned François, his cheeks rosy, his gray eyes baggy. "For someone who doesn't remember who they are, you play very well," he laughed.

Eli smiled at François. He thought there was something familiar about him. But Eli's smile faded when a fragmented memory of Cyrus flashed through his mind.

"You were at the front?" François asked, lighting his pipe.

"That is what I've been told," said Eli.

"Pity you don't recall. I would have liked your report. I'm a military man myself, you know—Foreign Legion. I fought the Nguyen Dynasty in Indochina—not by myself, mind you. Those little yellow men were a tenacious lot—nothing like the Hun, I suppose. But that was a long time ago, when I was a young man, like you," François said, not hiding his envy.

Eli warmly considered his new friend, then asked, "You remember all those things from when you were young?"

"Yes, like yesterday," François grinned as he puffed on his pipe.

Eli's brow furrowed. "I wish I could remember."

"Hmmm, it will come back, I suppose." François studied Eli, who filled the armchair and barely fit into the pants and shirt Michelle had given him. "Does your leg still bother you?" asked François, seeing it stretched to the side.

Eli nodded.

"Michelle said you were hurt quite badly."

"I guess so."

"My daughter is a good nurse?"

Eli's face brightened. "Yes, she is...wonderful."

François' bushy eyebrows gathered. He recognized the glimmer of love in the mysterious man's eyes and wasn't sure he approved.

"What did you do after you fought the little yellow men?"

François chuckled. "When I came back to Paris, I worked in a factory. My life was ordinary until I met a beautiful girl one day in the fromagerie. We fell in love," he smiled. "We got married. Soon we had our beautiful little Michelle LaRue."

Eli yearned for the joy he saw in François' face. "What was your wife's name?"

François' sad gaze drifted out the balcony door window. He pulled the pipe from his mouth and breathed, "Joséphine."

"You loved her very much," Eli observed, his blue eyes searching.

François' nod was slow and deliberate; his gaze fixed out the window. "She was my life." His chest heaved, and then he added, "Now Michelle is my life."

Eli turned his head when the apartment door opened, and Michelle entered.

François saw Eli's delight at seeing his lovely daughter.

"Bonjour," beamed Eli, struggling to his feet.

François's face dimmed when he saw his daughter's eagerness toward Eli.

"Elijah, you're standing on your own. Does your leg hurt terribly?"

Eli shook his head.

"That's marvelous!"

Eli watched as Michelle moved past him and kissed François on the cheek.

"Have you two had a good morning?" asked Michelle.

"He has beaten me at chess three times," sighed François.

"That's not such a feat. I can beat you in chess, Papa."

François shrugged.

"I have lunch. And I found a coat and some shoes that should fit you better," Michelle said, holding the wool coat up for Eli to see.

"Thank you, but I have no money to pay you for these things," said Eli.

"You need not worry," smiled Michelle. She laid the coat down, then set a baguette and a wedge of cheese on the small kitchen counter.

"No, with my pension and her exorbitant nurse's income, we are as rich as thieves," muttered François.

"Papa, Elijah is my friend," sighed Michelle as she cut cheese slices.

"And how long does your friend intend to beat me at chess?"

Eli looked at François innocently.

"Papa, I should think you'd like the company," said Michelle.

"And who says I do not? I simply ask the question. He is a soldier in the French Army. When does the Army come looking for him?"

Michelle stopped cutting the bread. She looked at Eli, unable to hide her worry, then at her father. "Elijah needs more care before he can return to the front."

"Clearly," François said, nodding to Eli's stiff leg. "Will they discharge him?"

"I don't know," shrugged Michelle as she resumed her meal preparation.

Eli's face filled with concern. "It seems I am putting you at odds."

"Don't be silly," sighed Michelle.

Eli shook his head helplessly. "I don't know what I should do. I don't know where I should be."

"You should be here with us until you mend," nodded François, moving past Eli to the kitchen table.

"Thank you, Papa," Michelle said with a loving smile.

"Then you should return to wherever you belong."

"*Papa*," breathed Michelle, shaking her head. When she saw Eli limping behind her father, she smiled and said, "You're getting on quite well, aren't you?"

"I have an outstanding nurse," grinned Eli. He sat at the table and eyed the cheese and bread as Michelle poured a glass of wine for him. He was about to reach for the food when Michelle took his hand in hers. Their eyes met, and Michelle warmly smiled. When François took his other hand, Eli turned to him in surprise.

"We're saying grace. You may have forgotten about that," François said with a hint of judgment.

AFTER HELPING Eli into her bed, Michelle pulled the blanket over him, placed a loving hand on his arm, and smiled. "You've done much today. You need to rest. Tomorrow...we'll see what happens tomorrow."

Eli watched as Michelle got up from the bed and closed the door behind her, casting him into darkness.

In the main room, Michelle moved to the armchair across from her father, who was reading the evening post.

"There is fighting in Turkey now. Gallipoli, it's called," François said, not looking up.

Michelle sighed. "I'm so tired of hearing of this war. Is there nothing else?"

François looked up from his newspaper. "No, sadly, there is not." He watched his daughter staring into the fireplace for a time, then said, "It has been very nice having you home these past two days. Will you return to the hospital tomorrow?"

Michelle gulped, and her gaze lowered to the floor. "I've left the hospital."

François set the paper down.

"I've had a problem with a doctor there. He's sending me to the front—to a field hospital."

"The front?" François frowned. He considered her news, then asked, "What kind of problem?"

"The usual kind," muttered Michelle.

"Oh." François' perplexed gaze returned to his newspaper.

"I rebuffed him and now face the consequences," fumed Michelle.

François angrily shook his head. "Despicable doctor."

Michelle studied the flickering flames. "But it's much more complicated than that."

François' eyebrows raised. "More complicated than that?"

"I've told you about Elijah's fantastic recovery."

"Every day for the past month," sighed François.

"The Army wants to experiment on Elijah! They want to know how he can heal so remarkably. I fear they will do whatever it takes to find out—despite Elijah's wishes or what's best for him!"

"From my experience in the Army, I don't doubt your claim."

"Father, I cannot allow it!" Michelle blurted. "You've been with him for two days now! You've seen his innocence and splendor! He is the rarest of men!"

"He's not himself," shrugged François.

"Just because he cannot remember doesn't mean he's someone he is not! He is a kind and gentle soul!"

"He is a large soul."

"I trust him completely and feel safe and at ease with him."

François eyed his daughter. He knew well of her stubbornness.

"I will not allow them to take Elijah and dissect him like some-some lab rat!"

"Do you think you have any choice in the matter?" asked François.

"What do you mean?"

"There is a war on. France is fighting for its life. The military will do anything. When they find out you have brought him here, they will come and take him, whether you approve or not."

Michelle's face paled at the thought.

"Does anyone know you brought him here?"

"No, I sneaked him from the hospital early in the morning. I'm sure no one saw us."

"They will suspect you."

Michelle gulped.

François couldn't hide his concern. "Once they learn you have not reported to the field hospital, how hard will it be to find where you live? They have only to ask your friends."

"What do I do?" fretted Michelle.

François feared his daughter's interest in Eli was more than being his nurse. It seemed clear to him that she had feelings for the man. "You have but two choices. Wait for them to come and find your friend, or take him somewhere they cannot."

"Where would I take him?"

François studied his daughter. "Your Elijah means this much to you?"

Michelle considered the question. "When I'm with him, I feel something I can't explain. He's like no other man I have ever known."

"Oh, my," muttered François.

Michelle looked at her father with helplessness.

"Why don't you take him to your uncle's château?"

Michelle's eyebrows raised at the idea.

"It's away from Paris, far from the war. He's always welcomed you there."

"Oh, Papa, that is a splendid idea! But..." Michelle's excitement faded. "I could never leave you here."

"Who says I want to stay here? Not with those nasty Germans knocking at our door."

Michelle nodded eagerly. "I have money saved! We could stay there comfortably for six months! By then, the war should be over!"

François smiled at his daughter's naiveté. "Very well. You can fetch tickets tomorrow, and we'll take the train to Gien."

"Thank you, Papa!" Michelle moved to her father and gave him a warm embrace. She gazed across the room, thinking of all she must do. "Tomorrow will be a big day. I think I will retire."

"So should I," François said, pushing up from his chair. "You may have my bed if you like."

"No, Papa, your bed is for you," Michelle whispered, kissing her father on the cheek.

François watched her disappear into her bedroom and close the door.

Inside her room, Michelle waited for her eyes to adjust to the dim light from the window. She smiled when she saw Eli asleep in her bed with his feet hanging out from the covers over the end.

After quietly undressing and pulling on her nightgown, Michelle let down her hair and tiptoed to the bed. She lifted the covers and slid under the sheets beside Eli. Then, with a contented sigh, Michelle closed her eyes.

THE MORNING LIGHT through the thin draperies stirred Eli from his sleep. His eyes widened when he realized Michelle was nestled against him with her head on his chest. Uncertain of what to do, Eli hesitantly touched her arm. When she didn't move, he nudged her shoulder.

Michelle shot up in bed. Her long chestnut hair was tangled, and the front of her nightgown was open, revealing the curves of her breasts. She stared at Eli, unsure of where she was.

"Good morning," said Eli, gazing at her with uncertainty.

Michelle gasped when she noticed her open nightgown and quickly gathered its loose pull strings. "How-how did you sleep?" asked the blushing Michelle as she slipped out of bed.

"Very well." Eli's curious gaze followed Michelle as she scurried to her wardrobe.

"I'm terribly sorry! I meant to wake up before you," Michelle explained. She opened the wardrobe door, grabbed her clothes, and darted from the room.

Not sure what had happened, Eli pushed aside the sheets, arose from the bed, and dressed.

When Eli emerged from the room, François looked over the top of his morning newspaper suspiciously. "Good morning, Elijah. How was your night?"

"Nothing happened, Papa," called out Michelle, cooking eggs over the kitchen stove. "As I told you, Elijah is a perfect gentleman."

"Hmm." François returned to his paper.

"These shoes fit very well," smiled Eli, clicking them together.

"I'm glad," replied Michelle, hastily preparing breakfast.

Eli turned to the open balcony door. The sheers on either side were a dazzling white in the morning sun and drew Eli closer. Strange images of men and women shrouded in white flashed through his mind.

"It's a beautiful morning, isn't it?" Michelle asked with a glance.

"Indeed, it is," Eli muttered, blinking in thought. Unable to make sense of his fleeting memory, Eli moved out onto the shallow balcony.

Three floors below, he saw Parisians busily moving along the walks while horse-drawn carriages and motor cars crisscrossed the street.

Michelle noticed Eli staring out the window. "Elijah, are you all right?"

"Yes," Eli nodded.

"It's time to eat."

Sitting beside François, Eli watched Michelle bring a plate of fried eggs, the last of the baguettes, and the cheeseboard to the table.

"Today, Elijah, we are leaving Paris," Michelle announced as she sat beside him and took his hand.

Eli turned to François, anticipating his hand, then bowed his head as François blessed the food. Afterward, Eli looked up and asked, "We're leaving Paris?"

"Yes, I'm taking you to the country. Away from all of this," said Michelle.

Eli's brow gathered in thought. He had heard them talking the night before and knew he posed some kind of problem for them, but he wasn't sure what.

"Where I'm taking you is beautiful. You'll like it there," smiled Michelle.

"I'm coming too," nodded François, tearing off a piece of bread.

MICHELLE HAD JUST REACHED her floor and was walking down the corridor when she heard the commotion. Hurrying to her apartment, she found the door open and screamed when she saw her father struggling with a man. Her eyes widened when she recognized the gaunt, stringy-haired orderly from the ambulance. "Papa!" Michelle dropped her bag of travel supplies and rushed to help her father.

When the hobbling Eli heard the commotion, he lurched from the bedroom toward the intruder, reaching the struggling François before Michelle. After grabbing hold of the scraggly Gik, Eli flung him across the room against the wall. The impact knocked Gik off his feet and a hanging picture from the wall.

Michelle gasped when she spotted the pewter blazerod she had taken from the ambulance rolling across the rug. Her eyes shot to the bookcase where she had hidden it. The shelf was empty, and a pile of books was on the floor.

"He's trying to rob us!" shouted François, sitting on the floor with one hand clutching his armchair and the other his chest. Michelle rushed to him.

Eli stood over the recoiling Gik, glaring down at the familiar intruder with clenched fists. "Who are you? What do you want?" he barked, trying to place the halfborn's ghoulish features.

Gik's sunken eyes darted from the looming Eli to the blazerod on the floor six feet away. He lunged for it, but when Gik landed on the floor, his clawing fingers were still inches short of the pewter cylinder.

"No! Don't let him get it!" cried Michelle as the hobbled Eli moved to stop the intruder. But he was too slow.

Clawing across the floor, the wild-eyed ghoul's bony hands grabbed the weapon. He rolled and pointed it at Eli.

"Elijah! Watch out!" yelled Michelle.

Eli jumped aside as the glowing blazerod shot a bolt of light past his head, cutting a smoldering hole in the ceiling.

"Elijah! Stop him!" Michelle cried as Gik jumped to his feet. When Gik pointed the weapon at Michelle, she gasped and pushed her father to the floor behind the armchair. But instead of firing at Michelle, Gik looked at her knowingly, much as he had in the ambulance.

After breaking from his trance, Gik turned the weapon back on the watcher. But before he could fire, Eli grabbed the intruder's wrist and bent the blazerod back. The released bolt grazed Gik's face, taking off his ear. The halfborn shrieked in pain, dropped the blazerod, and danced on the floor as he clutched his smoking head.

Eli kicked the blazerod across the room toward the fireplace and roared, "Who are you? Why are you here?"

François stretched out from behind the armchair and grabbed the rolling cylinder. With wide eyes, he pointed the blazerod at the still howling Gik, but nothing happened.

Gik's frantic eyes flashed to the blazerod in François' hand. With a shriek, the halfborn charged François and Michelle, crashing into the armchair and pinning them against the wall.

"NO!" Michelle screamed, feeling the wind of Gik's clawing fingers as she blocked him with the chair.

With fierce eyes and tightened jaw, Eli yanked Gik from the chair, swung him around, and hurled him through the open balcony door. The impact of the balcony's railing spun the bony creature in a kind of awkward cartwheel as he tumbled to the street, three floors below.

Michelle gasped when Gik's shrieks stopped with a *thud*. She rushed to the balcony past the stunned Eli and looked over the railing in horror as people gathered around the bent and twisted Gik. Her eyes widened when she saw the blazerod lying on the street beside him. "Oh, no! He has it!" Michelle turned to Eli, who was staring out the balcony, his chest heaving as he tried to understand what he had just done.

When Michelle looked back down at the street, she saw a man stooping and tending to the lifeless ghoul. She pointed when Gik moved. "He's still alive!"

Eli hurried to the balcony. He watched in dismay as Gik's contorted body twisted back into shape. After climbing to his feet, Gik's dark, sunken eyes glared up at Eli. Then, pushing the helping man aside, Gik grabbed the blazerod off the street, stumbled through the gathered crowd, and hobbled away.

When Michelle heard her father's moaning, she hurried back to the toppled armchair. François was lying on the floor. "Papa, are you okay?" she asked, her wide eyes searching him for harm.

Eli hurried to join them as François cringed in pain and clutched his chest.

"What happened, Papa?" Michelle asked, her voice trembling with emotion.

François' eyes flashed to her as he fought for air, his face twisted in pain and fear.

"Oh no, Papa, your heart!" gasped Michelle.

Eli pushed the toppled chair aside and kneeled beside them. He placed his hand against François' chest and felt his heart.

"Can you help him?" Michelle asked, tears welling in her eyes.

Eli looked at her blankly, his hand still on François' chest.

"Please help him if you can," she pleaded.

Eli's uncertain gaze returned to François.

"I love you, my sweet," François wheezed.

"I love you, Papa! Don't go, Papa!" sobbed Michelle.

François turned to Eli with glazed eyes and drooping lids. "Take care of my precious girl," he breathed before relaxing in Michelle's arms.

"No, Papa. No, Papa!" wept Michelle.

Eli removed his hand from François' chest, sank onto the floor, and watched the sobbing Michelle rock her father.

CHAPTER 15

THE OBSERVER

By French standards, it was not a large funeral. The Cathedral of Saint Croix was small and unimpressive compared to the magnificent Notre Dame, just blocks away, but it was suitable for Michelle and François' friends and neighbors to reflect on the fine man's life.

"I grieve for you," said a wrinkled old woman in a black hat and dress as she filed out of the small chapel. "François was an old friend. He shall be missed."

"Thank you," Michelle nodded, her face streaked by tears. She thanked and hugged the twenty others attending, then turned and sadly followed them out of the chapel.

"Mademoiselle Duvall," asked a lean, middle-aged man standing outside the church in a plain suit and hat.

"Yes?" Michelle asked, still wiping at her tears.

"Nurse Michelle Duvall?" pressed the man. He spoke with an Italian accent and had smooth olive skin, short dark hair, and a neat mustache.

"Yes," Michelle uneasily replied.

"I am Cleto Nazario. I write for *The Roman Observer*."

"I've heard of it. That's the Vatican newspaper. You're Italian."

"That's right. I am looking for a soldier you attended to in the hospital, Elijah Mansel."

Michelle gulped. "Yes, I remember him," she nodded, still dabbing at her tears.

"Have you seen him?"

Michelle's pulse quickened. "It was several days ago that I last saw him in the hospital," she said, which was true.

"What can you tell me about him?"

"Not much, I'm afraid. He was one of many patients I attended to."

"Is it true he healed from wounds that would have killed most men?"

"Yes...maybe a little," Michelle uneasily shrugged. "Now, if you please."

"He disappeared from the hospital the same day you were removed," persisted Nazario.

"I wasn't *removed*," glared Michelle. "I was transferred to the front because I refused to sleep with a loathsome doctor. Perhaps you should write a story about him!"

The reporter looked at Michelle with pleading eyes. "Please. This Elijah is extraordinary. I have been following him for years, but he is elusive. Any information would be helpful."

Michelle wondered what light the reporter could shed on her mysterious Elijah, but shook her head and said, "Please, let me be. My father has died."

Nazario's shoulders sank at her reluctance. "Of course. I'm terribly sorry for your loss. It's just that this is the closest I've come. Do you know of the Hermetic Order of the Golden Dawn?"

Michelle shook her head. "No. I'm sorry. I can't help you with your story." She wiped at her tears and started past the reporter.

Nazario stepped in front of her. "You don't understand. Finding him and others like him is now my life's work!"

Others like him? Michelle gulped. She wondered if she could trust the man.

"When you were with him in the hospital, did Elijah tell you anything about himself? Who he was, or where he came from?"

"No, I told you. Now, please, with all decency, let me be. My father has died!" Michelle sobbed, pushing past the reporter.

"I can tell you!" blurted Nazario as he stepped aside.

Michelle took a step, then stopped but didn't turn back to the reporter.

"He is one of a group of immortals God sent after the creation of the earth. They are called the watchers. They are prominent in the Book of Enoch, but the Church removed that book from the Old Testament in the fourth century. There are still some places where you can find their names. They divided at the time of the flood and have been at war with one another—fighting for the souls of men—ever since." Nazario moved beside Michelle and saw her wide, weepy eyes.

"Please, let me be," Michelle muttered.

"I'm sorry. Please contact me if you should learn of him."

Michelle tearfully nodded as she took Nazario's card, then turned and hurried down the street.

Michelle had stopped crying by the time she reached her apartment, but Nazario's words lingered. When she entered, she promptly closed and locked the door. Michelle turned and scanned the apartment with sad, lonely eyes. "Elijah?" she called out, fearing she might truly be alone. Her shoulders sank with relief when Eli emerged from her bedroom.

"I should have been there with you," said Eli, his face drawn, his heart aching for Michelle.

"No, it's just as I feared. They're looking for you. A reporter stopped me. I told him I didn't know where you were. The Army may come here next. They may already know," she fretted. Michelle considered asking Eli about what the reporter had said, but knew he remembered nothing of his past. She dismissed Nazario's story of immortal beings as fanciful imaginings of a religious fanatic. But then she remembered the ghoulish attacker. *Could some of it be true?* she asked herself. *How else could Elijah's miraculous recovery be explained?* Michelle pushed those thoughts aside as she locked eyes with the approaching Eli.

Eli felt a flutter in his chest as he moved closer. Michelle's beauty, even in sadness, had become overwhelming to him. He gently wiped a tear from her cheek. The mere touch of her flesh sent a thrill through him. Lost in the strange sensations, Eli's mouth held open, speechless.

"Elijah, we must leave. We must leave now." Michelle wiped away her tears and hurried past him to her bed and the suitcase she had already packed. When she returned, hefting the bag, she saw Eli hadn't moved.

"I should leave. I should turn myself in," said a worried Eli. "I can't let any more misfortune come to you!"

"No! I won't let them have you! I won't let them take you away!"

"But your father... I fear his death was my fault."

"No, you don't understand! If they find you, they will do things to you! I won't let them!"

"I don't know what to do," Eli muttered.

"You must come with me."

"But what of your father's burial?"

"I've said my goodbyes," Michelle said with a stoic nod. "We can't take a chance on them being there, waiting for us." Seeing Eli was still not convinced, she moved closer, took his hand, and with pleading eyes said, "You're not safe in Paris. Neither of us are. If they find us, they'll take you and arrest me! Come with me. We'll protect each other."

Eli's eyes softened. Since first meeting Michelle, he had known of her compassion and grace, but now he saw something else—her affection for him. A flash of heat surged through Eli's veins as he stood transfixed.

Michelle took Eli's hand and led him from the apartment. She paused before closing the door and looked back inside, memorizing the space as a thousand memories flashed through her mind. Then, with a sad sigh, she closed and locked the door.

Michelle exited the building first. She looked up and down the street for the reporter or any sign of the police, but she saw only the usual afternoon passersby. After glancing back at Eli in the doorway, she motioned for him. Hardly inconspicuous, at a head taller than every other man on the street, Eli carried Michelle's bag as he followed her down the walk. Neither of them noticed the stringy-haired Gik watching from the shadows across the street.

The halfborn stayed far enough away not to be seen as he followed them down the busy street. But when they turned into an alley, the wiry Gik ran to catch up with them. The halfborn's sunken eyes widened, and he lurched to a stop when he turned into the alley. A woman in a glowing white gown stood two feet off the ground before him. "Out of my way!" cried Gik, trying to get by her.

"You have no place here," warned Charmeine, her golden eyes burning, her voice smooth yet cutting.

"You cannot interfere!" protested Gik.

"I can interfere with *you!*" Charmeine glared.

"I must stop them!" The frustrated Gik backed away and tried to dodge the messenger, but she blocked him.

"You will not pass by me!"

With Eli and Michelle having disappeared down the alley's far end, Gik jumped up and down, pulled on his long, greasy hair, and howled in frustration. He feared he would be punished for losing them.

THE RHYTHMIC BEAT of the train was relaxing as Paris passed by the window, and fellow travelers softly chatted or read their books.

"Who was that man?" asked Michelle, sitting close to Eli.

Eli turned from the window, uncertain who she was referring to.

"You threw him from a third-story balcony. It should have killed him when he hit the street, but he got up and ran away as though he had just tripped. Who was he?"

Eli shook his head. "I don't know. I don't even know who I am."

Michelle gave a warm smile. "You are indeed a mystery."

Eli nodded, uncertain of how to take the comment.

They watched Paris pass by through the window. Michelle nestled her head against Eli's shoulder, and her eyes were closed within minutes. Eli felt contentment as he watched her peacefully sleeping.

Eased by the train's vibration, Eli's gaze returned to the passing buildings and streets beyond the window. His brow furrowed as images from another train ride flashed through his mind. Eli saw a man running from him through a train, clutching a bag. He saw the man's pale, ghoulish face glaring back at him and realized it was the same man from the apartment. *Who is he?*

Eli's brow tightened further when an image of a golden ball flashed through his mind. He saw a man with white hair talking to a policeman and felt him familiar. He saw the same man sitting on a rock atop a hill speaking to others. He saw the white-haired man lying dead on a busy street. "Cyrus," Eli muttered as a name without meaning came to his mind.

"What?" Michelle mumbled, stirring from his shoulder.

Eli strained to link the images, but they were blurred and jumbled. "I had a memory," he whispered.

Michelle sat up. "You remembered something? What was it?"

Eli stared out the window. "Just bits and pieces. I can't make sense of it."

With a loving smile, Michelle sighed and said, "Well, that's a start."

Eli turned to Michelle. "Why are you doing this for me?"

Michelle's eyes searched his. "Because...we're friends, remember?"

"But...what if I'm not a good person?"

"I'm not worried about that," laughed Michelle before placing a kiss on his cheek.

Eli felt his heart quiver.

"I'm more worried about other things," she added, turning away.

"Other things?"

"Yes. Is there someone that's missing you?"

"Missing me?"

"Yes." Michelle's smile faded. "A family. Your mother and father." She gulped. "Or maybe...a wife...maybe children."

Eli sighed. He wished he could remember.

"It doesn't matter. I've thought about it quite a lot. I'll take care of you for them. And if you do remember them, then I will-I will return you to them," Michelle said, fighting the downward corners of her mouth.

Eli looked into her warm chocolate eyes and smiled. "What if I never remember?"

"Then I'll keep you for myself."

Eli felt his heart pounding as Michelle nestled against him. Having no memory of prior love, Eli didn't know how to compare his feelings for Michelle. All he knew was that she was the kindest, most perfect, and beautiful person he could remember, and he never wanted to be apart from her.

Château de Bret
27 April 1915

THE BUDDING elm trees lining the gravel road were alive with the song of birds. Eli caught glimpses of a pond through the trees as he carried Michelle's suitcase up the gentle hill. He saw ducks gliding across the water, past the lily pads, rippling the reflected trees on the opposite bank. The birdsong, afternoon breeze, and serene view eased Eli.

"Isn't it lovely?" Michelle asked, smiling at Eli.

"Yes, it is."

"Stop and listen. Can you hear the frogs?"

Eli grinned at the deep *rub-bit*, *rub-bit* of the bullfrogs.

"Momma used to bring me here as a little girl. I would catch frogs and swim in that pond," Michelle said with a nostalgic grin.

As they topped the hill, the trees opened to a stately three-story manor with ivory walls, windowed balconies, and a slate roof lined with dormers. A lawn and well-manicured yard stretched to one side of the gravel lane, and trees along the other. Beyond the manor, a meadow and lush green hills rolled into the forest.

"Welcome to Château de Bret!" beamed Michelle, twirling.

Eli stopped and eyed the impressive manor. "Your uncle lives here?"

"My mother's brother. He's very wealthy and handsome. I used to pretend he was the King of France and I a princess," Michelle explained, her face alive with childhood memories. "I always felt very safe here. You shall feel safe as well."

"Is that your uncle?" Eli asked, nodding to a man in coat and slacks coming out onto the main balcony, its ivory pilasters splotched green with moss.

"Yes! Uncle Ronan! Hello!" Michelle yelled with the eager wave of a schoolgirl.

As Eli approached the white château, his mind flashed with the images of a much larger castle with men on horses in chain mail and gleaming helmets. He saw a battle raging with swords and flaming arrows arching through a smoky sky. His gaze returned to the present as Michelle and her uncle kissed cheeks.

"Uncle Ronan, this is my friend, Elijah Mansel," Michelle said, almost giddy.

"Good afternoon, Elijah. Ronan Bret," nodded the fit, aging man with brushed back wiry gray hair and an extended mustache. "Welcome to my home."

"Good afternoon, sir. Thank you," Elijah replied, shaking hands.

"Mansel," Ronan said with narrowing eyes. "Are you from Le Mans, perchance?"

Eli's expression dimmed. "I don't know."

"Uncle, Elijah was badly wounded at the front. He has amnesia and has forgotten everything from before his accident."

"Tragic," Ronan said with a sad frown. "You met him at the hospital. Cared for him, I'm guessing," he added with a sideways glance at Michelle.

"Very good," beamed Michelle. "Uncle Ronan is quite astute."

"Yes," nodded Eli. His eyes narrowed as he sensed something profound in the man. He somehow knew Ronan to be a kind, generous soul.

Turning to Michelle, Ronan's eyes widened, and he said, "Tell me of your father. He chose not to accompany you on this visit?"

Eli saw Michelle's pain as she lowered her head. "Papa...Papa died two days ago."

"What! Gracious me!" Ronan exclaimed. "I'm so sorry. I had no idea. But...why are you here then? His funeral."

Michelle wiped at her tears and forced a smile. "It was this morning. A lovely tribute with a few of his friends and neighbors."

"I'm so sorry. I would have come had I known," said Ronan with grieving eyes.

Michelle sighed, somewhat regretting that she had not stayed for his burial. "I had to leave Paris—*we* had to leave Paris."

After embracing his niece, Ronan's concerned eyes turned to the tall Eli. "You are, of course, welcome here. You may stay as long as you wish."

With his hands on the sobbing Michelle's shoulders, Ronan said, "I'm sure you must be tired from the day's journey. Madame Duguay will show you to your rooms; then we'll have dinner. I hope you will then tell me everything."

Michelle gave a tearful nod, then embraced her uncle again.

ELI STARED at the flickering flames inside the massive fireplace as disjointed images from his past danced in his head. Behind him, seated in matching paisley wingback chairs, Michelle told of the last few weeks while an engrossed Ronan puffed on his pipe. What she did not share, however, was her meeting the Catholic reporter, Cleto Nazario.

"How remarkable," Ronan said, glancing at Eli.

"The way he healed was nothing short of a miracle, really," sighed Michelle.

"And what of this character who attacked your dear father? How did he survive being thrown down to the street? And his lightning-spitting baton, what of that?"

"I don't know," Michelle whispered, her eyes fading in thought. "It's all so incredible; it gives value to the very word. I dare say, I would never believe or imagine such things had I not seen them with my own eyes."

"Exactly," Ronan nodded, holding his pipe.

"Elijah's remarkable recovery will no doubt extend to his blocked memories," Michelle said, not at all sure that was a good thing. "He's already beginning to remember—even now, staring at the fireplace, I'm guessing."

"I think that must be tragic to forget one's past," Ronan pondered. "Our memories make us who we are. They define us. We are creatures of memory, and to lose that...it must be akin to losing one's mind."

Eli half turned as he considered the words.

"Your father's death still grieves me," frowned Ronan. "But I am so happy that you thought of coming here."

"We're delighted you will have us." Fighting back the tears, Michelle added, "Papa wanted to come too."

Ronan nodded sadly. His curious gaze moved from Michelle to the contemplative Eli. "Something tells me your relationship is more than nurse and patient."

"Well...we are friends," Michelle awkwardly grinned.

"Perhaps more than friends?" Ronan asked with a raised brow.

Eli turned to see Michelle's response.

"Don't be silly," she blushed, her eyes flashing from Ronan to Eli.

The hurt and confusion in Eli's eyes were imperceptible as he turned back to the dying flames. But Ronan saw through Michelle's denial as he puffed on his pipe.

"Elijah is my patient," a bewildered Michelle tried to explain. "I can't stand the thought of any harm coming to him." Her worried gaze moved to the turned Eli. Her feelings towards him were much more than that.

"Of course," Ronan nodded. He puffed on his pipe, then asked, "What are your intentions?"

A distracted Michelle turned back to Ronan. "Sorry?"

"How long do you intend to stay?"

Michelle glanced at Eli. "I suppose until he's fully recovered and his memory has returned."

"And what of the Army? You said they might view him as a deserter," frowned Ronan.

"They should have discharged Elijah because of his injuries," Michelle insisted. "It isn't right."

Ronan's gaze turned to Eli, still watching the fire. "Elijah, you've been very quiet. What do you have to say on this matter?"

When Eli turned from the fire, his searching gaze fell on the befuddled Michelle. His heart swelled at the very sight of her chestnut hair and warm chocolate eyes. Eli knew she had feelings beyond what her words expressed, and it confused him. He wondered if he had ever felt such an attraction to a woman before. Eli's brow wrinkled when he remembered Ronan's question. "I don't know. The uncertainty I feel is overpowering. I fear I may be putting you both in danger."

"No, that's not true," said a concerned Michelle. But she knew it was true. She knew her father would still be alive had she not taken Eli in. The thought that the Army, a reporter, and a ghoul were after Eli was more than Michelle could bear. She felt a tightening in her chest as she imagined them hunting Eli down.

Ronan's knowing gaze moved from his niece to the brawny Eli.

Michelle tried to push away the worrisome thoughts, but her body and soul ached with the pain, emotion, and fatigue of the past days. "I think I should retire," she muttered, trying not to look at Eli.

Ronan stood from his chair. "Of course. Madame Duguay has shown you to your room?"

"Yes. Thank you," nodded a visibly drained Michelle.

"Good evening, then," Ronan smiled, his pipe in hand.

"Good evening, Uncle," Michelle moved to Ronan and kissed his cheek. She took a step toward the stairs, then turned back to Eli, her face sad and longing. "Good night, Elijah."

"Good night," Eli nodded. His captivated gaze followed Michelle as she went up the stairs.

CHAPTER 16
AMBROSIA

Michelle rubbed her face as she rolled out of bed. Robbed of sleep, she had spent most of the night thinking about Eli, of her feelings for him, and all they had endured the past few weeks. Nazario's fantastic claims had also lingered despite her dismissal of them. The final three hours of sleep left Michelle feeling a little more herself, but the uncertainty of Eli's feelings for her made her anxious.

Dressed and primped, Michelle closed her bedroom door and looked toward Eli's room as the smell of cooking eggs and bacon wafted up the stairs. While her feelings toward Eli were now unambiguous, Michelle still didn't know how to address them. The fear he might have a wife and family he couldn't remember was troubling, at best. But she worried not sharing her feelings with Eli might give way to him leaving —something she told herself she could not endure.

After smoothing out her dress and breathing in resolve, Michelle stepped to his door. She paused when she noticed it was ajar. "Elijah?" Michelle called into the room and pushed his door open. Her eyes widened at Eli's neatly made bed. Panicked by the thought he had left in the night, Michelle moved to the railing overlooking the great room, but felt no better when she saw the chairs by the fireplace and the sofa near the piano empty. She hurried down the stairs but slowed when she entered the dining room and saw her uncle reading the morning news.

"Ah, good morning," Ronan smiled, getting to his feet. "How did you sleep?"

"Fine," Michelle lied. She anxiously glanced into the kitchen, where Madame Duguay was preparing breakfast, and asked, "Have you seen Elijah?"

"Yes, he's gone for a walk. To the pond, I should think," Ronan replied.

Michelle gave a relieved sigh. "Oh, good. For some reason, I got it in my mind he left in the night."

Ronan grinned at her obvious infatuation with Eli. "He and I talked quite a lot last night."

"Oh? Whatever about?" Michelle asked with a forced smile.

"History mainly. The poor fellow seems to have an abounding interest in it. It's indeed a shame he can recollect so little of his own."

Michelle gulped. She wanted to ask if he had talked about her but didn't dare. "Is he coming back for breakfast?" she asked as Madame Duguay carried in a tray of fried eggs, bacon, and pastries.

"Of that, I'm not sure," Ronan replied, flipping open his table napkin as he happily received his breakfast.

Michelle glanced toward the great room, hoping Eli might come through the door, then sat at the table, fighting the urge to be somewhere else as Madame Duguay placed a savory plate of eggs and bacon before her.

"This is so very hospitable of you, Uncle," Michelle gushed.

"Nonsense, you're my guest," Ronan said pleasantly as Madame Duguay poured coffees.

As they ate, they exchanged pleasantries and discussed the day's weather and the worker shortage with the war on, but the Italian reporter's fantastic claims about Eli lingered in Michelle's mind.

After finishing her breakfast, Michelle saw Ronan again immersed in his newspaper and cleared her throat. "Uncle, do you have a Bible in your library?"

Ronan lowered the paper. "Yes, I believe I do."

"Thank you for a lovely breakfast," Michelle nodded as she pushed away from the table.

Moving into the great room, Michelle crossed the rug past the grand piano to the library. Inside, lit by rays of sunlight through the tall windows, sat two reading chairs, a billiards table, and a wall of books that reached the coffered ceiling. Michelle searched the titles until she found a thick, leather-bound book with the engraved words, Holy Bible. Michelle studied the worn book, her brow furrowed in thought. Moving closer, she reached for it, but her fingers stopped short of touching the holy text. *I'm being ridiculous. There's nothing in there that will tell me about Elijah.*

Michelle pulled back her hand, shook her head, and left the library.

ELI WAS SITTING on the hill above the pond, watching the ducks glide between the white-flowered lily pads, when Michelle emerged from the trees with a blanket in her arms. She moved down the grassy slope beside Eli. "Good morning," she said, eyeing him with uncertainty.

Eli turned to her, his blue eyes pensive. "Good morning."

"We missed you at breakfast," Michelle said, still trying to gauge Eli's mood. "May I join you?"

Eli nodded, and Michelle situated the blanket on the grass beside him.

"I'm sorry," said Eli, his face full of regret.

"They've saved some for you," shrugged Michelle, thinking he was talking about breakfast. She didn't notice his sadness until she sat on the blanket.

"No. Not that. I'm sorry about your father. He would still be alive if it were not for me."

Michelle's lonely gaze trailed off to the peaceful pond.

"You've been nothing but kind to me and are repaid by that."

"It wasn't your doing," whispered Michelle, turning to Eli.

"I'm sorry, nonetheless," Eli said, looking at her with pleading eyes. "I hope you can forgive me."

"There is nothing to forgive," breathed Michelle, swallowed up in his gaze.

Eli's heart was racing as he slid onto the blanket beside Michelle. He reached a hand to her flushed cheek. He felt his chest might explode when he touched her perfectly soft skin. The magical fever surged through Eli. He gently stroked her cheek, as if having never touched a woman before. He saw Michelle's longing, beckoning eyes and heaving chest. He smelled the sweetness of her fragrance. He wanted to kiss her but feared he could never stop if he did. His face, his lips, drew closer to hers. When they touched, Eli felt a strange tingling throughout his body. After remembering to breathe, he kissed her more passionately. When Michelle pushed up against him, hungry for the taste of his lips, Eli took her in his arms. Tingling all over, Eli felt all control leave him.

After some time, with his fever no less intoxicating, some of Eli's reasoning returned. He pried his lips from hers. Michelle lay breathless in his arms, her head rolled back on the blanket, her eyes serene from the same enrapturing inebriant. When Michelle unbuttoned her collar, Eli's mouth went to her neck, kissing and sucking as she writhed in pleasure.

It was the sniffing dog that stopped them. After pulling away from the yearning Michelle, Eli's eyes widened at the Berger Picard seated in the grass beside them. The shaggy, pointy-eared canine cocked his head as he eyed them inquisitively.

"Sébastien!" laughed a flush-faced Michelle as she sat up and pulled her unbuttoned collar tight. "What are you doing out here? Exploring?" she asked, looking through the trees for her uncle.

Eli gathered himself and buttoned his shirt that Michelle had undone.

"This is Sébastien, my uncle's dog," Michelle beamed, scratching the happy old dog behind his ears.

Eli's eyes narrowed as images of the war and a small, wiry man in uniform flashed through his head.

"Oh, I think you ruined Elijah's fun," Michelle joked, seeing Eli's pensive face. But her smile thinned when she recognized his look of fighting for a memory. "Do you remember something?" she asked, hoping the memory didn't involve another woman.

Eli's searching eyes returned to her. "I knew someone named Sébastien," he breathed.

"Who was it?" Michelle asked, leaning closer.

"He was a soldier. A friend, I think," frowned Eli.

Michelle smiled, reached a loving hand to Eli's cheek, and leaned in to kiss him. "It doesn't matter. None of it matters anymore," she sang, the ambrosia still coursing through her veins. "Not the war, not the Army, none of it—as long as I'm with you!"

Eli looked deeply into her warm chocolate eyes and smiled.

"THIS SMELLS DELICIOUS. WHAT IS IT?" Eli asked, eyeing the bowl of stew.

"Boeuf Bourguignon," replied Ronan, "One of my favorites."

"I'm so glad the beef shortage has not reached Gien," Michelle sighed.

"It soon will, I'm afraid." Ronan waited for the croissants to arrive, then asked, "How was your day exploring?"

"It was perfect, both exhilarating and relaxing," Michelle replied with a playful glance at Eli.

"Do tell," Ronan said, sipping his wine.

"We spent quite a lot of time at the pond. It's always so lovely there. Sébastien joined us."

"Did he?" Ronan laughed. "He's still an explorer."

"I was glad to see him," Michelle said, fondly remembering her adventures with the dog. But when she noticed Eli not eating, she turned to him and asked, "Is something the matter?"

Eli looked at Michelle in confusion. "Before we ate with your father, he thanked God for the food."

"Yes," Michelle nodded, "Father always preferred we say grace before meals. He did that for my mother, I think."

"Should we not thank God now?" asked Eli.

Somewhat embarrassed, Michelle glanced at her uncle.

"Well, it was Madame Duguay who prepared the meal, but I suppose giving thanks to God is always in good order," Ronan nodded. "Would you do us the honors, Elijah?"

"Yes." Eli reached for Michelle's hand beside him, then lowered his head. "Thank you, God, for this food Madame Duguay has prepared. Thank you for the generosity of Ronan Bret. Thank you for Michelle, for her kindness and compassion." Eli's brow furrowed in thought. "And please guide François' soul as he comes to you. Amen."

"Well said," nodded Ronan, returning to his meal.

"That was lovely, Elijah. Thank you," breathed Michelle, eyeing him.

"Are you a religious man?" Ronan asked.

"I don't remember, but I think perhaps I was."

Michelle's eyes were slow to leave Eli as she wondered what was going on inside his head.

AFTER DINNER, they sat before the large fireplace, Ronan in his wingback chair with his pipe, and Michelle and Eli on the couch moved from beside the piano.

"Elijah, tomorrow I would like to take you into town. I'm sure you would enjoy a change of clothes. I would share my wardrobe, but I'm afraid I'm a might smaller," Ronan grinned.

"That is very kind of you, but I have no money," said Eli.

"I will pay," said Michelle.

"Nonsense. It's the least I can do for a war hero," Ronan said, holding his pipe.

Eli considered his splintered memories of the fighting, but the images made no sense, with some seeming to come from different ages.

"Michelle tells me you are remembering more," said Ronan, taking a puff.

Eli stared across the room in thought. "There is a part of me that doesn't want to remember—that only wants to live from this day on."

"It is, in a way, starting life over," Ronan reflected. "I, for one, wouldn't mind doing some things over again—or at least forgetting the more painful parts."

"But didn't you say yesterday that our memories make us who we are?" Michelle asked, immediately wondering if those words might hurt Eli.

"Exactly." Ronan puffed his pipe.

They stared at the flickering flames for a time, then Ronan asked, "What will you do if the Army comes looking for you?"

Eli glanced at Michelle. "I don't know. Surrender, I suppose."

"I won't let you," said a troubled Michelle, placing her hand on his.

"How long do you suppose this war will last?" Eli asked, staring into the flames.

"It doesn't show any sign of letting up, I'm afraid," sighed Ronan. "This evening, I read that Allied forces are still stuck at Gallipoli. It seems the British grand plan of sneaking behind the Hun has met a snag, namely a hundred thousand angry Ottomans. Italy has joined the war on our side, but I'm afraid that will be another debacle. The Italians claim to have style, but they lack the taste and emotional competency of the French. I fear this war will wreck the world beyond repair."

Michelle sighed. "Can we talk of something else?"

"Yes, my dear. What shall we speak of?" Ronan asked with a tender smile.

"Anything else. How about puppies or pretty flowers or lovely days by the pond?" Michelle said, leaning her head on Eli's shoulder.

Eli reached a hand to her soft cheek and gently stroked it.

Ronan recognized Eli's affection for his niece and turned to the fire.

Michelle breathed in contentedly, then asked, "Would you like to go for a walk? There is a lovely moon out."

Eli smiled and nodded.

THE GRAVEL CRUNCHED under their feet as they moved away from the glowing windows of the château, Michelle's arm in Eli's.

As the glowing moon came into view, Eli had a sudden, vivid remembrance. He felt small in the memory, looking up into a moonlit sky. In it were two moons, one larger than the other. *It must be from when I was a boy*, he concluded, *but why would there be two moons?* After blinking away the strange memory, he turned to Michelle and smiled.

"It is a bit brisk out," she said, wrapping tighter around Eli's arm.

"Would you like me to go back for a coat?"

"No, you're enough to keep me warm."

After a few steps further into the moonlight, Michelle stopped and gazed skyward. Eli turned to her. To him, she had never looked so radiant. He stepped closer.

Michelle's breast gently heaved as she lost herself in Eli's blue eyes.

Eli lowered his head, and their lips met.

After several minutes of passionate kissing and embrace, Eli pulled away and looked into Michelle's tranquil eyes, his body bursting with restrained desire.

"What is going to happen to us, Elijah?"

"I don't know," Eli whispered, his eyes unable to get enough of her.

"I want to be with you forever," sighed Michelle, resting her head against his chest.

"The feelings I have for you..."

Michelle looked up into his eyes. "Yes?"

"They're like nothing I've ever felt before."

"That you can remember," she breathed.

"No. I would remember this," whispered Eli.

Michelle kissed him, then lay her head against his warm chest. "I don't ever want this to end. When I'm with you...I feel complete delight."

"You're trembling. You're cold," said Eli.

"I'm not sure if it's the chilly night air or the delight that's causing my trembling," she laughed.

With a loving smile, Eli took Michelle by the arm and led her back inside.

ELI STARED at the ceiling as he lay in his bed with his hands folded behind his head. The moonlight through the open window cast his smooth, muscular chest and thick biceps in a bluish hue as Eli considered Michelle's perfection. It had only been an hour since they had parted company, but he yearned to see her warm smile, feel her comforting touch, hear her loving words, and taste the sweetness of her lips.

When his door creaked open, Eli lifted his head. He recognized Michelle's silhouette in the doorway, the light from the corridor filtering through her nightgown. When she entered his room and closed the door, Eli sat up.

"*Shhh*," Michelle breathed as she edged closer to his bed.

Eli gulped as the moonlight revealed Michelle's face, her chocolate eyes wide, her perfect lips parted, her chest heaving with the rush of anticipation. Eli watched spellbound as Michelle's fingers moved to her nightgown. Their eyes were locked as she undid the tie strings. Eli didn't blink as Michelle pulled the nightgown from her shoulders and allowed it to fall to the floor. His eyes swelled at the graceful slope of Michelle's shoulders, her gently hanging breasts, and the elegant curve of her hips. His breathing stopped as she moved closer. Paralyzed, Eli watched Michelle pull back his covers and climb into his bed.

CHAPTER 17
THE APPARITION

Ronan surveyed the tall Eli, standing before the clothing shop mirror in his new suit, and nodded approvingly. "You do that suit justice."

"Thank you," said Eli, not hiding his embarrassment.

"It now fits you well, sir," added the balding tailor, looking over his glasses.

Eli ran a hand along the elegant wool sleeve and turned to Michelle, smiling at him from across the shop. "It is very nice, but more than I need."

"Nonsense, a gentleman needs to look like one, especially for dinner," Ronan replied, lighting his pipe. "I've been impressed with you this last month, Elijah. You've gotten on well with the other workers and seem to have a knack for leadership."

"I have enjoyed working in the vineyard and with the sheep," Eli nodded.

"I've noticed that. You have taken on even more responsibility than expected of you. That's why I want to make you my foreman. There would be a commensurate increase in pay, of course."

"Foreman?" Michelle moved closer to Eli and placed a loving hand on his arm. "That's splendid! Elijah is a very hard worker. He will care well for your estate."

"I'm sure he will," grinned Ronan. "And I hope it will keep you both here as long as possible. I've grown rather lonely in my old age and am so glad to have you. Of course, you are under no obligation to stay. As I told you from the start, you are welcome in my home as long as you wish."

"Industry benefits the working man at least as much as the proprietor," reflected Eli.

"Well said," Ronan nodded. "You accept my offer, then?"

"Yes, sir," Eli replied with a beaming Michelle hanging on his arm.

"Splendid!" Grinned Ronan. "It tickles me to have things work out so fortuitously. I can use the help, and you want the work."

After leaving the shop, Eli walked with Michelle to her uncle's carriage carrying two wrapped bundles of clothes, a pair of fine leather shoes, and new work boots. When an automobile puttered by, Michelle turned to Ronan and asked, "Do you ever see yourself in one of those contraptions?"

"I find them noisy and uncouth," Ronan replied, taking the reins as his mare glanced back at him.

The ride back to the château was relaxing with the rhythmic clopping of the old mare's hooves and birds happily chirping. Nestled beside Eli, with her head on his shoulder, Michelle thought it was the perfect day. She looked up at Eli and smiled contentedly. Michelle had never given herself to a man so completely. She felt more than a physical attraction to Eli, although that was strong. Michelle was drawn to his essence, a quality she had never known in a man. And while Eli was still largely a mystery, she trusted him implicitly.

After passing the vineyard and the front gates of the château, Michelle perked up in her seat and said, "Uncle, will you let us off here? We would like to walk the rest of the way. Doesn't that sound grand, Elijah?"

"Yes, it does," said Eli, helping Michelle out of the carriage.

Michelle wrapped her arm around Eli's as the horse and carriage continued up the shaded lane. After a few steps, Michelle turned to Eli, pulled his face down to hers, and kissed him.

It had been weeks, but the wonderful tingling ran through Eli still. He had never felt so much joy and peace. He wanted only to be with the radiant Michelle.

"Do you have any new memories today?" Michelle asked as they strolled up the gravel road. It was a question she asked less frequently now.

Eli considered the question. "A few, but they're all bits and pieces."

"Has that been terribly hard for you, not remembering?"

Eli sighed. "I'm not sure. It's all I know."

"I hope your memories of us being together are enough."

"They are," Eli said with a loving look. They walked awhile, then he asked, "What of your memories?"

"Mine?" Michelle glanced up at him lovingly.

"Yes. Do you think of your childhood? Do you think of your father and mother?"

Michelle considered the question. "Sometimes. I try to remember the happy times."

"Why not all the times?"

"Some bring too much pain."

"Your mother and father have both died, but you seem more troubled by your mother's death."

Michelle sighed. "I was younger then. I was a girl. It was—it still is painful for me. Not just that she died, but the way she died."

Eli turned to Michelle, his concern plain to see, "How did she die?"

Michelle was quiet for a time. Then, with emotion cracking her voice, she said, "It was cancer that took her. It was very slow and painful for her. For all of us."

"I'm sorry," said Eli.

"When she finally died, and the priest told me it was God's will, I hated him and God for it," Michelle whispered, wiping away her tears.

Eli stopped and turned to her. "Are you still angry at God?" he asked, his gentle eyes searching.

Michelle considered the question, then tiredly said, "I don't know. Are you mad at God for what he's done to you?"

Eli thoughtfully shook his head. "I think it was a German shell that took my memory."

"But you believe in God?"

Eli looked at the leaves of the trees and listened to the robins chirping. He saw Michelle's beauty and nodded. "Yes. I see God—I feel God in everything."

Michelle stared at the trees. "For a time, I doubted. I wondered, if God was real, why would he allow such terrible things? The war...such tragic deaths?" Michelle swallowed her emotions. "But if God has brought you to me, I am forever grateful, and I forgive him." Releasing the pain and heavy thoughts with a sigh, she wrapped her arms around Eli and said, "I only want to think of you now."

Eli held her tightly. "The feelings I have when I'm with you..."

"Yes?" she softly prodded.

"I love and adore you. I cannot see myself without you."

"And I adore you, my love," beamed Michelle.

Eli kissed her.

Michelle sighed when Eli pulled away, her gaze lost in his pensive blue eyes. They seemed to her sad and lonely. She noticed Eli's lips faltering, as if searching for the right words. Michelle tried to hide her concern as she ran a gentle hand along his cheek. "What is it, my love?"

"Marry me," breathed Eli, his eyes pleading. "Be my wife."

Michelle's face radiating with joy. "I will! I will!"

<hr>

CHÂTEAU DE BRET
7 JUNE 1915

THE WEDDING WAS a simple affair despite Ronan Bret's offering of an elaborate cathedral ceremony. When he learned that Michelle had long dreamed of a wedding on the back lawn of the château overlooking the pond, he was more than happy to oblige her. While Michelle insisted it be without frills, Ronan persuaded her to allow a violinist who floated sweet harmonies across the warm evening breeze with his bow's gentle motion.

When the priest in his black robe and white stole moved under the chestnut tree, Eli joined him in his buttoned-up suit and oiled-back hair. Eli's eyes widened, and his breathing stopped when the strikingly beautiful Michelle approached along the path of rose petals escorted by her uncle. Though her simple white dress and flowers were lovely, they were lost in her radiant smile.

As Eli and Michelle gazed into each other's eyes, Ronan found his seat beside a weepy Madame Duguay. He listened proudly as the bride and groom exchanged vows. When the priest pronounced them husband and wife, they kissed, and the violinist played "Clair de Lune."

CHARLEVILLE-MÉZIÈRES, FRANCE
GERMAN SUPREME ARMY COMMAND HEADQUARTERS
23 JULY 1915

STANDING IN THE SHADOWY CORRIDOR, Lu glared at the scrawny, trembling Gik. "Where have you been? It's been weeks."

Gik helplessly shook his head.

"You lost them?"

"Yes, master," the halfborn replied, his head down, his greasy bangs hanging.

"I trusted you to find and destroy him!" Lu fumed.

"I followed him, but a messenger of light stopped me," said Gik.

"A messenger?"

"The one called Charmeine."

"They are not allowed to interfere!" roared Lu.

"That's what I said to her! She said she could with me!"

"Because you are a useless, half-mortal waste of skin?" snarled Lu.

Gik hung his head and nodded at his worthlessness.

"Hand it to me."

Gik looked up at his master. "No...please," he whined. "I've been looking for him everywhere! He's vanished!"

Lu stepped closer and reached out his hand. "Hand it to me."

Wagging his head with worry, the halfborn reached into his satchel and removed the pewter blazerod. "Please, master, I tried," he groveled. Upon seeing Lu's wanting hand, Gik reluctantly handed the weapon to him, then took a step back and braced for the punishment he was sure would follow. Gik wondered if Lu would disorganize his matter into a cloud of atoms or simply return him to the abyss.

"I am not going to harm you," huffed Lu. "You haven't been altogether unprofitable. You destroyed two of the four I sent you after."

"Yes, I did, master," nodded Gik, timidly looking up.

"Besides, you're part of my flesh...which part, I don't know," Lu grunted.

"Yes, master."

"And I'm in a good mood. Now leave me!"

"Yes, master," bowed Gik before scurrying out the door.

With a tired sigh, Lu turned back to his quarters. He walked past a German sentry and a bank of windows, then pushed open the door to his darkened apartment. Inside, the sour smell of linseed oil clashed with lavender perfume as afternoon light splintered through walnut shutters.

After closing and locking his door, Lu stepped to his cluttered desk. He laid the blazerod beside a heavily marked map of France and Eli's rosewood box that held the golden orb. Lu opened his bedchamber door, removed his suit coat, and laid it across a chair. His hungry gaze didn't leave the hazel-eyed woman sitting up in his bed, hiding her nakedness with a sheet. Lu liked her auburn hair and olive skin. She had so far been the best he had enjoyed all week.

"There will be no more interruptions," Lu muttered, removing his shirt.

CHARLEVILLE-MÉZIÈRES
GERMAN OCCUPIED FRANCE
5 AUGUST 1915

GÉRAUD DUCHAMPS EYED the auburn-haired woman rummaging through the basket of picked-over cabbage and beets. "Not much left, is there?" he asked in a friendly tone.

The woman glanced at the short, stout man with a round nose. Seeing nothing appealing about him, she turned her back and poked through a crate of radishes. Still feeling Duchamps' eyes on her, she continued through the open-air market. Duchamps followed her.

The auburn-haired woman casually passed the last table of picked-over vegetables and continued along the street. But when she reached an alley stacked with crates and lined with trash cans, the woman pulled up her dress and bolted. She hadn't gone ten feet down the alley when a man with thick forearms jumped out from behind a stack of crates, blocking the way. "What do you want?" cried the woman as she spun around to Duchamps, her hazel eyes wide with fear.

"Just to speak with you," Duchamps reassured her with open palms. "You are Hélène Fabron."

"How do you know me?"

"It doesn't matter."

"What do you want?" fretted Hélène, seeing the thick-armed man moving up behind her.

"We don't want to hurt you," replied Duchamps. "We want to help you."

"Help me? How?"

Duchamps raised a halting hand, and the thick-armed man stopped. "We know you're sleeping with the red-bearded German."

Hélène gulped. "I don't know what you're talking about," she lied. She knew collaborating with the Germans had gotten more than one French woman killed.

"There are some who would hang you for what you have done. We can protect you."

"No one can protect anyone," Hélène sneered as she backed into the wall.

"You can help your country and save yourself," Duchamps explained.

"How is that? If I spy for you? How will you save me when the Germans find out and gut me like a pig?"

"If you do as we say, they won't."

"Leave me alone!" Hélène cried, trying to push past them, but the thick-armed Phillipe shoved her back against the wall.

Duchamps' eyes narrowed. "If you won't do it for yourself, maybe you will do it for your daughter."

Hélène gulped. "What are you saying?"

"I think you know."

Hélène's shoulders sank, and her face filled with fear. "Please, don't hurt my little girl. I'm only doing this for food for her and my mother."

"What happened to your husband?" grunted Phillipe.

"He was killed," she muttered.

"The dirty Huns killed your husband, and now you pleasure one of them!"

Hélène lowered her head in anguish. "Please...I'm only doing this to keep my child from starving," she sobbed.

Duchamps' eyes flashed to Phillipe. "If you do as we ask, we will take you, your daughter, and your mother away from here to Switzerland."

Hélène worriedly shook her head and wiped away her tears. "He will know. He will kill me, and my daughter will have no one."

"Not if you do as we tell you," Duchamps insisted.

Hélène gulped and eyed the two men in frantic thought. "You will protect my daughter? Even if something happens to me?"

"And your mother," said a stern-eyed Duchamps.

"You swear it?"

"I swear it on the graves of a hundred thousand dead Frenchmen."

HÉLÈNE STARED at the coffered ceiling above the bed as she considered what she must do. With her breathing shallow and hands clammy, she waited. When the red-bearded Lu began to snore, she slid out of bed and quietly dressed. But when he abruptly stopped, she froze, fearing she had awakened him. Hélène held her breath as she waited for Lu's eyes to open. When he resumed snoring, she breathed again.

After carefully gathering up her shoes and cloth sack, she tiptoed to the bedchamber door, something she had done several nights that week, but this time, she heard every creak and groan of the pine floorboards. Hélène quietly opened the door and glanced back at the still-snoring Lu before slipping through the doorway and pulling the door closed.

Hélène tiptoed through the darkened front room, where slats of light were cast across the ceiling from the shuttered windows. She moved to the window and opened the shutters, bathing the room in the streetlight's glow. Hélène gulped as she looked out the window to the cobbled square two floors below. Near a fountain stood two German sentries, their rifles slung, glowing cigarettes moving to and from their mouths.

After slipping on her shoes, Hélène moved to Lu's cluttered desk. She eyed the intricate rosewood box. It was just as Duchamps had described. Hélène glanced back nervously at the closed bedchamber door, then lifted the box's lid. Her eyes widened at the dull luster of the golden orb nestled in the velvet-lined box. She reached a trembling hand inside and touched the golden sphere.

In the bedchamber, Lu's eyes opened.

Hélène turned the door latch with a trembling hand. In the lighted hallway, she saw the German sentry standing by the row of windows not far from the stairs. Gulping, the auburn-haired woman stepped through the doorway and closed the apartment door. She froze with wide eyes at the loud *click* of its latch. After breathing in courage, Hélène turned to the guard and nodded as she passed, just as she had on previous nights. The soldier's eyes remained forward.

After pulling on his trousers, the glaring Lu exited his bedchamber. He moved to his desk, his powerful legs and feet clomping across the hardwood floor with each stride. Lu pushed aside two rolled-up maps and opened the rosewood box. His face filled with rage when he saw the orb was gone.

Almost to the stairs, Hélène stopped when she heard the apartment door open.

"Stop her," bellowed the shirtless Lu, standing in the darkened doorway, his green eyes glaring at the woman.

With her heart pounding, Hélène considered running. But her shoulders sank when she thought of her little girl. She would do what Duchamps had told her.

"Bring her to me," Lu demanded.

The sentry moved to the trembling woman, took her by the arm, and led her back to the glaring Lu.

"You have something of mine." Lu pulled the cloth sack from her hand and felt the shape of the precious sphere inside. With scornful eyes, Lu plunged his hand into the bag, but when he pulled it out, he held not the golden orb but a yellow onion.

"I'm sorry," whimpered Hélène. "I didn't think you would miss it."

Lu emptied the rest of the sack onto the floor. Out fell a bottle of cheap perfume, a handkerchief, and a half-eaten carrot. "Search her!"

The guard roughly ran his hands up and down her dress but found nothing.

"Where is it?" barked Lu.

Trembling, Hélène pointed to the onion in Lu's hand. He threw the onion down, smashing it on the floor. "WHERE IS IT!" he roared. "WHERE IS THE ORB?"

"I-I don't know what you mean," shuttered Hélène.

A seething Lu pointed at the guard and roared, "Take her away!"

After storming back to his apartment, Lu returned to his desk. His jaw slackened when he realized the blazerod was also gone. Furious, Lu searched the room. His darting eyes paused when he noticed the nearby shutters were open and the window was ajar. Lu pushed open the window to the moonlit night beyond. When he leaned out, he noticed a dangling rope that led to the roof, a floor above. "Guards! Alarm!" Lu yelled, seeing two sentries walking across the cobbled square below. "Search the premises for spies!"

The soldiers unslung their rifles and ran in opposite directions across the plaza.

Lu climbed out the window, yanked on the rope, then began climbing, his jaw tight, his green eyes determined. Halfway to the roof dormer, he spotted a man in civilian attire frantically edging along the narrow ledge, the slate roof raking steeply above him. "There! Shoot him!" yelled Lu, but the sentries had already disappeared around the building.

When Lu spotted his blazerod protruding from the Frenchman's pocket, he pulled himself up onto the roof and chased after him. The stone slate along the precarious ledge cracked and popped under Lu's weight.

Upon reaching a roof valley, with the fleeing Frenchman still on the ledge, twenty feet away, Lu spotted the shorter Duchamps clawing his way up the valley between two roof peaks. Knowing he could capture only one, Lu chose the man with his blazerod as Duchamps disappeared over the top of the roof.

Lunging in great strides along the narrow ledge, Lu was just feet from the scrambling Phillipe when rifle fire echoed from the other side of the building. Lu's chest swelled at the realization that the other spy had been shot. With the look of a hunter closing in on his prey, Lu leaped the final distance and grabbed hold of Phillipe, climbing through an open dormer window. The Frenchman fought back, but his strength was no match for Lu's, who yanked him out the window. Phillipe cried out as he fell the three stories, hitting the stone pavers with a sickly *thud*.

Lu grinned as the pewter blazerod rolled away from the sprawled Frenchman. After climbing to a copper rainspout, Lu scaled down a floor before leaping the remaining twenty feet to the square. The gloating Lu moved to the writhing Phillipe, who had blood coming from his ear and mouth.

"You will not win," sputtered the Frenchman.

Lu picked up the blazerod and aimed it at Phillipe's head. "I already have," he growled before firing a bolt and exploding the Frenchman's head.

With his chest swelling in triumph, Lu marched around the building to where he had heard the rifle fire. The fallen watcher's eyes narrowed when he approached the back garden and noticed three soldiers standing around a body. When he pushed past the soldiers and found the sentry who had taken Hélène lying in his own blood, Lu's face twisted with rage. The orb was gone.

BASILICA OF SAINT-PIERRE-AUX-NONNAINS
METZ, FRANCE
9 AUGUST 1915

GÉRAUD DUCHAMPS WAS SURGING with adrenalin when the door to the crypt creaked open. The Frenchman looked into the dimly lit burial chamber with a pistol in hand and a bag over his shoulder. The flickering candles at the far end, below a stone crucifix, cast strange shadows across the massive marble caskets. While it was not Duchamps' first time in the ancient crypt, hidden under the fifteen-hundred-year-old church, he still marveled at the elaborately carved sarcophagi. Each of the six nine-foot-long tombs rested atop large stone platforms and barely fit under the arched ceiling.

With wary eyes, Duchamps started down the black and white checkerboard floor that divided the crypt like a river cutting through a canyon. He searched the shadows between each of the giant stone tombs for a murderous Hun.

"You do not need that here."

Duchamps spun toward the resonating voice as the crypt filled with dazzling light. He raised a hand to shield his eyes and saw the silhouette of a man in a flowing white robe.

Duchamps swallowed his fright and put away his pistol. He tried to look manly but was unable to hide his amazement.

"You should not have coerced the woman with the threat of harming her child," echoed the shimmering apparition.

Duchamps gulped. "It was the only way to make her help us."

"She would have helped you, given a choice."

"She and her child are now safe." Duchamps took a nervous step closer, his eyes wide. "It was just as you said. Everything happened just as you said it would, except...we lost Phillipe. The red-bearded German killed him."

"Fewer will die because of your friend's sacrifice."

Duchamps gulped.

"You have it?"

Still shielding his eyes, the Frenchman stepped closer to the gleaming figure. He pulled his bag from his shoulder and removed a cloth bundle. Holding it in his palm, Duchamps opened the cloth wrapping to reveal the glistening golden orb. As his eyes better adjusted to the light, he saw the shimmering apparition had a white beard. "This will help us win the war?" asked a squinting Duchamps, holding out the ball.

"In time. The struggle will not be short." When Cyrus took the sphere, it came alive, filling the crypt with even more light and projecting strange glyphs across the arched ceiling.

Duchamps' eyes widened, and his jaw hung in wonder.

CHAPTER 18
A GHOST RETURNS

Château de Bret
10 August 1915

Eli contentedly listened to Michelle play "Clair de Lune" as he sat beside the grand piano in his fine suit. When she finished, he and Ronan clapped enthusiastically.

"Well done! Monsieur Debussy should be honored to have such a beauty playing his song," Ronan gushed.

"I wholeheartedly agree," Eli nodded, "whoever this Debussy fellow is."

"He's a very talented Frenchman," Ronan proudly replied.

"Play something else," urged a contented Eli.

Michelle leaned back on the bench and stretched her arms. "I thought it might be nice to go for a walk before bed."

Eli promptly got to his feet and reached for her hand. "Then we shall go for a walk."

"He's learning quickly," Ronan winked as he reached for his brandy.

The warm August night was perfect for a stroll around the pond. Michelle nestled against her husband as they took in the reflected image of the moon breaking through the clouds across the still water. Michelle took Eli's hand and led him to the bench beside the flower garden. They sat and listened to the song of crickets and croaking frogs as the moon disappeared behind a shimmering cloud.

When Eli leaned down to kiss Michelle, he noticed her restrained emotion. "Is everything okay?" he asked, still learning how to navigate the sometimes unpredictable waters of a relationship.

"Yes," Michelle breathed, looking lovingly into his eyes. "The past months have been the most magical of my life. I'm so happy to be your wife."

Eli kissed her. When he pulled away, he saw she had something more to say.

"I'm happy to be your wife, but I'm just as delighted to be a mother to your child."

Eli's eyes widened. "What?"

"We're having a baby," Michelle beamed.

A rush of emotions overcame Eli. Foremost, he was ecstatic at the news, and his expression showed it, but at the same time, he felt a tremendous dread and didn't know why. His face betrayed that emotion and Michelle saw it.

"Are you not happy to be a father?" she asked, feeling the weight of it all herself.

"No...I mean, yes. Of course I am! I just have never imagined such a thing," Eli reflected.

"Well, it was bound to happen," Michelle slyly grinned.

Eli gulped as he considered the responsibility of pending parentage.

"I think you'll be a splendid father. You're splendid at everything you do," Michelle said reassuringly.

Eli nodded, but his thoughts were on the world outside their happy hiding place. He felt a worry he couldn't explain. He feared it was a part of his forgotten past. "When will the baby come?" Eli whispered, as if out of breath.

"The doctor says in seven more months. The end of March." Her joy faded when she noticed Eli's worry. "What troubles you? The war? Or have you remembered something you haven't told me?"

Eli turned to Michelle and sighed. "My memory is the same. I could never be happier than to have a lifetime of memories with you. But...the war...and other things weigh on me."

"Other things?" Michelle fretted.

"The man who came after us the day your father died."

"That ghastly beast!" Michelle steamed. "I hope to never see him again. Twice in one lifetime is quite enough!"

Eli's brow tightened with concern. "But what if we do? What if he or the Army comes for me?"

Michelle shook the horrid thought away. She had tried to forget it all, including the Italian reporter and his absurd story. "No, they won't find us here. Perhaps...perhaps we should change our names. A secret identity would protect us, for sure!"

Eli looked into his wife's eyes with a newfound calmness and smiled. "No matter what happens, I will protect you and our baby."

The angst melted from Michelle's face, and she kissed Eli.

TWO DAYS PASSED, but thoughts of impending fatherhood were still very much on Eli's mind. While his duties at Château de Bret were many and occupied the better part of each working day, Eli had searched for even more to fill his time over the past few days.

Eli's bare chest glistened with sweat under his overalls as he mucked out the stable. He was laying down a fresh bed of straw when Gert, the mare watching in the next stall, began to squeal and nicker. "What's wrong, girl?" Eli asked, straightening up and leaning on his pitchfork. His brow furrowed as the horse shook her head and snorted with agitation. Eli raised his pitchfork and moved to the stable door. The midday sun was bright and left short shadows below the trees and stable. Eli listened for the sounds of an intruder, but heard only birds chirping and leaves softly rustling in the gentle breeze.

Eli's eyes widened when he turned to a man standing near the back of the stall. "Who are you?" he gasped, raising his pitchfork. "How did you get in here?"

"Do you not remember me, Elijah?"

Eli studied the lean, white-bearded man. He had seen him before, in the fragments of memory that often darted through his mind. "I recognize you," Eli muttered, noticing the faint aura around the stranger for the first time.

"So, it is true. You have forgotten everything," scowled the overseer. "Do you not remember Sarajevo?"

Eli shook his head. "No. I've been to Sarajevo?" he asked as images flashed through his head.

Cyrus examined Eli as if deciphering a puzzle, then muttered, "They granted you your wish."

"My wish?" Eli asked, still holding his pitchfork.

"Are you going to run me through, Elijah?" Cyrus asked, eyeing the spiked farming tool.

"Who are you?"

"An old friend visiting from a faraway place."

Eli shook his head, still not remembering. He leaned the pitchfork against the stall and studied Cyrus. Upon realizing his questions might be answered, Eli asked, "How do I know you? What's happened to me? Who am I?" each question growing in intensity.

"So many questions." Cyrus eyed Eli, then said, "If I told you, you would not understand. It is better to show you." The overseer removed the gleaming golden orb from his coat pocket.

Eli pulled back in amazement as the orb's flowing script shined off the walls of the stall. His eyes narrowed as he realized he had seen the golden ball before.

"Here, take this." Cyrus held out the glowing sphere.

"What is it?" gasped Eli.

"It is...your past. It is your future."

"It will tell me who I am?"

"Yes," nodded Cyrus. "But understand you have a choice."

"What is the choice?" asked Eli.

"To have your questions answered, to know who you are and *what* you are, or to remain in your mortal ignorance. Knowledge is never without consequences."

Eli's face dimmed. "I don't understand."

"Elijah, you have been given a life that is not yours. Why? I do not know." Cyrus's eyebrows raised. "You've taken a wife. And she carries a child."

"How do you know?"

Cyrus's eyes shifted in thought before returning to Eli. He held out the orb. "Take this, and you shall see. But remember, it will change everything."

Eli stepped closer. "What will it do to me?"

Cyrus's eyes narrowed. "It will guide you."

Eli gulped. "It will help me to remember?"

"Yes," Cyrus nodded. "But you must decide if that is what you want."

"How can one live not remembering his past?" fretted Eli.

"Your past is a part of you, but not as much as the present, for what you do next will determine the future."

"My future?"

"Everyone's future."

Eli studied Cyrus, still not understanding. But his desire to know was too great. Eli's eyes closed when he took the glowing orb in hand, and his body quivered as a wave of light rippled through him. In what seemed like years but was only seconds, Eli's memory returned. He saw the dawn of the First Age when the world was young, and the watchers were full of hope. He saw the good they had done and the aid they had rendered to ancient people. But he also felt the bitterness of failure as a once pure and majestic plan became corrupted, and evil spread. Eli experienced a hundred millennia in the blink of an eye. He saw his failure in Sarajevo. He saw his dead friends Jean-Pierre and Sébastien. He felt tremendous joy and terrible anguish. It was all revealed to him, but the weight was staggering.

When Eli opened his eyes, he found himself lying in the straw. He sat up and looked around, as if awakening from a bizarre dream. The visitor was gone, with only the mare staring down at him. Eli looked around the stall in bewilderment. *Was it all a fantastic dream?* he wondered. But when he looked down to find the golden orb shimmering beside him, Eli's heart sank, and his mouth fell open.

"ARE YOU NOT HUNGRY?" Ronan asked, seeing Eli had not touched his food.

"I think it was a long day for my husband," Michelle answered, but her real concern was that the news of their forthcoming child had upset Eli.

"Perhaps I'm working you too hard on my estate," Ronan said before sipping his wine.

"No," muttered Eli, coming back to them.

"Have you remembered something?" Michelle asked, always curious about what might come to his recollection.

Eli gulped. "Bits and pieces," he said, almost choking on the lie.

Ronan cleared his throat. "Eli, you have been working very hard as of late. Perhaps you should take some time off. You two could take a little holiday. Mathéo and the others can pick up the slack."

Michelle sighed. "It's difficult to holiday when there's a war on, and our boys are dying. It just doesn't seem right."

Ronan noticed Eli close his eyes as if wounded by the reminder. He considered saying more, but returned to his meal.

LYING IN BED, Michelle ran her hand through Eli's wavy brown hair as he stared at the ceiling. After caressing his cheek, her hand moved to Eli's broad, muscular chest. His scars were now completely gone. "What's the matter, my love?" she asked, worried for the answer.

Eli's mind was a whirlwind of thought and emotion. He wanted to tell Michelle who he was and how he had failed her and so many others. He wanted to explain why millions now suffered because of him. Eli yearned for Michelle to understand he wanted to stay with her. But pushing the world aside and neglecting his duty—even for another day —would only cause more death and suffering. But above all, Eli wanted to apologize for doing what was forbidden: falling in love with a mortal, taking her as a wife, and giving her a child. Eli wanted to tell her everything, but feared such knowledge would be their demise. "I'm not feeling well," he finally muttered.

Michelle pulled her hand away, and her brow tightened. "It's because I'm having a baby, isn't it?"

Eli shook his head in dismay.

"What is it then? Why have you been acting this way? You've pulled away from me since I told you of the baby."

Eli's heart ached as he looked into Michelle's troubled eyes. He saw not only her pain and worry but her inner strength and beauty. Eli's jaw slackened as he saw the light of her soul. She had a brightness and quality he had not before identified in a mortal. His puzzled gaze drifted as he tried to understand it all. Why the Holy and Great Ones had made him mortal, why they had taken his memory, and why they had given him to Michelle, Eli didn't know. "How fortunate I was to be placed under your care," he whispered. "How exquisite and beautiful you are. You are more than I could ever ask for. I would give up everything for you."

Michelle's expression softened. "Elijah, I'm your wife. We are bound together under God. I'm here for you. *Please* tell me what's wrong? What troubles you? Is it your failed memory? Because that doesn't matter. We will build our own memories together, our little family." Michelle's shoulders sank at Eli's blankness. "You're not going to tell me."

Eli sighed. "I cannot."

Michelle shook her head in frustration. "I don't know what to do, Elijah. I've given myself to you completely, more than any man before. You're my husband! I love you! But I feel us growing more distant, and it frightens me!"

"I will do everything I can to care for you."

"Why are you talking this way?" Michelle gasped, pulling the sheet over her chest. "I feel I know you less now than the day I met you!"

Eli's heart sank. Drawn in two directions, he felt as though he might rip in half. While Cyrus had told him he could not have both worlds, Eli was determined he would. He reached a hand to Michelle, who had turned away from him sobbing, but he stopped short of touching her. Eli breathed in determination. "My love, I must leave you for a time."

Michelle's gentle sobbing grew to near convulsions. When Eli touched her shoulder, she pulled away.

"Stay here with your uncle until I return."

"Where else am I to go?" she bitterly wept.

"I'm doing this for *us*," Eli said softly.

Michelle sat up, her eyes weepy, her tears streaking her flushed cheeks. "I don't understand! Help me to understand, Elijah! Don't you love me anymore?" She recognized Eli's anguish, but it was not enough.

"I love you more than you can know. That's why I must leave you."

Michelle's teary eyes widened. "You remembered something, didn't you? Do you have a family? Another wife?"

"No," Eli whispered, her heartache cutting to his bones. "You are the only one. You will *always* be the only one."

Michelle swallowed some of her pain and wiped at her tears. She somehow believed him. "How long will you be gone?" she asked, surprised when the words came from her lips.

"A few weeks. Maybe a month. I've already discussed it with your uncle."

"*A month!*" Michelle groaned. "Where will you go? You're not turning yourself into the French Army!"

"No," Eli said calmly. "I must go to the east. For now, you and our child will be safer with me gone."

"Will you be in harm's way?" Michelle fretted.

Eli's brow tightened with concern. "We are all in harm's way."

WHEN ELI ARRIVED at the clearing on the hill, the morning sun had yet to clear the oaks on the eastern ridge. Dressed in his suit and hat with a calfskin satchel across his shoulder, Eli looked back through the trees to be sure he had not been followed. After seeing he was alone, he kneeled and brushed the dead leaves and dirt from a large, flat rock. Eli cleared the soil from its edges and lifted the rock, revealing a foot-wide and deep stone box with the glistening orb resting inside. He reached down for the golden sphere, but pulled back when he heard a croak and a small toad hopped away from the orb. Gently lifting the little gray toad from the stone box, Eli set it in the dirt, then watched it hop away, somewhat envious of the amphibian's simple life and dual nature.

Eli's face filled with concern when he turned back to the stone box. He felt the weight of all that had come before and what was to follow. He breathed in resolve and reached inside. When Eli removed the golden orb, he felt its soft vibration as its inscribed characters glowed. He wondered why it had failed him before.

After replacing the stone lid and getting to his feet, Eli rested the gleaming orb in his left palm. The watcher's face tightened in concentration as he placed his right hand on top of the sphere. The glow from between his fingers grew in intensity until a growing circle of light split the space directly before him, like a shimmering, eight-foot-round doorway. Eli placed the orb in his satchel. Then, breathing in determination, he stepped through the rift and disappeared.

CHAPTER 19
REDEMPTION

Eli's brow tightened as men in khaki uniforms, stained from dirt and summer sweat, rushed past him down the narrow, chaotic street. Some were missing their peaked soldiers' caps, while others didn't even have rifles. Two more fleeing soldiers followed, carrying a wounded Cossack between them. Eli looked past an overturned wagon to a man and his son sprawled on the pavers in puddles of blood. The fleeing Russians had killed them for their horses, he sadly surmised.

As Eli continued down the street, he saw the fallen bodies of Russian soldiers whose retreat was cut short. He passed a field hospital empty of all but those who had died or soon would. Eli shook his head at the carnage as German artillery shook the ground and rattled the few unbroken windows.

A year and two weeks old, the war on the Eastern Front had already claimed a million Russian casualties but was no closer to finding its end. Once stretched along a thousand-mile front, the Russian Army had been in a state of retreat for months. The frontier fortresses of Kovno,

Novo-Georgievsk, Brest-Litovsk, and Grodno had fallen. With the advancing German Army on Vilnius' doorstep and the pungent stench of panic in the air, the fractured and dispirited Russian Army was again retreating.

As Eli followed the fleeing Russian troops toward the train station, he saw frightened and wary eyes looking out from the shadows. While many Lithuanians fled their beloved city when the brutal Cossacks arrived, most had stayed. With the Germans advancing and the Russian troops leaving, they wondered how much worse their lives would be.

Eli watched a frightened woman clutching an infant hurry across the street into an apartment building. He thought of his lovely Michelle. Soon she would be swaddling their baby. Eli fought against his loneliness. He wished he were with her, but knew what he was doing was for all.

Eli pushed away the sentiment and continued to the train station. He looked up as a German scout plane flew overhead, its dual wings dipping from side to side as it viewed the retreating army below. Eli knew he had much to accomplish and little time.

SAINT PETERSBURG, RUSSIA
2 SEPTEMBER 1915

THE GRAND BALLROOM was full of men in their most splendid officers' uniforms with tunics adorned in ribbons and shiny medals, and ladies in elegant evening gowns with their hair done up and necks and ears sparkling with jewelry. While couples waltzed to the orchestra's music, a few dour-faced generals holding cocktails stood to the side.

General Alexei Polivanov, a tall, balding man with a thick, bushy goatee, half-listened as another general complained. When he spotted the familiar Eli standing across the ballroom with several ladies eyeing him, he grinned and left the conversation.

Eli saw the general approaching and nodded politely to an eager countess with a string of rubies dipping into her ample cleavage.

"It's been a few years," said General Polivanov with an outstretched hand.

"Yes, it has," replied Eli in Russian as they shook hands.

The general turned to the lusty-eyed countess and, with a bow of his head, said, "Will you excuse us?"

The countess put a hand to her chin and turned her head, pulling her eyes from Eli.

The general led Eli away from the prying ears and asked, "Where is your associate, Cyrus?"

Eli considered how to respond. "He's passed on."

Polivanov's eyebrows raised. "Has he? You've taken his place?"

"Not very well, I'm afraid."

"He was a friend and trusted advisor to the Romanovs. He will be missed," Polivanov lamented.

"Yes," Eli nodded.

Polivanov's face grew serious. "Sadly, there are other voices of counsel that are not helpful. One in particular who bends the Tsarina's ear."

"Oh?"

"Perhaps you will meet him tonight. Despicable fellow," muttered Polivanov, gazing across the ballroom. "What are your thoughts on the war?" the general asked, turning back to Eli.

"Your forces are retreating."

"It was a necessary step. The salient was too long to manage. Falling back has shortened the front by four hundred miles."

"Victory through retreat," sighed Eli.

"It's a temporary setback. We are calling up two million more men. We have plenty."

"Not when your generals cast them into the fire like kindling. They need proper training. They need discipline."

"There have been some mistakes," Polivanov begrudgingly nodded, "but the Germans cannot possibly counter our army of fifteen million!"

"Farmers and boys commanded by nepotistic idiots," frowned Eli.

"They will fight," Polivanov insisted.

"They will die."

Polivanov gave a slight shrug. "So will the Germans."

Eli sighed. "I fear there is a larger problem."

"And what is that?"

"Tsar Nicholas has vowed to take control of the army. This cannot happen."

"I know. I've counseled him against it. He knows nothing of commanding large military forces, but he believes it will inspire the men and the country."

"It will not," Eli insisted. "Any military failures will be tied directly to him. It will be his undoing. The Russian empire is teetering. Even now, as we speak, forces are working to undermine it. If we fail, what comes next will be a thousand times worse than the Romanov dynasty. The Tsar has appointed you Minister of War. He will listen to you. You must make him aware of the risks."

Polivanov sighed. "I know you are right. I will speak to him again. I will plead for him to return power to the generals and stay in Saint Petersburg."

Eli studied the tired Polivanov. He feared the growing wave of evil was now too great to stop.

"Here comes that damn monk now," muttered the general.

Eli turned to see a slim man in a black cassock with dark, greasy hair and a long, wiry beard approaching.

"Grigori Rasputin," nodded the priest, his knowing, dark-ringed eyes fixed on the watcher.

Disgusted by the halfborn's presence, Eli fought to control his tongue. "How did you rise to such prominence? I understand you have captured the Tsarina's ear," fumed Eli.

"You shouldn't be surprised," smirked Rasputin. "We work for the same master on opposite sides of the coin."

"Hardly," Eli glared.

"You know each other?" asked a surprised Polivanov.

"This...*man* should not be trusted," warned Eli.

"Neither should he," hissed Rasputin. The halfborn's eyes lowered to Eli's coat pocket that held the orb. "We missed you. Perhaps now the balance can be restored."

Eli's eyes narrowed. "We first must fix the scale."

OYSTER BAY, NEW YORK
10 SEPTEMBER 1915

ELI'S NOSE wrinkled at the musty smell of oiled wood and taxidermied game as he waited in the large, walnut-paneled office. A bright Persian rug covered much of the wood floor. An assortment of chairs lined the room, and a mountain lion's head and skin lay before a couch. An elk's head with a giant rack was mounted on the wall above the couch. Leopard skins draped two other sofas while bison heads stared down from either side of the fireplace.

Eli turned from a painting of the Grand Canyon when a barrel-chested man with wire-rimmed spectacles and a shaggy mustache entered the room. "Thank you for seeing me, Mister President."

"I haven't been the damn president in six years! My friends call me Teddy. My question to you, Mister Mansel, is, are you a friend or a politician? If you're a friend, call me Teddy. If you're not, I don't have much time for you."

"I'm a friend," nodded Eli.

"Good. I've got plenty but can always use a few more."

"And we have met before."

"Have we?" Roosevelt squinted through his small round glasses.

"I was an associate of Cyrus. We met several times in the White House."

"Ah, yes. Now I remember. How is Cyrus?"

"He has passed," Eli replied.

"Shame. It happens to all of us—well, most of us," Roosevelt added, eying Eli. "Now, what brings you to Sagamore Hill? George tells me you've come all the way from France. To talk about your little problem over there, I wager."

Eli grinned at the fast-talking New Yorker. "Yes, sir. I would like to talk to you about your country's neutrality in the war."

"Seems to me you should be talking to the man living in my old house, Woody Wilson," Roosevelt huffed. "You know, I worked hard to build this country's military back up, but it's an uphill battle! Just when you get something done, another election rolls around, and someone like Wilson comes in and lets all your hard work go to hell! We should be helping those boys fight the Germans right now instead of twiddling our damned thumbs!" Red-faced, Roosevelt pulled down on his vest and grunted, "I'll get off my soapbox. What can I do for you?"

Eli's eyes narrowed. "I would like to speak with you about your preparedness movement."

"Why am I not surprised?"

"You have enlisted the help of many prominent bankers, lawyers, and industrialists and have argued that the United States must rebuild its military presence."

"They call me a war hawk like it's some kind of damn insult! A hawk is nearly as mighty as an eagle if you ask me, but I'm just looking out for my country. You don't do that by sticking your head in the sand! You go kick ass! Excuse my French."

"You speak softly but carry a big stick," grinned Eli.

"That's right; only sometimes you need to bark loudly and wave a shotgun!" Roosevelt exclaimed. He motioned to a round table near two arching elephant tusks. "Have a seat. Care for a drink? Coffee? Whiskey?"

"No, thank you," Eli said, moving to the table.

"You're a big fella, and you don't sound very French," Roosevelt observed, pulling out a chair. "More Canadian, if you ask me."

"I've lived many places," Eli replied.

"Well, let's get down to brass tacks. What can you do for me?"

Eli studied the former Rough Rider for a moment, then said, "I can help you understand the seriousness of the situation in Europe."

"I don't think I need much help. Your French friends got into a scrape with the Hun and now need a hand getting out of it. I understand that pretty well, but what I don't understand is how Germany and Austria, two countries smaller than Texas, can cause such a ruckus! You got all them Russians, and now even the Italians are in the fight. You should be able to squash them like a bug!"

Eli shook his head. "Russia has great internal strife. I fear a revolution will take them out of the war. The French generals think they can simply outlast the enemy, but they don't understand what is at stake and how powerful the forces at play are. If America doesn't join the fight, Europe will be lost. America will fall next. Like cancer, this unseen force will eat away at the world until there is only death and chaos."

An engrossed Roosevelt leaned back in his chair and ran a hand down his bushy mustache in thought. Then, with a serious nod, he turned to Eli and said, "You should've been a lobbyist. Hell, I'm already sold on the idea, but there are others that need to hear. I want you to meet some of my friends, General Wood, Elihu Root, Henry Stimson. I think hearing from you might just be the push we need. Maybe we can finally light a match under that worthless Wilson!"

NEW YORK CITY
29 SEPTEMBER 1915

AS ELI WALKED along the busy pier, with the blue sky and swirling seagulls overhead, he considered the smoke-filled chambers where he had sat. For too many days, Eli had listened to fat and balding men who had lost their prominence and power debate over America's place in the world. After two weeks of meeting with politicians, businessmen, and former generals, Eli was no closer to affecting the war. The obstacle was the popular notion that Europe's war was not America's problem. Unless something changed, America would remain neutral.

Eli missed Michelle. Nearly two months had passed since he had left the peaceful château, and Eli knew each day away from his wife was one he could never reclaim. He feared leaving her at all was a mistake. Eli had sent Michelle a telegram the week before, apprising her of his efforts, but had heard nothing back.

While Eli believed her safe in his absence, his time away allowed him to consider what Lu might do to accomplish his ends. But with each day of rejection, Eli questioned more and more what he was doing. Any influence he and the other watchers once had was now gone. Like a raging river, humanity was cutting its own course, and its ferocious torrent was consuming all in its path.

Eli ached to return to Michelle, and had twice tried to use the orb to travel back through the spacial rift just as he had come. But just as in Sarajevo, the orb now seemed unresponsive to him. Eli had followed its direction and could only conclude it meant for him to stay in America, but for how long it was unclear. Eli could wait no longer.

With a transatlantic ticket in one hand and his calfskin satchel over his shoulder, Eli walked up the ship's passageway to the freighter bound for England. With or without the orb's help, he was going home.

CHÂTEAU DE BRET
1 OCTOBER 1915

MICHELLE TIGHTENED the shawl around her shoulders as she sat on the hillside above the pond and stared across the rippling water. With a hand on her swollen belly and her face vacant, she watched the fall breeze stir the flaming elms across the pond, their dry leaves flying and spiraling. There was not a duck or swan in sight. Even the croaking toads and chirping birds had left her. Although her caring uncle and trusty Sébastien were never far, Michelle felt utterly alone. Her mysterious Eli had told her he would return in a few weeks. It had been more than six. She wondered if she would ever see him again.

Michelle looked down at her pregnant belly and wondered if her child would ever know its father. The pondering caused her heart to ache even more and an errant tear to break free.

With a forlorn sigh, Michelle wiped away the tear. She wondered what she would do when the baby was born. Michelle loved the château but felt she had already become a burden on her kind uncle. She questioned what she would do with the baby should she return to Paris. She wondered why Eli had left her, and if he ever truly loved her as she did him. Her chest swelled with angst and loneliness and grief.

Michelle looked down at the shaggy Sébastien beside her. After a lick and a wag, she scratched behind the dog's ear. "Oh, Sébastien...at least you haven't left me."

Michelle turned at the sound of crunching leaves. Her eyes widened with the possibility of it being Eli, then settled when she saw her uncle's gray hair under a hunting cap.

"There you are," Ronan said as he navigated the slope with the agility of a younger man.

"Hello, Uncle," Michelle sighed as she scratched the dog's head.

"I've been looking for you. I should have known."

"Should have known what?" Michelle frowned.

"That you'd be here. I have a telegram for you. Two, in fact," Ronan said, reaching inside his hunting vest.

"A telegram?" Michelle breathed, standing up.

"Yes. Apparently, the first arrived a week ago. I asked the messenger why it was not delivered, but he had no idea. Dreadful service, if you ask me."

With her eyes round, Michelle took the two letters and opened the first. "It's from Elijah!" she gasped, spotting his name at the bottom.

"What does he say?" asked Ronan with a tilted head.

Michelle's eyes darted across the text, too excited to read it. She gulped down her anxiousness and read:

Michelle Duvall, Château de Bret
Leaving New York today-STOP.
Hope to see you in one week-STOP.
Miss you terribly-STOP.
Affectionately Eli

Michelle's brow tightened in confusion. "It says he's leaving New York."

"Certainly, he means York—in England."

"No, it says New York," Michelle replied, looking up at her uncle.

Ronan pointed to the unopened envelope. "What about the other one?"

Michelle quickly opened the second telegram, her eyes wide with wonder.

<u>Michelle Duvall, Château de Bret</u>
In America to help with war-STOP.
Will return soon-STOP.
Hope you and baby are well-STOP.
Miss you terribly-STOP.
Affectionately Eli

"He's in America!" Michelle gasped. "I don't understand. He said he was going east."

Ronan stepped back. "What's he doing in America?"

"To help with the war, he says," Michelle replied, staring across the water.

"To help with the war?" Ronan pondered. "America is neutral, but they are rendering aid and supplies. At least they're trying. Half of it ends up at the bottom of the Atlantic, thanks to the damn German U-boats!"

Michelle half-heard her uncle. Her thoughts were on her bold and courageous husband. *He has not abandoned me!*

Ronan shook his head. "For someone who has no memory, he is quite ambitious. Your husband is a curious man." With a shrug, Ronan turned and walked back up the hill.

Elijah, who are you? Michelle wondered as she clutched the telegrams against her breast.

CHAPTER 20
THE BLACK BRINE

Eli's eyes narrowed as the cold brine sprayed up from the ship's bow. The lead-blue waters of the Atlantic stretched as far as he could see. Another freighter, a mile to the port bow, had led them the past two days, but no other vessel was in sight. With the sun setting to the stern and the biting October sea breeze growing brisk, Eli was about to go below deck. He turned when a man with a sailor's beard, wearing a wool navy coat and captain's hat, joined him at the railing.

"Evening. I'm Captain Lloyd," nodded the man, clenching a pipe between his teeth as he sized up Eli.

"Good evening, Captain."

"First time across the Atlantic?"

Eli considered saying it was his first time by boat, but knew that would lead to more questions. "No."

"I saw you day before last. You're a big bloke, hard to miss. I meant to natter with you. I like to know my passengers—it's easy when there's only twenty-two. You're English then? I can't place the accent."

"I have lived in England before."

"Have you now? Where do you call home?"

"France, for now," said Eli.

"Uh. Pity about the war. Have you seen fighting then?"

"Yes, I have," Eli replied, his gaze drifting across the water.

"You're a strapping lad. I wager those bloody Hun turned tail seeing you!"

Eli didn't reply.

The captain eyed Eli and puffed on his pipe. "Nice and smooth today," he said, looking over the bow. "Last trip was a mite rougher. She's a big water for a tin can like this."

Eli glanced back at the bridge's glowing windows and the billowing smokestack between the towering fore and aft masts. "It seems like a fairly large ship."

"The *Skawby*? She's just shy of five thousand ton. The big liners are upwards of thirty thousand, but she does the job for us," the captain nodded, proudly patting the railing.

"What is your cargo?"

"Well now, some of that's private information, but you look like a trusting soul, you do. This time around, we've got a hundred eighty barrels of fuel oil, a couple ton of good American wheat, and a little something to help our boys at the front, if you know what I mean." The captain's eyes widened, almost bulging from holding in the secret.

"I see. Have you made many of these journeys?"

"This is only our sixth transatlantic; Bombay to Liverpool for years before that. They moved us because of the bloody German U-boats. They like to sit in the Med and torpedo Allied ships coming out of the Suez Canal. Bloody cowards. Transatlantic is five days shorter, and the money's a mite better. That's two plusses if you ask me," shrugged the captain.

Eli looked from the chatty captain back across the dimming water. He missed Michelle more than ever, but Eli knew it could still be days before he could be with her. After porting in Liverpool, he would still have to find passage to France.

Eli felt the orb in the satchel over his shoulder. He went nowhere without it now, but the domain sphere had once again dimmed, and its silence perplexed him.

"I don't think you have to worry too much about the bloody U-boats."

Eli's gaze returned to the captain. He saw he was worried about the U-boats.

"It's not like we're the bloody *Lusitania* with all them passengers. That was a big, luscious target the bloody U-boat commander couldn't resist! No, we're a little dingy compared to it! Hardly worth a torpedo, if you ask me." The captain nervously puffed on his pipe. "Killed over a thousand of them rich passengers, including a bunch of Yanks. I thought for sure them Yanks would join the fight after that," the captain huffed. "Bloody cowards."

Eli backed away from the railing. "I think I'm going in for dinner."

"We port in Liverpool in the morning. You should sleep like a baby with these lovely waves."

As Eli walked away, the captain turned forward, placed his hands on the bow railing, and breathed in the crisp sea air.

The small, dim dining room smelled of fish and cabbage. Three round portholes to the gathering night lined one wall, a swinging door to a pot-clanging galley another. The tables and chairs were small and crowded with hungry passengers, and the teak floor was sticky. Eli had just sat at the last empty table when an attractive woman with blonde, done-up hair and an inquisitive gaze moved beside him. "Good evening. Do you mind if I join you?" she asked searchingly.

"Good evening. Please," Eli replied, standing. He wondered what was wrong with her other table as he motioned to the chair opposite him. Eli had noticed her eyeing him on the main deck earlier but thought nothing of it.

"Hello," she smiled, hiding a blush. "I'm Penelope Chamberlain."

"Pleased to meet you. Eli Mansel," he politely nodded.

Penelope coyly grinned as they shook hands.

Eli tried to hide his uneasiness as he returned to his plate. He felt the woman's loneliness and pain. She had not been treated well by men and was running from her past.

"Fish'n chips and cabbage," Penelope remarked with raised eyebrows. "Is it better than last night's fish'n chips and peas?"

"No," Eli grinned, brushing away her interest in him.

Penelope tasted her cabbage and eyed Eli. "If you don't mind me asking, where are you from?"

"France, most recently."

"Oh, *bonsoir*," flirted Penelope. "You speak excellent English."

"Thank you." Eli ate some of his cabbage.

"Do you speak more than French and English?"

Eli shrugged. "I can converse in a few other languages."

"That's splendid!" replied an impressed Penelope. She took a bite, then grimaced, "Oh, I think this is yesterday's fish."

"Probably," replied Eli.

Nothing was said for a few minutes as they ate, but Penelope's eyes didn't stray far from the handsome watcher. Seeing no ring on his large hands, she pushed out her chest, leaned closer, and said, "It's a dreadful thing, this war."

"Yes, it is," Eli frowned, staring at his last few potato wedges.

When Penelope noticed the weight of her simple comment, she turned away and cringed, wishing she hadn't spoken it. Eli was gathering his plate, about to leave the table, when Penelope, desperate to make a connection, blurted, "I've decided to go home to Manchester."

Unable to ignore the woman's pain, Eli's concerned gaze turned to her. "You're from there but lived in America."

Penelope's smile faded. "Well, yes. Nearly five years."

"You've left much behind, haven't you?" Eli sadly observed.

Penelope's face went blank. She looked down and nudged her cabbage with a fork. "How do you know that?"

Eli studied Penelope with blue, piercing eyes. She was pregnant but didn't yet know it. "You carry an important future."

Penelope shook her head. "I doubt that." Then, with fearful realization, she looked up and asked, "Did my ex-husband send you to bring me back?"

Eli's expression softened. "No. I could just see you're...troubled."

Penelope tried to hide her embarrassment with an awkward nod, then got up from the table and left the dining room.

. . .

LIEUTENANT CAPTAIN HANS WEGENER was a small, lean man, but his size belied his brutish cunning. He had risen quickly through the ranks of the *Kaiserliche Marine*, and in less than a year commanding U27 had twelve kills to his name and been awarded two Iron Crosses.

After maneuvering through the tight confines of the U-boat's control room, he ascended the ladder to the conning tower. Wegener's sharp gaze moved across the shimmering sea as he breathed in the cool, salty air. With only a waning crescent, he thought the moon was perfect for killing.

"Two freighters, two thousand meters to port, both with English flags," reported Lieutenant Ramm. "We've been tracking them for an hour. No other vessels in sight."

"I see it. And the second?" asked Wegener, peering through his binoculars. "There it is," he grinned slyly. "Too easy." After coming off a resupply with six torpedoes, he was eager to add to his resume.

"They're ripe for the picking," nodded Ramm.

Wegener scanned the horizon to be sure the ships were unescorted, then lowered his binoculars. "Come left to zero-six-zero."

"New course, zero-six-zero," echoed Ramm.

"Prepare tubes one and two for surface firing," ordered Wegener with the eyes of a hunter.

"Tubes one and two flooded," reported Ramm.

"All ahead full." Wegener watched the lead ship for a few minutes. Then, pulling down the binoculars, he barked, "Left full rudder, come to zero-three-zero. Standby to attack."

An excited Ramm repeated the command.

"Bow angle bearing zero-five-five; range, nineteen hundred meters."

"Left standard rudder, all ahead one-third, open bulkheads!" added Ramm.

"Lock on tube one. New bow angle, zero-four-zero," glared the captain. "Fire when ready!"

. . .

ELI WAS LYING in his cramped middle bunk, considering his life and how badly he wanted to return to Michelle when he heard the warning cry "German U-boat!" from outside his cabin door. The snoring man in the lower bunk lurched to consciousness when Eli landed on the deck to pull on his trousers and shoes.

"Lifebelts! Get your lifebelts and come on deck!" yelled another passing crewman as Eli opened the cabin door. He pulled on his shirt but didn't bother to button it as he hurried down the passageway to the main deck ladder.

"What's happening?" gasped the woman from dinner as passengers hurried by her cabin door.

"I'm not sure," Eli replied, moving past.

Penelope pulled tight her plush bathrobe and followed Eli.

When they emerged into the chilled night, their eyes widened. The freighter they had followed for days was engulfed in flames, lighting the blackened sea three hundred yards ahead. "What happened?" Eli asked no one in particular as crewmen frantically readied the ship's three lifeboats. On the ladder above Eli, the bearded captain stood at the door of the wheelhouse, searching the murky expanse with his spyglass.

The flash of a distant explosion, followed an instant later by a thunderous *BUHBOOM*, turned Eli's worried gaze back to the burning wreck.

"Bugger! She's going down!" gasped a wide-eyed crewman.

"TORPEDO STARBOARD BOW!" bellowed the captain. "FULL LEFT RUDDER!"

"Full left rudder, aye!" cried the wheel-spinning helmsman as two deckhands rushed to the railing and pointed across the darkness at the approaching torpedo.

Eli had to balance himself as the deck tipped. His eyes widened when he spotted the foaming, churning water behind the torpedo, forty yards ahead and to their right on a course to intercept them.

All eyes were on the underwater missile as it streamed toward the hard-turning ship. Cheers erupted when it propelled past the bow, missing by only feet.

"Where's the bloody U-boat?" cried a crewman, sliding along the gunwale as he peered into the night.

"It's still out there!" warned another.

"Where's the bloody Royal Navy?" exclaimed a third.

"Do we rescue the *Berkley's* crew, captain?" asked a man, pointing to the split-in-two cargo ship's burning remains.

"Only if we're sure the bloody Hun's gone!" shouted the captain, frantically searching the darkness for the German submarine.

"Captain, they're drowning out there!" pleaded a crewman.

"We can't bloody rescue them if we're drowning!" bellowed the captain.

"Should I lower the boats, Captain?" fretted another man, his hands on the lifeboat rigging.

"Not until I give the order!" roared the captain.

The third torpedo wasn't spotted until it was twenty feet from the starboard quarter. The violent blast rocked the ship, knocked Eli and the others off their feet, and ripped open the boiler room. The *Skawby* was dead in the water.

"Fire in the boiler room!" shrieked the helmsman as Eli helped the captain, who had fallen six feet off the bridge's ladder, to his feet.

"Is she flooding?" grimaced the captain, clutching his knee as the lights in the wheelhouse flickered.

"They blew a bleedin' hole in us, Captain!" cried the first mate as he stumbled along the deck.

"Get that fire out!" barked the captain, clinging to the ladder.

"Fire in the hold!"

The captain immediately thought of the barrels of oil and munitions they carried. "GET THOSE FIRES OUT!" he roared.

The crew darted about the groaning, listing ship, their training overriding panic as worried passengers, some half-dressed and others wrapped in blankets, helplessly watched. Eli saw Penelope's fear when their eyes met. He wished he could comfort her. He wished he could tell them all they would be safe, but he knew that would be a lie.

"The boiler room's flooded, sir!" reported the helmsman.

"What about the U-boat?" fretted a shivering passenger, his face a ghostly white.

"They won't spend another torpedo, not on us," said the wild-eyed captain.

"Will we sink, Captain?" gasped a terrified Irish woman, her crying teenage daughter wrapped in a blanket beside her.

The captain's frazzled gaze moved to the rear of the listing ship. He shook his head when he saw the stern low in the water. "Get the passengers to the lifeboats," he dejectedly ordered.

"Aye, Captain!" A deck mate turned to the gathered, worried passengers and hollered, "All passengers to the lifeboats!"

"What about my trunk?" fretted a gray-haired woman, fighting to keep her balance on the listing deck.

"Only what you can carry, ma'am. She may stay afloat, but you should be in a boat, just in case."

Upon remembering the orb still inside his cabin, Eli dashed down the ladder to the tipping passageway as the lights flickered. Toward the far end was a gurgling, growing pool of seawater.

After retrieving his coat and checking his satchel for the orb, Eli turned back to the cabin door. He had just reached the flooding passageway when the deck exploded beneath him. The force of the blast threw him and two other passengers against the overhead. The surrounding flames quickly faded as the ocean swept in, filling the torn-open cabins in seconds.

The bite of the frigid water was jarring. Clinging to his bag, Eli found a pocket of air and filled his lungs before pushing up toward the cracked-open hull and the glowing firelight above. He grabbed hold of an unconscious man floating in a crimson cloud. Eli clawed his way to the surface as bubbles, debris, and bodies floated around him. He looked down to see the rear of the ship falling away into the dark abyss.

When Eli's head finally broke above the surface, he gasped in air. He pulled the lifeless man up beside him and scanned the undulating sea. To Eli's left were patches of burning oil and floating debris. Ahead of him was a half-filled life raft with two crewmen pulling on a drenched passenger with a white lifebelt under his arms. To his right was the bow of their broken-in-two ship, jutting twenty feet into the cold night.

Eli spit out the salty water as he tried to keep the lifeless man beside him afloat, blood streaming down his face. He heard the cries and screams of those fighting to stay above the swells. He saw a crewman floating face down and a woman thrashing the surface. *Too many will die, but I can't help them all*, fretted Eli, knowing their strength and air were running out with each precious second.

"Over here!" Eli called out as he swam toward the lifeboat, the fire-light from the burning oil shimmering across the blackened sea.

"Help me!" choked the woman to Eli's left, her lengthy blonde hair obscuring her face. "It's cold!" she gasped before going under. When she came back up, Eli saw it was Penelope.

"Grab hold of something!" he yelled, seeing a splintered beam floating near her.

Penelope disappeared under the waves before fighting back to the surface, the weight of her plush bathrobe pulling her down. Her frantic face was a ghostly white as she gasped and sputtered, "I can't reach it!"

Still thirty feet from the lifeboat, Eli knew she had only seconds. He turned to the lifeless man under his arm. The gash in his forehead was no longer pulsing blood into the water, and his eyes were half-open and disjointed. He was dead.

Eli released the body and swam hard toward the drowning Penelope. As her thrashing arms lost the fight, her gasping face slipped under the waves. Eli was almost to her when the bag came off his shoulder. The watcher's eyes widened. Both the woman and his precious orb were sinking into the murky depths. He froze, not knowing which to save.

Torn by his choice, Eli lunged downward and chased after the sinking orb as it disappeared into the blackness. He reached with searching hands for his bag but felt only the cold, numbing water. When Eli kicked down even harder, his stretched fingers brushed against the bag's trailing strap. He grabbed hold, felt for the orb, and pulled the bag up and across his chest. Eli then turned and kicked his way back to the fire-lit surface.

Searching for Penelope, Eli angled his ascent to where she had been, but he couldn't find her in the murky, shifting sea. Nearly to the surface and out of air, Eli finally spotted her floating eight feet down, her open bathrobe flowing, her limp arms and legs extended, her golden hair weightless in the frigid, swirling brine. Desperately kicking down to her, Eli pulled the weighty robe from Penelope, grabbed hold of her arm, and dragged her to the surface.

Bursting out of the water with Penelope under his arm, Eli gasped for air. He fought to stay afloat as he searched for the lifeboat, but it had drifted farther away. "Over here!" he cried as he pushed through the swells toward it, the woman limp in his arm.

When Eli finally reached the lifeboat, two men, one balding in a dripping nightshirt and another with bent and twisted teeth, pulled Penelope on board. "She's drowned!" exclaimed the crewman, seeing her gray, pasty face. Eli grabbed hold of the boat's gunwale and pulled himself out of the water. When he rolled into the sixteen-foot lifeboat, drenched and gasping, the snaggle-toothed crewman had rolled Penelope onto her back across a thwart, her arms hanging, her nightgown pasted to her pale flesh. The crewman pushed on her abdomen while the seven other survivors watched.

"Someone pump her arms!" cried Snaggletooth as seawater dribbled from Penelope's hanging head.

The shivering bald man with his lifebelt still about him slid closer and began raising and lowering Penelope's limp arms like a bellows.

"Faster!" ordered the crewman.

Eli climbed past the wide-eyed survivors, slid beside Penelope, and gently pushed the arm-pumping man aside. After flipping his wet hair from his face, Eli placed a hand under Penelope's sagging head, filled his aching lungs with air, and placed his mouth to hers. All eyes were on the dripping watcher as he exhaled into her.

"What's he doing to her?" gasped the horrified teenage girl huddled beside her mother.

"I don't know," muttered the transfixed Irish mother.

The crewman pushing on Penelope's belly slowed as Eli forced another breath into her lungs. He had seen drowned men return when smoke was blown into their mouths, but never just air and never by touching lips.

After four more attempts, with the others in the boat growing more and more disturbed, Penelope's chest moved. She coughed a little at first, but it quickly turned to a hacking bark as seawater spewed from her lungs. Eli rolled her on her side as more water came out, and she gagged and retched.

"He brought her back to life!" declared the wide-eyed mother, looking at the rugged Eli in awe.

"He breathed life right back into her!" shivered the bald man in the dripping nightshirt.

"Mate, well done, you!" applauded a thick-bearded crewman.

"It were I who was pump'n her belly," grumbled Snaggletooth.

Eli sat the coughing Penelope up as she looked around in confusion, her color returning, but her lips still blue. "What happened?"

"The bloody Bosch sank us!" barked the thick-bearded crewman.

"He saved your sweet life, is what happened!" declared the Irish mother with a nod to Eli. "I saw it all! You went under, and he swam down and saved you, brought you back here!"

"You were dead, miss," added the bald man. "He breathed life right back into you!"

A shivering Penelope turned to Eli and, with chattering teeth, said, "Th-thank you."

After tipping his head to the enamored Penelope, Eli looked across the water. The patches of burning oil had spread far and wide; their light swallowed up between the night and the rolling blue.

"It-it's so cold," chattered Penelope. Dripping wet in her thin night-gown, she crossed her arms and shivered.

"IS THERE ANYONE ELSE OUT THERE?" called out Snaggle-tooth as he looked across the rolling water.

"I ain't heard no one for ten minutes," replied Thick-beard.

"I wonder if anyone from the *Berkley* made it?"

"Ain't seen a one of 'em."

"What about the capt'n?"

"I think he went down."

Eli sighed, his open shirt dripping, his satchel across his chest.

There was a long silence, then Thick-beard muttered, "Poor Capt'n Lloyd."

Eli's sad gaze moved across the undulating blackness as the crescent moon broke through the clouds and gleamed off the water.

"It's so cold," whimpered Penelope.

"Sorry. We don't have no more blankets," shrugged Snaggletooth.

"She can have mine," said the girl huddled beside her mother.

"That's very fine of you, miss," commended the bald man.

Eli nodded his approval and accepted the blanket. After straddling the shivering Penelope, he wrapped the blanket around her, then pulled her tight against his bare chest to warm her as the Irish mother and her teenage daughter watched.

"What's going to happen to us?" shuddered Penelope.

"We're just south of Ireland. Come morning, we'll see some ships. Someone will pick us up." nodded Snaggletooth.

"What time is it?" asked the shivering bald man.

"Maybe midnight," replied Thick-beard. "It was about eleven o'clock when that bloody Hun hit us."

"Six more hours," groaned the Irish mother.

"Gather close. Our bodies will warm one another," explained Eli.

The Irish mother promptly moved beside Eli and wrapped her arms around his broad back while her teenage daughter watched slack-jawed. Upon remembering her daughter, the mother turned and waved her closer. "Come here, you. We're keeping warm."

"It was a bleedin' miracle we survived," muttered the bald man.

"God must not have it in for us, after all," added the Irish mother.

"We ain't been bleedin' rescued yet," grunted Snaggletooth.

As the survivors huddled to stay warm, Eli couldn't help but examine their personas. While only one in the lifeboat was bound for greatness before the attack, all were changed by their brush with death. Eli had seen it all before: the grand matrix of life. Like a swirling, steaming stew, the experiences and connections of mortality—some random, some predestined—allowed greatness and mediocrity, prominence and fame or obscurity and insignificance. It both thrilled and pained Eli to watch the generations rise and fall, to see brilliance realized and greatness squandered. He wondered what treasures had been lost that night—drowned in the frigid Atlantic.

The watcher's eyes lowered to Penelope's shivering belly and the child she carried. Even as a fetus, Eli recognized its potential to change the world. He wondered how different mortals would be if they had such vision.

Eli's gaze moved across the shifting darkness. He thought of his forthcoming child and wondered when he would see Michelle again.

CHAPTER 21

THE FIERY RIFT

Not long after first light, an Irish fishing trawler spotted the bobbing lifeboat. Huddled together and desperate to keep warm, the haggard survivors waved and hollered as the fishing boat puttered toward them. The frazzled and shivering travelers joyfully thanked the thick-armed Irishmen in rubber chest waders who pulled them aboard the trawler. Eli was the last to leave the lifeboat and simply nodded his thanks as others told of their ordeal in a chorus of chatter.

Eli followed the survivors out of the cold down into the fishing boat's cramped hold. He watched as the weary travelers crowded in and sank onto piled fishing nets and buoys. The bald man with the lifebelt still about his thick middle struggled to hide his tears while the Irish mother and her daughter held each other. Snaggletooth and Thickbeard one-upped each other as they told the captain of their harrowing escape from the German U-boat. Seated not far from Eli, Penelope gave her rescuer frequent glances as she quietly shivered and pondered her future.

"We're turning back to Crosshaven," announced the captain in a thick Irish brogue, proud of his accidental rescue. "We'll get you fed and warmed up there."

"How do we get to Liverpool?" asked the bald man.

"You'll have to get to Dublin first," replied the captain.

"How long will that take?" fretted the Irish mother as a crewman handed out blankets that stunk of haddock.

The captain shrugged and went up the ladder.

It saddened Eli that some of them had already forgotten their brush with death and the fragility of life.

"What are you going to do?" asked Penelope, wrapped in a blanket, her tired eyes still yearning for the watcher.

Eli turned to her and said, "I'm going home."

"Back to France?"

Eli nodded.

"You have someone there?"

"My wife," Eli replied, feeling like an imposter for saying so.

The words sucked the hope from Penelope's face. She tried to disguise her hurt and attraction to Eli but couldn't. "What...what's her name?"

"Michelle," Eli whispered, not wanting to worsen Penelope's pain.

"She's fortunate to have such a man," Penelope replied, not taking her eyes off of Eli.

Eli's gaze lowered. He wondered if that was true.

"Won't you come with me to Manchester? I don't think I can go anywhere by myself ever again. I don't know what I was thinking ever leaving on such a voyage."

Eli stared at the deck, ignoring Penelope's attraction to him. He focused instead on her pain. While she was fleeing from a cruel past, Eli knew she had the strength to overcome it.

Penelope leaned closer when she saw Eli's reluctance. "You were planning on passage to France from Liverpool. Manchester's not much farther, a little over an hour by train. If you could escort me home, I would be forever indebted. I would even pay for your voyage. My father is a well-known Egyptologist. He'll reward you handsomely. As soon as we get to Dublin, I'll wire for money. Don't worry; I have plenty."

Eli tried to block out Penelope's excitement, fear, and desire; he just wanted to get back to Michelle. But the importance of Penelope's descendants, through a child that not even she knew about, was too great. "I will see you to the train station."

"Thank you," beamed Penelope.

Eli nodded, then looked across the cramped hold at the exhausted survivors. Two were already asleep. Eli considered his failings. He had answered the orb's call and done all he could, but none of it seemed to matter. Eli was tired. He was tired of fighting for a cause that now seemed lost. He was tired of trying to make a difference. Eli wanted to be released from his call. He wanted to return to his beautiful wife and live in the peaceful château near the lovely pond. Eli felt the orb in the satchel beside him. He wondered if he should have let it sink into the sea.

GIEN, FRANCE
6 OCTOBER 1915

MICHELLE TIGHTENED her sweater over her protruding belly as she perused the open-air market with a quarter-filled handbasket. With commodities scarce, she found it something of a game to help Madame Duguay collect what they needed for their meals. Beef was now nearly impossible to find, leaving poultry and lamb also in short supply. While her uncle had sheep, he felt it wise to save them, should meat become even scarcer.

Though there were days Michelle still felt sick, she was grateful they were less frequent. The looming question of what was to be, both with her coming child and the future of the world, left her disheartened. That the Germans were no closer to advancing on Paris was some consolation, but it was little comfort knowing the French and British had been unable to push the enemy back. While the front lines had changed little in months, the fighting and dying had not stopped. The stalemate, now more than a year old, steadily consumed men, material, and morale.

A week had passed since Michelle had received Eli's telegrams, and her anticipation of his return had grown with each day. She pushed from her head any notion of him not returning. He was her miracle man, and she believed nothing could stop him. But the Italian reporter's words still gnawed at the back of Michelle's mind. She often wondered about Eli's past and who he was. Michelle wanted to believe he was like any other man, knowing all the while he was not. Her time with him had told her as much.

Michelle had spent her lonely hours searching the Old Testament for clues, as the reporter had told her, but she found only vague references to "watchers" and "the sons of God." None of it made sense to her. Who Eli was—who he *really* was—was a question she didn't know she was prepared to have answered.

Gazing pleasantly about the busy market, Michelle held the weaved basket by the crook of her arm as Madame Duguay selected a few tomatoes. Across the square, from the shadows of an archway, a dark pair of eyes watched her.

LIVERPOOL, ENGLAND
7 OCTOBER 1915

DESPITE THE DRIZZLING RAIN, Church Street was abuzz with midday commotion. Men in suits and bowler hats with umbrellas walked under the dripping awnings as a horse-pulled beer wagon clopped past a stopped double-decker bus. Eli held the umbrella for the two of them as Penelope sashayed beside him in a new powder-blue dress, white feathered hat, and matching cape and scarf. While he had insisted against it, she had purchased him a new wool suit, wing-tipped shoes, and hat.

While thoughts of her past still pulled at her, Penelope tried to forget as she walked with Eli toward Liverpool Station. She hoped every minute Eli spent with her might be enough for him to forget his past as well. It wasn't just that Eli was tall and ruggedly handsome or even that he had saved her life. There was something else that, like a bee to a fragrant orchid, drew her to him.

"Shall we have some lunch?" Penelope asked with large, schoolgirl eyes. "I'm famished."

Eli knew she was stalling. His boat to Saint-Nazaire was leaving port in just an hour, and she wanted him to miss it.

"We ate breakfast not long ago," replied Eli.

Penelope's face grew pouty. They walked another block. When the train station came into view, Penelope turned and grabbed Eli's arm. "I don't want you to leave! I want you to stay with me!" she exclaimed, gazing up into his blue eyes.

"You know that's not possible," frowned Eli.

With a look of desperation, Penelope pulled Eli's face down and kissed him. "There, I've done it!" she gasped, her chest heaving, her eyes wide. But when Eli failed to respond, her face grew pouty again. Penelope had never known a man to resist her advances. She eyed Eli questioningly, then said. "Is there something wrong? Don't you feel anything for me?"

Eli sighed. "I told you—"

"Yes, I know, you're married, but...I'm here, and she's not."

Eli shook his head. "That doesn't matter."

Penelope gulped down her emotions and wiped away a tear. She wanted the upstanding Eli even more now. "I need...I need you! I need someone!"

"You will have someone," Eli calmly replied.

"I'm not going back to America! I'm not going back to him! He's an emotionless brute!"

Eli's face filled with concern. He saw in Penelope two futures, one dim and one bright. One in which she gives up her child to an orphanage. That choice would lead to pain and Penelope's death at her own hands. The second future involved Penelope keeping the child and raising her with the help of others. He saw the latter future held more initial pain but would also lead to tremendous joy. "Penelope, you carry with you great promise. You have an important future."

"With you, perhaps," she eagerly nodded.

"No. Not with me." Eli's eyes softened. "You will have a child—a girl. And she will have a child who will grow to influence many."

Penelope's face went blank. She feared she might be pregnant but had told no one. "How...how do you know this?"

"I can only tell you that your future will not be easy. There are many paths you may take. Some will bring pain. A few will bring you joy. It will take time to find peace, but that peace begins on this train to Manchester."

Penelope gazed blankly at Eli, trying to understand his words.

"Now, I must leave you," whispered Eli. "My journey is on another course." He handed the umbrella to her, turned, and left.

Standing in the gentle drizzle before the train station, Penelope watched Eli disappear down the street.

Château de Bret
9 October 1915

THE HILLS around the château were still. The elm and chestnut trees were bare, the flowers on the lily pads closed, and the deep croaking bull-frogs were silent for the winter. Orange and red leaves littered the lonely road to the château, and the gray sky licked at the barren trees as wispy clouds moved past in a slow, tumbling dance. If Michelle listened closely, she could hear the faint baaing of sheep in the back meadow. She pulled her coat tight against the icy afternoon breeze as she walked, crunching the once vibrant leaves into hundreds of tiny flakes.

Michelle looked down the lane. It ran downhill for seventy yards before turning out of sight. Every day on her walks, she imagined seeing her husband coming up the lane. Michelle missed Eli. She missed the texture of his hair, the firmness of his arms, the kindness of his soul. Michelle felt her belly through her coat. At four months pregnant, the coat was tight against her. She wondered what Eli would say when he saw her. She wondered if he would still be attracted to her. She wondered what their life would be like after the baby. The thoughts and uncertainty swirled in her mind as they had every day for weeks. Michelle was used to it now. The uncertainty didn't frighten her anymore. It was now a part of her.

Pausing at where the gravel lane met the country road, Michelle looked toward the vineyard. She missed the days she had visited Eli working there. Michelle breathed in the brisk fall air and watched the empty road, hoping for Eli to appear from around the bend. Ten minutes passed. With a lonely sigh, she turned and started back up the hill.

Michelle was halfway up the lane when she heard a rustling in the trees. She stopped when she heard the *whoo-hoooo, whoo-hoooo* of an owl. Michelle took another step but paused at the sound of leaves crunching and twigs snapping. She turned and scanned the line of trees that faded into the forest. Her eyes darted to the left when she noticed movement. "Is someone there?" she called out, her neck stretched, her body tense, her wary eyes searching the shifting shadows. "Sébastien? Is that you?" she called out, hoping to see her uncle's dog wander from the trees.

Michelle gasped when a doe emerged from the forest. "Oh, you scared me!" Michelle sighed with relief, then happily watched the doe scratch and nose around the straggly blades of grass. She thought it odd when the deer stopped and raised its head to look at her. Michelle's eyes narrowed when the doe darted back into the forest.

With a restless sigh, Michelle turned to start back up the road but screamed when she saw the loathsome Gik standing before her. "What are you doing here!" she cried, nearly falling as she stumbled backward.

The halfborn glared at her with dark, sunken eyes, his coat and slacks shabby, his oily hair dangling.

"What do you want? Leave me at once, or I'll scream for my uncle!"

"He will not hear you," leered Gik as he drew a long, curved knife out from behind his back.

Michelle screamed and raised a halting hand toward the halfborn as she stepped back.

"Where is he?"

"Who?" asked Michelle, pretending not to know as she clutched her pregnant belly.

Gik's dark eyes lowered to Michelle's protruding middle. "He did this to you?" With his dagger pointed, Gik crept closer. "He gave you a baby? I will take it from you."

"No! Don't hurt me!" whimpered Michelle. Clutching her belly, she backed toward the trees.

Gik's glaring eyes raised to the horrified Michelle. "Has he told you who he is? Who he really is?"

"I don't know what you're talking about!"

"Your Elijah is not what you think," Gik seethed.

"Uncle!" Michelle yelled, backing off the road. "UNCLE! SÉBASTIEN! HELP!"

Gik moved closer, eyeing her protruding belly. He waved the blade in a slow, carving motion and hissed, "I will *cut* it from you."

"NO!" Michelle turned and ran into the forest with Gik walking behind. She started up the hill but slipped on the rotting leaves and fell. Dazed by the hard landing, Michelle screamed when she looked back and saw the halfborn standing above her, his blade ready to plunge into her belly. Michelle rolled to her side as Gik stabbed the knife down. The dagger missed her by inches as it pierced the earth. Michelle scrambled to her feet and turned downhill, hoping to find safety on the country road, but that was still fifty yards through the trees. Gasping and sobbing, she ran as fast as she could, dodging the dreary trees and tripping on roots and stones. But as quickly as she moved, the slow yet steady Gik was only steps behind.

When the sobbing Michelle reached a ravine, she slid down its muddy side, but her feet sunk into the rotting ooze at its bottom. "Oh, no! Help me!" Michelle screamed as she fought to free her feet from the ankle-deep sludge. She clawed at the earthen wall as Gik watched from the other side of the ravine. Breathless and out of strength, Michelle turned to the leering halfborn. "Who are you? What do you want from me?"

"I must stop him," glared Gik.

"Why are you hunting us? Why are you after Elijah?"

"Because he is the last of the few."

With some of her strength renewed, Michelle turned and tried to move down the ravine, but the ground was like molasses, and after three steps, she collapsed against the muddy side.

Tired of waiting, Gik started into the ravine, the long, curved blade pointing at the exhausted Michelle, his dark, loathsome gaze fixed on her heaving belly.

Michelle screamed and jumped when a shotgun blast blew pellets through Gik's chest and knocked him into the ravine. She looked up as a staggering Ronan lowered the shotgun and clutched his bleeding side.

"Uncle!" she cried as he dropped to his knees. Upon seeing the motionless Gik face-first in the mire just feet away with the dagger beside him, she began clawing up the slope to her wounded uncle. Michelle was halfway up when she slid down again. After finding a root, she finally pulled herself free.

Gasping for air, Michelle's eyes widened when she noticed the bleeding knife wound and Ronan's pale, wilting face. "Uncle! No! You mustn't! Please!" she pleaded as she eased him into her muddy lap, the still-smoking shotgun on the ground beside him.

"I'm sorry I didn't protect you better," Ronan muttered.

"No, Uncle, you're going to be okay. I'll get you to a doctor," sobbed Michelle. She screamed when she glanced back at Gik rising from the muddy ravine. She had forgotten how he had survived the three-story fall from her Paris apartment.

A bewildered Ronan reached for the shotgun but was too weak to raise it.

Michelle climbed over Ronan, grabbed the shotgun, and pointed it at the steadily approaching halfborn. But when she pulled the trigger, nothing happened.

"You must change to the other barrel," huffed Ronan, weakly pointing to the lever atop the gun's chamber.

Remembering seeing it done, Michelle pushed the lever with a muddy thumb, raised the shotgun to the lumbering Gik, just feet away, and pulled the trigger. Nothing happened. "NO!" Michelle cried as Gik raised his dagger.

Michelle was sobbing with fear when she dropped the empty shotgun and grabbed hold of her dying uncle. Her body trembled as Gik inched closer, his glistening blade about to plunge. Michelle screamed when a large shadow burst through the trees, collided with the halfborn, and knocked him to the ground. "ELIJAH!" she gasped as the watcher wrestled with the bony Gik. Huddled beside her uncle, Michelle watched in horror as the halfborn viciously stabbed his dagger into Eli's ribs.

Finally grabbing the knife from Gik, Eli threw it aside, and with a single punch, dazed the halfborn. Wasting no time, Eli dragged the stunned Gik away from Michelle and Ronan to where he had dropped his satchel.

Gik's eyes widened when Eli removed the glowing orb from his bag. "What are you doing?"

"What should have been done long ago!" bellowed the watcher. With the sphere clutched in Eli's hand, its light filled the shadowed forest until a six-foot-round shimmering portal opened before them. Eli's jaw was tight, and his face determined as he set the orb down and grabbed the panicked Gik by his lapels.

"No! Not there!" cried Gik as Eli pulled the bony halfborn from the ground and hurled him through the swirling doorway. The fiery rift closed with a snap and a rush of air, leaving only the bloody dagger at Eli's feet.

Michelle, who had witnessed the entire incident, gaped at Eli as her legs wobbled.

With his chest heaving, Eli turned to Michelle as her eyes rolled back, and she collapsed to the ground. "Michelle!" Eli hurried to his unconscious wife and quickly examined her for harm. He knew she would be fine, but Ronan's life was slipping away.

After fetching the orb, Eli wiped the dirt from it and hurried to the groaning Ronan. Eli's shoulders sank when he noticed Ronan's bleeding, gaping wounds. He knew saving Ronan's life would be another violation of the Grand Precept—the code that had guided Eli for millennia—but he no longer cared. Eli had seen too many perish from his mistakes and couldn't allow another. He turned to the unconscious Michelle. Eli's heart swelled when he saw her protruding belly. She held their child—his most serious infringement of the code—but Eli wanted only to be with her and to live the life of a mortal.

Breathing in determination, Eli placed one hand on the orb and another on Ronan's head. As the orb began to glow, so did Ronan. It was a diffuse yellow light at first but grew brighter as it emerged from Ronan's eyes, mouth, and stab wounds. As Ronan's wounds closed, the light turned to a brilliant white. After gasping in air, Ronan's eyes shot open, and he jolted to life. When Eli released the orb and took his hand from Ronan's head, the light faded, and Ronan fell into a slumber.

Eli glanced back at his unconscious wife as he raised his hand to Ronan's forehead and said, "You will forget."

With a sigh, Eli moved to Michelle and kneeled beside her. Even smeared and caked with mud, her beauty took his breath away. He wished he had never left her. He wished for so many things. Eli considered taking the memory from her as he had Ronan. But then he wondered how hard it would be to live a lie. Eli wondered if it would be a lie should he denounce his calling. He wondered if he already had.

Eli hovered his hand over Michelle's face, then shook his head and muttered, "No, she's my wife. She will bear my child. She has earned the right."

After placing the dimming orb into his bag and pulling it over his shoulder, Eli kneeled, lifted his wife from the leaf-strewn ground, and started up the hill.

CHAPTER 22

ENLIGHTENMENT

When Michelle regained consciousness, she was lying on the sofa near the piano. Her face brightened when she saw Eli smiling down at her. "You've come home!" exclaimed Michelle, embracing him. But her face dimmed when the memory of what had happened returned. "Oh, Elijah, I just had the most terrible dream! That frightful man who attacked us in Paris, he..." She paused when she saw Eli's mud-smeared face.

"My dear, it was not a dream," Eli whispered.

Michelle looked down at her muddy dress. "But...I don't understand." She studied Eli, a thousand questions swirling in her head. "Uncle Ronan!" she cried, trying to stand.

Just then, the front door opened, and a muddy and bewildered Ronan entered with his shotgun in hand.

"Uncle!" gasped Michelle, seeing the blood on his shirt.

"Elijah! You've returned!" exclaimed Ronan.

Eli got to his feet. "Yes. Not long ago."

"Well, it's good to have you back. Strangest thing," frowned Ronan, scratching his head. "I was out hunting, but I can't for the life of me remember what I was hunting! I must have fallen and hit my head."

"Oh, Uncle!" fretted Michelle as she pushed past Eli to Ronan, her eyes fixed on his bloody shirt. "We must get you to the doctor!"

"Whatever for?" Ronan asked as Michelle pulled up his blood-stained shirt.

Michelle stopped and stared at his slight paunch. There were no stab wounds, only his white belly hair over smooth skin.

"I must have shot something; look at the blood on me, but what, I'm at a loss for," said Ronan, stroking his chin.

Michelle turned to Eli, her mouth gaping, her eyes wide. "He was..." Dying, she was about to say. But instead, she breathlessly asked, "Did you do this? Did you save him?"

Eli gulped, uncertain of how to respond.

"Thank you," Michelle whispered.

"Whatever happened to you two?" asked Ronan, eyeing their muddy clothes. "I know you're glad to see Eli, but couldn't you at least wait until you were upstairs?"

Michelle held back a stupefied laugh and watched Ronan go up the steps, shaking his head. She looked at Eli in dismay when she realized her uncle had no memory of the attack. The whirlwind of thought and emotion was nearly more than Michelle could bear. She told herself what she had seen in the forest was not possible. But then she remembered Eli's miraculous recovery in the hospital. Michelle had known from the day she met Eli that there was something fantastic about him. She thought of what the Italian reporter had said. Even the murderous halfborn had warned her that Eli was not who she thought he was. For an instant, Michelle was terrified. She wondered who this man was she had fallen in love with—who she had married. *Was he even a man?* But then, a strange tranquility overcame her. As Michelle looked into Eli's caring blue eyes, her heaving chest calmed, and her clenched fists relaxed. Her panic subsided until she saw only the man she so dearly loved and missed. With tears filling her eyes, Michelle rushed into Eli's arms and kissed him.

DAYLIGHT WAS FADING outside the bedchamber window as Eli lay beside his wife, gently stroking her naked belly, the corner fireplace cracking and popping, their muddy clothes strewn across the floor.

"Thank you for saving my uncle," Michelle whispered, running her hands through Eli's hair, her eyes searching his not in fear but wonder.

Eli humbly nodded.

"Thank you for saving me," she added with tears in her eyes.

"I could never let anything happen to you."

Michelle's smile pushed a tear down her cheek. "We missed you," she breathed, stroking her belly.

Eli's heart sank as he felt Michelle's pain. Two months passed in the blink of an eye to an immortal, but to an expectant mother, worried for her and her child's future, those same two months seemed an eternity. "I'm sorry I left you." Eli kissed her.

"I feared you wouldn't return," whispered Michelle, choking down her emotions as tears wet her pillow.

"I'm sorry I worried you." Eli wiped the tears from Michelle's cheek. "Have you been ill with the child?"

"Some. But I think it was mostly missing you."

Eli nodded. While there were human emotions he still struggled to understand, loneliness was no longer one of them.

Michelle stroked Eli's square jaw. "I worried you wouldn't want me with my fat belly." She giggled when Eli slid down and kissed her flush belly button.

They made love again, and Michelle wept with joy.

Sinking back into his pillow, Eli stared at the coffered ceiling as Michelle wrapped around him. "I should have stayed. It was all for nothing," he said with a sigh.

"I don't understand, Elijah. Where did you go?" Michelle asked, raising on her elbow to better see his face. "You said you were going east, but your telegrams came from America."

Eli grew pensive. "I was trying to stop this terrible war. Something I could have...*should have* prevented."

Michelle shook her head. "Elijah, how could you possibly stop it? How could you have prevented it? And who was that despicable man who wanted to kill our baby? Where did you send him? How did you save my uncle's life? Please, I have so many questions. I trust you completely, but I need to know."

Eli looked into Michelle's pleading eyes. He considered all that would change should he tell her. Eli got off the bed and moved to the wingback chair, where his satchel lay buried under his coat. He opened it and removed the orb.

Michelle sat up when she spotted the golden ball. She curiously watched as Eli climbed back into bed, holding it in his palm between them. "What is it?" she breathed, captivated by the orb's design and luster.

"It is called a domain sphere."

"I've never heard of such a thing," frowned Michelle. "Where did you get it? What does it do?" she asked, reaching a tentative hand to the strange, flowing text that wrapped the orb. She pulled her hand back before touching it.

"The sphere does many things. It's a source of power and direction. It harnesses and focuses the energy of this earth. There are portals around the earth—conduits that lead to other spaces and realms. The orb focuses their power to create travel conduits. It can open space."

"I don't understand," Michelle frowned. "Open space? What does that mean?"

Eli's brow furrowed in thought. "The cake Madame Duguay made for our wedding had different layers."

"Yes, four," Michelle nodded.

"Our space—the one you and I live in—is like the delicious crème frosting in one of those layers. There is frosting above us and frosting below; only we can't see it because of the cake."

Michelle lay back on the bed, struggling to keep the concept in her head. She looked at the orb. "Where did you get it?"

"It belonged to my mentor. There used to be more of them. This may be the last one."

"I'm so confused, Elijah. Who are you? Why do you have this ball?"

Eli sighed, wondering if he was making another mistake. "I'm not exactly like you."

Michelle was unfazed when she whispered, "I know."

Eli studied Michelle, impressed by her astuteness. "We were brought to this world long ago. In the beginning, when the process was complete, we helped early humans grow and learn. We gave them the skills to survive, to thrive."

"The process?"

"The creation."

Michelle's eyes widened. "Like in Genesis?"

Eli nodded. "That is one account. There are many."

"So...it's real?" asked Michelle, her face filled with wonder.

"The bible story is symbolic. The creation of life on this world took millions of years and much effort by the designers. We arrived when the younglings received the breath of life."

"The breath of life?"

"Their souls," explained Eli. "The light and intelligence that sets humans apart from the animals."

Michelle's lips parted, and her eyes drifted across the bedchamber. "So...there is a God."

"Yes, but not as you have been taught. They are the chief designers —the Holy and Great Ones. They are the creators of your soul—your inner self. There is the Divine Father, and there is the Divine Mother. It's the way of things throughout the universe."

A visibly dazed Michelle shook her head. "I must be dreaming."

"You are not," said Eli with tender blue eyes.

Michelle rubbed her head. After gazing across the room in thought, she turned to Eli. "If-if you've been here from the beginning...you must be...*old*."

"Ancient, by your reckoning, but because of our calling, we don't age the same as you."

"You're not...*human*?"

"I'm human, just different."

"You're immortal."

Eli sighed. "I no longer want to be."

"Are you an angel?" Michelle gasped and pulled the sheet over her. "My god, have I been sleeping with an angel?"

Eli wanted to laugh but only grinned. "No. Angels are simply messengers that pass through the layers of the cake. They can be quite annoying sometimes."

Oblivious to Eli's attempt at humor, Michelle's brow tightened. She felt her baby and asked, "Elijah, how many wives have you had? How many children?"

Eli gazed into Michelle's eyes and whispered, "None before you. You're the only one."

"How could that be?"

Eli shrugged. "It was against our directive. That wasn't our task. We were only to guide. We are forbidden to interfere. We cannot take or preserve a mortal life. We're only to teach and advise."

"But my uncle?"

Eli looked down and sighed. "I've watched too many suffer and die because of my mistakes. I couldn't let him perish."

"Your mistakes?"

"There are dark forces at work in the shadows of this world whispering secret plans into the ears of those who crave power."

"I don't understand."

"Not long after we arrived, there was a rebellion. Sides were chosen. Most of our order stayed on the designed path—to guide and elevate humankind. But one called Semjaza wanted more."

"Semjaza...he's like you?" asked a wide-eyed Michelle.

"He is of my order, but he is not like me," frowned Eli. "Semjaza and his followers abused their power. They used their abilities to manipulate mortals—to feed on their basic human instincts. Greed. Power. Hate. Semjaza recognized that by instilling fear, they could have power over the mortals and become more than guides and teachers. They could be masters. They could be gods. It happened gradually. We thought we could manage it, but we couldn't. Wars ensued. They raged for a thousand years. When all was thought lost, the last hope to save humanity was the great cleansing."

Michelle's eyes shifted in thought. "The flood?"

Eli nodded. "Those not destroyed were cast out. Or so we thought. After the new beginning, there was a betrayal. The abyss was opened. Lu, one of Semjaza's disciples, returned to your world and brought others."

"Others?" asked Michelle, unable to hide her amazement.

"Yes. Like the one who tried to harm you."

Michelle gulped.

"After that, there was much debate. Some thought the balance between good and evil was necessary. But good is often naïve and evil cunning. The evil ones never intended to maintain the balance. They wanted only their power and dominion back. By then, it was too late. The Great Ones vowed not to interfere again...until the end times, when the process is complete, and the *Ihidaya* returns."

"The *Ihidaya*?" asked Michelle.

"The Chosen One who will make all things right, free the damned, and usher in this world's end."

Michelle stared across the bedchamber for a time, then muttered, "So, he was right."

"Who was right?"

"Before we left Paris, after my father's funeral, a reporter—his name was Nazaro, I think—asked about you." Michelle's brow furrowed in realization. "He was telling the truth."

Eli nodded. "Cleto Nazario."

"You know him?"

"He is...tenacious. He writes for the Vatican newspaper, but seeking us out is his passion." When Eli saw Michelle's concern, he added, "He's harmless."

"So, he's not like that terrible man who tried to kill our baby?"

"No."

"Who was that dreadful man? Is he one of them?"

"He's their servant." Eli's gaze turned to Michelle's swollen belly. He wondered how she would respond if she knew Gik was the offspring of a watcher and a mortal.

"How many of you are there?" Michelle asked, her eyes wide.

"There were two hundred in the beginning. A third were cast out."

"But they've returned?"

"A few of them. Lu is now their leader. He's the one behind this war."

Michelle shook her head. "Why? Why would he want something so terrible? This war has caused only misery, suffering, and death!"

Eli sighed. "That's how some try to bring about change. Creation through destruction. Control through fear. It's about power—wanting it and keeping it."

"How many of the good watchers are there?"

"I don't know. Lu has destroyed many."

"He tried to destroy you!"

Eli nodded.

"Who betrayed you and brought Lu back?"

Eli's brow furrowed. "I don't know."

Michelle embraced her husband and kissed his forehead. "Will the Great Ones punish you for helping me? For saving my uncle?"

"I don't know."

Michelle's eyes narrowed in thought as she caressed Eli's back. "When I met you in the hospital, you were badly wounded and remembered nothing. How can that be if you are truly immortal?"

Eli shook his head. "I don't know what happened to me. When we failed at stopping the war—"

"There were others beside you trying to stop it?"

"Yes. Cyrus, the grand overseer. Lu tried to destroy him." Eli's gaze trailed off. "I thought he was successful..."

"But how? If you're immortal?"

"We're not impervious to all things. Lu used a blazerod, an ancient weapon from the First Age—before the cleansing. They were used to remove...the impure."

"The silver rod that ghoul tried to kill you with in the ambulance—that he took from my house!" exclaimed Michelle.

Eli nodded. "It was after that—after we failed in Sarajevo—that I noticed it."

"Noticed what?"

"I began to bleed. It happened slowly at first, but my body began to change. It was as though I was becoming mortal." Eli shook his head. "It was both exhilarating and terrifying. I blamed myself for the war. I tried to run away but knew I couldn't. I realized I had to do something, even though I might die. I hated myself. By the time I got to the front, I only wanted to die! I wanted to pay for my failings!" Eli sighed. "Out of the millennia I have lived, out of the thousands of lives I have guided, I learned more about myself and humanity in those few months living in a muddy trench as a mortal than ever before."

Michelle's face was full of compassion as she placed her hand on Eli's.

"Then fell the German shell. It killed my friend and took my memories." Eli locked eyes with Michelle. "That's when I met you. I don't know why the Great Ones allowed it. I don't know if it was a punishment or a reward, but it comforted my yearning soul. It was the realization of my dreams. You are my dream come true. I will give everything up for you. To live and grow old with you. To one day be laid in the ground and change to dust with you. To be in the next realm with you."

With tears running down her cheeks, Michelle leaned into Eli and kissed him. She sat back and looked at the orb with sad, knowing eyes. "But Elijah, how can that be? What you have done—what you are meant to do—is more important than—"

Eli placed a hushing finger on Michelle's lips. "All of my existence, I have tried to make a difference. I have tried to inspire good. I have tried to counter evil, but it has all been for naught. Mankind continually chooses destruction over creation, death over life, evil over good. I have failed," he sighed. "I want the responsibility no more. I only want to be with you—to live away from the world, to have *a family*, and finally have peace."

Michelle wiped away her tears as Eli caressed her protruding belly. "I love you," she breathed.

Eli was steeped in thought when his stern gaze turned to the dulled orb. With a determined sigh, he gathered up the sphere and walked across the bedchamber to a steamer trunk. He opened its lid, pushed aside folded clothes and blankets, and buried the orb inside. Then, with a look of finality, Eli let the lid fall closed with an echoing *thump*.

Château de Bret
11 December 1915

MICHELLE STROKED her growing belly as she gazed out the bedchamber's frosty window across the back lawn to the misty forest. She glanced back at the empty bed and wondered where her husband was. She exited their bedchamber and looked down over the railing to the great room. The manor was shadowed and quiet, with the early morning light glowing through the library windows. Her head turned at the faint sound of Madame Duguay at work in the kitchen.

Michelle was about to return to the bedroom when she noticed the door at the end of the hall open. She stepped across the cold wood floor and stopped when she spotted Eli sitting in the darkness, his legs folded and his eyes closed. She had seen him meditating more lately and wondered if it was a reason for concern.

Michelle quietly made her way back to the bedchamber. She eyed the welcoming feather bed and wondered if she might fall back to sleep. When Michelle felt a draft, her gaze turned to the steamer trunk across the room. She moved to it, opened its lid, and removed a shawl. Michelle froze when she saw the golden sphere resting between folded sweaters.

Michelle studied the orb. She remembered the glowing characters on it when Eli first showed it to her. It was a dull gold now, lacking in its previous luster. Gulping, Michelle reached down to it. Her fingers hovered an inch from its smooth surface.

The orb came to life when Michelle touched it, flooding her with its golden, shimmering light. She gasped, and her eyes widened as the room grew into a vast expanse. She viewed the world and the millions of suffering, frightened, and confused souls that filled it. More than that, Michelle felt their pain. The view quickly changed. She saw the limitless universe as if traveling like a photon of light. She viewed the energy that joins and moves matter everywhere.

Michelle pulled her finger from the orb and sank to the floor, her breast heaving.

"What did it show you?"

Michelle looked up to see her husband filling the doorway. "I'm sorry. I shouldn't have touched it," she breathed, her face filled with wonder.

Eli's brow furrowed, knowing most mortals would experience nothing touching the orb. "That's all right," he said in a loving tone. "You saw something when you touched it."

"Yes," Michelle gulped. "How did you know?"

"I felt it from the other room."

Michelle was still catching her breath as she looked down at the dimmed golden orb resting in the trunk. "I saw..." She gulped and looked back at Eli.

Eli moved to Michelle, took her by the hand, and led her to the bed where they sat. "It's okay. Tell me what you saw."

Michelle's eyes welled with tears. "I saw *everything*," she breathed.

Eli held her hand.

"It was as though I was a bird flying around the world and then out into space through the stars," she whispered. "I saw...I felt something."

"Yes?" Eli prodded.

"I felt an energy I've never felt before...a connection," she whispered.

"Yes."

"It was...it was love."

Eli nodded warmly.

"I have never felt such a thing in all my life." Michelle's eyes welled with tears. "I...saw...*my mother*," she barely managed, her voice straining with emotion. "She was young and happy and out of pain."

Eli marveled at the radiance of Michelle's being.

"I saw *her* mother too." Michelle's awestruck gaze moved across the room. "And *her* mother before her. And *her* mother next. There were dozens of mothers—maybe fifty of them—going back to..." Michelle's eyes shifted in thought. "We all shared a bond. They were all young, like me—together in the same space. We were all connected. It was as though we were in a place without time. I saw myself in all of them. I saw my soul. It was like a light bursting through me," Michelle joyfully laughed. But then she again turned serious. "And then...I saw something else." Michelle's eyes moved back to Eli's. She wiped away her tears and gulped. "Did I have a hallucination? I've treated soldiers who have had them. What's wrong with me, Elijah?"

Eli's face brightened with a smile. "There is nothing wrong with you, my darling." He held Michelle closely as she sobbed.

CHAPTER 23
THE CALL

The snow was falling outside the tall window, leaving the grounds of Château de Bret pristine and white. Inside the great room, Michelle sat awkwardly at the piano, her large pregnant belly ballooning before her otherwise slender form as she played Chopin. Before the cozy fireplace, Ronan puffed on his pipe while Eli read a book on Roman history, chuckling and frowning at the miswritten parts he had witnessed.

Michelle was in the middle of Debussy's "Rêverie" when she stopped playing and released a painful groan.

"Are you all right, my dear?" asked Ronan, looking around his wing-back chair.

Michelle cringed as she held her belly, and nodded when Eli got up from his chair and approached. "I'm okay...I think. I get these pains from time to time."

"Is the baby coming?" asked a concerned Ronan.

"I hope not. The doctor tells me I have four weeks more. But look at me! I'm already about to pop!" She looked up at Eli and laughed, "I think I have a giant in here."

Eli couldn't hide his worry. He had seen too many moral women perish birthing a watcher's child. Eli had told himself Michelle was different, that she would be fine, that she was strong and brave. But in the shadows of his thoughts, Eli feared his act of love might destroy the most precious thing in his life. He refused to imagine living without Michelle. *She'll be fine*, he had told himself over and over. *Even if she has complications, I have the power of the orb to assist me.* But the finicky orb had abandoned Eli more than once, and now he had abandoned it. With the watcher trying to forget his duty, he had not touched the mystical sphere since burying it in the trunk four months before. He hoped he would never have to look at it again.

"I'm better now," Michelle said breathlessly.

Eli studied his wife; she seemed faint and unsteady, with beads of sweat on her brow. "Can I help you to bed?"

"I think I'll be fine," Michelle stubbornly replied. But when she took a step, her legs faltered.

Eli caught Michelle as her legs gave way. He cradled her in his arms as she looked on in embarrassment.

"I don't know what happened," Michelle nervously replied.

"You're with child, is what happened," said Ronan, still watching from his chair.

"Elijah, you should put me down. I'll break your back."

"Don't be silly. I'm taking you to bed," replied Eli.

"That's what got you into this predicament in the first place," smirked Ronan, turning back to the fireplace.

Michelle laughed. "Quite right, Uncle. And it will all be worth it once I'm swaddling our lovely child!" She wrapped her arms around Eli's neck, kissed him, and looked into his caring eyes.

Eli forced a smile as he carried Michelle up the stairs, her dress and legs draped over his arm. After entering their bedchamber, Eli gently laid her on their bed, but Michelle kept her arms around his neck and pulled him in for another kiss.

"Thank you for taking such wonderful care of me—and my uncle too."

Eli nodded.

"I'm the luckiest woman in all the world to have a husband like you," she whispered, her wonder-filled eyes searching his.

"I'm more fortunate to have you," said Eli, his loving concern visible through his smile.

With a sparkle in her eye and a contented sigh, Michelle lowered her head onto the pillow. She patted her round belly and groaned, "Look at me."

"You have never looked more beautiful. Now you must rest."

"If you say so," sighed Michelle, settling into the soft comforter.

When Eli came down the stairs and returned to his chair by the fire, Ronan asked, "How is she?"

"Tired," said Eli, trying to hide his worry.

Ronan nodded and puffed on his pipe. After staring at the flickering flames for a time, he said, "It's been some time since we've had a little one roaming about. Michelle may have been the last one, in fact."

Eli turned to Ronan, studied him for a moment, then asked, "Was it sad for you to have no children?"

Ronan shrugged. "It was not our choice. God, in his infinite wisdom, saw fit to give children to indolent paupers instead. My Bridget would have been a wonderful mother, but God decided to take her as well."

"I'm sorry," frowned Eli, feeling Ronan's forgotten pain.

Ronan shook his head. "It's all part of this miserable life." He turned to Eli. "Don't misunderstand; I have prospered greatly," he said, motioning to his lovely home. "I'm referring to the misery all around us. It is as though we are on an island surrounded by an ocean of pain and mindless bloodshed. The war is no closer to ending. Men fight and die on both sides and for what? When it does end, what will it mean?" Ronan looked Eli in the eyes and said, "I fear for the next generation—for your child. What will they inherit? What misery will they be forced to endure at the hands of mindless politicians and monarchs?" Biting on his pipe, Ronan turned back to the fire and quietly seethed.

Eli could not hide his sadness as he studied the flickering flames.

An hour later, Ronan pulled up from his chair and announced his retirement for the night. Eli nodded and returned to his somber ponder-ing. His book was open, but his mind was far away.

It was a little before midnight, and the fire had burned down to glowing embers. Out the great room window, the light of the moon shimmered across the new-fallen snow. Eli stirred from his thoughts when the shadowy great room brightened. He turned in his chair, and his eyes widened when he saw a gleaming white Cyrus standing before the tall window.

"Elijah, why do you hide?" asked Cyrus, his face and eyes shim-mering as if from within.

Eli sat up. "I'm not hiding."

"Your memories have been returned. You possess the sphere, yet you bury it. You do nothing while the world bleeds."

Eli's jaw tightened. "It doesn't matter what I do. I tried. I went where the orb took me, but no one would listen! Lu and his minions have grown too strong." He looked down and sighed. "I fear mankind is lost."

"You left America before it was your time. Your haste to return to your woman jeopardized the world!"

Eli tried to hide his frustration. "I can only do what I know."

"Mankind is only lost if we allow it! There is good still in this world. The end time is not yet. There is still much that must be done," Cyrus insisted.

"But how? How many of us are there left?"

"Few."

Eli shook his head. "We were hundreds! How many of *them* are there now?"

"Far more," frowned Cyrus. "Their numbers grow with the half-born, and their cunning message is sweet in the ears of the power-hungry."

Eli helplessly shrugged. "What are we to do? What can *I* do?"

"You can persevere for the cause of good. Evil will only triumph if good allows it to grow unchecked."

Eli turned back to the dying embers.

"The sphere has been calling you. Why do you not heed it?"

"I cannot. I relinquish my call. I want only to live as a man with my wife and our child."

Cyrus's eyes narrowed. "You know that cannot be. The die has been cast. Your path is not as a mortal. You have a higher role."

Eli sighed. "There's nothing I can do." He turned to Cyrus and asked, "What will happen to Michelle? Will she survive giving birth?"

"Her future is undecided. It depends on you. You must make a choice, Elijah. If you forfeit your call, you may save Michelle, but the world will be lost!"

Eli stared blankly at the overseer. "And what if I heed the call?"

"Then you will allow mankind another chance."

"But...Michelle?"

Cyrus shook his head. "She will be taken from you."

"I don't understand why I can't have both! Why am I being punished? After all that I've done? Why can't they let me have peace?"

Cyrus eyed the watcher. "I've long feared your interest in mortals would be your downfall. But I didn't foresee it would cause the end of humanity. I'm surprised by your selfishness and shortsightedness," seethed the overseer. "You would have made only an average mortal."

"What do you want from me?" fumed Eli.

"Is the great Elijah rethinking his retirement?"

Eli sighed. "Why must it be so difficult?"

"To live as an immortal? To never fear the taste of death?" scoffed Cyrus. "Mortals aspire to such heights!"

"The *taste* of death will not leave my mouth," glared Eli. "I have witnessed it for far too long. And it's only the promise of life that allows me to endure it."

"You think too much like a mortal," frowned Cyrus. "You should know better. Their passing is just a doorway to the next realm. Though their end might be violent or calm, it's nothing more."

"But to be robbed of the sweetness of this life! For boys to go to war, never to return! Never to know love—*true love*, never to have a family, to learn and grow old. That was the plan!"

"You are a naïve fool, Elijah." Cyrus watched Eli turn to the fire, then said, "If you fail to heed your call, the balance will be completely upset. It will prematurely usher in the end time. Those who might have been will be lost. The future of this mortal race will be cut short. Are you so selfish to allow such a thing? Do not believe your Michelle and her uncle and everyone else you pretend to love will be spared. All will be lost!"

Eli stared at the dying flames, then shook his head in defeat. He knew Cyrus was right. He could no longer hide and shirk his duty. "Very well," Eli muttered, his head down. "What must I do?"

"As much as I detest saying so, it is up to you," scowled Cyrus.

Eli sighed. "I will do what I must."

"Very well. There is one man who can make a difference; he can inspire and guide millions for good. He can help save the world and spare hundreds of millions of lives from what is to come...*if* he survives. The next twelve hours are critical. Time is drawing short."

Eli watched as the light dimmed and Cyrus disappeared. He sank into the chair and buried his face in his hands. Eli knew it was folly to believe he could abandon his call. Eli wondered if he could still protect Michelle and his child or if they would be just another tossed out of the revolving door of mortality.

After trudging up the stairs, Eli quietly entered their room. He saw Michelle asleep in their bed by the glow of the shimmering moonlight through the window. The watcher moved to the trunk in the corner of the room, kneeled, and lifted its lid. The light from the shimmering orb grew as he removed the clothes and blankets from the trunk. With an anxious sigh, Eli took hold of the glowing sphere. The swirling characters on its side changed at his touch. When he lifted the orb from the trunk, its golden light illuminated Eli's face and much of the room.

Michelle stirred in the bed, then sat up and groggily asked, "Elijah, what's happening?"

Eli's worried gaze moved from the glowing orb to his wife. He had to tell Michelle, but feared how she would react.

Eli got to his feet. He cradled the glowing orb as he moved to her bedside.

"What's it doing?" Michelle asked, now fully awake.

"It's calling for me," Eli whispered, watching for her response in the golden light.

"Calling for you?" Michelle's face filled with worry. "What does that mean?"

Eli gulped. "Cyrus came to me tonight. Something terrible is about to happen. Something only I can prevent."

"Oh, no, Elijah," groaned Michelle.

"I'm sorry, my love. I must leave you, but I won't be long," Eli whispered.

Michelle shook her head as her eyes welled with tears. "Last time you said that you were gone for months! I'll have this baby soon! What will I do if you're not here?"

"I'll be here, I promise," Eli assured her, fearing he might not.

Michelle wiped at her tears, her cheeks quivering. "It's important?"

"It could mean the difference," breathed Eli.

"It could end the war?"

Eli gulped. "Cyrus says it could save hundreds of millions from misery and death."

Michelle sank back into her bed. "I-I cannot stop you. It's too great a thing! Go. Go quickly, but you must promise to come back to me. You must promise to come back to both of us!"

With tears filling his eyes, Eli nodded and kissed Michelle. After moving to his wardrobe, he changed into wool trousers, a sweater, and boots as Michelle quietly sobbed from their bed. After pulling on his coat, Eli returned to his heartbroken wife and placed his hand on her swollen belly.

"Ah! The baby jumped at your touch!" Michelle tearfully exclaimed.

Fighting back emotions Eli had never known, he kissed Michelle again. Then, with the orb in hand, he moved to the middle of the room.

Michelle watched unblinkingly as Eli placed his right hand on top of the glowing orb. She gasped, shielding her eyes from the brightness as a round, shimmering doorway appeared. Michelle's jaw slackened when she saw a darkened field through the opening. She wondered how such a thing could be in the middle of their bedchamber. "I love you!" she cried as Eli glanced back at her with sad, longing eyes. Feeling the draft from the cold, dark field, Michelle watched as Eli stepped through the rift. With a *snap* and a gust of air, the doorway closed, leaving Michelle sobbing alone in her bed.

CHAPTER 24
NEVER SURRENDER

PLOEGSTEERT WOOD, BELGIUM
28 FEBRUARY 1916

The bitter night air had frosted the barren trees white. Below the stumps and blast-splintered oaks, men in drab wool coats and blankets huddled in the trenches to keep warm. Eli surveyed the shivering British soldiers, their flat helmets icy, their grumbling breath billowing before them. A few of them curiously watched the large Eli walk up the crowded support trench in civilian attire, the weight of his boots snapping and cracking the ice between the duckboards.

As Eli made his way through the network of trenches, he thought of his time at the front. A year had passed. While the battle lines had changed little in those months, tens of thousands more had died. Eli had learned much about himself and humanity in that year. It saddened him humanity had learned so little about itself.

"Hey mate, wha' you doin' here?" grunted a ruddy-faced, pug-nosed sergeant.

"I'm here to see your Sixth Battalion commander," Eli replied in English.

"Well, you jus' don't come walzin' up here like that. This is the bleedin' fron' line. In case you haven't noticed, there's a bleedin' war on! You should go back to your pigs and sheep before you get hurt," scowled the sergeant.

Eli didn't move. "I'm here to interpret for the colonel."

"You're an interpreter?" scoffed the sergeant. "The Royal Scots Fusiliers don't need no bloody Flem to interpret; we does our talk'n with bullets and bloody bayonets! We know bloody good and well what them damn Bosch are sayin' when we tear their guts open!"

Behind the sergeant, bundled soldiers with frost glistening off their helmets nodded and grunted their support.

Unfazed by the sergeant's bluster, Eli shrugged and said, "Then I'll let you deal with the colonel."

The belligerent sergeant's posturing faded as Eli turned and started back down the icy trench. "Wait."

Eli kept walking.

"I said, wait!" barked the sergeant. "The colonel sent for you?"

Eli nodded but didn't stop.

"Well, why didn't you say so!" gushed the sergeant as the other men watched with bent brows. "Come on back, mate. Let's get you up to the colonel."

Eli stopped and turned to see the ruddy-faced sergeant backed against the wood planks with a muddy coat arm pointing up the trench. "Jus' continue up the way. Take a right on Bristols' Avenue, then go up to Red Fanny. The command post's 'bout twenty paces past that on the left."

"Thank you," Eli nodded as he moved past the smaller men, who were impressed by his size.

"Don't you want a helmet, mate?" asked a corporal.

Eli paused and turned. "I was at Reims. Tin pots do nothing against a German shell. They're only good for keeping the bird dung off you."

"Blimey," muttered a round-eyed private.

The sergeant's gaze lifted through the splintered trees to the clear morning sky as Eli continued up the support trench.

Maneuvering by tired and bored soldiers smoking, eating, and nervously chatting, Eli crossed planked-over shell craters and passed blood-spattered sandbags. He saw frosted strips of cloth hanging from tree branches in the still morning air, but heard no rifle or artillery fire.

When Eli came to the roughly made sign, *Red Fanny Way*, he turned down a side trench.

"What can I do for you, mate?" asked a mustached captain outside the sandbag-reinforced command bunker.

"I'm here to assist the colonel as an interpreter," Eli reported.

"An interpreter?" frowned the captain. "I wasn't aware. HQ sent you up? Let me see your orders."

"I have none," sighed Eli.

"Well, I can't let you in without papers," insisted the captain. "You're not even in uniform!"

"I must speak with the colonel," Eli persisted.

"And what's that in your bag? You could be a bloody spy with a bomb, for all I know!"

Frowning, Eli pulled his satchel from his shoulder, opened it, and held it before the wary captain. When the gold light from the glowing orb illuminated the officer's face, Eli looked into the captain's spellbound eyes and sternly said, "I must see the colonel. Now."

Blinking, the captain nodded. "Right. I'll take you to the colonel."

In a dark corner of the command post bunker, separated from the other officers by a rat-chewed curtain, a round-headed colonel with a receding hairline sat on the edge of his bed, staring at the dirt floor. On the thin, sagging mattress beside him lay his service pistol. Weighed down by his failures and the loss of life they had brought, the colonel's forlorn gaze drifted to the revolver. He saw no way back. The war would rage on, but he would not make another mother childless.

Choking a swallow down his parched throat, the colonel reached for the pistol. He studied its smooth barrel and bullet-filled cylinder. He thought it a cruel irony he had sent so many to their deaths but had never himself fired the revolver in anger. His life would be its first.

With bleak determination, the colonel raised the revolver to his temple. After filling his chest with his last breath, his finger tightened on the trigger. He hoped his wife and children would forgive him.

"Sir," the spellbound captain called from the other side of the curtain.

The colonel's eyes opened. Irritated and yet relieved, he lowered the pistol. "What do you want?"

"I'm sorry to bother you, sir. I have someone here for you from HQ."

Eli stood behind the captain with his head bent under the low beams. He glanced back through the smoke-filled bunker at the officers gathered around the map table. The hanging lantern shadowed their drawn faces as they eyed Eli.

"Who is it?" barked the colonel, buttoning up his tunic behind the curtain.

"He's an interpreter, sir," replied the captain, coming out of his spell and wondering what he was doing.

With his satchel over his shoulder, Eli watched as the curtain snapped open to the round-headed officer. Eli's eyes narrowed. He saw the man's pain and his potential.

"Lieutenant-Colonel Winston Churchill," grunted the dire man as he looked up at the foot-taller Eli. "What do I need a bloody interpreter for?"

STILL IN HER nightgown and robe, an exhausted Michelle held her pregnant belly as she carefully descended the stairs to the smell of eggs, porridge, and coffee.

"My dear, are you feeling better?" Ronan asked, setting down his paper and standing. "Madame Duguay could have brought you breakfast."

"I'm better today," Michelle nodded, not at all looking like it.

"I haven't seen Elijah yet this morning," Ronan said, snapping his newspaper open.

Michelle gulped. "He had to leave early."

"Oh? Into town?"

"No. Farther," Michelle replied, unable to hide her worry.

"Oh." Ronan's brow furrowed, not understanding. "For how long?"

"Not long, he said. He needed to help with the war effort," Michelle shrugged as she gingerly sat at the table.

"Poor fellow. He can't go back and fight but wants to make a difference. Commendable," Ronan nodded. "Has his memory come back fully then?"

"Yes," Michelle replied as Madame Duguay placed a steaming coffee before her.

"And no skeletons in the closet?"

Michelle's face paled. "I-I don't know what you mean."

Ronan studied his niece. "No dark secrets or surprises? He doesn't have a harem, or is a wanted train robber?"

"No, nothing like that," Michelle awkwardly laughed.

"Well, that's good. But his timing isn't, is it?" Ronan eyed Michelle's belly as if it might burst at any moment.

When Michelle felt Madame Duguay's disapproving gaze, she sat up and forced a smile. "It's a very urgent matter, it seems, and I support my husband wholeheartedly!"

Ronan nodded. "As you should, but I hope he isn't gone too long. He still has duties here, even in the winter."

Michelle felt the baby kicking inside of her. "I'm sure he won't be long."

Winston Churchill's dour face and sagging brow remained unchanged as Eli spoke from across the small, makeshift table. The dwindling candle between them dripped wax onto a letter to Churchill's wife as it flickered off the golden orb. With only the rat-chewed curtain separating them from the rest of the command post, Eli's words were quiet but direct.

Churchill sat back on the bench, his questioning gaze moving from the dull luster of the curious orb back to Eli. "What you're telling me... it's a mite hard to swallow," Churchill frowned as he chewed on a cigar. "A year ago, I was First Lord of the Admiralty, for God's sake. Now look at me. I'm buried in a rat's hole, waiting for a German shell to drop on my head. But you're telling me I have some grand purpose?" Churchill shook his head and laughed. "I might have believed you a year ago, before Gallipoli...the crowning work in my catalog of blunders."

"What you have experienced—all you have been through—will prepare you for what is to follow."

"I don't believe you," Churchill grunted. "My parliamentary days are over. The thousands of boys crying from their graves will see to that."

Eli studied the failed leader for a moment, then said, "This war will end, peace will return, but it will be a shallow peace. The world will remain in unrest. Opportunities will arise for both good and evil. Choices will be made. You will have to choose as well. But if you do not survive this war or fail to embrace your destiny, what follows will be far worse."

"Another war, no doubt," Churchill grumbled. "History is replete with them, and they will assuredly carry on with or without me."

Eli's blue eyes narrowed. "Do you believe in evil?"

Churchill shrugged. "Yes, I see manifestations of it daily."

"Then you must also believe in good."

"Of course. I think they are both in our nature."

Eli nodded. "You are correct, but tell me, are there two more opposite forces?"

"Good and evil? I should think not."

"What causes one person to care for the misfortunate and another to take advantage while a third does nothing?"

Churchill pulled his chewed cigar from his teeth. "I should think it dependent upon the person. Some are more charitable than others. Self-preservation—selfishness and greed are certainly empowering forces. I have seen them firsthand."

"If evil is inherent in all, why do only some succumb?"

"I think given the right opportunity, one might choose either path or, most easily, none at all."

"You are correct again," nodded Eli.

"You're quite a philosopher, aren't you?"

"I have known many philosophers, but I am not one. But let me ask another question. Of the two, which is more common?"

"I should hope good, but I fear the answer is evil," frowned Churchill.

"Which comes most naturally to man?"

Churchill considered the question for a moment. "Unlike my Church of England friends, I believe we are born good but learn to do evil."

Eli gave a subtle nod, and his eyes narrowed. "From the beginning, it was intended for humankind to live in balance. Good—love and charity—are in your divine nature, but you are subject to evil forces as well, such as hatred and greed. The test was to learn and grow from one's choices and the consequences they brought. But the balance was disturbed. The test was corrupted. Some of those entrusted to teach and guide humankind unleashed the hidden powers of darkness. Like cancer, these dark powers eat away and disfigure the human body. If unchecked, they will consume and destroy all."

"If this is true and there is a God, why does he not put a stop to it?"

"Once introduced into the equation, these forces cannot be removed; they can only be countered. These forces for evil are now part of the test."

Churchill chewed on his cigar as he studied Eli, then grunted, "Poppycock. I have nothing more to offer my country. I will finish my command, whether alive or dead."

Eli glanced at the revolver on the colonel's bed. "You are too valuable a soul to squander your life."

Churchill's brow tightened. "There can be honor in death."

"There is more honor in living and fulfilling one's destiny."

Still unconvinced, Churchill sighed. "If I survive...I will return to Oxfordshire with my dear Clementine and see if I can be some kind of father to my children. My political life is finished."

Eli studied the colonel.

"You are indeed an interesting chap, and it has been a rather invigorating conversation, but if you'll excuse me, I have some rather important business to attend to." Churchill gave a parting nod and began to stand.

Seeing no other way, Eli placed his right hand on the sphere; it immediately came to life, glowing between his fingers.

Churchill's eyes widened at the shimmering orb as Eli placed his other hand on the colonel's arm. Churchill sank back on the bench; his jaw slackened and his face paled as glimpses of unparalleled warfare and destruction flashed through his mind. In an instant, he saw the blood-red Nazi flag, millions of German soldiers standing in formation, acres of tanks the likes he had never before seen, and a sky darkened by bombers. He saw burning cities, piles of bodies, miles of tattered, fleeing refugees, and the crying faces of starving children.

Churchill gasped, and his cigar fell from his mouth. His frazzled gaze moved from the still shimmering orb to a calm Eli, and he breathlessly asked, "What did I see? The future?"

"You saw *a* future. There is much still in motion—choices to be made—decisions that will shape the world for decades to come." Eli looked into Churchill's eyes. "Despite your flaws, you have the unique talents to help save this world—not by yourself, but with the help of others."

Churchill's eyes flashed in thought as he tried to fathom the stakes. He wondered how he had come so close to taking his own life. "I've always believed I had a destiny," he whispered. "I assumed my course was altered. That my failures had done me in."

"Failure is the ladder that leads to one's destiny," Eli explained. "But you mustn't look too far ahead. The ladder of destiny can only be grasped one rung at a time."

Churchill's brow wrinkled, and he shook his head in dismay. "What must I do?"

"You must never give up on yourself. You must never give up on your nation or the world around you. You must never surrender."

<hr />

CHÂTEAU DE BRET
6 MARCH 1916

THE HILLS above the château were quiet as millions of tiny shimmering crystals floated down through the empty trees.

Eli's boots crunched on the white blanket of snow as he entered the clearing. He paused and looked through the gently swirling snowflakes to the leafless trees that surrounded him. They stood tall and proud, and he felt them judging him. Eli turned to the gentle mound of snow in the center of the clearing. He moved to it, kneeled, and wiped the snow off the smooth stone lid. He then carefully moved it aside.

Eli stared into the empty stone box as he considered his counsel to Churchill. He imagined Cyrus standing before him and giving the same counsel. Eli told himself he wasn't giving up. He told himself he wasn't quitting. He was beginning. Eli told himself he had done enough for the world; now it was *his* time.

Eli pulled the satchel from his shoulder and opened it. The domain sphere was dark within. He considered removing the orb, but instead placed the entire bag inside the stone box. Then, his face tight with determination, he replaced the stone lid.

Eli's shoulders sank as he felt the burden lifted from him. But his billowing breath of relief was lost in the sudden gust that sent the gentle snowflakes reeling sideways. Eli looked up at the trees, their branches waving fingers of scorn.

The surrendered watcher climbed to his feet, turned, and left the clearing as the forest whistled its disdain.

Eli hadn't been gone long when Lu emerged from the swirling snow. The fallen watcher's red beard was bent in the wind as his fierce green eyes moved to the stone box.

CHAPTER 25
THE BARGAIN

Château de Bret
7 March 1916

It was a dull and quiet night. Ronan was reading the evening paper in his chair before the fireplace, and Michelle was listlessly playing the piano when the front door opened.

"You're back!" exclaimed a surprised Ronan as Eli entered with his boots in hand.

Eli's worried gaze quickly found his pregnant wife at the piano.

"You're home!" Michelle gasped, stumbling across the rug to her husband.

Eli dropped his boots and rushed to Michelle. He felt her joyful sobbing as they embraced. "I'm home, and I won't leave you again," he whispered, holding her tightly.

Ronan held the lapels of his dinner jacket as he awkwardly watched. "Well, mission accomplished?" he asked, sitting in his chair by the fireplace.

Eli turned to Ronan, taken aback by his comment.

"I-I told Uncle of your war efforts," beamed Michelle. But her exuberance waned when she saw Eli's uneasiness. "I'm so glad you're home. It's been a week! I feared it would be much longer—that you wouldn't be here for the baby."

"I told you I would be." Eli struggled with a smile, the uncertainty of his decision to give up immortality weighing on him.

"What was it you accomplished?" asked Ronan, lighting his pipe.

"Oh, Uncle, I think Elijah might be weary from his travels," said Michelle.

Eli saw his wife's worry and forced a smile. "I just needed to cheer a friend up. The war had gotten him down, and he needed to know how important he was."

"I'm afraid this war has gotten us all a bit down," nodded Ronan. "Was he just back from the front?"

"He's there now," replied Eli.

"Oh, I see," frowned Ronan, not really understanding.

"How have you been feeling, darling?" Eli asked, turning to a tired but radiant Michelle.

"Like I'm ready to have this baby," she laughed, patting her belly. "But the doctor says it might be *three* more weeks! Look at me! I look as though I've swallowed a watermelon!"

Eli fought to conceal his worry at the terrible risk she faced. "Let's get you off your feet. What can I get for you?"

"Nothing," beamed Michelle, a tear running down her cheek. "I have everything I need with you now here." But she had no sooner said that than her face grimaced in pain.

Eli placed a hand on Michelle's stomach and felt the baby lurch at his touch.

"Oh, I think he's *very* excited to have you home!" gasped Michelle, still feeling the contraction.

"Good gracious! Are you all right?" Ronan asked, leaning from his chair.

"How long does the doctor take to get here?" Eli asked.

"Twenty minutes, once given the word," an increasingly concerned Ronan replied. "Should I send for him?"

Madame Duguay was out of the kitchen now, watching with wringing hands.

Michelle blew out the pain, then looked up at Eli and huffed, "I think-I think it's passing."

"I don't believe the baby will wait three weeks," frowned Eli.

"I don't either," breathed Michelle, reaching for a chair as her legs gave way.

Eli swooped Michelle off her feet and said, "Please send for the doctor," as he carried her up the stairs.

"Oh, I don't think I need him yet," countered a brave Michelle. But she had no sooner said that than another contraction forced a grimace.

"Please inform the doctor she's having pains," urged Eli.

"I'll do that. I'll go for him myself!" Ronan exclaimed, getting up from his chair.

Their eyes were locked as Eli carried the panting Michelle into their room and gently laid her on the feather bed. His face filled with worry when he saw her pain. "Are you all right, darling?"

"Yes, I think it's going away now," she breathed.

Eli gently stroked Michelle's cheek as her eyes closed and her breathing calmed. "I'm sorry I had to leave you," he whispered.

"I'm just happy you've returned," Michelle smiled, her eyes still closed. "I've had this terrible dread that I would have to raise our child without you," she whimpered, a tear streaking down her cheek.

Eli gulped.

After a few minutes, Michelle was breathing easier. "There, it's not so bad now," she smiled, trying to sit up, but Eli gently laid her back down. Michelle's glistening face filled with concern as she looked into his blue, caring eyes. "Elijah, what will become of us?"

"What do you mean?"

"I'm a woman, and you...you're like a god."

Eli furrowed his brow and shook his head. "I am not like a god."

"What will happen when I'm a wrinkled old woman, but you're still a handsome young man?"

"I want to grow old with you."

"But you won't, will you?" Michelle asked searchingly.

Eli sighed. "I don't know."

"Will our son be like you?"

Eli shrugged. "I don't know."

"But you said it's happened before, those like you and women."

Eli nodded. "Some of them are like mortals; some of them are not."

Michelle's eyes widened in realization. "That man who attacked me. The one you cast away who looked so ghastly...he was one, wasn't he?"

Eli's face went blank. He considered lying to her but couldn't. "Yes, he was. How did you know?"

Michelle shrugged. "I just did."

Eli gulped.

"Was he quite old?"

Eli nodded.

"As old as you?"

Eli shook his head.

"Will our son be so ugly?"

Eli laughed. "It's not possible with such a beautiful mother."

"And handsome father," she grinned, pushing another tear down her cheek. Her smile faded, but more tears followed. "Elijah?"

"Yes, darling?" replied Eli, gently stroking Michelle's arm.

"Will I die having our baby?"

Eli's heart sank at the question, and he couldn't hide his despair. "No," he finally managed. "I won't let you."

Michelle placed her hand atop Eli's, forced a weepy smile, and closed her eyes.

DOCTOR NOBERT, a thin man with a bushy mustache and rolled-up sleeves, closed the bedchamber door and moved to the worried Eli, standing in the hall. "It's been eight hours, and the labor is very difficult for her. The baby is large, and she is small." He sighed. "She's losing strength. If she cannot deliver on her own in the next few hours, I'll have to take the baby, but not here. We'll have to move her to the hospital."

Eli ran a hand through his hair, anxiously nodded, and turned away. He knew the too frequent results of mortal women birthing a watcher's child and wondered why he had thought Michelle would be different. Eli closed his eyes when Michelle shrieked in pain. The watcher agonized at knowing he was to blame for her suffering.

The doctor eyed the worried Eli for a moment, then returned to the bedchamber where his nurse was comforting the groaning Michelle.

Eli moved to the railing and looked down over the great room. He didn't see Ronan gazing up from his chair with concern. He didn't see Madame Duguay wringing her hands from outside the kitchen. To Eli, there was only his lovely Michelle writhing in their bed, her life slowly but inevitably slipping away. He hated himself for what he had done to her. The thought Michelle would be better off having never met him tore at Eli, for she had given him everything. More than all the mortals over the thousands of years, she had given him life and a reason to be.

Eli shook his head as he wondered what he could have done differently. Nothing would have changed had he left her when his recollections returned; Michelle already carried his child.

Eli considered the Grand Precept, the body of guiding principles that had shaped the world. He had spent millennia adhering to its law. Guiding humans without interfering was a tenuous task, but he had done all the Great Ones had asked. That all changed after Sarajevo. Eli had lost count of how many times he had violated his oath since then. Lu and his followers had long before rejected the law; Eli now wondered if he was no better than them. In Eli's mind, he had betrayed everything he knew to become something he was not. The thought that his precious Michelle would soon pay the ultimate price for his mistake was more than Eli could bear.

Turning from the railing, Eli marched to the bedchamber door, opened it, and bellowed, "Take her to the hospital and take the baby from her!"

"It's too late! The baby is coming!" cried the nurse.

Eli's face filled with concern when he saw the tortured Michelle, her legs bent and back arched.

"Go out and close the door!" snapped the nurse, but Eli couldn't move.

After twenty more minutes of screaming and pushing, Michelle collapsed from exhaustion. Eli's eyes widened when the doctor raised a bloody baby boy by his feet, his umbilical dangling from his chubby belly. After coughing and sputtering, the baby gasped and then cried. Eli gulped, his eyes wide in astonishment as the doctor passed the baby on to the nurse.

Amazed by the miracle of birth—something the watcher had never witnessed in his tens of thousands of years—he failed to realize the screaming infant was *his* child. Instead, Eli's thoughts were on his sweet Michelle, who lay drenched in sweat, her face pale, her chest heaving.

"She's bleeding," warned the doctor.

"You shouldn't be in here!" scolded the nurse as she bundled the screaming baby.

"I'm her husband," muttered Eli, as if reminding himself.

"Nurse, help me!" called the doctor as he frantically worked on Michelle.

"Can-can I see my baby?" panted Michelle, trying to lift her head.

"Stay down and rest, dear," ordered the nurse as she handed the doctor gauze.

"I can't stop the bleeding!" Dr. Nobert blurted as the baby wailed.

Eli's eyes widened when Michelle's pale face rolled to the side in unconsciousness. Knowing time was short, Eli burst from the bedchamber, dashed down the stairs, and out the front door past a wide-eyed Ronan.

The icy morning air was thick with fog as Eli raced up the hill and through the barren trees. Unable to see more than fifteen feet ahead of him, Eli dodged the trees as they came into view, his harried breath puffing by him like a locomotive at full tilt.

The choking fog strained the morning light as Eli burst into the clearing, dropped to his knees, and slid across the snow to the stone box. After pulling open its lid, Eli thrust his arm inside to retrieve his satchel and orb, but the box was empty. Eli gaped into the stone box with round, panicked eyes. "Where is it?" he gasped.

"You seek this?" asked Lu, emerging from the fog with the shimmering orb in his palm.

Eli glared at his red-bearded nemesis with pulsing blue eyes. "What are you doing with that?"

"I have simply claimed what is mine, what was taken from me," shrugged Lu.

"It is NOT yours!" seethed Eli, getting to his feet.

Lu's eyes narrowed. "You think it belongs to you? A watcher who has impregnated a mortal? Who has defiled his standing and violated the Grand Precept?" the smirking Lu shook his head. "I don't think so."

"Give me the orb!"

"It is bitingly ironic, don't you think? The great Elijah, who has spent so many millennia decrying my sins and the sins of my brothers, has himself become a sinner. You are no better than I am," sneered Lu. "You are now just another apostate. *A heretic.*"

"You and I are nothing alike. We have never been alike!" fumed Eli.

"Says the would-be mortal who, even now, has a wife paying the mortal price for his sin. Your hypocrisy is astounding."

"I didn't know who I was when it happened! My memories were taken from me!"

"Really, Eli. It's difficult to listen to you and your pathetic justifications. You should own up to your mistake. You should embrace your impurity."

"I've done all those things, and I'm willing to give up my call to live the life of a mortal."

"To live the life of a mortal?" scoffed Lu. "You're truly delusional even to think such a thing! To live like a bug waiting every day to be squashed underfoot? You would trade what you have for that? Just to live with a mortal woman who will be old and gone in a few blinks of an eye? You can have thousands more like her. One for every day of the week!"

"There are no others like her!"

"Please, you make me wretch," cringed Lu.

Eli's jaw tightened. He was running out of time. "Give me the orb, or I'll take it!"

Lu laughed. "I will give it to you on one condition."

"What is that?" frowned Eli.

"That you join me and my cause."

"Your cause? You have no cause! Only unraveling all that we have done! You seek only to destroy this world and the plan of peace!"

"There was never such a plan!" roared Lu. "Chaos is the only way! Destruction and tribulation lead to life!"

"You mean *power*," glared Eli.

Lu nodded. "Power and dominion *is* life. If you join me, nothing can stop us!"

"I will never join you!" fumed Eli.

"Then your Michelle shall perish," shrugged Lu.

When Eli stepped toward Lu, a bony figure emerged from the mist. It was Gik, pointing the glowing blazerod. "I cast you out," seethed Eli.

"And I brought him back. You can do that with these," smirked Lu, holding up the orb in his hand. "Think of the army I can raise—just like before. There are plenty waiting, and they'll do anything I ask."

Eli shook his head. "Give me the orb!"

"I give you one last opportunity," Lu said with narrowing eyes.

When Eli lunged toward Lu, Gik stepped forward and fired the blazerod, but the bolt shot past the dodging Eli. Gik quickly re-aimed and fired again. The second bolt grazed Eli's shoulder and spun him back onto the snowy ground beside the stone lid. Sprawled on his back, clutching his wounded arm, Eli's eyes flashed from Lu to the closing Gik.

"Too easy," scoffed Lu. "You are even beginning to think like a mortal. What a waste." Lu nodded to Gik. "Finish him."

When Eli pushed back in the snow, he felt the edge of the stone lid.

Gik stepped closer and raised the blazerod to Eli's head as Lu placed his other hand atop the orb. When the shimmering rift formed beside Lu, Gik's distracted gaze turned to it.

Eli grabbed the stone lid and hurled it at Gik, striking him in the chest. The impact toppled the halfborn backward as the blazerod shot a bolt into the air and flew out of his hand.

Eli scrambled to his feet and charged Lu, who was about to enter the rift with the orb. The force of the collision knocked Lu sideways and dislodged the golden ball from his hand. Eli and Lu traded blows as they wrestled in the snow beside the sparkling portal, the glowing orb half-buried four feet away. As they fought, a dazed Gik sat up and searched for the blazerod that had disappeared in the snow.

"Destroy him, you fool!" yelled Lu from beneath Eli as the fierce-eyed watcher's punches rained down.

Gik climbed to his feet and frantically searched for the blazerod as Eli continued to dominate Lu.

"Get him off me!" wailed Lu.

Unable to find the blazerod, Gik leaped onto Eli's back, pulling his hair and slapping his head.

Eli reached behind him, grabbed Gik by his scruffy collar, and pulled him off. But the change in momentum was to Lu's advantage. Lu wrestled his way back on top of Eli, but before he could land a punch, Eli wrapped his legs around Lu's neck and bent him backward.

Eli had just regained the advantage on the weakening Lu and was about to land a knockout blow when he felt the cold alloy of the blazerod pressed against his temple.

"Get off of him!" growled the halfborn, his bony arm trembling as he clutched the ancient weapon.

Still straddling Lu, Eli's shoulders sank in defeat. He released his hold on the battered watcher as Gik stood over him with the blazerod pointed. The fuming Lu pushed Eli off of him and climbed to his feet as Gik laughed and shook the weapon in Eli's face. Kneeling in the snow, his shoulder wound smoking, Eli hung his head, anguished at the thought of failing his wife and child.

As the noble watcher awaited the blast that would end his existence, he considered all he had done, all the lives he had touched, and the world he had helped guide into being. Eli told himself he would miss this world, but he would miss Michelle the most. Eli wondered what would happen to their newborn son. He hoped he could find Michelle in the next realm.

"Do it!" barked Lu, glaring at the surrendered Eli. "End him now!"

A vile smug filled the halfborn's face as he aimed the blazerod.

Bowed and kneeling in the snow, Eli closed his eyes, awaiting his end.

A shotgun blast fractured the stillness and blew Gik sideways into the snow.

Eli's eyes shot open, and he spun as Ronan stepped into the clearing, the empty shotgun barrel smoking, the second barrel at the ready.

Lu backed away from the stunned Eli as Gik writhed in the snow.

"What in the devil!" exclaimed a wide-eyed Ronan, eyeing the shimmering rift as Lu staggered toward the half-buried orb. "Elijah, are you all right?"

"Stay back!" barked Eli as he jumped to his feet and lunged for Lu, tackling him just short of the orb and the sparkling portal. Eli's head snapped back when Lu viciously kicked him in the face. A kick to Eli's shoulder wound caused him to cry out in pain.

After fighting free from Eli, the battered Lu lurched to his feet and staggered toward the sphere. Eli crawled through the snow, desperate to reach the orb first, but his shoulder gave way, landing him face-first in the snow.

Lu was a foot from the glowing orb when Eli felt the blazerod in the snow. He grabbed the ancient weapon and rolled on his side, shooting wild bolts of energy that missed the fleeing Lu by inches.

Eli pushed up on his knees, steadying his arm to fire as Lu snatched up the glowing orb, stumbled forward, and dived through the open rift. "No!" Eli cried. He lunged for the shimmering doorway with all of his strength, but in an instant, the rift was closed, leaving Eli sprawled in the snow, staring into the misty forest. "NO!" he roared, knowing the orb was gone, and with it, any chance of saving his beloved Michelle.

"Elijah. Elijah, are you all right?" gasped Ronan, unsure of what he had just witnessed, his shotgun forgotten in his hands.

When a furious Eli turned the blazerod to the wounded halfborn, the terrified Gik darted into the mist. Ronan raised his shotgun to fire, but the creature was gone.

Eli lowered the blazerod, fearing he had doomed his dying wife. With the last gasps of hope, the watcher staggered to his feet and raced through the mist to the château.

After bursting through the front door, a wet and weary Eli raced through the great room and up the stairs. When he reached his bedchamber, his chest heaving, his shoulder wound charred and raw, Eli slowed to a stop. His devastated gaze moved past the sobbing Madame Duguay to the nurse quieting the crying infant before settling on the doctor, pulling the bedsheet over a gray-faced Michelle.

"No!" cried Eli as he staggered to Michelle's bedside, shaking his head in disbelief. "NOOO!" Eli didn't hear the doctor's somber explanation as he pulled back the bloody sheet. Tears streaked down Eli's face at the sight of Michelle's gray and empty shell. He sank to his knees and took her limp hand in his. Eli closed his eyes and focused all his might, just as he had when using the orb to save Ronan's life, but her hand felt just as cold.

"I'm sorry," sighed Dr. Norbert. "I-we did everything we could."

The sound of Ronan huffing up the stairs turned the doctor and nurse, but not Eli. Ronan's shoulders sank when his eyes fell on his life-less niece. Sadly shaking his head, he turned away.

"Please...please," muttered Eli as he fell against the bed with Michelle's hand in his. "I'll do anything. Please..."

The saddened nurse hovered for a time with the now quieted newborn in her arms before leaving the bedchamber. Outside the room, she carefully handed the baby to a still-sobbing Madame Duguay. The exhausted doctor gathered his medical bag and followed.

Eli didn't hear the door close. He didn't hear the ticking of the mantel clock above the fireplace or the popping and cracking of the burning logs within. Eli heard and felt nothing as he clutched his wife's icy hand. Instead, he thought of the dream that was never to be. His vision of living as a man with a woman who loved him, raising children, and growing old was a fantasy. He thought it cruel to have been given a taste at all. But then again, life was cruel, Eli reminded himself. He had seen it take from the best and give to the worst too many times. He now thought its promises empty and vain.

After gently laying Michelle's hand on the bed, Eli kissed her fore-head. He thought of her loving smile, her tender caress, and her warm body. "Is this my punishment?" Eli tearfully groaned. "Is this the penalty for what I've done? I'VE DONE NOTHING BUT SERVE YOU!" he bellowed.

With his head buried beside Michelle's, Eli didn't see the room brightening around him.

"Elijah."

"Go away, leave me," Eli muttered, thinking it was the nurse at the door, but the door was closed.

"Elijah," repeated the voice as the room grew brighter still.

Eli gasped when he looked up to see Charmeine hovering to the side of the bed in her flowing white gown. His eyes widened when two more angels appeared on either side of her.

"Why do you mourn?" asked the angel, her eyes aglow.

"Because...she's gone," groaned Eli.

"You have witnessed the passing of millions upon millions in your time," Charmeine reminded him.

"She was different," breathed Eli.

"She was the daughter of a man and is now in the next realm."

"She was different to *me*."

"Elijah, why did you not agree to Lu's demands? He would have given you the orb. You could have saved her yourself."

"To follow him would be a betrayal of all I know—all I have worked and stood for. It would be against my very core," said Eli, his head hanging.

"So it would be," nodded Charmeine, her glowing face full of compassion. "Elijah, you know well the agency of man, but you have failed to understand your own freedom of choice. Even Watchers of the Holy Order are bound to the consequences of their actions, just as mortals."

"I know," muttered Eli. "I have failed."

"Elijah, you have not failed. You have done what no other watcher has before. You have tasted the fruit of power and remained true."

"But I have not remained true. I've wanted to become a mortal. To be something I'm not."

"You have yearned for the mortal life, for the common desires of the flesh, but you remained unwavering when tempted by Lu. There could be no truer test."

Eli hung his head.

"Elijah, you have been granted your wish," breathed Charmeine.

"To live as a man?" Eli shook his head. "It is all for nothing without my dear Michelle."

"She will be restored to you, but at a price."

Eli looked up with wide eyes and a slack jaw. "Yes! Whatever the price, I will do anything for her!"

Charmeine studied Eli. "Would you give up your immortality for her?"

"Yes!" Eli replied without hesitation.

"That is true love, to sacrifice one's self for another," a visibly moved Charmeine replied. But then her face grew serious. "You must choose carefully and know the consequences of your decision. To live as a man, you would grow old, and the world would pass you by. You would lose your power of influence, of discernment."

"What of the world?" Eli asked as the angels watched him.

"The world will no longer be your concern; it will continue for good or for bad. Your sphere will shrink to your family."

"There are others who can take my place?"

"There are but few."

Eli's eyes shifted in thought as he tried to comprehend his choice. His sad perception that he had lost any influence he once had for good swayed him. Eli tiredly shook his head. "I have grown weary in my work. I choose Michelle. Though our time may be short, I choose her!"

"So shall it be," announced Charmeine.

Eli watched in wonder as the three angels placed their hands on his wife's lifeless shell. One touched Michelle's still-swollen belly while another touched her breast and Charmeine her head. "Awake," commanded Charmeine.

Michelle's gray face warmed until it was a rosy pink. Then, with a back-arching gasp, she breathed in.

Eli sank back on his knees as Michelle stirred, as if emerging from a deep slumber. "Thank you, thank you!"

"It is not we you should thank," Charmeine reminded him with a tender smile.

Eli bowed his head. "I give all credit and glory to the Holy and Great Ones." He looked up as the accompanying angels disappeared, leaving only Charmeine hovering beside the bed. "What does this mean for me—for *us*?"

"That is your choice."

"And what of our son?"

Charmeine studied Eli. "I will tell you of his future."

"Will he grow to be a normal man?"

"The child shares your essence, but he also carries the blood of his mother."

"Yes, I know. He's a halfborn," Eli said in shame.

Charmeine shook her head. "The child is not a halfborn."

Eli's brow furrowed in confusion. "What do you mean?"

Outside the bedchamber, the nurse and a weeping Madame Duguay comforted the newborn while the doctor spoke to a sad Ronan about what to expect. Men would soon come to take Michelle's body. A heart-wrenching funeral would follow. Then the difficult task of raising a child without a mother would begin.

Back inside the bedchamber, Eli looked up at the angel with wide eyes as she finished her explanation. "But how can that be?"

"It has been foreseen and foretold."

Eli gulped. "What of Lu? Will he leave us in peace?"

"As long as he does not know or perceive you as a threat."

"How can I, as a mortal man, now protect my wife and child?"

"That is a consequence of your choice," explained Charmeine. "Pre-pare yourself, for the bowels of the earth will upheave at his knowledge. Do not despair; you will receive help, some from unlikely sources. But be wary, for all is not like it seems."

"Thank you," breathed Eli, weighed down by all he had heard. He kissed his sleeping wife on the forehead.

When Michelle opened her eyes to Eli, Charmeine gave an approving nod and faded away, dimming the bedchamber to the light of the table lamp and the flickering fire.

"There's my miracle man," Michelle weakly smiled.

"How are you feeling, darling?" beamed a teary-eyed Eli.

"Exhausted. I had the most unusual dream," she frowned, strug-gling to remember.

Eli leaned down and kissed Michelle's lips. "I thought I had lost you," he whispered.

Michelle's smile faded as she looked around and felt her flattened belly. "The baby! Is the baby all right?"

Eli tearfully nodded. "Yes, our son is safe."

"A little boy! Just as you said! Please fetch him for me. I want to see him," whimpered a tearful Michelle.

Breathing in his new reality, Eli moved to the bedchamber door. He paused, his hand an inch from the door latch as he considered what he would say. Unable to formulate an idea, Eli pulled open the door. In the hallway near the railing, he saw the sad doctor speaking in hushed tones with Ronan. A few steps away, Madame Duguay bounced his whimpering son while the nurse coached her.

"Elijah, I'm so terribly sorry," groaned Ronan.

Eli moved past the two men to his bouncing son.

The nurse instinctively moved to block Eli, having seen rage-filled fathers lash out at their surviving baby following the mother's death. But she stepped aside, recognizing the loving fascination in his eyes.

"Your son," sobbed Madame Duguay, presenting the chubby baby.

Eli gulped as he beheld his infant son. He had his mother's olive skin but Eli's blue eyes, and a thick tuft of blonde hair that seemed to come from neither. "My own flesh and blood," breathed Eli.

Carefully taking the swaddled baby in his arms, Eli gently brushed his finger along the infant's fat cheek. The sight of the helpless, squirming baby seemed out of place with the greatness Charmeine had spoken of. Eli looked deeply into his son's eyes, expecting to witness his promise and potential, but he saw only a whimpering baby. Eli felt blinded by his sudden loss of insight but relieved at the lifted weight. With a sigh, he turned back to the bedchamber.

The others sadly watched as Eli returned to the dimly lit room.

"This will help him heal, but someone should stay with him...just in case," warned the mournful doctor.

After exchanging helpless looks with Ronan, Madame Duguay started for the door. But when a gleeful woman's laugh came from inside the bedchamber, she looked back at the others in dismay. "That sounded like Mistress Michelle!"

Ronan rushed past her and pushed open the door. His jaw slackened at seeing his niece sitting up in the bed, cuddling the round-eyed infant. "My God!" he gasped. "She's alive!"

The doctor quickly joined him, rubbing his head in confusion at a beaming Michelle holding her newborn. "I don't understand. She was dead," he muttered.

Ronan shook his head. "Tonight, I have seen many things I don't understand."

CHAPTER 26
THE PREDATORS

Château de Bret
August 1916

The leaves of the chestnut tree softly rustled in the midday breeze as cottony clouds billowed in the bright blue sky. The tranquil pond at the base of the hill mirrored the clouds and sky where the lily pads were not. Michelle breathed in the fresh summer air as a hummingbird hovered nearby, as if inspecting her and the toddler in her arms. After laying out a picnic blanket in the shade of the tree, Michelle set six-month-old François, or Franny as they called him, onto the blanket, then looked across the meadow to where Eli was working. She waved but doubted he saw her. Michelle wished her husband wasn't always so busy and could spend more time with them, but then reminded herself Eli's sense of duty was one of his attractive traits.

Michelle kneeled beside the curly-haired Franny, who had outgrown his romper, and watched him study the gingham blanket's pattern. She opened the wicker basket and removed a baguette and a plate of cheese. Michelle glanced at the curly-haired Franny, watching a robin pecking in the grass, then hurried back to the house for the rest of their supplies.

Not far away, in the shadows of the forest, Gik's dark, sunken eyes peered through the trees. The halfborn closely watched as Franny moved onto his knees and crawled off the blanket into the grass toward a dandelion. Gik's eyes narrowed when Franny continued on hands and knees toward the forest. From his position in the trees, fifty feet away, the halfborn could see the bending blades of grass as a two-foot-long asp slithered toward the baby. Gik's eyes widened when Franny stopped and sat up, just feet from the coiled snake.

The curious Franny pointed at the hissing asp. He turned his chubby arm when a second and third poisonous viper slithered toward him.

With eyes bulging, Gik knew the child was easy prey. He was about to spring from the trees when a humming Michelle appeared from the château carrying a water pitcher and a bowl of grapes. The halfborn sank back into the shadows as she approached the vacant blanket. Gik's eager gaze returned to the seemingly unafraid Franny, calmly pointing at the angry, hissing snakes. "The prophecy," Gik muttered as he watched in amazement.

"Where are you going, Franny?" called out Michelle when she spotted him on the grass fifteen feet from the blanket. But her smile vanished when she noticed three gold and black coiled and hissing snakes surrounding him. "FRANNY! ELI!" she cried as she dropped the water and grapes and dashed to her baby.

Eli was returning from the meadow when he spotted Michelle racing across the lawn.

Thinking only of her child, the charging Michelle reached down and scooped up Franny as two of the snakes struck. Michelle felt the bite on her ankle and cried out in pain as she hobbled away from the vipers.

"What is it?" yelled Eli from forty yards away.

"Snakes!" exclaimed Michelle, clutching Franny as she limped back to the blanket.

Eli spotted a garden spade leaning against the stables, grabbed it, and sprinted toward his sobbing wife. But by the time Eli arrived, two of the snakes were streaking through the grass toward the trees. The third snake, defiantly coiled, hissed at Eli as he raised the spade. With a quick downward thrust, he chopped the viper in two. "Are you all right?" Eli called out as he rushed to Michelle, sobbing on the picnic blanket as she clutched a concerned Franny.

"I think Franny's okay, but it bit me!" she whimpered.

Eli took the infant and quickly surveyed his chubby arms and legs for bite wounds, but the unbothered Franny was free of harm. When Eli kneeled beside Michelle, his brow furrowed at the fang marks on her red and puffy ankle.

"What happened?" Ronan yelled as he raced from the house with a shotgun in hand, a fretting Madame Duguay waddling behind.

"An asp bit her," replied Eli, pointing at the severed snake.

"An asp?" gasped Ronan, surveying the sobbing Michelle.

"There were three of them! They tried to kill my baby!" she cried, pointing to the trees.

"Send for the doctor!" Ronan barked as he raised the shotgun and stomped into the forest.

When Gik, who still carried shotgun pellets in his neck and cheek from his previous encounter with Ronan, spotted the determined man marching toward him with his shotgun pointed, he quickly disappeared into the shadows.

Eli had just handed Franny to Madame Duguay and lifted Michelle from the grass when a shotgun blast, followed by another, rang out.

"Is Franny all right?" asked the weepy-eyed Michelle, traumatized more by the snakes attacking her son than the pain of the bite.

"He's fine. Not a scratch on him," Eli assured her.

"I killed the other two," huffed Ronan as he followed them into the house. "There must be a nearby nest. Very unusual."

DOCTOR NOBERT RUBBED his bushy mustache as he closed the bedchamber door and turned to Eli and Ronan. "She needs to rest. While the snake that bit her is venomous, it is rarely deadly."

Ronan eyed the doctor. "You say rarely, but I see you're concerned."

The doctor shrugged. "There are always risks, but from what I have witnessed with her, I doubt she will have any problem."

Ronan glanced at Eli and nodded.

"Anything I should do?" asked a worried Eli.

"She has a slight fever, which is normal." Dr. Norbert shook his head. "If anything, I should be coming to you for medical advice."

Eli looked down uncomfortably.

"Just watch her. She should be fine. Good day," the doctor nodded, gathering his bag and putting on his hat.

Eli's gaze was distant as the doctor left down the stairs. Unable to hide his worry, Eli entered the bedchamber and approached his resting wife. "How do you feel?"

Michelle sighed. "I have a head and ankle ache."

"The doctor says you should be fine."

"At least I didn't die again," Michelle said with a teary smirk.

Eli gulped. "Yes. Thank you."

Michelle's uncertain gaze drifted across the room. "That was so unusual. In all of my summers here, I only remember seeing one other snake, and that was down at the vineyard. There were *three* snakes, Eli! Three deadly asps tried to kill my son!" She wiped away tears and whimpered, "Is this what our life is going to be like? Fending off snakes and ghastly men trying to destroy us?"

Eli considered Charmeine's warning the night Franny was born: that the bowels of the earth would upheave at his knowledge. He wondered what more would come.

"Will you check on Franny? I can't stop worrying about him," fretted Michelle, wiping away her tears.

"He's in the nursery with Madame Duguay," replied Eli.

"Please go check on him. I'll be fine."

After kissing his wife on the forehead, Eli departed the bedchamber and turned toward the nursery. At the end of the hallway, beyond the railing that overlooked the great room, the nursery held Franny's crib, changing table, and rocker on a large woven rug with some of his toys. Eli thought nothing of the shadow moving within the nursery as he approached, but he knew something was wrong when he heard Madame Duguay's voice downstairs. Eli hurried to the nursery to see if someone was inside. He stopped in the doorway when Franny pulled himself up in the crib and pointed to the open window. Eli turned to the drapes stirring in the afternoon breeze. *Was that what I saw?* he wondered, eyeing their shifting shadows. Eli moved to the open window and gazed across the back lawn to the forest. He breathed easier when he saw all was still.

But just feet away, on the slate roof outside the window, crouched a wide-eyed Gik, his gangly form pushed up against the house out of sight from the nursery. The halfborn's nostrils flared as he searched for the watcher's scent.

Eli scanned the shadowy forest as Franny watched, his arm still pointing at the window. With a sigh, Eli turned to the crib. His brow furrowed when he noticed a dusty footprint on the rug that was not his own. His wary gaze followed the faint trail of forest twigs and dirt leading to the window. After another search of the yard and forest, Eli closed and locked the window. Then, hiding his worry with a smile, he gathered up little François and left the room.

APRIL 1917

ELI HELD the bushy sheep on its side with one hand as he clipped its thick fleece with his other. With sweat glistening off his brow, Eli worked while the sheep tirelessly bleated. Beside him, another worker gathered the clumps of sheared wool and pushed them into a burlap bag. Eli looked up into the blue sky and wiped his brow as a cloud moved before the sun and darkened the meadow. Three other wooly sheep nervously bleated in the pen beside him while the dozen already shorn played in the meadow.

When Eli finished the clipping, he stood and stretched his back, allowing the trimmed sheep to jump to its feet. Eli's eyes narrowed when he noticed a shape slinking in the shadows of the forest just beyond the meadow. Thinking it may be the wolf that had killed a sheep the week before, Eli glanced at the shotgun leaning against the fence ten feet away. But when Eli turned back to the forest, he saw only trees. He wondered if the heat of the day was playing tricks on his eyes. He wondered if it was a wolf or something else.

A year and a month had passed since Eli's son was born. The former watcher had hoped his choice to live as a man would set him free, but Eli felt the opposite had happened. Every day he lived with the worry that Lu or one of his halfborn would come after his wife and son. While Eli's powers were gone, he had already seen signs that young François was no ordinary child. Eli wondered how long it would take Lu and the others to find out. He feared they were already watching.

Eli felt for the blazerod on his hip. He carried it in a lambskin holster even though he was unable to use it. Not a day had passed that he hadn't tried to fire the ancient weapon, but as with his other abilities, the power of the blazerod was now a memory. Eli hoped showing it off would be enough of a deterrent to keep anyone who knew of its power at bay, and so far, it had.

After finishing the last sheep and helping the other workers pack the trimmed fleece into bags, Eli started back toward the château. He heard laughter from the back lawn as he rounded the stables. Eli's face brightened when he spotted Michelle, wearing a flowery dress and summer hat, standing under the chestnut tree where they were married. Ronan sat nearby in a folding chair with his pipe, laughing at the toddling boy chasing a squirrel.

"He is quite the little explorer," beamed Michelle as Franny waddled across the lawn.

When the boy wandered too close to the shotgun leaning against the table, Ronan promptly moved the gun and chuckled, "Not for a few years yet, my boy."

Michelle's smile faded as she eyed the long-barreled weapon. "I wish we didn't always need to have that nearby."

"It's for your protection, my dear, from wolves and other things," Ronan reminded her.

"Yes, I know, but I still don't like it. What if Franny should get hold of it?"

"It would be quite a feat for him to turn the safety," said Ronan before puffing on his pipe.

"I'm afraid that little boy is full of surprises," sighed Michelle. "Don't forget who his father is."

"Of that, I'm sure." Ronan nodded. "He's quite a boy, and I'm so glad you named him after your father. A noble tribute, I should think."

Michelle smiled. "I wish Papa could have seen him."

"I think he might be watching him now," Ronan winked, thinking back to the fantastic things he had seen.

Michelle sighed. "I do hope so."

"Ah, here comes Elijah."

"Hello, dear," beamed Michelle, shielding her eyes from the lowering sun as Eli approached. "How were the sheep?"

"Very warm and wooly," replied Eli.

"I should think they would be grateful to be rid of their coats on such a lovely spring day," said Michelle with one eye on her exploring son.

"Someone should have explained that to the sheep," sighed Eli as Michelle approached to kiss him.

She paused a foot away. "Oh, you smell rather..."

"I smell like dirty wool socks. I know," nodded Eli.

"That wool will help our boys at the front," said Ronan, puffing on his pipe.

"Oh, I wish this dreadful war was over," fretted Michelle. "Sometimes I can go all day without thinking about it. Those are the best days."

"Some good news in that regard," perked up Ronan. "I read in the paper this morning that America has declared war on the Bosch! Did you have anything to do with that, Elijah?" Ronan winked. While Michelle knew much about Eli, Ronan only knew what he had witnessed and surmised.

Eli shook his head. "I was there more than a year ago."

"Surely, you had some influence," Michelle insisted.

Eli gave his wife a wounded look. "I'm afraid whatever influence I may have once had was lost long ago."

Michelle studied Eli. She knew something had changed with her husband but didn't understand all he had sacrificed for her.

"I hope America's entry makes the difference, and we can finally end this damned war!" huffed Ronan.

"Amen to that," nodded Michelle as she picked up her son. "Franny, did you see your papa is here?" she asked, presenting the toddler to Eli.

"Papa!" beamed the boy.

"Hello, little man. Have you been helping Uncle and Mama today?" Eli asked, taking his son in his arms.

"Papa!" cried Franny, kissing his father despite the sheep stench.

Eli tossed his son into the air a few times to hear him squeal, then stood him back on the grass. "So, the Americans are coming to fight."

"Yes, but it may be some time. Apparently, their military is in shambles."

Eli looked down in thought. At his and Cyrus's prodding, President Roosevelt had built up the US Navy. He thought it a shame that Wilson had let it dwindle.

"How long can our boys hang on at the front?" asked Michelle.

"The lines haven't changed much since Verdun, six months ago." Ronan shrugged. "Probably because each side lost half a million men!"

"Oh, can we please talk about something else?" groaned Michelle.

"Yes, my dear, but first, let me ask Elijah: do you hear anything from your old war acquaintances? Are they making any inroads?"

Eli shook his head, fighting through guilt. "I'm afraid I've lost touch with them."

"Hmm, yes. You are a family man now," Ronan nodded.

Eli tried to hide his frustration as he turned to the house, but Michelle saw it.

"Elijah? Are you okay?" Michelle asked.

Eli only half turned to her when he said, "I'm going to clean up for dinner."

"Okay," said Michelle, still uncertain of his mood.

As Eli walked, he considered the war. While it had not yet ended, the French and British forces had given the invading Germans all they could handle. The fighting in Eastern Europe and the Middle East had also slowed. Eli surmised Lu had two war strategies. His overarching goal was for the four nations and twenty-five million men of the Central Powers to conquer the thirty-six million men of the Allied Powers. If he couldn't do that, Lu would be content with causing as much death and destruction as possible. With the unrest in Russia, Eli knew it was only a matter of time before their twelve million soldiers stopped fighting. While a victory for the Central Powers was not in sight, Lu's second goal was in full swing: the world was crumbling under the weight of chaos, suffering, and death. As Eli entered the house, he wondered how Lu would respond to the four million Americans preparing to join the fight. A part of Eli wished he could still make a difference.

From the shadows of the forest, the bony Gik watched the little boy wander from his mother. The child's guardians had grown lax, the half-born concluded, as he considered the ease of seizing him. Gik's dark, sunken eyes narrowed as he scanned the yard.

Gik was about to stand when he caught the smell of a sheep. His gaze moved to the meadow and the shorn beasts roaming the distant hill. But when Gik turned back to the child, he gasped when he felt the unforgiving alloy of the blazerod against his head.

"What are you doing here?" snarled Eli, clutching a weapon he could no longer use.

"I-I am here for the child," Gik stammered.

"Why? Why can't you leave us alone?" seethed Eli.

Gik's sunken eyes turned sideways to Eli, but he remained otherwise frozen.

"I will not let you harm my son. I will destroy you or anyone else who comes near him," Eli growled, bending Gik's head with the blazerod.

"No-no, you-you don't understand!" Gik stammered, "I'm here to protect the child!"

Eli glanced at the yard and saw Michelle carrying their son back into the château. "I don't believe you. I won't fall for your tricks!"

"It is not a trick," whimpered Gik. "He is the foretold one!"

Eli's eyes widened. *Does he know?* "I won't let you harm him!"

"No! Please, lower the blazerod. I swear to you, I-I mean no harm this time."

"This time, what about next time?" barked Eli, jabbing the blazerod against Gik's head.

"No! The child has changed everything! You don't understand!"

Eli's eyes narrowed, and he lowered the blazerod. "Tell me."

Gik gulped, and his sunken eyes moved from the blazerod back to the stern-eyed Eli. "Among the halfborn, there is a foretelling of the Awaited One, one who will set free the outcast and close the gulf! One who will bring the worlds together in a final peace! One who will usher in the end times and welcome the *Ihidaya*—the sovereign to end all sovereigns!"

Eli studied the bony Gik. "Why do you think my son has anything to do with this?"

"Because...his father is a watcher and his mother is..."

Eli's brow tightened. "Is she not a mortal? Just like your mother?"

"No." Gik breathed, slowly shaking his head. "She is more than that. She carries royal blood."

He knows! Eli jabbed the blazerod back against the halfborn's head. "Tell me why I shouldn't end you right now?"

Gik recoiled and raised his bony hands. "Because-because I have been here from the beginning—since the child was born."

"You tried to kill me the day he was born!" growled Eli.

"That-that was before the angel told me!"

"The angel?"

"Charmeine," Gik nodded.

"She came to you that night?"

"Yes, I didn't understand before. I only knew what my master had told me!"

"How can I trust you?" glared Eli.

"I-I sit outside his window each night! If I meant to harm him, I would have. I am here to protect him!"

"Protect him from who?"

Gik gulped. "From those who would do him harm."

"Other halfborn?"

Gik slowly shook his head.

"From Lu?"

"He does not yet know of the child's promise. There are other things. The dark elements."

"The dark elements are a myth! I don't believe you!" snarled Eli.

"They are not a myth! How else will the bowels of the earth rise against him?"

Eli's jaw slackened. *Those were Charmeine's words.* "The snakes."

"Yes! Believe me! It is true! I have seen the dark elements in the abyss!" cried Gik, recoiling behind his bony hands. "I wish only to protect the child!"

Eli studied the cowering halfborn, then shook his head. "I can't trust you."

Gik's bony face sank in defeat. He looked into Eli's blue, discerning eyes and shook his scraggly head. "You are right. I do not deserve to protect the child. You should finish me."

Eli shook his head when Gik slumped on the forest floor like a dog submitting to its master. He remembered Charmeine's promise that he would receive help from unlikely sources. *Could this wretched soul be that help?* Eli's gaze lowered to the blazerod, and he replaced it in his holster. "I'll let you be for now, but you must swear an oath not to harm my son."

"I swear it! I will protect him!"

"Very well."

"You are merciful," breathed Gik as he pulled himself up from the ground with dirt and twigs in his greasy hair.

"We'll see," frowned Eli as he got to his feet.

"I will be your servant now! I will watch over the child!" Gik eagerly nodded.

Eli studied the groveling halfborn. "You can watch from the trees, out of sight. Your appearance will frighten the others."

"I *am* hideous," nodded Gik.

Eli sighed. "It's not that you're hideous...well, you are that, but you've attacked my wife at least twice, and she won't be so understanding."

"I will attack only those who try to take or harm the child," Gik replied, bowing down.

Satisfied, Eli nodded, then took a step back. He started to turn, then raised a stern finger at the cowering Gik. "I'll be watching you."

"Yes, master," nodded Gik.

"Stay out of sight of the others!"

"Yes, master." Gik watched Eli leave, then turned to resume his vigil.

CHAPTER 27
REVELATIONS

CHÂTEAU DE BRET
JULY 1917

The draperies gently stirred in the morning breeze as the summer sun poured through the window across the bedchamber rug. Lying in bed beside Eli, with the lacy strap of her nightgown falling off her shoulder, Michelle ran her fingers through his wavy hair.

"Good morning," Eli smiled as he rolled on his side. "Have you been up long?"

"A while," Michelle grinned, studying his features.

"What have you been doing?"

"Looking at you...and wondering," she whispered.

"Wondering about what?" Eli asked, rubbing his face.

"About you. Are you happy, my love?"

"Yes, of course." Eli tried to smile, but his expression belied his words.

Michelle sighed. "I know there are many things I don't understand about you. Things you won't talk to me about, but I know you're bothered. I can tell."

Eli shrugged. "I'm happy caring for your uncle's estate, watching our son grow, and loving you. It's what I've always wanted."

Michelle tried to smile, but she saw the worry burdening Eli. She rubbed his thick arm. "They haven't called for you for some time."

Eli closed his eyes. "No. I don't think they will again."

Michelle glanced at the blazerod on the nightstand. She knew well its deadly force and was glad it was never far from Eli's grasp. But the strange orb Eli had used to save her uncle's life was still a mystery to her. It had been over a year since she had seen the golden sphere. Eli had since seemed reluctant to speak of it, and Michelle wanted to know more. "I haven't seen your magical ball for the longest time."

Eli sighed. He considered lying to Michelle but realized that would be *too* mortal of him. "It was taken away."

Michelle pulled back in surprise. "Taken away? Were you... punished?"

Eli drew in a ragged breath and lay flat on his back, his eyes squeezed closed as if in pain.

Michelle wondered if she was pushing Eli too far, then reminded herself she was his wife and had a right to know. She gently ran her fingers over the comet-shaped scar on Eli's chest and shoulder. "You got this that night. The night Franny was born."

Eli gulped and nodded.

"Elijah..."

"Yes?"

"What happened that night?"

"Our son came into this world," said Eli with a smile not forced.

"And I left this world," Michelle said with a furrowed brow.

Eli's smile faded.

"You saved me. You brought me back," she whispered, kissing Eli's chest.

Eli sighed. "No, I didn't."

"What do you mean?" Michelle asked with searching eyes.

Eli's chest swelled as he breathed in resolve. He felt it was time to tell Michelle. "When I knew I was losing you, I went for the orb. I had hidden it in the forest after my last task. I told myself I was done with it, but it was the only way to save you. When I got to the hiding place, the orb was gone."

"Gone?" Michelle gasped, clutching her breast.

"Lu had found it."

"Oh, no!"

"We fought for it, but he escaped with the orb."

Michelle stared at Eli in confusion. "Then...how did you save me?"

Eli gulped. "Angels came down. They saved you."

"I don't understand."

"I traded my life for yours."

"Your life?" Michelle's gaze moved across the bedchamber, wondering what he meant. "Your immortality?"

Eli sighed. "It's all I've ever wanted. To have someone to love and love me back, to live the life of a man, to have a child. You've made that all possible for me."

Michelle sat up as the full impact of his sacrifice hit her. "But you'll die!"

"Just as you," Eli nodded.

"What of your work? Your call as a watcher?"

Eli shrugged. "I have relinquished my call. I have served my time."

"There are others that can do the work?"

Eli looked away. "I fear no one can stop the evil force that has seized this world—no man nor watcher."

Michelle sank back on the bed beside Eli. "What does that mean for us? For our son?"

"I will protect you."

"While the rest of the world burns," Michelle whispered, horrified by the thought.

Eli turned to Michelle, unable to hide his bewilderment. "I did it for you."

Michelle's eyes filled with tears as she muttered, "I know you did... but at what cost? Elijah, the world..."

"What are you saying?"

Michelle sat up, her weepy eyes filled with the painful realization of the true sacrifice. "I cannot bear the thought of the world suffering more because of me! What have you done?"

"I saved you, just as you have saved me," insisted Eli. He reached for his wife, but she was already out of bed, pulling on her robe.

"All this time..." muttered Michelle.

Eli shook his head in confusion. "I did it for you! For our son! For us!"

"Yes, I know, but can't you see? The world is now suffering because of it! The war might be over now if it weren't for me! How many mothers will lose their sons? How many wives will lose their husbands for me to be alive?"

"No! Don't you see? There was nothing more I could do! Humanity has chosen its course! Our influence is no longer wanted!" Eli insisted as he followed her out of bed.

"How do you know?" asked Michelle, wiping away her tears. "How do you know the world wouldn't be better with your guidance?"

Eli's shoulders sank. "Darling, you don't understand. I've been doing it for so *very* long. Look at the world. None of it has made a difference!"

"No, Elijah! It is you who doesn't understand!" sobbed Michelle as she pulled her robe closed and rushed from the bedchamber.

Eli sank back into the bed and rubbed his face in frustration.

TWO DAYS PASSED, and Michelle was still visibly upset with Eli. Even Ronan noticed it. While Eli had spent millennia guiding and mediating mortal affairs, trying to prevent wars and suffering, none of it had prepared him for how to deal with an angry wife. He had tried twice to talk to Michelle, but she was not ready to hear him.

Weary from working in the vineyard and the afternoon sun's baking heat, Eli was returning home when he spotted Michelle and Franny coming down the path toward the pond. Dressed in her frilly skirted bathing suit and straw hat, she held their son's hand in her right and a shotgun in her left. "Are you going swimming or duck hunting?" smiled Eli, stopping before them. While Michelle was capable with a shotgun, he knew her disdain for weapons and was happy she had it.

"Swimming," replied a still-befuddled Michelle, looking from her husband down to their fast-growing son.

Sweaty and grape-stained, Eli nodded as he considered what to say next.

"Was it hot down at the vineyard?" Michelle asked, glancing up at Eli.

"Yes."

"We're just going down to the pond for a swim. If you'd like to join us..."

"Yes, that sounds refreshing," replied Eli, unable to hide his relief at the invitation.

The conflict and burden Michelle felt were evident as she looked at her husband, sighed, and said, "Well, why don't you fetch your trunks? We'll be at the pond."

Eli's troubled gaze didn't leave Michelle as he moved aside on the trail for them to pass. When Franny looked up at him and squeaked, "Bye, Papa," Eli's face lit up, and he waved back. Eli watched them continue down the trail for a moment, then hurried to the house.

When Eli got to the pond, he found Michelle and Franny in the water on the grassy side, where there were fewer lily pads. Michelle's hat and towel rested on the picnic table a little way from the beach. A shotgun hung from a nearby tree branch out of Franny's reach.

Eli pulled off his shirt and smiled at Franny, laughing and splashing in his mother's arms.

The water was refreshing to Eli as he sank in and waded toward them. He watched Michelle closely for a sign she was no longer mad at him, but her eyes met his only fleetingly.

"We swim, Papa!" cried the splashing Franny. At only sixteen months, young François looked and acted more like a two-and-a-half-year-old, something neither Michelle nor Ronan were surprised about, given his father's DNA. Eli wondered what abilities the boy had inherited from his mother.

After swimming and splashing together for a time, with hardly a word uttered, Michelle turned to Franny and asked, "Do you want to play in the grass and look for frogs while Momma and Papa swim?"

"Look for frogs!" Franny eagerly splashed.

Eli sank under the water as Michelle made her way to the grassy shore twenty feet away. The water was soothing to Eli's tired body and troubled soul.

As Michelle waded back into the pond, Eli watched his son playing with a stick in the mud of the beach, stooping as he moved stones and searched for bugs and frogs. Eli's gaze shifted to a cheerless Michelle as she drew closer. She surprised him when she wrapped her arms around his neck and rested her head against his shoulder. Eli sighed when he felt the warmth of her body against his, releasing days of angst.

"I'm sorry," Michelle whispered. "I'm sorry for being so ungrateful. You were faced with the most impossible choice. All of your life, you have had this weight. It's something I could never understand."

Eli felt Michelle's chest rise and fall as she clung to him.

Michelle's eyes welled with tears. "I should be so grateful that you chose me—that you saved my life—and I am." She pulled back, looked into Eli's loving blue eyes, and breathed, "It just makes me feel so...*so selfish*."

"I'm sorry I caused you this pain. That's why I didn't tell you before."

Michelle tearfully nodded, her arms wrapped around Eli's neck. She swallowed her anguish and whispered, "Will you please forgive me?"

"There is nothing for me to forgive, my love." Eli's face filled with remorse. "Will you forgive me?"

"Of course. You are my everything. How could I not?" whispered Michelle. Floating in Eli's arms, she closed her eyes and kissed him.

When Franny gleefully called out, "Doggy!" from the shore, Eli pulled his lips from Michelle's. They turned to see their little boy on the beach a little way from the picnic table, pointing a stick at a large gray wolf emerging from the trees forty feet away. The toddler seemed unafraid as the wolf crept closer, its snarling head down, its fangs showing.

"FRANNY!" shrieked Michelle as she turned and clawed her way through the water toward her son.

"Franny, don't move!" cried Eli as the hungry wolf crept closer, unconcerned by the splashing in the pond.

Eli quickly passed the panicked Michelle as he raced to protect his son, but still thirty feet from Franny, the wolf was only two lengths away and about to pounce on the child. As Eli frantically pushed through the water, he spotted a shadow moving in the trees to the right and feared it was a second wolf.

Unafraid, Franny was still pointing his stick as the wolf lunged. But in that same instant, a dark, wiry figure charged from the forest. A wide-eyed Gik leaped through the air and collided with the attacking wolf as its jaw snapped inches from Franny's outstretched hand, breaking his stick in two. Gik's collision knocked the wolf on its side with a startled yipe. But the surprised wolf was not long distracted. It angrily jumped to its feet and pounced on the halfborn, latching its fangs into his bony arm. Wailing in pain, Gik punched and slapped the wolf as it violently shook him.

Gik's sunken eyes were bulging when Eli grabbed the wolf by its coarse scruff and yanked it away. The startled wolf yipped in pain and spun on its hind legs before jumping back to its feet. Growling and snarling, its dark and ferocious eyes moved from the writhing Gik and the threatening Eli to the little Franny running for the pond. The wolf charged after Franny but lurched to a stop at the shotgun blast and the storm of lead that tore through its hide.

Halfway to his son, Eli stopped and turned to see Michelle with the smoking shotgun pointed at the wolf. Eli realized killing the ravaging beast might be the only answer and was about to tell her to fire again when the wolf turned and limped along the shore and into the forest.

"François!" Eli cried, rushing to the pond's edge, where his son stood bravely brandishing another stick. "Are you okay?" he gasped, scooping the child up and surveying him for harm.

"Bye, doggy!" yelled an unfazed Franny.

Eli's eyes widened when he turned back to Michelle and saw her shotgun barrel in the face of the back-crawling Gik.

"What are you doing here, you monster?" she seethed. "You killed my father! I won't let you harm my son!"

"NO! PLEASE!" blubbered Gik, the flesh from his bony arm hanging as he raised a blocking hand. "I am here to protect the child!"

"No, you're not! You're here to take him!" she cried.

"No, only to protect him. To protect you!" the halfborn pleaded.

"I won't let you hurt my son!" bellowed Michelle, her face red, her eyes filled with tears, her trembling finger on the trigger. Michelle gasped and staggered backward when Eli pushed the shotgun's barrel up and took it from her hands.

"He's telling the truth," said Eli, eyeing the terrified Gik.

"He killed my father!" sobbed Michelle, staggered that Eli would defend the creature.

"No! No, I didn't kill him!" Gik protested. "He died after!"

"But you caused it!" insisted Michelle. "Elijah, he tried to kill you!"

Gik sank back into the grass with a look of sad realization. He shook his stringy-haired, pellet-laden head, looked down, and muttered, "I am bad. You *should* shoot me."

After laying the shotgun on the picnic table, Eli took his sobbing wife in his arms and whispered calming words.

"I don't want *that thing* here," sobbed Michelle.

"He saved Franny's life," Eli reminded her.

Michelle was wiping away tears when she noticed her son curiously eyeing the halfborn. She tried to pull away from Eli as Franny lowered his stick and moved closer to the still-cowering Gik, but Eli held her close. They watched as the toddler kneeled beside Gik and reached his chubby little hand to the halfborn's torn flesh. Michelle's frustration faded when she saw her son's compassion. Her eyes widened when Franny pushed Gik's torn skin back into place. Her jaw slackened as the toddler held the halfborn's bloody arm, and his torn flesh joined the untorn, mending before her.

"Thank you," Gik breathed as the blood and bruising faded. But it wasn't only the halfborn's arm altered by young François' touch; Gik's countenance lightened, the shotgun pellets pushed out from his healing skin, and his haggard features softened. His dark and sunken eyes seemed more normal, his greasy hair less stringy, and his gaunt and ghastly appearance less disturbing. Even Gik's yellow and crooked teeth seemed whiter and more uniform.

"What has he done?" breathed an astonished Michelle.

"He's healed him," replied an equally amazed Eli.

"I told you," bowed Gik. "He is the foretold one."

CHAPTER 28
THE PLAGUE

D octor Sieghard Lorenz, a tall, thin man with large ears and high cheekbones, looked up from the microscope when the laboratory door swung open. "Yes, may I help you?" he asked, squinting at the two blurred figures in the doorway. Lorenz pulled on his wire-rimmed glasses to see a tall, sturdy man with a red beard and piercing green eyes. Beside Lu stood the hospital director, Colonel Hilbert, in his double-buttoned, stiff-collared officer's tunic.

"This is Herr Stormbrewer. You will stop what you are doing to assist him," ordered the colonel.

Lorenz couldn't hold back his frustration. "Colonel, I'm in the middle of an important experiment!"

The fallen watcher entered the laboratory dragging a heavy canvas bag that left a bloody trail. Over his shoulder, he carried Eli's leather satchel. "Doctor Lorenz," Lu boomed, "Your experiment is concluded. You have new work to do."

Outraged, Lorenz turned to the hospital director. "Who is this man? I'm doing valuable research for the army!"

"You're now doing more valuable research for the emperor!" barked the colonel. With a crisp nod, Hilbert left the lab and closed the door.

Lorenz gulped as Lu dragged the heavy canvas bag closer. "What's in there?" he asked, his wary eyes shifting from the oozing bag to the menacing Lu.

"Tell me what you know about Yellow Fever?" Lu asked with the look of a quizzing professor.

"The emperor has Yellow Fever?" gasped the scientist.

Lu's green eyes narrowed. "No. What do you know about Yellow Fever?"

"It was discovered in Cuba twenty years ago. It is an illness transferred to men by mosquitos," explained the lanky scientist.

"Very good," Lu nodded. "What causes the illness?"

Lorenz's eyes swelled with excitement. "It's something we're just learning about. In fact, I'm experimenting with Tobacco Mosaic disease right now!"

"Were you?" Lu said with a condescending grin.

"Yes," Lorenz eagerly nodded. "It's a new pathogen! We call it a virus. Quite different from a bacterium. It's a living germ!"

"Is it now?" grinned Lu. "And this living germ, this *virus*, you call it; it can be transmitted—by a mosquito, for example?"

"Yes, such is the case with Yellow Fever," Lorenz replied.

"Such is the case," nodded Lu.

Lorenz's gaze lowered to the heavy canvas bag. "May I ask what you have in there?"

Lu pushed the books, papers, and lab equipment on the table aside, then hefted the bag onto it. After opening its end, he emptied a bloody and bloated pig onto the table, its glazed eyes staring at the scientist, its swollen tongue hanging to the side.

Lorenz recoiled in disgust at the black and oozing carcass. "What is it?" he gasped, plugging his nose at its rotting stench.

"It is a pig," said Lu, unimpressed by the scientist. "*Was* a pig."

"It's clearly diseased," grimaced Lorenz.

"This illness afflicts some of your farmer's livestock. When it strikes, it can destroy an entire herd."

"Black swine," gasped Lorenz, trying not to gag.

"Very good," Lu nodded. "I want you to take the essence of Black Swine and transfer it."

"Transfer it... To mosquitos?" frowned Lorenz.

"You may if you wish, but birds would be more suitable. Chickens, more precisely."

"Chickens? But...for what purpose?" asked an intrigued Lorenz.

"For killing, of course. You will be creating a weapon, a plague the likes of which the world has not seen for a very long time."

"To use on the French and British?"

"We will unleash it on the meddling Americans."

Lorenz's eyes swelled, and his jaw fell open as he considered the idea. He shook his head and looked up at Lu. "It's not possible."

Lu's eyes narrowed. "It *is* possible."

"Even if it were, once transmitted to humans, what would stop it?"

"An ocean," replied Lu.

Lorenz frowned. "But diseases travel. If it spreads to other birds—or humans—they will carry it elsewhere."

"Precisely."

"But they could bring it to Europe—to Germany!"

"Yes, they could," shrugged Lu, unbothered by the notion.

Lorenz sighed. "If it is possible, I don't know how. I'm sorry, I can't help you."

Lu nodded knowingly and pulled the satchel from off his shoulder. He opened it, removed the golden orb, and rested it in his palm. The sphere glowed when he placed his other hand on its top, casting its light onto the astounded scientist's face.

"What-what's that?" gasped Dr. Lorenz.

Lu's stern gaze moved across the lab as a churning spot of light expanded to a shimmering round doorway.

Dr. Lorenz staggered backward, nearly falling over a chair as he looked through the portal to a strange landscape beyond. When another burly man dressed in seventeenth-century breeches, a waistcoat, and a baggy shirt stepped into the lab through the portal, it was all Lorenz could do to stand.

Lu embraced the grinning man, who wore a sword strapped to his side and his dark hair pulled back in a bun. The fallen watcher turned to

Lorenz and said, "Doctor, this is my friend, Gadreel. He is an expert in such matters. He will show you how it is to be done."

<hr />

BUCKEYE, KANSAS
FEBRUARY 1918

MILTON BROTHERS FARMS was an American success story. Started by two brothers ten years before, they now provided poultry to butcher shops from Wichita to Kansas City. But the customers the two brothers were most proud of were the fifty-thousand soldiers they fed at nearby Fort Riley. The farm had grown by acres in the past nine months to satisfy the demand, just as Fort Riley had. The brothers had built six new henhouses, and chicks, which would one day be fried or mixed with carrots and dumplings, were hatching at an unprecedented rate.

Henhouse number five held twenty-thousand chickens in rows of cages stacked six feet tall. Despite the thousands of roosting chickens, the henhouse was quiet in the dark hours of the morning. When a glistening portal appeared near the stack of feed bags, the scattered light rays stirred the chickens in their crowded cages. Tired clucks followed as the sturdy Gadreel stepped through the portal. Dressed in black leather boots and a seventeenth-century greatcoat, the banished watcher had a sword at his side and carried a shiny copper tank. On the three-foot-tall cylinder's domed top was an angled brass valve. What looked like a brass bicycle pump with a wooden handle was attached to the tank's side.

Gadreel's cunning eyes scanned the henhouse as the portal's shimmering light cast strange shadows across the cages and stirring fowl. With his dark pulled-back hair glistening in the shifting light, Gadreel lugged the heavy spray can to the middle aisle between the rows of cages. He set it on the straw-laden floor with a *thunk* and pumped its wooden handle.

With a clever smirk, Gadreel lifted the copper tank and opened its valve. A whistling rush of air followed. When a pungent mist shot over the cages and rained on the half-slumbering fowl, they began clucking madly. By the time Gadreel walked down both sides of the row, every chicken was cackling or clucking.

Gadreel was re-pressurizing the spray tank for the next row when a door at the end of the henhouse burst open, and a light flipped on.

"What in the hell is goin' on in here?" barked an eye-rubbing farmer, the corner of his bib overalls hanging over his barreled chest, a shotgun in one hand. "Chester! Are you in here botherin' the damn birds again?" he yelled, his voice echoing as he strained to see through the dim light. When the farmer saw the shiny copper spray tank on the floor between the row of cages, he grunted, "What in *thee* hell?"

The farmer turned down the aisle. He was just feet from the can when he passed the towering Gadreel standing in the shadows. It was then the farmer noticed the portal's shimmering light the next row over, its strange radiance filtering through the cages of nervous chickens. The farmer crept closer to the stacked pens and squinted to see through to the other side. "What the hell?" he muttered, not understanding what he was looking at.

"You should not be here."

With a gasp, the farmer spun around to see the foot-taller and broader Gadreel glaring down at him. Before the startled farmer could raise his shotgun, Gadreel placed his palm against the farmer's forehead. With the touch of the watcher's hand, the farmer's eyes crossed and then closed as if falling asleep, and his shotgun dropped to the floor.

Gadreel chuckled as the farmer swayed on his feet. With the jab of his finger, the farmer toppled back against the cages.

After returning to his spray can, a smirking Gadreel turned the nozzle on the dozing farmer and showered him with the deadly pathogen. He then sprayed the remaining three rows of the henhouse.

Within ten minutes, the copper tank was empty, and Gadreel was exiting through the shimmering portal, leaving thousands of nervously clucking chickens and the sleeping farmer in the shadows.

CHÂTEAU DE BRET
27 FEBRUARY 1918

BUNDLED IN A COAT, hat, and scarf, Eli had just finished feeding the horses in the stable when he turned to the pile of hay in the corner. His gaze moved to a board with knots that looked like glaring eyes. Eli squared up to the board and stared it down like a gunslinger, then lifted his wool coat and pulled the blazerod from its holster. He pointed the pewter cylinder at the knots, closed his eyes, and strained in concentration. The end of the weapon faintly glowed, but no bolts of light fired. Eli fought back his frustration, holstered the blazerod, and resumed his chores.

While the former watcher cherished his mortality, there were things he missed. Eli wished he could still make a difference in the world, bring about good, and inspire the best in mortals. He often reminded himself the world no longer wanted him and his time had passed.

That Eli's existence was now finite didn't bother him; in some ways, he thought immortality a curse. To Eli, the most exciting part of mortality was its uncertainty. That he or Michelle could perish from disease, accident, or physical harm made every day precious. On top of that, each day had its own challenges and problems—some he found laughable. Simple things he would have scoffed at as an immortal now seemed epically troubling.

But the grandest and most concerning part of Eli's change was fatherhood. Despite Eli's vast knowledge and experience, he often wondered if he was up to the task. He feared he might not be enough to prepare and protect his son, especially in light of Charmeine's declaration.

The gray winter light was fading when Eli pushed out of the stable and looked across the meadow to the wooly sheep. He turned and waved to the other workers as they lumbered down the path to the road.

Eli was about to turn back to the house when he noticed an unusual glow over the trees on the hill. It came from the clearing above the meadow—a place he had not visited since his son's birth. Eli studied the glowing light. He considered ignoring it but then started up the hill.

When Eli entered the clearing, he wasn't surprised to see a glowing

Cyrus standing near the open stone box, its lid ten feet away, half-buried in decayed leaves. Eli's jaw tightened at Cyrus's judging gaze.

"I'm disappointed in you, Elijah."

Eli sighed. "Yes, I'm sure you are."

"What have you done? You've sold yourself for the fleeting life of a mortal!"

"That was two years ago," frowned Eli.

"You're even reckoning as one," scoffed Cyrus.

"You told me once I'd make a poor mortal. I thought I'd try it."

"An attempt at humor," huffed Cyrus.

Eli raised his palms.

"Despite your fascination with mortals, I never thought it would lead you to this."

"I'm sorry my imperfection offends you."

Cyrus's eyes narrowed. "We were never meant to be perfect, only to rise to our calls as teachers and guardians of this world."

"And what if they no longer want our guidance? What do we do when they reject us at every turn?"

"When a child disobeys, it is disciplined—guided back onto its intended path. That is how you teach it."

"But when the grown child strays, then what? Force it?"

"If necessary," Cyrus nodded. "There are always consequences."

"There's nothing we can do! They've rejected us!"

"No, you have abandoned them."

Eli sighed and shook his head.

"You've been granted what you wanted. I hope you're satisfied."

Eli nodded. "I have the love of a woman and a son. I will live out my life as a mortal and then go the way of all living things."

"You make it sound so easy. You should count yourself lucky your woman survived birthing a halfborn. She lives while the world suffers!"

Eli's eyes narrowed. *He doesn't know Charmeine saved her.* "The war is ending. Lu's forces are losing. It's only a matter of time."

"They have not lost yet," frowned Cyrus. "Gadreel has joined Lu!"

Eli's jaw slackened. "You exiled Gadreel to the abyss! I saw it!"

"Lu has learned to harness the orb to bring exiles back."

"As *he* was brought back," Eli muttered, trying to make sense of it all. "Who freed Lu from his prison? He was bound in Naraka. Who summoned him from the abyss? As grand overseer, you were the keeper of the orb!"

"You forget there were other domain spheres—and travel portals."

"But they were all locked after the Great Purge. You oversaw it!"

"I don't know all things," bristled Cyrus.

A fuming Eli shook his head. "So, besides his army of halfborn, Lu has Gadreel."

"Others may follow," Cyrus grimly added.

Eli gulped. "But not Semjaza?"

Cyrus shook his head. "The Dark One is locked away for the eternities. I've seen to that."

"So was Lu," frowned Eli.

Cyrus's gaze lowered.

"What does Lu mean to do?"

"What he's always meant to do."

Eli stared across the clearing.

Cyrus studied Eli. "You are correct that this war is ending. Lu's forces have lost their potency. The German and Austrian people are weary of the price they've paid. But Lu will not go out with a whimper. Gadreel has unleashed a plague the likes of which this world has not seen in millennia. It will take more lives than the war."

Eli's shoulders sank at the sad realization of what was to follow. "Then it *is* the end time."

"Not yet. Our work is not complete," glared Cyrus.

"What Charmeine said about my son... It all makes sense now."

Cyrus's eyes narrowed. "Charmeine came to you? What did she tell you?"

Eli studied Cyrus, puzzled by his reaction. *He doesn't know about Franny.*

Cyrus composed himself. "From my place in Elysium, I'm afraid I'm lacking in recent information. It's all I can do to get here and urge you on."

Eli eyed Cyrus. While there was much he didn't know about the realms beyond, Eli was surprised Cyrus could travel so freely. "How is it you're able to return from there?"

"Your mortal mind is already failing you. You've forgotten I was the grand overseer of this world."

"But when Lu destroyed you, you became an out-of-phase entity. I thought such—"

"That I'm allowed to return doesn't matter. It's what I'm here for that matters. To assist you."

Eli nodded. He recognized he needed help. "One of Lu's halfborns pledged himself to me. He told me of the prophecy of the prince—a child who would usher in the return of the Chosen One."

"I'm familiar with the prophecy," frowned Cyrus. "But that child will come at a future time. When we have made the world ready."

Puzzled by Cyrus's response, Eli considered saying no more, but he knew Cyrus's wisdom could help him protect his family.

"What is it you're not saying?" questioned Cyrus.

"Charmeine told me...*my son* is that prince."

Cyrus pulled back, astounded by the declaration. "Charmeine said that? Your child is nothing but a halfborn! The bastard child of a watcher and a mortal woman! There are a thousand others like him!"

Eli's jaw tightened. "You're wrong. My son's mother is no ordinary woman. She died giving birth, and Charmeine raised her!"

"That's not possible! Charmeine would never do such a thing... unless..."

"Michelle LaRue Duvall is no ordinary mortal," replied Eli. "She carries a royal bloodline. Charmeine told me my wife is a descendant of the great Emmanuel, the *Ihidaya*! He who sacrificed himself to change this world! How do you not know this?"

Cyrus's eyes widened. "She is the one," he breathed, his gaze fading in thought. "The child is the Harbinger. How can that be? I was not told." He turned back to Eli. "If it is true, they will seek to destroy your son!"

"Yes, I know," Eli grimly nodded.

FORT RILEY, KANSAS
4 MARCH 1918

IT HAD BEEN NEARLY a year since America had declared war on Germany, but U.S. forces had yet to enter the fight. To train the proposed six-million-man army, existing U.S. Army facilities across the country had grown, and new ones sprung up. Fort Riley was no exception. With the addition of the adjacent Camp Funston, it had increased by nine hundred buildings and two thousand acres. The men of the 89th Infantry would be among the first Americans to fight and die in the war. But some of them would die before ever getting to France.

Colonel Horace Palmer, M.D., shook his head as he walked down the hospital ward floor. The white surgeon's mask covering his face stood out against his olive officer's tunic and flared breeches. "How many more men today?" he boomed, his voice deep and direct.

"Nine more, sir. Two died last night," replied the masked captain, watching the colonel with concern.

"How long ago did those two present?"

"Three days ago, sir."

Colonel Palmer's bushy eyebrows gathered as he looked over the crowded hospital ward. Every bed was filled with groaning and wheezing men, some shivering from fevers, others sweaty and delusional. "I've never seen anything like it," muttered the colonel.

"It presents like influenza: chills, fever, fatigue. Some men are only mildly affected, while others get violently ill—nosebleeds followed by rapid-onset pneumonia. Their lungs fill up, and they drown."

"How many cases altogether?"

"Seventy-three...so far."

"Seventy-three? Where have you put the others?"

"The less sick are in a field tent outside."

The colonel nodded his approval. "Seventy-three out of fifty-thousand men, that's a drop in the bucket."

"With six dead, sir."

"Acceptable casualties. In battle, we would consider that a miracle," nodded Colonel Palmer.

"But they're not in battle, sir. Not yet."

"Yes, I know. They're due to ship out to New York and then France in a month. Like other influenzas, this one will run its course. They'll then be fit as a fiddle and ready to fight."

"Should we issue a quarantine?" questioned the captain.

"Quarantine?" glared Palmer. "Whatever for?"

"To keep it from spreading, sir—into the community," insisted the captain.

"Nonsense. It would only create a stir. Besides, the men will be fitter for having it. They'll have stronger constitutions."

The captain's concerned eyes narrowed. "Sir, six out of seventy-three have perished so far. If it spreads to all fifty-thousand men, it could kill more than four thousand! If it spreads outside the camp..."

"How do you know that's not where it came from?" The colonel shook his head. "You said it yourself. It's mild in some cases. You could look at it as God's way of weeding out the weak. He wants only the fittest to kick the Hun's asses!"

"Yes, sir," the captain grimly nodded. He stepped forward when the colonel turned to leave. "Sir, the new hospital building at Camp Funston is sitting empty. Can I at least move these sick men there and keep this smaller ward for regular patients?"

The colonel paused, looked across the filled hospital beds, and nodded. "That would be fine. Oh, and Captain."

"Yes, sir?"

"Make sure word of this does not leave this camp," the colonel frowned.

"Sir?"

"We are at war. Such information would damage morale and aid the enemy."

"But what of the deaths?" questioned the masked captain.

"Keep track of the deaths, but wait to release those numbers. That's an order."

"Yes, sir," the captain muttered as Colonel Palmer turned and left the crowded hospital ward.

CHAPTER 29
THE APPRENTICE

Ronan chuckled as the small, curly-haired boy ran through the great room, flying a toy biplane in his hand.

"Franny, fly your airplane to Father. You mustn't bother Uncle," gently chided Michelle.

"Oh, he's no bother, my dear. I enjoy the life he's brought to my dreary old home. Besides, it's his birthday!" grinned Ronan. He fondly watched Franny run around the furniture, his small arm rising and dipping the French-badged biplane as he made little-boy engine noises.

While young François was only two, he could have passed for a three-year-old in stature and intellect. An obedient and cheerful child, Franny was also fearless, giving his watchful parents one more reason to worry. Though the strange attacks on their son were less frequent now, Eli knew more would come, especially once Franny's eminence became known. Eli knew he was no longer a match for Lu and hoped enlisting Cyrus's help would be enough to prepare for the brewing storm.

Sitting on the couch near the piano, Eli laughed as Franny ran into his arms.

"Maybe he will be a famous French flying ace when he grows up," Ronan chuckled.

"Oh, I hope this war is long over before then," groaned Michelle.

"It's just a matter of time now, with the Americans in the fight," nodded a confident Ronan. "The Germans are running out of steam."

After pulling away from his father's arms, the eager Franny looped and dived his biplane around the piano. But when he passed the French doors at the back of the room and noticed the dark figure outside, he came to a sudden stop and pointed. "Look! Monsieur Gik!"

"Let him in," said Michelle, forcing a smile. While the halfborn's ghastly appearance had softened, and he now worked for Ronan, she was still uncomfortable in his presence.

"Happy birthday, young prince," nodded Gik as he presented little François with a small unwrapped shoebox.

"Oh, how nice. What is it?" Michelle asked with a nervous smile as she moved beside her beaming son, fearing it might be a captured rat or a dead snake. Her eyes narrowed when Gik opened the box to a handful of small stones and two lengths of worn twine tied to a small woven pouch. "What is it?" she asked, more intrigued than nervous.

"A sling," Gik grinned with yellow, crooked teeth.

"A sling?" Eli asked, coming closer.

"Yes," Gik eagerly nodded.

"Like the one David slew Goliath with?" joked Michelle.

"Yes! It *is* the sling that killed the giant called Goliath."

Michelle's eyes widened. "You knew Goliath?"

"I hated him. He was a terrible bully," frowned Gik.

Confused, Michelle turned to Eli, who offered only a shrug. "It's true then?" she asked searchingly. "David killed Goliath?"

"Mostly," nodded Eli as a stupefied Ronan moved closer. "The stone didn't kill the giant; it was the sword that separated him from his head."

"That's how you kill a halfborn," muttered Gik, holding his neck.

"Oh, that's awful!" grimaced Michelle, pulling Franny against her.

"That's why I'm here, to protect the young prince," nodded Gik.

Michelle's worried gaze moved to her husband.

Eli hoisted Franny in his arms, kissed his cheek, and squeezed him.

12 April 1918

ELI SCANNED the rows of green-sprigged grapevines that dipped and climbed the rolling hills. Just ahead of him, a laughing Franny chased after a grasshopper. Eli savored the fresh spring air as he considered the weeks spent pruning and cultivating the vineyard to prepare it for another growing season. He thought there was something especially fulfilling working with his hands. While grapes grew in the wild, it was man's collaboration with nature—the addition of human ingenuity and perseverance—that allowed them to grow and flourish at such a grand scale. Eli sighed as he considered the collaboration he had abandoned. He knew the vineyard would quickly decline without his and the other caretakers' efforts. He doubted humanity could decline any more than it already had without him.

While Eli missed serving humanity, he cherished his mortal life. The joy and happiness he now experienced were even more than he had imagined as a watcher—but so were the difficulties and heartaches. Like a robust French wine, he thought mortality was worth every bit of effort put into it.

Eli watched as Franny happily ran down the row of greening vines. He knew if Michelle were with them, she would want Franny closer, but Eli thought it was good for the boy to run free. Just the same, Eli kept an eye on him as he ran up the hill.

After kneeling to retie two vines that had come free of their posts, Eli stood and looked for Franny. While he could hear his voice from over the hill, he could no longer see him. Unalarmed, Eli continued along the row, stooping to tie another vine. By the time Eli neared the top of the hill, he could no longer hear the two-year-old. Quickening his pace, Eli crested the hill. He paused when he spotted Franny talking to a white-haired man. When he recognized it was Cyrus, Eli's concern faded. Too far away to hear the overseer's words, Eli watched as his son quietly listened. It wasn't until Eli was twenty feet away that he realized Cyrus's unusual glow was absent. Eli dismissed the change as the overseer turned to him.

"Franny, I see you've made a friend," said Eli, unsure of the reason for the overseer's visit.

"I hope he will call me a friend," nodded Cyrus, silhouetted in the morning sun.

"What brings you to us?" asked Eli.

Cyrus studied Eli. "The child is as you said, but I fear for him."

Eli sighed.

"You fear for him too. How many attempts have there been on his life?"

Eli's eyebrows gathered in thought. "Since his birth, eight, that I know of."

Cyrus nodded. "These were not Lu's forces."

"No."

"The dark elements," Cyrus concluded, eyeing the boy.

"Before, I thought that was a myth," shrugged Eli.

"Mortals believe we're a myth." Cyrus's gaze grew more serious. "The dark elements cry out for him and what he will bring. Even now, the earth could open and swallow him."

Eli's concerned gaze lowered to the ground. "What stops these dark elements from doing so?"

"There are countering forces—even at the molecular level, the balance must be maintained. Those forces preserve him, but for how long, I don't know."

Eli eyed Cyrus. He sensed something unusual in the overseer.

Cyrus's gaze moved to the blazerod holstered on Eli's hip. "I see there are some things you cling to. Another mortal flaw. Do you feel better carrying a weapon you can no longer use to protect him?"

"How do you know I can no longer use it?"

Cyrus studied Eli. "You have power remaining?"

"I will do whatever I must to protect my son," replied Eli.

Cyrus shook his head. "You have no idea what Lu will do to him and your wife, do you? You cannot stop him. Let me take the boy."

"Take him where?" frowned Eli.

"To a place where Lu cannot find him."

"And where is that? You never told me how you can return to this world so easily."

"You question me?" bristled Cyrus. "I'm offering the only sure way of protecting your son. If I take him, they will not find him."

"No," Eli replied, shaking his head. "He's staying with us. We will protect him. Charmeine promised me assistance in times of need."

"Charmeine," huffed Cyrus. "How do you know I'm not that assistance?"

Eli's eyes narrowed, surprised by Cyrus's disdain for the angel. "Franny, come to Papa," Eli directed, his eyes not leaving Cyrus.

When Franny started toward his father, Cyrus placed a restraining hand on his shoulder.

Eli's jaw tightened. "Let go of my son."

"You act as though you do not trust me," frowned Cyrus.

Eli's hands clenched as he eyed the overseer.

"I am offering my assistance. I will protect the child until he is ready to fulfill his work. It is the only way."

"It is *not* the only way," glared Eli. "Let go of my son."

"Elijah, you are even more foolish than I supposed. You have not seen the future of this child as I have. You cannot understand the way I do. If you fail to protect him—if he does not live to usher in the Chosen One—all will be lost. Humankind will disintegrate on the ash heap of time without a reckoning."

"Franny, come to Papa," said Eli, glaring at the overseer.

When Cyrus lifted his hand, and the boy moved to his father's side, Eli's fists loosened.

"Then you have decided," seethed Cyrus.

The overseer's indignant response surprised Eli. Something had changed in Cyrus, but he didn't know what. Not taking his eyes off the overseer, Eli took Franny into his arms and sternly said, "I will care for my own. I no longer need your advice or assistance."

"Very well," huffed Cyrus. With an angry wave of his hand, a shimmering portal opened in the row between the grapevines.

Eli's eyes widened. As an out-of-phase being, Eli had wondered how Cyrus was traveling without the orb's help. *He's learned to harness the energy himself!* Eli watched slack-jawed as a glaring Cyrus stepped through the portal and disappeared.

Pasewalk German Military Hospital
1 May 1918

THE TRAUMA WARD'S beds were filled with bandaged and moaning men who had returned from the front. Due to the shortage of chloroform and ether, some surgeries, including amputations, were performed without anesthesia, leaving the conscious wounded curled in their beds, covering their ears as shrieks and screams echoed from down the hall.

Such cries of agony didn't bother the red-bearded Lu or his black-haired associate, Gadreel, as they moved through the wounded and writhing, as if looking for a lost goat. While Lu sported a tasteful suit and vest, the extravagant Gadreel wore a German military dress uniform with shiny black calf-skin boots, a spiked helmet, and his ever-present watcher's sword.

Lu was near a steamy window when he sensed a particular presence. Like a hound honing in on a downed duck, he moved to a bed where a skinny soldier lay in pajamas, his face and eyes bandaged, with only his straight black hair and mustache showing. Lu hovered over the young soldier, who appeared to be awake yet unbothered by the sounds of pain and suffering.

"Is someone there?" asked the skinny young soldier, his voice abrupt and faintly quivering with fear. "Nurse? Is that you?"

Lu studied the wounded soldier. He liked the darkness he felt within him. "No. It is not the nurse."

"Who is it?" the skinny soldier snapped. "I can't see! I've been blinded by mustard gas!"

"You were at the front?"

"No! I was playing in my grandmother's backyard. Of course I was at the front, you idiot!"

"Do you always have so little regard for those you speak to?"

The bandaged soldier sat up in his bed. "Wait, you're not an officer, are you?"

"I am a friend," grinned Lu.

"My friends are dead," seethed the bandaged soldier. "The damned

British are to blame. They're the reason for this war! They should have minded their own business!"

Lu chuckled as Gadreel joined him beside the bed. "You have quite an opinion, don't you?"

"All I know is that I would have run this war much differently. MUCH differently," huffed the bandaged soldier.

"I'm sure you would have," nodded Lu. "You have quite a lot of pluck for a private."

"I'm a corporal!" snapped the bandaged soldier. "Corporal Adolf Hitler! I've been wounded twice and received eight medals, including the Iron Cross! I should be a damned major!"

Lu grinned. "Young Adolf... I like you. Follow me, and I'll make you more than a major."

"That's just fine, but there's only one problem. WHO NEEDS A BLIND SOLDIER!" bellowed young Hitler.

Lu glanced at the smirking Gadreel, opened his coat, and removed the orb from a pouch under his arm. He held it in one hand and placed his other on Hitler's forehead.

"What are you doing?" barked a squirming Hitler.

"Quiet. I'm restoring your eyesight," snapped Lu as the orb glowed. After a moment, Lu lifted his hand and removed the gauze from the skinny soldier's face.

Hitler squinted from the surrounding brightness as he tried to open his eyes. "I still can't see!"

"You will." Lu returned the orb to the pouch under his coat.

After adjusting to the light, a blinking Hitler laughed when his eyes focused on the tall, red-bearded Lu. "I can see! I can see again!"

With an approving nod, Lu turned away, and Gadreel followed.

"Wait! Who are you? How did you do that? How do I thank you?"

Lu stopped and turned back to the stupefied Adolf Hitler with a cunning smirk. "We will come again. Don't worry; there will be plenty of time to pay us back."

NIGHT HAD FALLEN IN PASEWALK. The few gaslights that lined the cobbled street left long shadows as Lu and Gadreel drove in their open-topped automobile. When their headlight beam fell upon a dark-cloaked man standing in the road with a raised, halting hand, Lu stopped the car. The cloaked figure pulled back his hood to reveal glistening white hair and beard.

"Cyrus," glared Lu.

"You should have run him over," snarled Gadreel.

"It wouldn't make any difference," scowled Lu as Cyrus moved to his side of the car. "I thought I got rid of you," Lu said with a look of disdain.

Cyrus's stern gaze moved from Lu to Gadreel like a disappointed father.

"What do you want?" snapped Gadreel.

"I've come to broker a peace," replied the steely eyed Cyrus.

"Peace?" huffed Lu.

"You will not win this war. While your plague has killed thousands, it did not stop the Americans from coming. Thousands more of them are joining the fight each day."

"Yes, I know," Lu proudly replied. "And they are bringing the sickness with them. It will kill millions—perhaps more than the war."

"That is your calculus? To destroy the mortals who would serve you?"

"There is no end to them," shrugged Lu.

"There is an end," glared Cyrus. "Your cause is lost. The world will soon rejoice at your downfall."

Lu drew in a furious breath. "Our cause is not lost! When this horse dies, we will mount the next one!"

"We have many in our stable," smirked Gadreel.

"Besides, our forces greatly outnumber yours, especially with the sanctimonious Eli out of the race," fumed Lu.

"You think he would have known he could have a mortal anytime he wanted and given up nothing," laughed Gadreel.

"To go through all of that and still kill her with his child," Lu added, shaking his head. "How deliciously tragic."

"But she is alive," frowned Cyrus.

Lu's eyes narrowed. "His woman didn't die?"

"She died but was brought back."

"By Eli? Impossible, I had the orb!" cried Lu.

"The messenger, Charmeine, restored her," explained Cyrus.

Lu's green eyes shifted in thought. "How can that be? Why would Charmeine meddle? Why would she restore a mortal to life? It violates the law they hold so dear!"

"Because Michelle is no ordinary mortal. She is the heir. She is a descendant of Emmanuel."

Lu's jaw fell open. "And she has mated with a watcher."

"The prophecy," muttered Gadreel.

"Yes. And as word spreads, who do you think your halfborn serfs will follow?" questioned Cyrus.

Lu gulped.

"What of your army now?" mocked Cyrus.

"We must destroy them before it's too late!" exclaimed Gadreel.

Lu's puzzled gaze moved to the overseer. "Why do you tell us this?"

"Don't you see?" grinned Gadreel. "The grand overseer has found the taste of power to his liking. When the Chosen One returns, the book will be closed, and Cyrus's purpose—his power as overseer will cease...forever."

"And so, you come to us," grinned Lu. "Our subterfuge and cunning appeal to you. You wish us to teach you."

Cyrus's countenance darkened. "Who do you think it was that freed you from the abyss?"

Lu's brow furrowed in thought before he looked up at Cyrus and gasped, "It was you? But you cast us out! You had me imprisoned in Naraka! Why would you bring me back?"

Cyrus laughed. "You are both so naïve. Do you not know you were groomed to do this?"

"By Semjaza, perhaps," frowned Lu.

"Who do you think prepared Semjaza?" sneered the overseer.

Lu's eyes shifted in thought before he turned to the equally confounded Gadreel.

"You have done just as I had hoped," said a proud Cyrus. "Chaos, conflict, blind hate—a divided people are much easier to rule and control. How can they grow and progress themselves when they are more worried about hating their neighbor?"

Gadreel laughed at the irony. "You've manipulated us just as we have them!"

A rare grin formed on Cyrus's white-bearded face. "You are beginning to see."

"And thus, the master purveyor reveals himself. You wish to ally with us," concluded Lu.

"I grow tired of working my puppets from afar," replied Cyrus.

An eager Gadreel leaned forward. "Will you bring others from the abyss? Will you return Semjaza?"

Cyrus's face dimmed. "No. Semjaza is too dangerous. He would destroy everything."

Lu's green eyes shifted in thought.

"But what of Eli and the others?" asked Gadreel.

"Eli has renounced his calling. He has lost his power and lives as a man. The world will be ours once the woman and child are gone."

"And the prophecy?"

"It will die with them."

"Can we even kill them?"

Cyrus's eyes moved to the bulge under Lu's coat. "You have the power of the orb. We need only separate them."

"And what if we expose you?" questioned Lu.

"To who? The other watchers are all but gone, thanks to you," smirked Cyrus. "They would never believe you if you did."

"The balance has been broken. The watchers have succumbed, and we will henceforth reign!" gloated Lu.

Cyrus's stern gaze moved from Gadreel to Lu. "We must first rid ourselves of what stands in our way."

CHAPTER 30
EVIL AWAITS

The cool night air gently stirred the bedchamber's window sheers as dim moonlight glowed across the feather comforter. Nestled in bed, Eli and Michelle soundly slept. Outside, crickets happily chirped as the light breeze rustled the forest leaves like the soft, rushing surge of the sea. On the back porch, the old dog, Sébastien, lay sprawled on his bed. His baggy eyes pulled open when the crickets stopped their song, and he raised his head at the faint scent of an intruder.

Michelle's eyes shot open at Sébastien's bark. When she shook Eli's arm, he catapulted up in bed and gasped, "What is it?"

"Something's wrong. Sébastien's barking," Michelle fretted, staring out the window into the night.

"That dog is too old to hear himself bark," groaned Eli, lying back down. "Maybe Gik scared him."

Knowing the halfborn lurked around the estate at night was no comfort to Michelle. "Do you trust it?"

"Gik is a him. And yes, I trust Gik more than most mortals. He hardly sleeps. He spends his nights watching after our son."

Perched on the ledge outside of Franny's window like a gargoyle, Gik's sunken eyes scanned the darkened forest as Sébastien relentlessly barked. The shadows were in motion with a stirring breeze and only a crescent moon to light the inky night. After a time, Gik returned his head to his pulled-up bony knees, but his wary gaze was slow to leave the shadowed forest. When the agitated old dog hobbled to the forest's edge, Gik took notice. He sat up, his nostrils flared, but breathed only the barking dog's scent. Gik's sunken eyes narrowed when Sébastien's barking stopped. The halfborn lowered his head, assuming the intruder —a rabbit, a fox, or even a wolf—had left, but he continued to watch the dog sitting at the forest's edge. Slowly, Gik's eyes closed.

The sound of a broken forest twig opened Gik's eyes. With a gasp, he stiffened on his perch. Where there were before only long, empty shadows stood two dark and foreboding figures, their green eyes gleaming in the blackness. The hackles on Gik's neck stood as he breathed in the scent of his former master, Lu. The halfborn's eyes swelled when Gadreel's glimmering sword swept down and lopped off the old dog's head with barely a yipe.

Inside the bedchamber, a sleepless Michelle shot up at the sound. "Elijah! Did you hear that?" she gasped, launching out of bed in her flowing nightgown. "I'm checking on Franny!"

After rolling out of bed in his pajama bottoms, Eli shuffled to the window overlooking the yard to the darkened forest. His sleepy eyes widened when he saw a grinning Gadreel in the moonlight. The banished watcher stood near the forest's edge, holding the dog's severed head in his outstretched arm. "MICHELLE!" shouted Eli, racing to Franny's room. Eli was in the hall when he remembered his blazerod on the nightstand. He dashed back for it and grabbed the useless weapon when Michelle screamed from the nursery. Eli charged down the hall to find his frantic wife standing over Franny's empty bed. Eli's broad chest was heaving as his worried gaze turned to the open nursery window.

"What is it?" gasped Ronan, hobbling into the nursery in his nightshirt.

"They took Franny! They took my little boy!" cried Michelle.

With blazerod in hand, Eli climbed through the open window onto the slate roof. He saw no sign of Gik and feared his trust in the halfborn had been a mistake. After sliding down the roof, Eli dropped to the grass. His jaw tightened, and his fists clenched when he saw Lu standing near the forest's edge, holding a calm Franny in his arms. "PUT MY SON DOWN!" roared Eli, fighting back his fury as he stormed toward the fallen watcher.

"I'm sorry, Eli, I won't be doing that," grinned Lu.

"Don't let them take my son!" exclaimed Michelle as she burst through the back door and charged off the porch toward them. A hobbling Ronan followed close behind with his shotgun in hand.

Eli grabbed Michelle when she raced by and pulled her against him. "Stay back. Let me handle them," said Eli, his blue eyes glaring at the banished watchers.

Gadreel laughed and tossed the dog's head aside as the furious old man approached with his shotgun raised to fire.

"What did you do to my dog?" bellowed Ronan, just feet away.

"Ronan, stay back!" warned Eli.

"I sliced him like a sausage, just as I shall you," snarled Gadreel, raising his sword.

"Baby, it's okay!" cried a frantic Michelle, still in Eli's grasp, reaching for her son.

Franny showed his first hint of worry at seeing his mother's distress.

"Let my son go!" ordered Eli. "He's an innocent child! He's no concern to you!"

"On the contrary," grinned the cunning Lu. "He's very much a concern to me."

"So, you birthed the Harbinger," grunted Gadreel, unbothered by Ronan's shotgun pointed at his head.

"He's my son! Put him down! Let him go!" demanded Eli.

"You know we can't do that, Eli. If you believe in the prophecy— and I think you do—you know how dangerous he is," glared Lu.

"What are they talking about?" fretted Michelle, trying to break free of Eli's grasp.

"You haven't told her?" laughed Lu.

"Told me what?" gasped Michelle.

"That your child is not a typical halfborn, bred by an empyrean watcher and a mortal whore," sneered Gadreel. "He is the Harbinger, the forerunner. It is prophesied that the scion of a watcher and a woman of the divine lineage will usher in the end time and the return of the Chosen One."

"That is something we cannot allow," glared Lu. "We have come too far and worked too hard."

"Please, I just want my son back!" pleaded Michelle.

"I won't let you take him," fumed Eli.

"And how are you going to stop us?" Lu's eyes lowered to the blazerod clutched in Eli's hand. "Using that? Have you forgotten how impotent you are now? You relinquished your power. You're now like any other weak and worthless mortal!"

"You'll think me weak when I blow your damn head off!" roared Ronan. He raised the shotgun and fired into Gadreel from eight feet away. The storm of lead knocked Gadreel back and blew holes in his waistcoat and frilly shirt, but the buckshot barely penetrated his flesh.

"Ronan! No! Get back!" warned Eli as Gadreel shook off the blast and angrily raised his sword.

With Gadreel storming toward him, a round-eyed Ronan stepped back and lifted his gun to fire again, but when he lost his balance and fell, the second blast flew high.

"NO!" cried Eli as Gadreel raised his sword above his head. But before Gadreel could bring it down on the helpless Ronan sprawled in the grass, Eli crashed into Gadreel and knocked him off his feet. Gadreel swung the sword, narrowly missing Eli's legs as Michelle screamed, and Lu laughed.

After pinning Gadreel's sword arm down with one hand, Eli used the blazerod as a club and smashed it against Gadreel's head. The blow did little damage but released Gadreel's hold of the sword. When Eli grabbed for the sword, Gadreel quickly pulled him back. The change in momentum was enough for Gadreel to gain the upper hand, and he rolled Eli onto his back.

Lu laughed as Gadreel and Eli wrestled and threw punches in the grass while a concerned Franny pointed at the brawl. Lu noticed when the blazerod came loose and rolled onto the lawn beside them. It was the last tool he needed.

Ronan's round eyes moved from the sword lying in the grass to the loose blazerod just feet away. He scrambled for the rod on his hands and knees.

When the struggling Eli reached for the sword, Gadreel viciously headbutted him, dazing Eli.

Lu was halfway to the blazerod when a determined Michelle charged him, grabbing for her son. Lu turned Franny out of Michelle's reach and roughly shoved her to the ground. But when Lu turned back for the blazerod, it was gone.

With the blazerod in hand, Ronan scrambled to his feet as Lu scooped up Gadreel's sword. The Frenchman was frantically eyeing the ancient weapon when an agonizing jolt pierced his back. Ronan gasped with barely a sound as he looked down at the bloody sword protruding from his chest.

"NO!" shrieked Michelle.

Ronan's eyes bulged, and his mouth gaped as he slumped to his knees. With a wheeze, the blazerod dropped from Ronan's hand as he fell on his face, the sword still lodged in his back.

Perched atop a beaten Eli, Gadreel savored the violent slaying. But young Franny, who had before been mostly unfazed by the attack, was now distraught. He fought against Lu's retraining hold and reached for his dead great uncle as Lu eyed the blazerod. The fallen watcher was stooping to claim the prized weapon when a high-pitched shriek came from the forest. Lu had barely turned to see what ferocity was approaching when the bony Gik leaped from the shadows onto his back. Gik savagely clawed at Lu's face and eyes before burying his yellow teeth into the watcher's ear.

"Get off me, you worthless dreg!" howled Lu as Gik bent him backward. Unable to fend off his former servant with only one arm, Lu dropped Franny to the grass.

Beaten and bludgeoned, a panting Eli gathered his strength as Gadreel sat on top of him, enjoying the assault on Lu. Eli's eyes widened when a shimmering circle of light appeared, and a portal opened. "Cyrus!" Eli cried out as the overseer stepped forth, "Help us!"

With all eyes on Cyrus, Franny jumped to his feet and scampered to the lifeless Ronan, his small arm extended. But before the child could reach him, Cyrus snatched him up.

"Don't let them take our son!" gasped Eli as Gadreel climbed off him.

Still clawing at Lu's face, Gik hissed at the white-bearded overseer.

"Please, give me my son," sobbed a heartbroken Michelle as she approached with outreached arms, but Cyrus clung to the boy.

On his feet, Gadreel moved to the dead Ronan. With a snarled lip, he placed his boot on the Frenchman's back and pulled his gleaming sword free.

The savagely clawing Gik was on Lu's shoulders when Gadreel's sword sliced through the air. Gik's wild, sunken eyes were still bulging when his head landed on one side of Lu, and his gangly body dropped to the other.

After kicking Gik's head across the lawn, Lu's glaring green eyes turned to Cyrus and the distressed child. "I will take him now."

"No!" sobbed Michelle, pulling on Cyrus's arm.

"Cyrus! Help us!" pleaded Eli as he staggered to his feet.

Standing with the sword, Gadreel laughed at the teetering Eli's shock when Cyrus handed Franny to Lu.

"Give me my son back!" cried Michelle as she charged Lu, only to be knocked back to the ground beside her dead uncle.

"Cyrus, what have you done?" gasped the battered Eli, his sweat-glistening chest heaving.

"I'm maintaining balance. I'm protecting this world from *him!*" glared Cyrus, pointing at the distraught Franny still reaching for Ronan.

"He's a little boy!" sobbed Michelle from the grass.

"HE IS THE ENDER OF WORLDS!" roared Cyrus.

With the frightened little boy clamped under his arm, Lu reached into his coat and removed the orb. It glowed at his touch, and a shimmering crimson portal opened before the trees.

"NO! NOT THE ABYSS!" cried Eli as Lu started toward the scintillating doorway and the dark dreamscape beyond. With the last of his strength, Eli lunged. He smashed into the back of Lu's legs and brought him down with Franny, six feet short of the shimmering red portal.

While Lu kept his hold on the child, the faintly glowing orb broke free and rolled across the grass. Eli reached for it, but his hand fell inches short.

"Don't let him get the orb!" shouted Lu as he fought for it.

Gadreel raised his sword and swung it down on Eli's outstretched arm.

"ELI!" screamed Michelle.

Eli pulled back his arm as the glistening blade chopped into the lawn, just missing his fingers.

Horrified, Michelle watched as Gadreel pulled the embedded sword from the earth and, with both arms, raised it over his head. She knew, in an instant, that her Elijah would be gone. When Michelle felt the warm pewter of the blazerod near her uncle's hand, she turned and grabbed it, raised it in her arms, and pointed it at the fierce-eyed Gadreel.

Cyrus was watching the scene unfold when a white bolt of light shot from the blazerod through Gadreel's chest. "What?" gasped Cyrus. His stunned gaze turned to Michelle, wondering how a mortal could harness the weapon's energy, but then he remembered Michelle was no ordinary mortal.

Eli lunged for the orb when Gadreel dropped the sword and collapsed on the grass. The faintly shimmering sphere came to life at his touch, and Eli felt a jolt radiate through his body.

"Get the orb!" yelled Lu, reaching for it with one hand as he held the squirming Franny against him with the other.

A teary-eyed Michelle pointed the blazerod at Lu and roared, "LET GO OF MY SON!" But Lu held the reaching Franny before him like a shield as he climbed to his feet.

Eli cried out in pain when Cyrus's boot stomped on his wrist. After prying the domain sphere from Eli's hand, the overseer stood triumphantly. When Michelle shot a bolt at him, Cyrus dodged it.

Lu took advantage of the distraction, turned to the glowing crimson portal, and hurled Franny through it.

Ten feet away, Eli reached for his son as the boy disappeared into the dark abyss. "NOOO!" bellowed Eli, clawing across the grass toward the red-shimmering doorway.

Michelle leaped to her feet and charged Cyrus with the blazerod.

Cyrus was closing the portal with the domain sphere when Michelle grabbed it from him and dashed for the shrinking doorway. She dived through it with orb and blazerod in hand.

"Michelle!" gasped Eli, still feet from the collapsing doorway. But in an instant, the shimmering portal was closed, and his wife and son were gone, leaving Eli staring at the shadowy forest.

Staggered by what had just happened, Lu turned to Cyrus. "You let her take the orb?" Lu bellowed. "Now what do we do?"

"I no longer need it," huffed Cyrus, shaking off the mishap as he backed toward his still-open portal.

Lu's face was red, and the veins in his neck bulging as he marched past the writhing Gadreel and grabbed the sword from the grass. He turned to the devastated Eli, still on his knees, raised the sword over his head, and charged.

"Wait!" barked Cyrus, about to step through the portal.

Lu stopped just feet from Eli, the sword's long glistening blade ready to strike.

"Leave him. The pain he will feel as he lives out his days as a mortal is more than a watcher's sword will ever bring."

The seething Lu lowered the glistening blade and kicked Eli onto his back. Lu then turned to the wounded Gadreel and pulled him to his feet. With sword in hand, Lu gave his nemesis a final hateful glance as he helped the groaning Gadreel to the shimmering doorway.

"You've beaten Eli, and the child is gone," said Cyrus, eyeing the sobbing Eli from the portal's threshold. "We can now reign with impunity!"

"But what of her? You said we must separate them!" glared Lu.

"Those in the abyss will see to that. She is lost forever."

"But she has the orb!" insisted Lu.

"She is now of no concern!" barked Cyrus, glaring at his doubting pawn.

Still questioning their victory, Lu helped Gadreel through the shimmering doorway. When the portal closed, Eli found himself lying in the dim moonlight.

Eli's face filled with anguish as he stared into the dark, starry night, his chest rising and falling, his tears streaking from the corners of his eyes. He waited for another light to appear, for Charmeine to come to his aid, but there was no light or rescuing angel. Eli groaned, unable to move. His Michelle, the love of his life, the one he had given up everything for, and his child, who was to change the world forever, were gone, and Eli knew of no way to bring them back.

Eli closed his eyes to the star-filled heavens. He didn't hear Madame Duguay sobbing from the porch or the warm summer breeze rustling the forest leaves. The former watcher felt nothing, not his aching muscles and joints or the stinging of his sweat and tears in the cuts and scrapes on his face. Eli's world, his life, was gone.

EPILOGUE

Rue Petrelle was a dirty street. Soot darkened the beige limestone exteriors of the four-story buildings. The bars on the clouded, street-level windows intended to keep thieves out protected little of worth within. Eli stopped and scanned the littered street. He looked down at a tipped-over wine bottle and a discarded newspaper. Though pasted to the walk by the morning's rain, he could still read the bold headline, "ARMISTICE IN FORCE. GERMANY DEFEATED!"

Eli looked up as two French soldiers leaning on each other rounded the corner and staggered down the street with a third wobbling behind. He watched as they stumbled by, yelling war slogans and waving wine bottles.

While most of the world celebrated the end of the bloody four-year conflict, proclaiming it the war to end all wars, Eli felt little joy. He knew it was only the beginning.

Eli's despondency was two-fold. He had witnessed the greatest of treachery. How Cyrus, the grand overseer, could turn away from all they stood for was unfathomable to Eli. He had seen power corrupt the best humans and average watchers, but he would have never imagined Cyrus succumbing. Eli wondered what hope there was for humanity.

As painful as the world's bleak future was for the former watcher, Eli suffered most over his lost wife and son. He had given up his immortality and calling to live as a man, love a woman, and be a father. For that, Eli had no regrets. He thought Michelle the most remarkable woman he had ever known, but she was gone now, and so was their son. Eli agonized for them both.

Eli blamed his shortsightedness. He had envisioned watching their son turn into a man and him growing old with Michelle. Despite observing mortals for millennia, Eli had failed to understand how life could be so fleeting—how dreams could be crushed or changed on a whim of chance.

Eli's dispirited gaze raised to the dirty building's third-floor balcony, where a bright blue, white, and red French flag hung. He pulled the three-year-old letter from his coat pocket, checked the address, then crossed the street to the weathered door. After entering the small foyer, Eli stepped over a man and woman sleeping on the dirty tile floor, the stem of a small French flag still clutched in the woman's hand. Eli looked up the staircase and began climbing.

Upon reaching the second floor, Eli found the door he was looking for and knocked. A tired-eyed woman with gray hair pulled back in a bun, wearing a drab day dress and sweater, answered, "Yes?"

Eli's face filled with pity. "You are Jean-Pierre's mother?"

The middle-aged woman nodded somberly.

Eli studied her. He saw her hidden pain, her still fresh anguish at losing her child more than three years before. "I knew your son."

"How did you know him?" the mother asked, her voice frail with restrained emotion.

"I was with him...at the front."

The mother forced a dry swallow. "Won't you come in?"

"Yes, thank you," Eli replied as she opened the door.

Eli's nostrils flared at the musty smell of poverty and burning coal. He followed her past the cracked plaster wall with a grainy family picture to a worn floral couch. Eli sat across from her, filling the armchair.

"Would you like some coffee?" she asked, remembering her manners.

"No, thank you."

The mother's thin, bony hands fidgeted as she forced a smile, and tears welled in her eyes. "You knew my Jean-Pierre?"

"Yes," Eli nodded. "He was my friend."

"I had three sons," the mother whispered, her cheeks quivering with sadness. "Now, I have only one."

"I'm sorry," Eli replied.

"I am not the only mother in France to grieve," she managed.

"Too many have made the ultimate sacrifice," frowned Eli.

The mother pulled a handkerchief from her sleeve and blotted her eyes. "You seem very kind." She forced another smile as she tried to hold back her grief. "Jean-Pierre didn't always have kind friends. Some said he was a bad boy, but...he was my son."

"He was my first real friend," Eli reflected.

After choking down a swallow, the mother's lips parted as if to ask a question, but she couldn't form the words. Eli listened to the mantle clock tick fifteen times before she finally asked, "Were you with him when..."

Eli sadly nodded. "I held him as he died."

The mother's shoulders shook as she lowered her head and sobbed, "I wish I could have been there with him."

Eli's chest heaved at her suffering. "Before he died, Jean-Pierre asked me to tell you he loved you...and he was sorry." Eli gulped down his sorrow as the mother placed her face in her hands and sobbed.

After a time, the mother looked up, wiped away her tears, and said, "Thank you for coming. Thank you for telling me."

Eli nodded. "I have something for you." He reached into his coat, removed a small coin bag, and set it on the low table between them.

"What is this?" she asked, tearfully eyeing the bag.

"Something to help."

The weepy-eyed mother reached for Eli's hand when he stood to leave. "God bless you. I will pray for you."

"Thank you." Eli's brow tightened. "Pray for us all."

SEATED AT AN OUTDOOR CAFÉ TABLE, Eli set his tea down beside the half-eaten Croque Monsieur as his empty gaze drifted. He paid no attention to the flag-waving revelers crowding the street or the Eiffel Tower standing proudly in the distance. Eli was glad the war was over, but his mind weighed heavy, and he had nothing to celebrate.

As the midday sun broke through the clouds, rays of light poured down on the crowded street of reveling Parisians. Hoots and cheers echoed as a parade of soldiers marched down the avenue, the hundreds of waving French flags making their own wind.

Eli considered returning to Gien and the peaceful Château de Bret. He had accomplished what he wanted in Paris. In the days before, he had visited his friend Sébastien's mother and had a similar reception as he had with Jean-Pierre's. Eli stared into his murky tea. As a mortal, he now understood what it meant to grieve.

Eli thought of Château de Bret, its vineyard in the valley, meadow and rolling hills, adjoining forest, and the lovely pond he and Michelle had so often enjoyed. It was all his now, willed to him by Ronan. Eli told himself he would never sell it. It was Michelle's favorite place in the world. He knew that if she somehow found a way out of the abyss, she would return there. Eli choked the sadness down his throat as he swirled his tea. There was plenty to do there, he told himself. He could live a fulfilling life working the vineyard and tending to the sheep. He could live there to his dying day. He wondered when that would be.

When Eli felt another's presence, he looked up to find his lovely young waitress standing at his table. She wore her dark hair pulled back, and her blouse buttoned low.

"Can I get you anything else, Monsieur?"

Eli saw beneath her flirtatious grin a sad and battered soul. Forced to sell herself to survive in the city, she had been abused by not a few. Eli's heart swelled at her bravery. Despite all she had endured, she had not given up. But she was confused and afraid. He could hold back no longer. "You should leave here at once."

"Monsieur?" the waitress asked, uncertain of his meaning.

"You will not survive much longer in Paris. You deserve better. You should go home to your family in Nantes. They will welcome you back. Here are twenty franks." Eli pulled the bills from his wallet.

Aghast, the young waitress stepped back. She looked at Eli in wonder. "How-how do you know I'm from Nantes?"

Eli's brow furrowed, and his gaze drifted as he considered her question. "I don't know...I just do."

The young waitress choked back her tears as she took the money, nodded her sincere thanks, and ducked away from the table.

Eli looked at those celebrating around him. It was easy to sense their joy and excitement over the terrible war's end, but there was a cacophony of other stimuli that felt overwhelming to him. It had been years since Eli had been forced to filter his perceptions. He wondered what was wrong with him.

Eli stared at his hand, picked up a fork, and jabbed it into his finger. He grimaced at the pain. Four pinpoints of blood emerged when he pulled the fork free. But his grimace faded when the wounds sealed and the blood disappeared. Eli shook his head and gazed across the crowded street. *How can this be?* he wondered. His mind flashed back to the terrible night Michelle and Franny disappeared. He remembered fighting with Lu and then lunging for the orb. In the chaos and ensuing grief, Eli had forgotten what had happened when he touched the domain sphere. He had forgotten the jolt it had sent through him. *Is it possible?*

Eli looked back across the crowd. He saw the people. He saw their hopes and their fears. While overwhelming, it was comforting to him, like an old pair of shoes.

With his heart pounding, Eli looked down at his hands. His work was not yet done.

I hope you enjoyed *Elijah's Awakening.*
I would love to hear what you think about it.
REVIEWS MAKE A DIFFERENCE!
Please leave a review so other readers can follow
Elijah and Michelle's journey!

I⊤ is 1933. Elijah has been searching for the vanished Michelle for fifteen years but is no closer to finding her. Frustrated by his lost ability to influence mortals, the shattered Eli can do nothing as Lu and the rogue watchers guide Hitler into power.

When the persistent reporter, Cleto Nazario, shows up with information from the Vatican's secret archives that might help him locate Michelle, Eli must decide whether he can trust him.

Meanwhile, trapped in a dark abyss, Michelle must fend for herself. But as the frightened mortal searches for a way home, she begins to realize her true potential.

In separate worlds, Eli and Michelle fight to unlock the cryptic mysteries of the past and stop the evil watchers. The fate of both worlds lies in their hands.

Buy your copy of *Elijah's Quest* today!

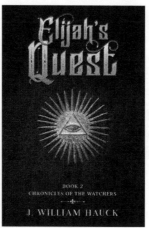

Please enjoy these excerpts from *Elijah's Quest:*

The driver opened the rear door opposite the red-bearded Lu, and the released prisoner, a thirty-five-year-old beady-eyed Austrian, slid into the back seat holding a basket of his belongings.

Adolf Hitler curiously eyed the shadowed Lu seated beside him. "It was you. You had me released." Hitler had wondered how he was freed after just six months of his five-year sentence.

Lu, who had discovered the wounded Hitler in a German hospital at the end of the Great War, waited for the sedan to drive away from the prison, then turned to his sunken-eyed apprentice. "You have much to learn, young Adolf."

Eli exploded in rage, grabbed Cyrus's lapels, and threw him against the wall as the French president jumped back. "This man is a traitor! You shouldn't listen to anything he says! He's behind it all!"

Unbothered by the assault, Cyrus raised his arms and knocked Eli's hands loose. Then, extending his palm in a halting gesture, he hurled the larger Eli against the opposite wall without touching him. "I'm disappointed in you, Elijah. So much promise squandered. I hope you're enjoying your mortal torment."

Frantic to find her child, Michelle climbed to her bare feet, her white nightgown all but lost in the inky night. "Franny, where are you?" This time, the groaning was more of a growl. Michelle stepped back. She stopped when she felt something against her. Gasping, Michelle spun around to the prickling arm of a dead branch. "Where am I?" she muttered before calling out again, "Franny! Come to Mama! It's okay, my sweet!"

Michelle gasped when she noticed something move in the shadows. She frantically scanned the darkened earth for the orb and blazerod she had lost on impact as the sounds of approaching footsteps and heavy breathing drew closer. *Oh, where are they?*

Made in the USA
Middletown, DE
05 August 2024

58559604R00189